UNDER THE KNIFE

A DI FRANK MILLER NOVEL

JOHN CARSON

DI FRANK MILLER SERIES

Crash Point
Silent Marker
Rain Town
Watch Me Bleed
Broken Wheels
Sudden Death
Under the Knife
Trial and Error
Warning Sign
Cut Throat
Blood from a Stone
Time of Death

Frank Miller Crime Series – Books 1-3 – Box set
Frank Miller Crime Series - Books 4-6 - Box set

DCI HARRY MCNEIL SERIES
Return to Evil
Sticks and Stones
Back to Life
Dead Before You Die
Hour of Need
Blood and Tears

Where Stars Will Shine – a charity anthology compiled by Emma Mitchell, featuring a Harry McNeil short story – The Art of War and Peace

MAX DOYLE SERIES

Final Steps
Code Red
The October Project

SCOTT MARSHALL SERIES

Old Habits

UNDER THE KNIFE

Copyright © 2017 John Carson

Edited by Melanie Underwood
Cover by Damonza

John Carson has asserted his right under the Copyright, Designs and Patents Act 1988, to be identified as the author of this work.

This is a work of fiction. Names, characters, places, brands, media, and incidents are either the products of the author's imagination or are used fictitiously. Any resemblance to actual events, locales, or persons, living or dead, is coincidental.

Without limiting the rights under copyright reserved above, no part of this publication may be reproduced, stored in or introduced into a retrieval system, or transmitted, in any form, or by any means (electronic, mechanical, photocopying, recording, or otherwise) without the prior written permission of the author of this book. Innocence is and

All rights reserved

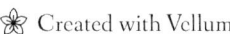 Created with Vellum

To the memory of my mother, Margaret Dods

ONE

Detective Inspector Paddy Gibb pulled up in his car, parking behind the patrol cars, their blue lights spinning in the early morning light. It was warm already, the August sun well on its way to give a red tan to the unwary Scots.

'Please, God, tell me this is all a mistake,' he said to Detective Constable Frank Miller.

'I wish it was, sir, but it's real.'

'Walk slow, I need a fag.'

They were in Saunders Street in Stockbridge. The flats looked like they had been built in the 70s. It was a nice neighbourhood. *Or had been,* before they found the body, Miller thought.

'What's your initial take on this, son?' said Gibb, lighting up. He sucked hard, before blowing out a plume of smoke.

'I think she was taken down one of those sets of steps.' He pointed to the steps closest to them. A tunnel ran under the bridge above. 'There's another set of steps on the other side. The road on the bridge is one-way with a cycle lane. As you see here, it's residents parking only, so even if he was here late, there's a possibility of somebody looking out of their window, getting pissed off and calling us to report suspicious activity. It's easier to park up on India Place and drag a body over to the top of the steps.'

'It's still a bit risky. What about from the other end of the path?' They started walking past the mortuary van, a huddle of uniforms, and an ambulance crew.

'The only other place to join the Water of Leith Walkway is to come in from Dean Village. Unless she was killed in one of the posh houses in Moray Place and they humped her over the back wall of their garden and dragged her here.' Miller shrugged, dismissing the idea.

'Don't discount it. I've seen stranger things.'

'I'm not. Some uniforms are already up there knocking on doors.'

'Good.' They walked towards the short tunnel. A female uniform was standing with one of her colleagues.

'Good morning, sir,' PC Carol Davidson said.

'Morning.' They carried on through. 'That's your girlfriend, isn't it?' said Gibb.

'It is sir, yes.'

'Harry Davidson's daughter?'

'Yes, sir.'

Detective Superintendent Harry Davidson was the head of CID.

'He'll rip your nuts off if you mess his daughter about.'

'I don't intend to.'

'And then his other daughter, the pathologist, will have the pleasure of opening you up on her stainless-steel table.'

'Julie Davidson might be one of the city's pathologists but she likes me,' said Miller with a smile.

'I'll have that engraved on your tombstone.'

A black plaque, attached to the stone wall on the other side of the tunnel, said *The Dene*. Meaning *Valley*. They then went through the arch under the other set of steps, and continued round the path. Officers were on the road above, stopping people from coming down onto the path.

'You think somebody dragged her along here? Not killed her where she was found?'

'Not killed where she was found; there's no blood, so it seems obvious that she was killed somewhere else and transported here.'

'How long have you been in CID, Miller?'

'A few weeks.'

'You liking it? Think you'll stick it for the long haul?'

'Yes to both counts.'

'Good. Some come here thinking it's all fun and games, then one of them gets an eye out and goes running back to uniform.'

'I'll remember to duck.'

They walked along the Water of Leith footpath that ran alongside the river, which flowed all the way from Balerno on the outskirts of the city, to empty into Leith harbour and into the Firth of Forth. A canopy of trees shaded them from the expensive town houses up above, arguably the finest houses in the New Town. Firemen were in attendance, standing next to two sets of ladders that had been tied together and placed over the railings, connecting the pathway to the base of the statue.

'I wonder why he chose St. Bernard's Well to dump her body?' Gibb said, puffing furiously on his cigarette. 'I'd better get this out before the Wicked Witch pisses her pants.'

Gibb's pet name for DI Maggie Parks, head of forensics. He nipped the cigarette and slipped it back into the packet with a sleight of hand any magician would be proud of.

'A random place he thought he wouldn't get caught?' Miller said.

'Or he knows the place.'

The open dome was held up by nine stone pillars. The mineral spring was discovered in 1760 and it became a visitor' attraction. The well itself was designed by local artist Alexander Nasmyth, and inside was a statue of Hygeia, the Greek goddess of health.

The woman had been found at the base of the statue. Paddy

Gibb reflected that the well hadn't been particularly good for this woman's health.

Detective Sergeant Andy Watt was talking to a uniformed sergeant when they walked up. One of the pathologists, Jake Dagger, was attending to the deceased at the base of the statue. He waved over to Gibb before getting back to work.

'What's happening?' Gibb said to Watt.

'Uniforms forced open the museum underneath the statue and there's no sign of blood in there.'

Gibb looked at Miller, thinking that Watt was taking the piss. 'Museum?'

'It's a little place where the actual well is. It's technically a pump room. It was capped a long time ago and it's only open certain times of the year. Like this month, it's only open on a Sunday.'

'Somebody has regular access?'

'Yes. We're trying to trace the keyholder now.'

'He's going to be upset you booted his door down before waiting for him to bring the key,' Gibb said, looking at Watt. '*Museum.*' He shook his head. 'What's round the back?'

'There's a wooden boardwalk that runs the length of the building, out over the river, before cutting back in.'

Gibb walked down the steps to the entrance of the pump room.

'Sorry, Andy,' Miller said.

'Don't worry about it, pal. Fuck old grumpy drawers. His wife buggered off and he needs a good night out. Until then, he's shagging all of us.'

They followed Gibb down to the pump room. The stone lintel above the door bore the inscription, *St. Bernard's Mineral Well.*

'A bit like Michelangelo's but only better,' he said, looking up at the ornate décor on the domed ceiling. A gold, smiling face of the sun looked back down at him.

The pump was like a small, marble obelisk standing in the middle of the room with a stone urn on top. On one side was a small, gold

Lion's face above what looked like a sculpted half sink. The spout. And to one side was the pump handle.

'Same name as the pub across the road but I bet this stuff doesn't taste half as good.' Outside, a pathway led off to the right while an opening led onto the boardwalk. Gibb looked across the river to the trees beyond and saw somebody looking back at them.

'What's over there?'

Miller consulted his notebook. 'Dean Gardens. Open only to members. There's an entrance at Eton Terrace just over the Dean Bridge, and there are pathways that come along here, and there's another gate at Ann Street.'

'We have uniformed patrols stopping anybody going in,' Watt said.

Gibb turned to him. 'Well, they're not doing a very good job, are they? I want that woman spoken to, the one who's taking an unnatural interest in us.'

'Sir.' Watt walked away.

'She won't be able to see much with the forensic screen up.'

'Let's go and see what Doctor Death has to say for himself.'

Back up the steps to the path. 'It wouldn't have been easy for him to get the corpse to the base of the statue,' Miller said, pointing to the ladders. 'Unless he had put his own set there, but it's doubtful.'

Gibb looked. 'He could have gone in the way we went and heaved her over the railings there.'

'He's fit, we know that.'

'Hey, doc, how's things this very fine Tuesday morning?'

Jake Dagger came across and stood looking down at them. 'Pray tell why you wanted to join this rabble?' he said to Miller. He was in his early thirties with an unruly mop of hair and a boyish charm that made him look like a teenager.

'Don't you bloody well start. We can hardly keep them in CID as it is,' Gibb said.

'That's not what you said at the interview, sir,' Miller said. 'You told me they were beating a path to get in.'

'I lied. We had to make it look like we were doing you a favour, not the other way around.'

'They need to up the pay scale,' Dagger said.

'Just remember one thing, Dagger; you have a boss too and I'm good friends with him,' Gibb said. 'Give us what you've got instead of standing there making chit-chat.'

'I can tell the Russian Bride site didn't pan out.' He grinned again. Gibb made a face.

'Well, she was killed somewhere else,' Dagger said, but stopped when Gibb put up a hand.

'Miller already told me she wasn't killed here, and he didn't go to medical school.'

Dagger kept on grinning. 'It was me who told him. Anyway, she's been cut open and sewn back up again.'

'What? Sewn back up? Like a doctor would sew somebody up?'

'It's a bit rough but basically, yes, like a doctor.'

'What about time of death?'

'No more than twenty-four hours.'

'Sometime on Monday then.'

'Gee, thanks for working that out for me,' Dagger said.

'I get enough from this lot without you adding to it. And where were *you* on Monday?'

'Funny,' he replied. 'But she's clean. As in, been cleaned up after whatever he did to her. No blood, nothing. He would need time to clean her up and then dress her.'

'Is she big built? As in body shape.'

'No, she's medium build. It would have been difficult for somebody like you to carry her, but not so hard for somebody who worked out.'

'What makes you think I don't work out? Cheeky bastard.'

'Please. You almost have a hernia taking your cigarettes out. You only lift pint glasses and fish suppers.'

'If I didn't know you better, I'd swear you've been talking to my ex-wife.'

'I have a keen eye for the human anatomy, Paddy, that's all. Plus, I've seen you in the pub. Never with your hand in your pocket, mind.'

'Again; cheeky bastard.' He looked at Miller. 'Is it my fault if my subordinates clamour to buy me drink?'

'I wouldn't say no to somebody wanting to buy me drink,' said the DC.

'Don't encourage him, Frank,' Dagger said. 'Norrie nae mates there still has a ten bob note in his wallet.' He laughed as Gibb stuck two fingers up at him.

'When will you be able to look at her on the table?'

'I called the prof when I got here to update him, and we have a sudden death to deal with later this morning, so probably this afternoon,' Dagger replied.

'Not gracing us with his presence, then?'

'Like you, he wouldn't normally climb a ladder, never mind one that was hanging precariously over railings.' He looked at the leading firefighter. 'No offence.'

'None taken.'

'Right, tell him to give us a call when she's ready to be opened up for the second time.'

'Will do.'

Watt came walking back along the pathway. 'I told the uniforms at both entrances to those gardens over there to make sure they corral any onlookers who were nebbing over the wall.'

'Well, don't go upsetting any of them for God's sake. It's only those with dosh who apply for entrance to them, so we don't want to tread on any toes.'

'Maybe one of them is the murderer, back to look at us working the scene. It happens.'

'You've a lot to learn about the gentry,' Gibb said.

'Don't worry, we won't use any bad language in front of them. And if we have to invite any of them along to the station, we'll have cucumber sandwiches and tea, with scones and jam for afters.'

'You've never had an upper-class girlfriend before, have you? I've known some who would give you a knee trembler just for starters. Don't knock it 'til you've tried it, son.'

Dagger laughed. 'That's you told.'

'Shut up, Dagger. Like you would know,' Watt said.

'I've had my fair share.'

'Yes, but they're usually in a fridge by the time they would take a fancy to you.'

'Enough, kiddies. Let's start getting everything together. Witnesses. Statements. Then I'll give your father the good news,' he said to Miller. 'Jack's in charge while our esteemed boss is burning his white bits in Spain. He's going to love this; a big one goes down while he's off on a hooly with the missus. Let's make him proud.'

They watched as the corpse of the unknown female was put in a body bag and loaded onto a stretcher to make it easier to handle her while they lowered her down the ladders to the pathway and onto a gurney.

Nobody said anything, showing respect for the dead.

Gus Weaver, one of the mortuary assistants, was waiting for the firemen. 'The van's in Saunders Street, lads,' he said, leading the way.

The detectives followed.

'I hate it when somebody thinks they can fuck with us like this,' Gibb said.

'We'll do everything we can to nail the bastard,' Miller said.

'That we will, son, that we will.'

TWO

'Paddy Gibb wants me down at the mortuary after lunch,' Miller said, pushing the plate of fish and chips away from him.

'Lost your appetite?' Carol Davidson said, tucking into her own fish and chips.

'You know something, we're used to getting called out to road accidents, sudden deaths where an old person has gone to sleep and doesn't wake up. People commit suicide or fall out of a window, but murder is always different.'

'I know it is.'

'It's the intent behind it. Somebody sets out to intentionally take another person's life. Not like a road-rage fight, but they've taken a life on purpose and they're being sneaky about it. Does that make sense?'

'Perfectly.'

'That woman who was murdered; she's somebody's daughter. Maybe somebody's mother, wife. And this bastard came along and took it away from her. I never used to let myself feel personally involved, but seeing this woman taken away in a body bag just got under my skin.'

'It's something we're going to have to get used to. I don't have long before I'm joining CID, and I understand there's a transition. Some uniforms think it's an easy number, then you do it for yourself and suddenly, things start to eat away at you.'

'I've been to murder scenes before, but when you're on the front line, it's different.'

'Have they identified the woman yet?' she asked.

'Not yet.'

Carol reached over and put a hand on his. 'Never mind, in a couple of weeks, I'll be in the department, holding your hand.'

He laughed. 'I never thought I'd be working with my girlfriend.'

'A lot of romances start in the office.'

'Some people don't think it's a good idea to start a work romance. What if it goes bad?'

Carol took her hand away. 'Too bad, Miller, you're stuck with me now.'

He smiled. 'Just as well I'm madly in love with you.'

'Oh, would you two love birds give it a rest?' Andy Watt said, putting his tray down on the table. 'You don't mind, do you?' He sat down without waiting for an answer.

'It's fine, boss,' Miller said.

'Jesus, Frank, keep that sort of talk for that radge, Gibb. Just call me Sarge in front of the others, otherwise, it's Andy.' He looked at Carol. 'You, young lady, can still call me Almighty One.'

'Yeah, watch me.'

Watt forked some fish and chips into his mouth and pointed his fork at her. 'Our life is going to be hell, Frank, mark my words. You'd be better off running away with old Betty behind the counter there. I heard her old man's looking to trade her in for a newer model.'

'Frank's just fine where he is, thank you very much,' Carol said.

Watt looked at Miller. 'You said that without moving your lips.'

'Despite your wisdom, I think I have to agree with Carol.'

'You're going down a slippery slope there, my son.'

'I think Betty has her eyes on you anyway, Andy.'

Watt screwed his face up. 'I wouldn't touch her with yours.' Looked at Carol. 'Sorry. It's how we talk in CID.'

'It's how we talk in the patrol car too, Andy,' Carol said. 'I'm thick-skinned just like the rest of them.'

'Good to know.'

'Do you have an ID for the victim?' Carol asked. She knew it was protocol for forensics to take prints from the deceased when there was nothing to identify them with at the scene.

'Maggie Parks normally couldn't find a gas leak with a box of matches, but she did get the prints sent through pretty sharpish and we're running them now.'

Carol looked over at Miller with raised eyebrows.

'What?' Watt said, eating more food.

'Gas leak with a box of matches? I heard she was pretty good.'

'She's okay. Bit snippy but she does loosen up when we have a do at the police club. Just don't piss her off or drop anything at a crime scene.'

'I wish I was going to the mortuary with you lot,' Carol said.

'You're joining us in a couple of weeks or so, aren't you?'

'Yes. It can't come quick enough.'

'Wait 'til you get to my age, then you start thinking like that about retirement.' More fish and chips. 'You on 'til three?'

'Yes.'

'Part timer.'

'Cheeky sod.'

'Hey, I'm a sergeant, remember. It's *cheeky sod, sir*.' He smiled and ate more lunch. 'There are very few times when a murder scene will put me off my food, and today wasn't one of them, thank God. And they do this fish twice a week, Friday being the obvious other day, for all the bible thumpers.'

'Have you seen anything like this murder before, Sarge?' Miller said.

'One or two, but to be honest, not one where she was cleaned before being dumped.'

'Obviously getting rid of any forensics,' Carol said.

'Unless he's some religious nut and thought he was cleansing her in the Styx or something.'

'Did anything pan out from the women in the Dean Gardens?' Carol asked. 'One of my colleagues was part of the team who were tasked with talking to them.'

Miller shook his head. 'One of them was just looking over the wall at all the activity. She didn't see anything.'

'Didn't see anything until she had a good gander at the woman lying next to Hygeia. That's our fault though. We didn't realise people were in there already, but that's no excuse.'

'I didn't think there would be any witnesses, but we know that she was dumped there through the night, unless somebody came along late last night and saw her but didn't say anything.'

'I'm not sure there are any normal folks who walk there at night after dark. Probably hoors and junkies but not Mr and Mrs Snooty from Moray Place up the hill.'

'My guess is he would have dumped her in the middle of the night when it's quiet. Less chance of anybody seeing him.'

'You're right, Frank, and if he parked up at India Place, then he could have quickly carried her down the steps and along before anybody spotted him.'

'What about the door-to-door in Saunders Street?' Carol asked.

'Yielded nothing. Nobody was up having a pish at three o'clock in the morning. Except me of course, but I don't live down that way.'

'Where *do* you live?' Carol asked.

'Hear that, Frank? Where do I live? Next thing, she'll be kicking you into touch.'

'Piss off, Andy, I was only asking.'

'Clovenstone, for now,' Watt answered, washing down his lunch with coffee. 'This fish likes to swim.'

'Clovenstone, eh? Nothing wrong with that.'

'I never said there was.'

'Oh, I meant... just that...'

'You expected a high-flying detective like me to be living in Barnton.'

'Something like that.' Carol could feel her cheeks starting to burn.

'It's a mate's flat. He's away on business for a while – and he said I could crash there while he's away. My missus kicked me out. God knows why. Regular wages, nine-to-five hours, always coming in sober. Well, two out of three ain't bad.'

Which two, he didn't elaborate on.

'I'm sorry to hear that, Andy,' Carol said.

'Don't be. It was my own fault. It's not as if she hadn't been telling me for years. I tried, I really did, but the job gets like that sometimes, if you let it.' He looked at Miller. 'If I ever hear you've been messing this lassie about, I'll boot your baby-making bits right over the back of your head.'

'She doesn't have to worry about that.'

'Glad to hear it. But Clovenstone is a stepping stone for me. God bless those who live there and all that, but it's not for me.'

'Where did you live before that?' Carol said.

'Baberton Crescent. Bungalow. Her mother's minted and practically bought the house for us when we got married. I'm the one who decided to go. She can keep the house. I liked living there and God knows I'd love to go home, but her mother's still kicking about and I swear to God I think the old boot dabbles in Black Magic. She has a black cat, just to keep up appearances.'

'Any chance you two can resolve your differences?'

'Fat chance, Carol. What's done is done. I'm moving on now. Onwards and upwards.' He felt around in his pocket and brought his phone out. Looked at the screen. Put it back in his pocket. 'We're wanted down at the mortuary. They're going to start in half an hour.'

They scraped their seats back.

'I'll see you back at the flat,' Carol said.

'I've told you, not in front of Frank,' Watt said, picking his tray up.

'You should be so lucky.'

'Amen to that, sister.'

THREE

Detective Chief Inspector Jack Miller was an imposing figure at six foot five. In contrast, head pathologist, Professor Leo Chester, looked like he belonged in a circus.

Jack, Watt, Gibb, and Miller were dressed in plastic throwaway aprons.

Jake Dagger and Julie Davidson were on the other side of the stainless-steel table with Chester. They stood facing each other, like they were about to go into battle.

'Well, this is a Kodak moment,' Watt said.

'Plenty of photos have been taken, Andy, but I don't think her family will be putting them in an album any time soon,' Jack said.

'Without further ado, I'd like to get started,' Chester said. He was unflappable, a smaller man who carried a big, invisible stick.

The detectives stood back and watched while Julie stepped forward and cut a Y incision in the woman's chest, then downward, paralleling the stitches that were holding the front of the corpse together. When Julie reached the groin area, the corpse was opened up.

Chester nodded for Gus Weaver to step forward with the

autopsy saw, as if he'd been waiting in the wings for his act to be announced.

The detectives all stood back while the older man took the woman's skull cap off.

Then the pathologists got to work, detailing what they were doing, recording every word, while the policemen looked on.

'How are you finding CID, son?' Jack said.

'Fine, sir. It's seeing things from the other side, as it were. Not just attending a call, but being a part of it all, that I like.' He didn't mention his earlier conversation with Carol.

'You'll get to see every inch of the depraved side of Edinburgh. God knows why they took hanging away.' He nodded over to the cadaver. 'And you can see the results.'

'The people who do this are either mentally unstable or else they don't think they'll get caught. In my opinion. Hanging wouldn't be a deterrent for them.'

'No, but it would stop the bastard from ever doing it again, once we caught him.'

Jack put a hand on Miller's arm, leading him away to a corner. 'Your mum's pleased that you're moving in with Carol, but all I'm asking is that you cut her a little bit of slack. It's going to be a new way of life for her from now on. Maybe come around for your dinner sometime. You and Carol both. She looks on her as a daughter.'

'I will, Dad. It's not as if I'm moving to the other side of the country.'

'As soon as you're out the door, it will seem like you've moved to the moon, for your mother.'

'That's fine. Luckily, Carol loves coming round.'

'You want my advice?'

'What?'

'Put a ring on her finger as soon as you can.'

'I don't think she's going anywhere.'

'Still. A woman wants to feel secure.'

'I intend to, but I haven't moved in yet. I'm doing that this weekend, but I need to move some stuff. Oh, I forgot. I need to borrow your car.'

'What? Sod off.'

'Carol has her Beetle, but it's not the same. I have a lot of stuff.'

'Oh, laddie, you have a lot to learn. You want to keep two women happy? Take some of your stuff for now. Get it bit by bit. You don't need your Airfix kits just now.'

'You're funny.'

'This way, Carol isn't overwhelmed by all your junk and your mother doesn't see you move out all your stuff at once.'

'My teddy bear will be lonely if I leave him in my old room.'

'Don't be a smartarse.'

'Okay, okay, have it your way. Little bit at a time.'

'Good man. And remember that Carol is the boss's daughter and you'll do just fine.'

'Does he know about this?'

'What, you moving in with one of his daughters or the dead woman?'

'Take a guess.'

'He's up to speed. No doubt he would read it in The Sun while he's sunning himself, so better it coming from us. Besides, you're not the only one he'd rip apart when he came back if we kept it from him.'

'Carol's mum won't be happy that he's running the case from the beach.'

'He's not running anything. Besides, it's the bar, not the beach. He said he'd use their phone at night to call me. Just don't mention it to Carol or it might get back to her mother.'

'Gentlemen, if you would,' Leo Chester said. Jack and Miller turned back to the table.

'Is that what it looks like?' Jack said.

'It would appear so,' Jake Dagger said. 'This woman has had most of her internal organs removed.'

'God,' Paddy Gibb said, taking a step forward.

'No need for formalities, Paddy,' Chester said. 'Just call me professor like everybody else.'

'That's a first,' Miller said. 'I don't recall reading about any killer who's done that.'

'I'm sure somebody in America thought of it first,' Chester said. 'They have so many, how shall I put it, creative minds over there.'

He put his hands into the woman's open cavity where once a beating heart was dominant but which now was an empty shell. He pulled out a small, rectangular object, thin with dried blood on it.

'Now we know who she might be,' he said, holding up a driving license by the edge. 'Iris Napier, 96 Hillpark Crescent, Edinburgh.'

Jack turned to Watt. 'Get onto it and see who's at that address. Take Frank with you.'

'Sir.' Watt motioned for Miller to leave the PM suite with him. 'Thank God,' he said when they were out in the fresh air.

'You'd think we were bloody Barbarians,' Miller said, 'the way some of us treat other humans.'

They got in the car and Watt drove out into the afternoon traffic in the Cowgate, heading in the direction of the Grassmarket and Lothian Road.

Connecting with Queensferry Road, Watt headed for Ravelston and down to Craigcrook Road.

'You said you're moving in with Carol this weekend?' Watt said.

'I am. I need to start shifting my stuff.'

'You know, in this job, you quickly learn how to read people, and I don't mean in uniform, I mean when you're in CID and start to interact with the dregs. And I can see that lassie is head over heels with you, Miller.'

'I love her too, Sarge.'

'Cut that *Sarge* shite out when we're in the car. You know after a few years I'm going to be calling *you* boss.'

'What? Pish.'

'It's true, Frank. I'm already at the top floor. I've been too outspoken for the longest time, and the top brass don't like it, and although I haven't fucked up royally, I've made my opinion known one too many times. If there really was a ton of uniforms beating a path to the CID door, I'd have been out on my arse a long time ago. But as I was saying, Carol thinks you walk on water. Don't fuck it up like I did with my missus.'

'In here,' Miller said, and Watt turned into a side street. He looked at the older sergeant. 'I won't mess things up with her. I've had a few girlfriends and nobody even came close.'

'Watch the trap,' Watt said, pulling up to the end of the road. They were looking at house numbers.

'Left,' Miller said. 'What trap?'

'Working together. I've seen it few times. A mate of mine was a bus driver with Lothian Buses, and so was his wife. Admittedly, he met her there, left wife number one for wife number two. They weren't with each other all the time, but they were on the same shift, and when he saw her flirting with other men, he went mental.' He looked at Miller as he pulled into the side of the street outside number 26. 'He forgot that's how he met her. Wanker. She was a nice girl, real fun. I don't know what she saw in the baldy bastard myself, but it went sideways. They worked together in Central depot at Annandale Street, and he ended up transferring to Longstone. He hated it there and he ended up leaving. My point is, remember to take a step back at times.'

'She's out on patrol with her partner all the time and it doesn't bother me.'

'Just keep that thought when she's working with us. She won't be out with you all the time. Sure, we'll gather at crime scenes together, but like now, we split up. Don't go all *baldy bastard* on her.'

'I won't.'

'Right, let's get knocking on that door and see if...'

'Uh oh,' Miller said, opening the car door and stepping out, followed by Watt.

A man had opened the front door of the bungalow. And he was standing holding a baseball bat. 'If she sent you two fuckers round to sort me out, then one of you bastards will go home with a broken kneecap.'

Both detectives pulled out their batons. 'Police. Put the fucking bat down and we can talk,' Watt said, taking his warrant card out.

'Police?' the man said.

'Yes. Drop it.'

The man threw the bat into the front garden and walked back inside, leaving the door open.

'For fuck's sake, keep your eyes peeled. He might be in there getting a shooter,' Watt said.

Miller was about to step over the threshold when Watt put a hand on his arm. 'Me first. Cannon fodder we used to be called in the army.'

They stepped into the hallway, leaving the front door open.

'Through the back,' the voice said. Miller's pulse was racing and he was starting to sweat and it was nothing to do with the afternoon heat.

Through the back was a kitchen. The man had his back to them and Miller gripped his baton like he was trying to squeeze the life out of it. In case the man was holding a gun. Watt was in front of him.

'You can put those away. I've nothing more dangerous in my hand than a kettle. It just went off. You want coffee?' He turned to face them.

They both declined. Put their batons away. This was the first death message Miller had ever delivered whilst being prepared to fight the recipient.

'You are...?' Watt asked.

'Sit down. You're making the place look untidy.' He poured hot water into a mug and added milk from the carton in the fridge.

They all sat at a dining table. Miller looked at the man; short, unkempt hair, stubble, dressed in an old golf shirt with torn jeans.

'I'm not usually dressed like a scruff, but I'm doing a bit of DIY.'

'What, hitting in nails with a baseball bat?' Watt said.

'Yeah, well, sorry about that. But that cow said she would send a couple of blokes round to smack the shit out of me for shouting at her. We're selling up because of the divorce and things have been a bit heated recently.'

'What's your name?' Miller asked.

'Sandy Napier.'

'And this cow you're talking about?' Watt asked.

'Iris, my wife. Why? What's this all about? Has she been telling you I was shoving her about? Because if she has, it's a load of nonsense. My lawyer will ream her if she's been making stuff up.'

'It's not about that,' Watt said, looking briefly at Miller before carrying on. 'I'm sorry to tell you that we found the body of a woman this morning who we believe to be that of your wife, Iris.'

Napier looked at him in dumb silence for a moment. 'Iris? Dead?'

'We believe it's her, but we'll need a formal identification.'

'What happened to her?'

'She was murdered.'

'Murdered? Where? How?'

'Mr Napier, get your stuff together. We need to have a talk at the station.'

Napier nodded.

FOUR

The afternoon wore on. Carol had sent Miller a text, asking what he wanted for dinner. He had forgotten she had finished almost an hour ago. He had been put on the spot and couldn't think. Usually his mother would have his dinner ready if he was on earlies. If he had been on late or night shift, he would have just fired something into the microwave.

Surprise me! he had told her.

If she cooks you fuck all, that'll be a surprise, Andy Watt had said when Miller told him. He had a point.

'Right, let's go and have a chat with him,' Jack Miller said to Paddy Gibb. 'Frank, come in and stand in a corner and observe.'

'Sir.'

'A baseball bat, eh? Little bastard.'

Sandy Napier was sitting with a plastic cup that had held water, but now he had torn it and was unfurling it.

'About time,' he said.

'We had some things to check, Mr Napier,' Jack said.

'Yeah? Like what?'

'We'll do the questions. Now, can you acknowledge you don't want a lawyer present?' The tapes were running.

'I've nothing to hide.'

Jack was sitting next to Gibb, opposite Napier, with Frank near the door.

'Why don't you start off by telling us about your relationship with your wife, Mr Napier?'

'As you already know, we were getting a divorce.'

'Can you tell us why?'

Napier took a deep breath and let it out slowly, making eye contact with Jack. 'It wasn't always like this, but she turned into a whore.'

'Can you elaborate?'

'I'm sure you know what a whore is, Inspector. Iris and I have been married for a long time. Coming on 20 years this year. She started going out with her friends, more and more, especially at weekend nights. Then she started staying out overnight, staying with a friend, she said. But one weekend, she didn't come back until the Saturday afternoon. I had been out shopping, getting something in for Saturday's dinner as I wanted to cook her something nice. I bumped into the friend she was supposedly staying with. I acted all coy, like, when she came in. Asked her how her night was, and she said she stayed over with the friend, and I confronted her about it. She went off her head.'

'Then you had a big fight?' Gibb said.

'Not a physical fight. It was never physical. But a big argument. I told her we were finished. That I wouldn't stay married to a woman who was going to stay out all night. Then she told me her boyfriend was a better fuck than I was.' He looked between the two detectives. 'Her words, not mine.'

'What happened next?' Jack said.

'I moved out into a little rented flat. Then I met somebody and moved in with her.'

'When did this happen?'

'A long time ago. Maybe close to a year and a half.'

'You haven't lived with her in all that time?'

'No. That's why I'm doing up the house to sell. She lived in it but it's getting sold so we can split the proceeds. But it needed a little TLC first.'

'Was it acrimonious?'

'Most divorces are, aren't they? But the shouting had stopped a long time ago. We accepted the fact that we weren't going to get together, and we had both moved on.'

'Where were you yesterday, Mr Napier?'

'With my girlfriend.'

'All day?'

'Yes. She had to go into work today, but we spent all weekend together.'

'We'll need her details.'

Napier nodded.

'What was Iris's profession?' Gibb asked.

'She was a staff nurse at the Western.'

'Where do you work?'

'At the Southern Scottish Insurance company on Lothian Road.'

'Do you know if your wife was in a relationship at the moment?'

Napier shook his head. 'I don't know. We were civil to each other but we didn't tell each other everything.'

'What's your address?'

Napier told him.

'Did Iris have anybody special in her life?'

'Not that I know of, but she might have. She didn't tell me.'

'Do you have kids?'

Napier shook his head. 'Neither of us wanted them. What's the point? I mean, what would they have grown up into? Bloody hooligans. No, we were quite happy having a good social life and a nice house. Until it went tits up, of course.'

Jack looked over at Miller for a moment. He couldn't think of a better decision in his life, having his boy.

'Did Iris have any family that we can inform?'

'Just an uncle over in Dunfermline and his brood. Bunch of knuckle-draggers. Her folks are gone though.'

'We're going to get you to write your girlfriend's details down, Mr Napier. And if you have details for your ex-wife's family, we'd appreciate that. We'll have Fife Constabulary tell them. We'll ask you to wait here while one of my officers does that.'

'Am I a suspect?'

'Everybody is until we rule them out, so the quicker we can rule you out, the better.'

'Fair enough.' He started writing on the pad in front of him.

'Can we get you a coffee or something while you're waiting?' Gibb asked.

'Yes, thanks. Milk and one.'

'We're also waiting for the mortuary staff to let us know when she can be viewed. I can have somebody take you down there. I'd also like permission to look around your house.'

'Go ahead.'

Jack stopped the interview and the detectives left the room. Out in the corridor, he looked at Gibb. 'Get Maggie Parks and her team down to the house and crawl over it to see if she was killed there.' He looked at Miller. 'He gave us permission, which made it easier, but if he hadn't we would have found something to hold him back while we got a warrant.'

'Okay.'

'Right, let's get moving. Paddy, deal with that, and get Parks to give me a call when she's there. Then I'll have somebody take him down to the mortuary.'

'Aren't we still waiting for them to call us?' Miller said.

'They already did. I don't want him to know that just now. Meantime, go with Andy Watt down to the Western and talk to her colleagues.'

'Will do.'

In the incident room, a whiteboard was being set up with a photo of Iris Napier at one side.

'Andy, you and I have to go to the hospital where the victim worked,' Miller said as he went into the incident room.

'Right. I don't mind going to the hospital as long as it's not in the back of an ambulance. Isn't that right, Tam?'

DS Tam Scott looked at them. 'I have to agree. Better to put somebody *into* an ambulance than *be* put into one.'

'Maybe Lothian and Borders should use that in the recruitment drive,' Miller said.

Tam Scott smiled. 'As long as you hear the sound of your front door clicking shut every night, that's what counts.'

'Talking of which, it's almost knocking off time, so get the fucking boot down,' Watt said to Miller.

FIVE

The sun was high above the Western General Hospital as Miller drove the car up Porterfield Road, the access road that led onto the hospital's grounds.

'Should we see if we can find a parking spot in there?' Miller said, pointing down to where the car park was.

'Will we fuck,' Watt said. 'Pull up to the front doors.'

Miller did and saw the *No Parking* sign at the double yellow lines.

'Here's fine,' Watt said. He saw the look Miller gave him. 'Listen son, we're Serious Crimes Unit, which means bugger all to most people, so when they ask, give them our old moniker; tell them we're murder squad detectives. They sit up and take notice then. Park the car here on the double yellows and put the police sign in the windscreen.'

'And if we get a ticket?'

'Sir Leslie Lyons will wipe his arse with it. He was murder squad at one time, and if there's one thing the Chief Constable hates more than murderers, it's traffic wardens.'

'Can't say fairer than that,' Miller said as they got out of the car. The air was warm and he loosened his tie a little bit, just enough so he could feel the fresh air but not enough that people would think they'd been out on the lash.

Inside, they were directed upstairs to the human resources office. After Watt explained what had happened, he was directed to the ward floor where another staff nurse took them into an empty office.

'My God, that's terrible,' she said. 'What happened to her?' Tears sprang into her eyes.

'We can't go into details,' Watt said. 'We just need some background information on her.'

'Have you spoken to her ex-husband?'

'We have. He told us that Mrs Napier liked to go out socialising quite a bit.'

'We all do.'

'He said that she liked going out with a lot of men.'

The nurse turned around so fast that Miller thought she was going to smack Watt. 'Oh, I get it; this urban myth that every nurse wants to get you in bed. That we're all sluts. If we go to a pub, we want to get shagged. If we go to a singles club, our knickers are in our handbags before we leave. Well, let me tell you something, you coppers put it about as well, including the married ones! But does anybody call you names? No. Call you wankers? No. Look at him, he could be a real wanker.'

She looked at Miller and he felt the red creep into his face.

'Finished?' Watt said. He stayed calm.

'Yes.' Her breath was coming in gasps she had been speaking so fast.

'Neither of us were making judgement on Iris, we're just going by what Sandy Napier told us.'

'You want to hear about him, do you?' the nurse said. 'Couch potato. That's what he was. Sat on his arse at the weekend, and only got up to go out with his pals to the pub. Iris was always on at him to go out with her, but oh no, he couldn't be bothered. So she started going out more and more. And then she met somebody in a bar one night and got talking to him. And I don't fucking blame her one little bit. Prick.'

'Do you know who this man was?'

'I can't remember his name now, but that was a long time ago. The point is, she started going out and enjoying herself. Started to see that there was life out there. And that was the end of their marriage.'

'Sandy wasn't happy about that. He told us all about her playing away from home,' Miller said.

'And who could blame her? All she wanted was to have fun with her husband, but he couldn't be bothered.'

'Did she have a regular boyfriend or...?'

'Or did she put it around?'

'Or did she have... you know... more than one... or did she...?' Miller said.

'Yes, we mean did she put it around?' Watt said, coming to the rescue.

'Yes. She liked the company of men, but it didn't make her a whore.'

'Nobody's saying she was a whore, but we need to know if she pissed off anybody so much that he would kill her. Now are you getting the point?'

The staff nurse looked at him as if she was preparing for a fight, then suddenly there was no wind under her wings anymore. 'Look, we have a stressful job, and it's nice to just go out and have a drink with your friends. Maybe flirt with some guy.'

'Did you go out with her at all?' Miller asked.

She held up her left hand, showing the ring. 'I like to have a drink, but I don't play around. I love my husband. But not all of us are married. I did go out with the group sometimes but not as much as the single ones.'

'You mentioned singles clubs,' Miller said, 'do you know if she ever went to the clubs in town?'

'No, but she did go to the singles night in the little hotel in Stockbridge. The *Dean* hotel. I've been a few times, but just for a laugh. Nobody takes it seriously. We would wind some men up and one or two of them actually gave some blokes their phone numbers.' She put a hand up to her mouth as if she was going to stifle a scream. 'You don't think one of them is a nutter?'

'It could be anybody. We just wanted to know if she'd ever had a problem with any man. Like if she had gone out with one and it turned sour.'

'I don't think so. Not that I know of anyway.'

'Do you know when she was there last?'

'Last Friday. I was there too.'

'No problems with anybody?'

'I would have said if there was. No, we only stayed for a little while then we got a taxi up town. And no, there wasn't any wanker following us.'

'Did she have any male friend that she regularly met for a drink?'

'Not that I know of.'

'What about here at work?' Miller asked.

'There's a group of us who go out, but it's just for fun.'

'Can you give us their names?'

'Yes.' She took a notepad out and scribbled some names down.

'If you remember anything else, can you give us a call?' Watt said, handing her a business card.

'Sure. And no doubt you'll be getting your end away next time there's a Treble Nine ball at the police club.'

'I don't think my wife would be too chuffed about that.'

They walked back the way they had come. 'I wasn't going to tell that torn face I'm not married,' Watt said when he was sure they were out of earshot.

'I bet guys are lining up to buy her a drink at the club.'

'She had you pegged right away though; wanker.' Watt laughed as the lift came.

'She meant it in a general way, Andy.'

'Yeah, keep telling yourself that, son,' he replied, grinning.

'Oh, fuck off,' Miller said as the lift doors closed.

SIX

'Now, don't be a stranger,' Beth Miller said, pouring two mugs of coffee and bringing them through to the dining room.

'I won't, I promise,' Carol said, taking one of the mugs. 'In fact, you won't be able to keep me away. I have a great recipe for mac and cheese with bacon.'

'Feel free to come around and cook it here any time you want. I can lend a hand.'

'Sounds great, mum.'

Miller smiled as he took one of the mugs. 'Mac and cheese is my favourite. I'm quite a dab hand in the kitchen.'

'Don't listen to him, Carol; he burns water,' Jack said.

'That's a slur on my character,' Miller said. *Although not as bad as being called a wanker by a staff nurse.*

'It's true. Maybe Carol will teach you a thing or two. Start with the basics, like putting bread into the toaster.'

'And you're Gordon Ramsey.'

'I can find my way around a kitchen. But never mind that. Carol doesn't want to hear how you don't know one end of a ladle from the other.'

'I'm sure Frank will do just fine with Carol's guidance,' Beth said.

'I'll teach him everything I know. In fact, I'd like to swap recipes with you, mum.'

'Come through to the living room and we can discuss them,' Beth said, and the two women left the dining room.

'She's a cracker, son,' Jack said, whispering. 'Put a ring on her finger.'

'One day, dad.'

'How long have you been going out with her?'

'A year.'

'What are you waiting for? You love her, don't you?'

'Of course I do.'

'Don't let her get away.'

'I'm moving in with her.'

'I'm just saying. Women like that don't come along all the time.'

'Duly noted, Chief Inspector.'

'Get a couple of beers out of the fridge and tell me what you found out about Iris Napier at the hospital. I want to hear it before morning briefing.'

Miller took a chilled bottle of Stella Artois out of the fridge, with a Coke for himself, and sat across from his father at the dining table. 'I'm driving.'

'Cheers anyway.'

'She liked going out with her friends from work. They all liked going out for a drink and a laugh at the singles night, along at the *Dean* hotel in Stockbridge.'

'That's why I want you and Carol to go there on your way home.'

'You don't think Paddy Gibb or Andy Watt will be put out by us doing this?'

'Who's in charge? I couldn't care less if they're put out. If they want to talk to me about it, they can feel free. Somehow, I don't think they'll give me any hassle.' He took some of the cold beer. Put the bottle on the table, making sure it sat on a coaster. 'It's a steep learning curve, but you're doing fine. I'm not saying this job gets easier, but you learn how to do it better as time goes on.'

'I like Paddy and Andy.'

'Watt shot himself in the foot a long time ago, him and Tam Scott. Both of them had a mouth. Tam not so much as Andy, but he clocked an inspector one night after a fight broke out. Tam was drunk and let fly about what he thought of the brass. That was his career halted right there. He was lucky he kept his job.'

Miller drank some of the cold Coke and felt it course its way down to his stomach. 'What about Andy?'

'It's more of an insubordinate thing with him. He didn't get on with some lad we had in a while back. A university grad who was on the fast track. He and Watt got into an altercation. It wasn't long before the grad outranked Watt and he started making life difficult. Andy was in the same boat as Tam Scott was. Dinosaurs from the old Lothian and Borders, who weren't going to get further up the ladder, despite having a wealth of experience.'

'Where's the grad now?'

'Down in London. After he messed up Watt's promotion chances, he buggered off.'

'Typical.'

They drank in silence for a minute. 'Give me your take on this killer,' Jack said. 'Just between you and me.'

'I think he hates women. He saw his chance with Iris and he made plans to kill her and carried them out.'

'Why do you think it wasn't just random?'

'Everything was calculated and executed to his plans, if you'll pardon the pun. No blood, cleaned up before he moved her. He dressed her again. Laid her out in a place that was secluded so he could get there and away again with little chance of being seen, yet in a place that she would be found.'

'Good. What else?'

'It's sort of like, *Game on*. Whether he's thinking this subconsciously or not, he's challenging us. Showing the world what he can do and how he can get away with it. He clearly thinks he's superior to us.'

'What about stitching her back up again? Do you think he's a surgeon?'

'There's no doubt. Each of the organs that was missing was taken out by a skilled hand.'

'Or maybe he wants you to think he's skilled.'

'Could be, although the job wasn't rushed. The cuts were precise.'

'He's clever though,' Jack said. 'Let's not underestimate him. Very planned, very efficient. And if we get to arrest him, don't turn your back on him. I've been in fights with sneaky bastards before and this guy is more than sneaky.'

'I'll bear that in mind.'

'And don't think she's the first. If this was just a killing, then he wouldn't have played this game. And he's going to get better at it. They always do. It's like taking up golf; your handicap gets better the more you play.'

'Are you boys talking shop?' Carol said, coming into the dining room.

'Talking about golf,' Miller said, smiling.

'Liar.'

Jack laughed. 'She knows you already, son. But to be fair, we were comparing our killer to taking up golf.'

'Fair dos.' She went over to a cabinet and took out a packet of biscuits. 'Carry on, gentlemen. We just needed a little something to go with the coffee.'

'What about the location?' Jack asked when Carol was out of the room.

'He knows the area. Whether he worked there or lived there, he knows it well. It would have to be somewhere he felt comfortable. He knows Stockbridge, either from the past, or now. He'll start getting more confident and move further away, but right now, I think if he strikes again, it's going to be within the vicinity.'

'You're right. Killers have proved this time and again. They don't want to be far from home. It's the comfort factor, until he gets more confident.'

'Which means we're going to have to pull out all the stops on this one, before he strikes again.'

'I have a feeling unless he makes a big mistake, that we're not going to get him until we have more victims. Sometimes, somebody kills in anger, and it's very unorganised, and we get him. Sometimes we don't get them and cases drag on for years. This game is a roll of the dice.'

'And right now, we have the odds stacked against us.'

They drank some more, Jack enjoying his beer more than Miller was enjoying his Coke. 'Your mother feels better about you just taking a few bits of your stuff. I told you she would.'

'My wise and wonderful father. How ever will I follow in your footsteps?'

'You won't. You'll come close though.'

'If your head gets any bigger, you won't be able to fit through the door.'

'Just telling it like it is, son.'

'And still you keep on about it.'

They went through to the living room where the women were debating the issue of whether basil should or shouldn't be added to a certain dish.

After another half hour, Miller and Carol left, heading for the *Dean* hotel.

'I'm excited about joining CID, Frank.'

'It's a bunch of suits going round pissing people off, mostly.'

'Oh, don't bloody ruin it for me.'

Miller laughed. 'You know what's going to happen, don't you?'

'What's that?' Carol said, driving down Drum Brae to connect with Queensferry Road.

'We'll be working with each other during the day, so we'll look forward to spending time apart.'

'It's called having our own space, Frank. Not a lot of people work together so they don't know what it's like, but we can make it work. We have two bedrooms, and there's a desk in there with the computer, so you can go there or into the bedroom for some privacy.'

'I know. We both can.'

'And we have our friends. You can still go out with your pals for a beer, and I'll be going out.'

'Great.'

'And don't worry, I won't nag you when you come in drunk.'

She drove down through Comely Bank and parked the car in their street. The hotel was five minutes from where they lived.

It was a detached two-storey building on the corner of Comely Bank Road and Portgower Place. There was a small wing on either side of the main façade. It took up a corner of the Edinburgh Academicals Sports ground. There was a beer garden out front with wooden tables. It was busy, the warm evening air encouraging drinkers outside.

Inside, Carol and Miller walked to the reception desk and took out their warrant cards.

'Is the manager in?' Miller asked.

'I'll call him,' the young woman said, picking up the telephone and talking to somebody. A few minutes later, a bald man who looked no older than Miller came into the reception.

'How can I help you, officers?' he asked. His accent was East London.

'Can we talk somewhere more private?'

'Sure. Come through to my office.'

He led them off to one side of the reception and into his office.

'Tony Hawkins. Drink?'

They both shook their head. 'Are these your normal hours?' Carol said as Miller closed the door behind them.

'There are two of us. I'm the duty manager for the back shift. The general manager is here from seven in the morning. Please, sit down.'

They sat in chairs opposite him. 'We just wanted a word about your singles night on Fridays.'

'Oh, yes? Fancy coming along?' He grinned at them.

'Not for the reasons you think,' Miller said. 'We want to know if you've had any problems with any of the men who come here.'

'Problems? Like drunk and disorderly?'

'No, I mean with any men giving women problems.'

'We have doormen to see that none of them get out of hand, but of course, there are the usual troublemakers. Some of them get drunk and start annoying the women but they're dealt with swiftly.'

'What about CCTV cameras?' Carol asked.

He gave a wry smile. 'People come here for a good time. Some come for a bit of fun on the side, just harmless fun where they can hook up with a member of the opposite sex. We don't tell them how to live their lives. We don't have much bother here, not like the clubs up town, so instead of having cameras, we have doormen. We're discreet here.'

'Is the singles night every Friday?' Miller asked.

'It is indeed. Good music, reasonably priced drinks. Not like those highway robbers up town.'

'What about last Friday? Anything out of the ordinary happen?'

'Like what?'

'I don't know. Something happening that normally doesn't happen. Like maybe somebody getting booted out who wasn't too happy about it.'

'It happens from time to time, but I would have heard about it if that was the case. I'm not here until closing. The bar staff close the function hall, but there's somebody at the desk all night at the weekends, so there's plenty of staff. None of them said anything unusual happened.'

'Are there regulars here, do you know?' Carol asked.

'I see a few faces, yes. Decent, working class people who like to let off steam.'

'Like nurses?' Miller said.

'I see a few from the Western in here, plus I've spoken to a few of them from the other hospitals.'

'You're here for a little while on a Friday?'

'I finish around ten o'clock, so I see some of them coming in. It starts at nine until four. Some of the lonelier ones get here at nine. Some women who think of this place as the last chance saloon. Some people think of these places as the next step from taking out an ad in the paper. Or going on one of those *safe* dating sites. *Date a rapist dot com* more like.'

'There are some desperate people out there looking for love,' Carol said. 'Some people prefer to go online and find romance.'

'Talking from experience?' he said with a smile. 'I don't think a good-looking girl like you would have any problem finding a man.'

'I didn't. In fact, he's sitting next to me.'

The manager looked at Miller. 'Oh, no offence squire.'

'None taken,' Miller said.

Carol looked at the man. 'Not everybody who comes to these places is desperate though?'

'Of course not. You see, we cater to different groups of people; those who come for a laugh, just to have a good time, a drink and a dance. Then we have those who are looking to get it away with a married person. Quick shag, back to the spouse.' He looked at Carol. 'Excuse the French. Then there's the men and women who come here hoping they really will find the love of their life. But I've yet to be invited to any weddings.'

'Who would you say is mostly here?'

'Mostly those who want to have a good time. Sometimes they

might get lucky without having looked for it. But we have a good clientele in here. Some are regulars who know me by name. We cater for a good time.'

'What about the guests? Aren't they bothered by the club?'

Hawkins sat back in his chair, smiling. 'We have the music loud but it's well insulated. We've had a few complaints over the years, but we've comped them a dinner or two. Nothing drastic. None recently.'

Miller had looked for any reports for the police being called to the hotel but there was only a couple of instances a few years back.

'Does the name Iris Napier mean anything to you?' Miller said.

'No. Should it? Oh, wait, wasn't that the woman who was found dead along at the well this morning? I heard it on the news earlier.'

'That's her.'

He leaned forward again. 'You're not telling me she was here?'

'We don't know.'

'But you think she might have been.'

Miller took a photo out of his inside pocket. It was a photo that Sandy Napier had provided. He showed it to Hawkins.

'This her? Bloody hell, I do know her.' He looked up from the photo, looking at each of them in turn. 'She's a regular.'

Miller took the photo back and put it away. 'Would you know if she was here last Friday?'

'Yes, she was. I was talking to her. I didn't get away until about ten-thirty. Some problem with a guest – nothing to do with the club – and I was late getting away. I was chatting with her outside. They come out for a fag 'cause there's no smoking in here. She was nice, always let on to me. One day she was with another bird, also a staff nurse, but this other one, she had a face like you make when you've stood in something. I think she batted for the other team. Never saw *her* go home with a man. She always left with the group she came with, the ones who were leaving without having hooked somebody. Sometimes I've had to stay overnight if the night auditor's called in sick.'

'Do you know if Iris left with anybody on Friday?'

'Sorry. I was away. But there is one thing.'

'What's that?' Miller said.

'When she was here, she used a completely different name.'

'Can you remember what is was?'

'Not off hand. But I remember the name of a bloke she left with a while back; Calvin.'

'No. They were walking out of the gateway onto the pavement and I heard her call him by his name. I don't know if he had thrown her some line but that was the name she called him.'

SEVEN

It had been three days since they had discovered the body of Iris Napier, and leads were drying up already.

'The drinks are on you, Miller,' DS Andy Watt said. 'Friday night, out with the lads, blowing your pay cheque.'

'As much as I'd like to, I've moved in with Carol, as you fine well know. We have a lot to do, emptying my boxes and the like.'

'Jesus, you're not under the thumb already?' He weighed up each hand, moving them up and down like scales. 'Night out with the boys, versus a boring night in with the girlfriend. I would have thought that was no contest.'

'Aren't you spending a night in with your missus, Andy?' DCI Paddy Gibb said.

'We're doing our own thing now, as you well know. She's probably spending her Friday night giving some young jockey a good…'

'Oh, hi Andy,' Carol said, coming up behind him. She had finished her shift and had changed into civvies.

'Game of darts. I was going to say, game of darts.'

'Sure you were. I heard you trying to persuade my boyfriend to join you in an evening of debauchery.'

'I don't know how to even spell that, never mind take the bait.'

Carol laughed. 'As much as we would love to join you, Frank really is going to be very busy this weekend.'

'I hate people who invite themselves out for a drink. You've just ruined my night out. I hope you're happy.'

'I am actually.'

'Well, just remember lover boy there is on-call. Any crap that comes in, he gets the phone call. Him and those other dafties that are further down the food chain.'

'Of which I will be one, remember? Next week is my last full week in uniform.'

'When I used the word *dafties*, I wasn't including you of course.'

'I saw your name's on the list, Andy,' Miller said.

'Don't bother calling me, son. I'm a senior officer in Serious Crimes. All the other twaddle is down to you guys. The peeping Tom is still on the loose. Not been any sightings for a few weeks, but you never know. He always appears on a Friday night. Right, unless the *Surgeon* is roaming the streets of Edinburgh tonight, I'm going to get pished.'

'What was that, Watt?' Paddy Gibb said.

'I said, I'll be at home, sitting by the phone in case it rings.'

'You bloody well better be sober this weekend.'

'Aye aye, Captain.'

They left the High Street station, home of Serious Crimes – soon to be the Major Inquiry Team – and Central Division CID.

'What do you say we stop for a quick drink at the local then we can get food delivered and crack a bottle of wine to celebrate?' Carol said.

'I think I should be like Andy Watt, sitting by the phone, waiting for it to ring.'

'Andy will be half-jaked by ten o'clock.'

'Go on then, you've twisted my arm, but just so we're clear, I won't have you taking advantage of me.'

'Yes, you will.'

'Yes, I will.'

Outside the station in the High Street, performers were giving free shows and handing out leaflets for their gigs. The place was bustling with tourists.

'I love August,' Carol said, 'it's my favourite time of the year. The Edinburgh Festival in full swing. The nice warm evenings. The whole atmosphere is brilliant.'

'I know what you mean. My career could have gone either way; police officer or clown.'

'Some people don't think there's much difference, unfortunately.'

'Except they don't call the circus when their house gets broken into.'

They walked up to George IV Bridge to catch a bus down to Stockbridge, Miller carrying Carol's holdall with her uniform jacket in it. He had his suit on, carrying the jacket over his arm. It might be August, but the weather could turn in a heartbeat.

'Nothing has panned out at all, has it?' she asked. They both knew she meant the *Surgeon*. Even the Edinburgh Evening Post was calling him that.

'Nothing. We were checking CCTV all week, but we didn't see Iris on anything.'

'I think the hotel should bloody well have cameras. This is just crap, trying to protect the identities of cheaters. All they've done is protect the possible identity of Iris's killer.'

'Everybody's alibi checks out, including her ex-husband's. Forensics went over every inch of her house and it's clear she wasn't murdered there.'

'We have to accept that sometimes killers get away with it, Frank.'

'Not this time. He's not going to stop at one.'

They caught a number 29 and chatted as the Lothian Buses double decker trundled down Frederick Street over the setts in the road. It was busy with commuters going home. It was a warm summer evening and despite the hopper windows being open, the bus was roasting.

'To be honest, I'm excited that you've moved in permanently,' Carol said after they got off the bus in North West Circus Place. The evening air was warm with only a hint of a breeze.

'Me too. It's like going on a Boy Scout trip without the midges.'

Carol laughed. 'You've got most of your stuff moved in, your mother's cried her eyes out at her wee boy moving out and it's all done bar the shouting.'

'In all honesty, I think my mother had just been cutting onions.'

'Aw, her wee lamb is being taken away by that harlot. Living in sin. It would bring the tears to my eyes too.'

'There's no tighter bond than between a mother and her son.'

'Hopefully I'll get the chance to find out.' She took his hand. 'I told you what my favourite time of the year is,' Carol said. 'What's yours?' She realised that even though they were going to be living together, there were still some things that they were going to find out about each other.

'Christmas.'

'Why Christmas?'

'It was always special when I was a wee boy. I loved it when my mum and dad put up the tree and the anticipation of Santa coming. Typical kid stuff, but the feeling always stayed with me.'

She smiled as they crossed over the old bridge that spanned the Water of Leith. They turned into Dean Terrace and he saw the sign outside one of the terraced houses, the *Savoy* hotel. The hotel had been a Georgian house originally.

Up ahead, they saw a woman shouting at a man. He was dressed smartly, with his back to them. The woman looked to be in her late twenties and Miller couldn't hear exactly what was happening, but he saw she started hitting the man with her handbag. He put up an arm in defence and as the bag came at him again, he ducked and the woman was off-balance and fell over.

The man ran without looking back and jumped into a Range Rover.

Miller and Carol walked up to the woman, thinking that she was a drunk. She was sitting crying, the contents of her bag spilled across the pavement. They weren't given any assistance from the patrons who were standing on the steps leading into the hotel.

'What's the problem here?' Miller asked, showing the woman his warrant card.

'You're a policeman?' she said, and Miller noticed her American accent.

'Yes. Detective Constable Frank Miller. This is Officer Carol Davidson.' He could tell that she wasn't drunk and this didn't appear to be a domestic. 'Was that man trying to mug you?'

She sighed and stopped crying, taking Carol's offered hand. 'No, I was bothering him.'

'Why were you arguing with him?'

'Long story.'

'Do you live round here?'

She nodded to the hotel. 'I'm staying there.'

Carol saw the woman had cut her knee and it was bleeding. 'Come on, let's get you in and we'll get you tidied up and you can tell us what was going on.'

She nodded as Miller started picking up the contents of her bag. Carol led her into the hotel, followed by Miller a few minutes later.

The bar was heaving. Locals, tourists, and maybe some guests thrown in for good measure. Edinburgh at festival time was a melting pot.

Carol got the attention of one of the barmen, Miles Laing.

'Hi, Carol. Frank. Good to see you again. What you for?'

'One of your guests was involved in an altercation outside. She's cut her knee. Do you have a first aid box?' Carol said.

'In reception. I'll take you through.' He asked the other barman to hold the fort. 'I'll catch you later, Robert,' he said to a patron at the bar. The man raised his glass, finished his drink, and walked in front of Miles, leaning heavily on a walking stick.

'Sherri, love, what happened?' he said as he came around the bar.

'I fell.'

They led her through to the reception area of the hotel. The man called Robert was slowly walking up the stairs to his room.

'Goodnight, Robert!' Miles said.

'Good night, my friend,' the man said.

'Come on, let's get this knee cleaned up before we get a plaster on it,' Carol said, leading her into the toilet.

Miles walked behind the reception desk and took a first aid box from a cupboard and gave it to Carol..

'What's Sherri's full name?'

'Judd.'

'Has she been here long?'

'A few days. She's very nice. She'll sit in the bar and chat away. She mentioned she was here to meet her boyfriend, but I didn't realise it was like that.'

'Like what?'

'Like he was an older guy. He seems a bit of a tosser. They started arguing and then he stormed out and she followed him.'

'And we know the rest.'

The women came out of the toilet.

'Now, why don't you all go through and sit in the dining room and I'll bring some drinks through,' Miles said to Carol.

'Cheers, Miles. Just an orange juice, please. Frank?'

'Bottle of Becks, thanks.'

'I'm fine,' Sherri said.

'It's on me. How about a Coke?'

'Okay then, thanks.' As if the fact that it was free had twisted her arm.

'You feel okay now?' Carol asked as they sat at one of the tables.

'I'm fine now, thanks to you two.'

'You can talk to us, Sherri.'

'I'm sorry I caused a disturbance in the street. Am I in trouble?'

'No.'

'Believe it or not, I don't always act like that, but I've travelled a long way.'

'Who was that man?' Miller asked as he sat opposite her. He emptied his pockets of the stuff he'd picked up off the street that had fallen out of her bag, including a paperback. A little glass vase sat empty in the middle of the table, waiting for the evening dinner sitting. The white tablecloths were fresh and he could imagine how busy this room would get at dinner time.

'I don't know.' They looked up as Miles came in with a tray, balancing their drinks on it.

'Oh, thanks Miles. You're a doll,' Carol said.

'We'll need to have a proper celebration for Frank moving in, but for right now, this is just your starter for ten.' He gave them their drinks. 'I'll be through in the bar if you need me. Sherri, give any of the staff a shout if you need any help. I mean it. I'll let my dad know what happened.'

'Thank you, Miles, you've been very kind.'

'We aim to please.' He walked away with the tray.

'We're here to help, Sherri,' Carol said.

Sherri looked down at her lap for a moment, one hand holding the glass of coke. 'I met a man online. We fell in love.'

'And he wanted you to come over here for a visit?' Miller said.

'No, this was my idea to come over.' She looked at Miller and took a sip of the soft drink.

'Did he know you were coming?'

'Not until a few days ago. I wrote to him and told him I was coming over. He got angry and said not to. He was busy and was sorting himself out.'

'But you decided to come anyway?' Carol said.

Sherri nodded. 'I had given him everything I had. All my savings, every penny I had. I even sold one of my cars, keeping the old runabout.'

Carol looked at Miller: *catfish*.

'I know what you're thinking,' Sherri continued, 'that I must be off my head to send a man money, but he was in trouble financially. One of his financial backers had pulled out. He said the money was a loan, but I knew it wouldn't make a difference when we were married.'

'Did he ask you to marry him?' Miller asked.

Sherri shook her head. 'I suggested it. He could come over to America and live if he wanted, but he said he couldn't leave his sick mother. I suggested I come over so we could be together, but he kept putting me off. There was always something going on, some reason he couldn't talk to me, or wouldn't be available when I wanted to talk on screen.'

'How did you recognise him?'

'He sent me photos of himself.'

Carol drank some of her orange juice and put a hand on Sherri's. 'Then you decided to come over and meet him in person.'

'Yes. He was angry. He wouldn't message me so I emailed him. He told me not to come yet as his mother had been taken into hospital. She was elderly and not well at all. But I suspected something was not right with him. I booked a flight and came over here.'

'How did you get him to meet you?'

'I wrote to him and told him I wanted to speak face to face or else I would come to his house. I Googled him.'

'What's his name?'

'Perry MacKinnon. He's a doctor.'

Jesus Miller thought but kept quiet.

Carol looked at her. 'Is he married?'

'He's in a loveless marriage. He and his wife are living under the same roof, but he's basically split up from her.'

'How old are you, Sherri?' Miller said.

'Twenty-seven.'

'How old is he?'

'Forty-two.'

'If he's a doctor, how come he needed you to send him money?'

Sherri took a deep breath before looking between the two police officers, like she was trying to find the answer without feeling foolish, and knowing that her answer would sound that way anyway.

'He asked me to invest in his new premises. He just needed a few thousand to finalise things, and it was only a loan. I wired him money.'

'And now he doesn't want to have anything to do with you?'

Sherri nodded.

'Do you know if these new premises actually exist?'

'No.'

'I wonder why he sent you his home address if he had no intention of meeting up with you?' Miller said.

'He didn't. I Googled his name and paid for a search. That's when I wrote to him telling him where I'd be staying and when I wanted to meet him.'

'Why did you choose this hotel?'

'He had mentioned it a few times. He said he sometimes came for a drink here. I thought he wouldn't feel so bad coming here to meet me. You know, him being in familiar surroundings. But he was very defensive when he came in. He asked me what I wanted and denied even knowing me. I asked him flat out if he was still married and he'd been stringing me along, but he kept talking to me like I was insane and to leave him alone.'

'You know what a *catfish* is, don't you?' Carol said.

'I think so.'

'Men and women go on the net, pretending to be somebody they're not, and often they'll lie to get money out of somebody. Like this guy did to you.'

'He seemed like such a nice man. I fell in love with him.'

'What are you going to do now?'

Sherri looked at them both in turn. 'I really have no idea. There's nothing to go back to. I didn't have a boyfriend, I jacked my job in. Sold my other car. Gave up the lease on my apartment. I know it sounds foolish, but I thought if he saw me in the flesh, he would see that everything would be fine.'

'How long are you booked in here?'

'Two weeks.'

'Do you have a return ticket?'

'Yes, but the date is for a month from now. I just put in any date to return, not intending to use it, because it was cheaper than a one-way ticket.'

'What will you do now?'

She gave a brief smile. 'I really have no idea. I paid for the room but after that, I'll have to go somewhere. I have a couple of weeks to think about it.' She tapped the book that sat on the table. *Triple Code* by Len Chatter. 'At least I'll be able to see this man. When I saw he was going to be at the book festival tomorrow night, I thought I'd go and see him. I'm a big fan of the *Ben Goode* thrillers.'

'Really?' Miller said. 'Us too. In fact, I have two tickets for tomorrow night as well.'

'You do?' Carol said.

'It was supposed to be a surprise. Dinner then the talk.'

'Great.' She looked at Sherri. 'Why don't you come along with us?'

'Oh, I don't know about that. I appreciate the offer, but this is a night out with your boyfriend.'

'How did you know he was my boyfriend?'

She smiled a brighter smile. 'I see the way you look at him.'

'He just moved in with me.'

'That's even more reason for me to go on my own.'

Carol looked at Miller.

'It's fine,' he said, 'you're welcome to join us.'

Sherri looked at them both in turn. 'I've only known you for a few minutes and yet here you are, inviting me along to your night out. Well, the book part. I don't want to spoil your dinner.'

'Anybody ready for another?' Miles said. 'Oh, Len Chatter. I'm a big fan of his.'

'We're all going to see him tomorrow. Sherri had a ticket and Frank got ours.'

Sherri fished into her bag. 'Two tickets.' She held them up and looked at Miles, her eyebrows raised.

'Miles, I do believe you've been invited along?' Miller said.

'And I graciously accept. It's my night off and I was going to be drowning my sorrows in some dive bar somewhere. Well, I'd be propping up my father's bar and the old sod would have roped me into working. So, if you're sure, that would be great.'

'I'm sure.'

'Then that's settled,' Carol said. She and Miller stood up. 'How about we see you both inside the Spiegeltent around seven? The show starts at eight.'

'Sounds good to me,' Sherri said. 'I looked at the beer tent online and it looks wonderful.'

'Good seeing you again my friend,' Miles said to Miller. The men shook hands.

'Likewise.'

He shrugged. 'Let's go home and have a nap. I feel knackered.'

'As chat up lines go, it's not one of your better ones.' She laughed and took his hand, her other one holding her holdall. 'But it'll do.'

EIGHT

'Vincent!'

Aw, what is it now? Vince thought, just as his fingers were hovering over the keyboard.

His mother was shouting at him from upstairs. He looked at the clock sitting on the mantelpiece. Just after seven-thirty. Half a fucking hour after he'd sat down at his desk, and she was shouting down to him.

'Vincent!'

Vince slammed the keyboard drawer into his desk and shoved the office chair back.

'Vincent!'

For fuck's sake. There was no way he could ignore the screeching from above. He'd get more peace if he moved his desk into the middle of the M8. He stormed out of the living room and walked towards the stairs. 'I'm fucking coming,' he said, stopping short of shouting it.

'What did you say?'

'I said I'm coming.' Radar ears. *This had better be good.*

He stomped harder on the stairs.

'What is it?' he said, pushing the door open wide. Mother was sitting up in bed, a knitted shawl wrapped round her shoulders.

'I need the remote for my TV.'

'Where is it?'

'Over there. By the TV.'

'Couldn't you get up and get it yourself?'

'I don't feel well today. My back's hurting me.'

Vince let out an exaggerated sigh and walked over to the TV, picked up the remote and handed it to her. 'Anything else?'

'Why are you in such a bad mood? You took the day off, didn't you?'

'Yes, I did.'

'You've been moping about down there all day.'

'Not moping; writing.'

'Oh, yes, I forgot, playing around downstairs, pretending you're Ernest Hemingway.'

'Oh, we're back to this then. I don't know why you're so against it.'

'Why you have these fancy ideas in your head, I don't know. I mean, it's not as if you picked up reading from your dad.'

'Look, I told you I wanted to write a book in the evenings so I could self-publish my books. Make some money.'

'Another flight of fancy.'

'No it's not.'

'Of course it is. You'll never make any money. Everybody's at it nowadays.'

'Not everybody.'

'Your head's in the clouds, laddie.' Mother pouted her lip for a moment and reached into the box of chocolates that was by her side.

'I've already told you this a million times, yet here I am having to explain things again. I work Monday to Friday in the office and then in the evenings, I'm a writer. I sit from seven until ten, every night. I only stop for a coffee or a pee.'

'Oh God.' She clasped a hand to her chest. 'Where did you pick up such language? It certainly wasn't from me.'

'It's only pee.'

'You didn't get that from your father, either. He was a real gentleman.'

Oh here we fucking go. 'Yes, I know, but that was a different generation.'

'When your father first brought me to this house, his mother and father lived here. Your father didn't bring me up to this bedroom until the day we were married.'

'I know, I know, you've told me all this before. Only on your wedding day did he bring you up here to show you his,' finger quotes, '*true love.*'

'You don't have to make it sound mucky.'

'As much as I'd love to hear all this again, I have to…'

'Everything was fine in this house until you brought that woman home.'

'She was a nice girl, Mother, and she loved coming around here, until you scared her off.'

'She's not here, is she?'

Vince screwed his face up. 'What? Of course she's not f… here. She broke up with me five years ago.'

'She wanted to get her hooks into you, my lad. Take all your money and bleed you dry.'

'Is that why you called me up here, to talk about Dawn?'

'No. I want you to stop this writing nonsense.'

'Not going to happen. Today, I want to finish a project I'm working on. I'm seeing Len Chatter tomorrow and I want to give him my manuscript. He's going to co-write some of his new books with other authors. It's not nonsense.'

'And this Len Crapper's going to pick you?'

'Chatter. His name's Len Chatter.'

'I've never heard of him.'

'Who cares? He's not going to know I exist unless I try.'

'There's a difference; those other writers are good.'

'Well, thanks a lot. How do you know my stuff isn't any good?'

'When you're at work, I go down and read the stuff you've printed off the night before. Utter drivel.'

'You wouldn't know good writing if it smacked you in the face. The only thing you read is the back of a cereal box.'

'Why don't you stick in at work and get up the ladder? You're good with computers, aren't you?'

'That place is a dump. A dead end. As for computers, I know how to switch one on and use a keyboard, I don't know how to research quantum theory.'

'It pays money every month. It pays the bills. This writing lark won't do that.'

'Not yet anyway.'

'They love you there, Vincent.'

He'd told her that, but the truth was, they couldn't wait to see the back of him, and he couldn't wait to tell them all to fuck off. Except Jimmy, his pal.

'Do you think I like seeing you like this?' She was talking to him but not looking at him.

'Like what?'

'Like this; skulking about the house like you're just out of prison.'

'I'm a writer! We skulk. We talk to ourselves. It's what we do.'

'If your father was here, he'd give you a stern talking to, young man.'

'Good God, I'm not twelve.'

'I bet your friends at work think you're silly wanting to give up your day job to do this hobby of yours.'

'They're all very supportive.' Except Duncan Wood, his boss, who thought he was an obnoxious wanker who should have left years ago. Vince looked over at the clock: 7.40 pm. Christ. She'd done it again; distracted him with her nonsense.

'Right, as much as I'm riveted with this conversation, I want to go and do some writing.'

'Why don't you tell Jimmy that you can't make it tonight and stay in with me and Beckett? We could watch some TV and you could make us popcorn.'

'As much as that sounds outstanding, I just said I want to do some writing before I go out.'

He tried tuning her out as he went back downstairs. He knew he wouldn't get any more writing done before he went out, but he had polished the first three chapters so that Len wouldn't be anything other than impressed.

Beckett rolled in on his wheelchair. 'You off out tonight?'

'Yeah, buddy. Sorry you're stuck in with old fanny upstairs.'

Beckett was five years younger than Vince, *my little accident* as his mother put it. The age gap didn't bother Vince. Beckett was his brother and he loved him like one. After Beckett had left the army, he'd been working in London, and God knows why, but he had decided to come back to Edinburgh to live.

Beckett laughed. 'Don't worry about it. I heard her lecturing you again. Just ignore her.

I've read your stuff after she left it lying about. I think it's great.'

'Yeah, well, if she would let me be, I might find some inspiration sometimes.'

'You'll get there. Are you still going to see that writer tomorrow?'

'Yes, I am.'

'How about I come along with you?'

Then Vince smiled. 'That would be magic. It would get you out of the house for a while.' He looked down at Beckett's leg, still in its brace. 'If you feel up to it, of course.'

'Of course I do. I'll use my crutches, even though I sweat like a builder's arse using them.'

'Great. I'd love you to meet Len Chatter. Especially since he's taking us for a meal afterwards. He's a great guy. He's moving up here permanently.'

'Sounds like a great guy.'

'He is. I consider him a mate now.'

Beckett smiled and started to wheel away. 'I'll put the popcorn on as soon as you're gone, then she'll be down in a heartbeat.'

'Good man.'

At nine o'clock, he left to go and meet Jimmy. The one bit of sanity in his life.

NINE

'Cheers!' the crowd shouted in the large room.

Calvin Baxter smiled as they all clinked their champagne glasses in toast to Carter's success.

'Senior manager!' Ben Mathers said. 'You should be proud, my old son.'

'Oh, I am, Ben. I've worked hard, but now the board have seen fit to promote me to head of department, there will have to be changes around here.'

Mathers laughed. 'I hope my job's safe. You never want to forget who was with you on the lower rung and who was by your side when you were climbing.'

'You got that right. I won't forget you, Ben, don't worry.' Calvin held the smile and slapped the man on the side of the arm. *You'll be the first one out of here, that I can promise you. Fucking tosser.*

'I knew I could rely on you. Where's Bree?'

Calvin was looking across the room at a woman who was standing chatting with one of the older partners. 'What? Oh, away on a business trip.'

'You should bring her round for din–' he started to say, but

Calvin wasn't listening. He was making his way over to the other side of the room.

'Congratulations again,' the woman said as he approached.

'Thank you.' He smiled and the older bloke moved away. 'How are things with you, Marcie Lincoln?'

Marcie Lincoln. Christ, just saying her name got his heart beating faster.

'Looking up, Mister Baxter, sir.'

Calvin laughed. 'You don't have to call me sir, you know that.' She looked fantastic in the little black number she was wearing. Was it still called a *little black number* nowadays? Things changed so much, so fast.

'What should I call you?' She smiled, her cherry red lipstick glistening from the champagne.

'Call me sometime,' he said, with rehearsed practice. It sounded corny now he'd said it out loud, but it usually got a laugh, generally when they'd had too much to drink, but Marcie hadn't had too much to drink. She'd said she wanted to enjoy the performance. She'd also said that to him the first time he'd fucked her.

The first time he'd seen her, he'd known he had to have her. Gorgeous, intelligent, smart, she was the whole package.

'This has been a great party,' Marcie said. 'What a day for you.'

Perfect teeth. They must have cost a fortune, but it was the icing on the cake. 'It's been a long one,' he said.

'Where's Bree?'

'In Hong Kong. Or Australia. Who cares? Where's Norman?' He grinned.

'In London. As you well know, mister Calvin Baxter.' She stuck her tongue between her teeth in what she thought was a provocative gesture, but he found it extremely annoying.

He had known Marcie for three years, and he'd been sleeping with her for more than two of those.

He'd met her in a bar one night. He hadn't been looking to

sleep around but his wife was a flight attendant with British Airways and was away for days on end sometimes. It had been winter, and Bree, his wife, had been stuck at JFK airport in New York, and while the snowploughs were beavering away clearing the runway, he was stuck on his own in a cold, wet miserable Edinburgh.

And into the bar walked Marcie.

He'd known her to say *hello* to, but had never had a conversation with her before that night. He'd hoped he didn't look like some sad lush who was propping up a bar before heading home to his mother.

He'd kept looking over at her and more than once, she'd caught him looking at her and had smiled back. After an hour or so, her friends had left and she'd come over to the bar where he was sitting.

'Fancy buying a girl a drink, Cal?' she'd said.

He was surprised that she knew his name. 'You have the advantage,' he'd said.

'I do, don't I?' She'd grinned at him and sat down on the stool next to him, assuming his answer was going to be *sure*.

'Scotch and whatever the lady is having.'

Champagne, of course.'

He'd paid for the drinks. 'So, you have the advantage,' he'd repeated.

'Marcie. I'm in legal on the fourth floor.'

'As you know my name, I'm sure you know which department I work in.'

'Accounting on six.'

'I've never seen you in here before,' he'd said. The *Caley* bar was in the Caledonian hotel, on Lothian Road. Formerly a station hotel when there was a railway station underneath many years before, it was a jewel in Edinburgh's crown, sitting in the shadow of Edinburgh Castle.

It was only a stone's throw from their office building that sat on the corner of Lothian Road and the West Approach Road. A big piece of modern architecture that the Georgian architects would have boaked over.

'Some of my department were coming for a drink here and they didn't fancy mixing with the riff-raff in *Shakespeare's*. Their words, not mine. I happen to love it in there. It's got great atmosphere. But some of my co-workers are snobs. So the *Caley* it was.' She'd taken a sip of the Champagne. Held up her glass in a *cheers* salute. 'Is this your regular haunt?'

'Sometimes I come here when I want a quiet pint before heading home. The bus stop is just around the corner.'

'Bus? You don't have a chauffeur?' She'd giggled.

'I'm working on it.' He had smiled at her, completely captivated.

'You now wanting to go home to the wife?' she'd asked.

'My wife is out of town.'

'My husband is, too. He's a travelling salesman. He knows the M6 better than he knows me.'

And so the dance had begun; she'd wanted to know if he was married, and she'd wanted him to know that *she* was married. Whatever they got themselves into after that, they weren't going in blind.

And what they had got into was a black cab.

Along to her townhouse in Pinegrove Gardens, off Maybury Road at Barnton.

Had he been on the market for a townhouse – and had one been for sale – he would have been impressed enough to put down a deposit and make an offer, but the only thing he had been interested in was her bedroom.

The house was on three levels, and if he'd had more to drink, he would have run out of steam before he even made it up to the top floor. But as it was, he'd done more talking to her than drinking, and that helped enormously. He could only imagine how fit her husband had to be, going up and down all these stairs.

Calvin was nearing forty and yearned for his twenties again. A time when running up the stairs wouldn't have winded him. Now his dodgy knee, which he'd twisted when he was drunk one night, was reminding him to not fuck with it, or else it might just give the kneecap a little dislocation.

Luckily, neither of them had to worry about a spouse coming in, so Marcia had suggested they have a little night cap. The living room was on the first level – base camp, as Calvin would come to think of it – and a nice antique drinks cabinet sat against a wall. The living room was divided by a wall with a fire in it, and although the central heating was on, she'd put the fire on too.

It had turned out that on that first night, he didn't even get to see her bedroom.

The big, leather couch was the first place they'd ever made love. And what an accomplished lover she was.

Christmas was knocking on the door and it was soon time for the office party. Each department was doing their own thing, but he had found out where Marcia's crew were having theirs, and he had "bumped into her" in a nightclub in Lothian Road, at that time of the night where the little groups were splitting off, like platoons going into battle, only this battle was being fought by drunken lawyers looking for a Christmas quickie.

That had been two and a half years ago.

Now they alternated between houses, and tonight it was his turn to get the sheets dirty.

'So, what are you doing after the party?' Marcie said, taking a sip of her drink and grinning at the same time, a feat only mastered by drunks and serial flirters.

'I thought I'd head off home. Have an early night. What about you?'

'Same.'

As the promotion party broke up, Calvin slipped out of the building into the warm night air. Marcie came out with some of their co-workers.

'Fancy sharing a cab?' she asked Calvin.

'Sure. Why not?' They walked to the rank on Lothian Road outside the Sheraton and jumped into a fast black.

'Balerno. I'll give you directions when we're there.'

They sat back and giggled like a pair of teenagers as Calvin nuzzled her neck.

Marcie playfully slapped him. 'Stop. Somebody will see.'

He laughed and sat up.

His house was a large pile past the turn off for the village. The driver got a large tip.

Inside the house, it was stuffy. Calvin opened one of the bedroom windows when they went upstairs with the glasses and champagne bottle.

'I've been waiting on this all day,' he said, popping the cork.

'Don't wait any longer,' Marcie replied as he grabbed her and reached round to pull down the zipper on her dress.

TEN

Ten minutes later they were in Carol's flat in Comely Bank Terrace. He would have to get used to thinking of this as their street now, not just Carol's.

'I hope every weekend isn't going to be like this,' Miller said.

'At least we'll be on the same shift again.'

'You really can't wait to be called detective now, can you?'

'You were like a wee boy on Christmas morning when you put your suit on that first day. You stayed over, remember and your mother gave you a hard time.'

'How could I forget. Just as well she loves you as much as I do.'

'I love your parents. Although it's going to be hard, both of our fathers working in the same department. It will be like they're watching over us.'

'Your dad is mostly office-based now, and he'd only come out when he felt like he had to look at something up close. Same with Jack; the grunt work is down to us now. He said they were out in the field more at the moment because they're short staffed.'

'How can they be short-staffed?'

'Believe it or not, a lot of uniforms join CID then find they can make their way up the ladder quicker back in uniform. It's not for everybody.'

'I'm glad you're not on-call all weekend,' Carol said.

'Me too. We can have wine over dinner when I take you out tomorrow night.'

'That was a nice surprise, getting tickets to see Len Chatter. And I'm glad you didn't mind me inviting Sherri along.' She put her arm round his waist and they stood looking down at the bowling green of the Dean Bowling Club. Members were starting to appear, dressed in their blazers, ready for a game and a drink afterwards.

'I feel sorry for her, being duped like that. And by a bloody doctor, no less.'

'Except it wasn't the doctor who duped her, was it?'

Miller shook his head. 'No. I suspect it was somebody pretending to be him. Those trolls on the net know what they're doing. But I want to find out more about this Perry MacKinnon anyway.'

'Just Google him.'

'I will. Then I'll run him through the system.'

'Just to be on the safe side, run Sherri too.'

'You tell me that *after* inviting her along to the book signing?'

'I didn't see the harm; she was going anyway and it's a public event. Hopefully she won't be weird.'

'Miles said she's been sitting in the bar all week, and he says she's okay. Unless she has a cauldron in her room, we should be alright.' He looked at his watch. 'Almost time for dinner. What do you fancy?'

'I fancy a quiet night in with my boyfriend. You choose the food.'

'Sounds good to me. You do like seafood, don't you?'

'You know I love it.'

'Good, 'cause there's a decent chippie along the road.'

'I wouldn't want you to go to that expense.'

'Money's no object when it comes to you, my darling.' He laughed and they kissed in front of the window, then thoughts of Sherri flashed into his mind and he felt guilty for a moment.

'Let's sit down. I don't want any of the old codgers keeling over after seeing us snogging at the window.'

'It'll give them something to talk about.'

Miller had started moving his stuff in less than a week earlier, but he felt as if he'd lived here for years. He knew some guys who'd moved into their own place, and he had given it thought, but if he had to be honest with himself, he'd been lazy. It was convenient to be living at home with his folks. Carol had been right; his mother had cried when he had told her he was moving out. Jack, his father and a murder squad detective, had told him it was about time. Not in a bad way, but he knew his son should be out on his own.

Miller loved Carol, he knew that, and barring some catastrophic event, he could see himself settling down with her. He was in it for the long term, and although he'd had other women in his life, nobody had had the pull that Carol had.

After dinner and some TV watching, they decided on an early night. *To christen their bed* as Carol put it. Miller didn't argue. But he wanted to shower first.

He was in the bathroom and opened the medicine cabinet with the mirror on the front. His razor and can of foam was sitting on the sink. Carol had promised to clean out some of her stuff so he could fit it in.

He opened it up and saw there was a space on a shelf for his stuff. Then he saw it. Tucked away behind Carol's deodorant.

A man's razor. Not his.

He picked it up, thinking that it was a lady one, even though it wasn't pink like the other ones, and he saw it was a man's.

The hot water ran into the sink, causing steam to rise. He stood looking at the razor like he had discovered a blood-covered knife. Carol had said that she had boyfriends before, and he hadn't expected her to be like a nun, but thinking that another man had stayed over took him aback.

Listen to you, Miller, all self-righteous. Remember the girl from

Gayfield Square who you took home one night after a party and you stayed over? his reasoning side said. *Yes, but I didn't leave my razor in the cabinet.*

So now what? End your relationship right now and go running back to mummy? Tell her you thought you were ready for the real world and now you know you aren't?

He held the razor. It wasn't new, the black plastic handle now tarnished, the colour faded. How long had it been there? How come he hadn't seen it the last time he stopped over?

It was in there behind her stuff. She wasn't hiding it.

He put it back in the cabinet. Used his own razor to shave.

After his shower, she was waiting for him, wearing some sexy nightwear.

He climbed into bed and lay staring up at the ceiling.

'What's wrong?' Carol said.

'Nothing. I just can't help thinking about that dead woman.'

'Sometimes you just have to leave work behind, my love.'

Oh, so I'm your love now? Not Mr fucking razor man, whoever he is.

'I'm sorry, I feel completely bushed,' he said.

'Never mind. We can spoon. Besides, I'm on early tomorrow.'

He fell into a fitful sleep.

ELEVEN

'I'm raring to go tonight, Vince boy,' Jimmy said, one leg bouncing up and down as they sat at a table in the function hall of the *Dean* hotel in Stockbridge. It was heating up nicely, with plenty of women dressed up for the evening.

'I can tell.' Vince sipped at his pint, watching everybody go about their business of slowly drinking themselves into a stupor.

'I don't mind telling you, they'll be fighting over me tonight.'

'For fuck's sake, get a grip of yourself.'

Jimmy took his hand out of his pocket. 'What did you do with your day off?'

'First of all, stop bouncing your fucking knee. You're making me sea-sick. The girls will think there's something wrong with you. And secondly, I had a shite day off, but thanks for asking.'

'Jesus, mate, cheer up. We're out on the pull. There's a couple of girls over there giving me the beady eye.'

'*Beady eye*? Who the fuck talks like that?'

Jimmy laughed. 'Or her glass eye. If she rolls it over here, I'm in.'

'Manky bastard. If it's got a pulse, you'll shag it, right?'

'At least I have *some* scruples. Unlike you.' Jimmy stood up. 'You want a chaser to go with that?'

'Cheers.'

Jimmy always made Vince laugh, but tonight, he didn't feel much like laughing. His mother bringing up Dawn had put him off his game. God, he hadn't seen her in the longest time. The last he'd heard, she was living in London and had a baby. That could have been him, if it wasn't for the old boot expressing her opinion at every opportunity.

Dawn. Just even thinking about her made him feel sad.

She had been the nicest woman he had ever gone out with, and the only one who had stuck around long enough to get to know him better. She had a loud laugh, but nothing embarrassing. And a figure to die for. He recalled the night he had made the mistake of taking her home to meet his folks.

He had thought the old coffin dodgers would scare her away, but she didn't give up easily. Dawn had laughed at his father's jokes and smiled at all the right times.

Then came the big question that Vince had been dreading; *What does she do for a living?* His mother had asked the following day.

A dancer Vince had replied.

What kind of dancer? She was dressed in a pink twinset with fake pearls round her neck, and she was twirling them.

Oh fuck, he had thought, looking at father sitting in his big, comfy chair that nobody else was allowed to sit in. Father just smiled back at him, as if he knew.

An exotic dancer he had said, and father giggled a bit and looked over to see if Mother had seen him. She hadn't, but her lips pursed in a way that Vince described as her *duck's arse* impression.

Well, what are my brothers going to think? They have kids who are happily married to professionals. All of them. They have wives who are doctors, lawyers, and by God, my lad, one of them is a surgeon!

If Mother had swallowed her pearls, they would have come out like machine gun bullets, she was talking that fast.

A stripper? A stripper? She fanned the flames of a hot flush.

A job so good, they named it twice, Vince thought.

I'll never live it down. What are the neighbours going to think?

I don't give a f–

Well I do. Your father and I are pillars of the community. We go to church.

Only for Communion.

And we put ten pounds in the collection, thank you very much. That's not the point; I will not have a woman of ill-repute in my family. How could you do this to us, Vincent?

Mother had got up and left the room, crying.

Now see what you've done? Father had said. *You've upset your mother.*

Didn't you like Dawn?

Of course I did, but it's not me you have to worry about.

He'd left the house. He had gone out to see Dawn that night, and had told her what a pair of old twats his parents were, but she'd assured him that it didn't matter to her.

They'd carried on with their relationship for two years. The dancing had been a way to help pay her way through college and then she got a job as a nurse. Then Dawn had asked him to come to London with her. His younger brother Beckett was in the army and getting on with his life, so why didn't he, Vince, do the same?

Dawn told him about the new job, after she got notice that the hospital was closing. She got a bit part as an actress, a non-speaking part in *EastEnders*. It wasn't much but it was a start. He had been so excited. He would get a job in an office somewhere. He worked for the Civil Service so he could get a transfer. The *DVLA* had offices all over, and he could work in London no problem.

He had felt excited for the first time in his life. Dawn managed to get them a small flat in the East End, promising him it was just until they got on their feet. He had laughed and said it didn't matter.

Then the stroke came.

Vince's father was retired so he and Mother skarted about doing their own thing. Father got up to shave. He wouldn't even go to the supermarket without wearing a shirt and tie, so there was no way he was going down to Portobello with Mother without having a shave first.

He had gone down like a stone, in the bathroom, trapping himself between the wall and the toilet. Mother had called Vince's mobile phone but he hadn't answered. He had been in bed with Dawn, celebrating their move with a bottle of champagne and morning sex.

By the time his mother stopped faffing about and called a neighbour to help her, time for his father was running out. The neighbour saw right away that father had had a stroke and called for an ambulance. That was on the Wednesday, a few days before they were to leave for London.

On the Saturday, Dawn got the train from Edinburgh to King's Cross, and he promised her he would be there as soon as he knew what was going to happen to his father.

The bleeding on the brain was the foremost cause of death. A side effect of the clot busting drugs they'd given him to try and save him.

Father had never woken from the coma. They were told that he would be on a morphine pump until he passed. Which was the following Tuesday, in the middle of the night.

Beckett had been in Germany on an army base and had been flown home. He'd come in to see father in his last few hours. Then they had escorted Mother along the quiet 3 am corridor to say goodbye, but his father was already gone.

After the funeral the following week, Vince had a bad feeling in his guts. Mother had made a snide comment about *that woman* not coming to the funeral. She was filming that day, he explained.

Mother didn't understand. The lawyer, the doctor, and the surgeon, all smartly dressed in black dresses that might have made them look attractive if they were at a nightclub instead of at their uncle's funeral, were in attendance with their husbands. They were the *proper girls'* contingent. Dawn obviously couldn't make it for the *whores* contingent, of which she was the exclusive member.

It was after the funeral that things started to go downhill. After tea and sympathy at the hotel around the corner from the crematorium. After he and Beckett had taken father to scatter him in the river in his Borders boyhood hometown. After Beckett had gone back to his unit. When he and Mother were alone.

That's when it all went out the window.

Don't leave me, Vincent! she had wailed when he had started talking about booking his train ticket for London. She needled away at him, poking at his resolve like tiny needles poking at his eyeballs, until he couldn't take it any longer.

He had called Dawn and told her he needed a bit more time at home. She understood, but obviously, he couldn't expect her to understand forever.

She understood the second time, and almost understood the third time. By the fourth time, she didn't return his call. Days stretched into weeks, weeks into months. He didn't need to be told by Dawn herself that they were over, but he had to hear her voice again.

Her phone had been answered by some moron called Nigel. *Nigel the sound engineer* she had called him in her letter. Vince had to read it four times to make sure he hadn't skipped over anything, that there weren't any pages missed out.

Nigel had moved in. Sleeping in the bed that Vince would have been sleeping in. Sitting in the chair that Vince would have been sitting in. Watching the TV that Vince would have been watching. Vince couldn't bring himself to think of anything else that Nigel was doing that he, Vince, should have been doing.

Dawn had moved on and was getting on with her life and her

career. Vince stayed at home to look after Mother. And he'd been here for the five years it had been since Dawn had dumped him. No, not *dumped*. She had *re-evaluated her life*. Which sounded a whole lot better than telling people that he had been flushed down the toilet.

It was the *Aw, poor Vince* he couldn't stand from his mother's friends. Like he was five and had cut a finger. *I'm the one who dumped her* he told anybody who would listen.

Except Jimmy. The wee man had been there for him, had lent him a shoulder to cry on and had paid for the prostitute that he, Jimmy, regularly visited, but Vince hadn't told him he had only sat and talked about Dawn. And cried.

Now, five years later, here he was out at a singles club with his friend, thinking about the love he had lost.

Jimmy came back with the drinks, sat down and started seat dancing to the fast tune that had come on.

'Again, they'll think you're only allowed out under supervision if you keep this up,' Vince said.

'There's a couple of women over there who've been smiling at us all night.'

'They're probably thinking, *look at that poor bastard, got stuck with taking his special brother out.*'

'Or they could be thinking, *take us home and give us a good–*'

Vince nudged him in the ribs as a woman stopped next to Jimmy.

'Can I buy you a drink?' she asked him.

He beamed a smile at her. 'You took the words right out of my mouth. Thank you, that would be most acceptable.' He stood up. 'This is my friend, Vince.'

Vince reached out and shook her hand. It was clammy. He smiled and wiped his hand on his trouser leg when she wasn't looking.

'I'm Candy. I'm here with my friend.'

'The one with the rolling eyeball,' Vince whispered to Jimmy.

'There she is. Flo! Over here!' Candy shouted.

Dowdy. Ugly. Face like a skelped arse. All these similes were going through Vince's mind when Flo fought her way across the dance floor. She was none of those things. Flo was a looker. From a distance. Then she got up closer and he could see how the wonders of make-up could knock years off. That combined with the eye-of-the-beholder's alcohol intake.

Vince tugged at Jimmy's jacket and waited for his friend to lean over. 'Go with her to the bar and make sure she doesn't slip something in it. And mine's a pint.'

'For God's sake, she doesn't look like a serial killer.'

'She's looking at you,' Vince said, making like a ventriloquist.

'Did you say something?' Candy said.

'I said, I can come up to the bar and help you carry the drinks. But Vince's paying.' He turned and grinned at his friend.

'Tight bastard,' he said, reaching into his pocket and taking a note out. 'Get yourself one for going. And I want the fucking change.'

'This is my friend, Flo,' Candy said, smiling.

'Jesus,' Vince whispered, standing up.

'Do you mind if we join you?' Flo said.

Vince shook his head slightly at Jimmy. He was okay with his friend going with this woman but he himself wasn't in the mood.

'Be my guest. My name's Jimmy. That's Vince.'

'Ooh, a nice tough name, that,' Flo said, laughing. It sounded like a squeaky wheel.

Fuck me, Vince mouthed at Jimmy when the women weren't looking.

Jimmy shrugged his shoulders.

'Flo and I are just going to powder our noses,' Candy said. 'Be a love and get the drinks in. Back in a tick.' They told Jimmy what they wanted to drink before they scooted off into the darkness through the flashing coloured lights.

'Christ, you could have just sat with her without inviting the other one,' Vince said, sitting back down.

'What's wrong, man?' Jimmy said.

'I'm not in the mood for all this pish tonight, Jimmy.'

'It's just a laugh. Even the women don't take this place seriously. A few beers and a dance. Maybe get lucky later on. It's just a laugh on a Friday night.'

Jimmy left to go to the bar.

Is this what my life has come down to? Vince thought. *Getting pished with Jimmy on a Friday night and taking a couple of slappers home?* There were worse things in life, but he should be settled by now. Christ, thinking about Dawn had really got under his skin.

Jimmy came back with the drinks. And handed Vince some notes and coins.

'Is that all? Did you buy fucking shares in the place?'

'Have you seen the bar prices? Of course you haven't, what am I talking about?'

'Don't forget who just paid for this lot.' He lifted the two pints and two drinks with umbrellas in them.

'What's this?' he asked.

'Pina Coladas.'

'Fuck me. If Randy Candy wants to buy us a drink, don't stop her.'

'That's not how we're going to impress them, if we let *them* buy the drinks,' Jimmy said, slipping the tray under the table.

'Hey, listen, you carry on mate, but I have no intention of touching Flo. Besides, they've probably had a better offer by now.'

'I don't think so, my fine friend,' Jimmy said, laughing, standing up as the two women joined them again.

'Ooh, fancy,' Flo said to Candy, 'but I would have preferred something with a nice cherry.'

'Well, here's to us,' Jimmy said, shooting Vince a warning glance. He held up his pint glass.

Flo was beside Vince while Jimmy sat down and put an arm around Candy.

'So, you sisters?' Vince said.

Flo laughed and Vince tried his best not to wince. 'Smooth talker. Candy's my daughter.'

'No. Really?' Flo laughed again and looked at Candy. Vince looked over at Jimmy and mouthed *You're a fucking dead man.*

TWELVE

'I told you he was a no-good twat,' Maureen said on the other end of the phone. 'Do you want me to come over?'

'No, I'll be alright, Mo. I just needed somebody to talk to, that's all.' Ruby Maxwell stood in front of the mirror that hung above her fireplace and shook her head when she saw the smudged mascara under her eyes. *Bastard.* She'd make the fucker pay for this.

'You know you can talk to me any time you need to, darlin', you know that.'

Mo was like a sister to Ruby. Somebody she could always count on, not like that wank she had booted to the kerb. *Ritchie.* The name made her want to puke. Her father had been right. *Twitchie Ritchie* he'd called him. There was no love lost there, and Ruby wondered what the wedding reception would have been like, father itching to give Ritchie a good belting, or at least a member of Ritchie's family. Maybe his brother, daft Cliff. She supposed that she wouldn't mind if Cliff got his nose broken. But Ritchie was the one in the firing line. That was one shitehouse who deserved a good kicking. Ruby had made the mistake of voicing this opinion to her dad one night, after she'd come in late. She was drunk, and her dad, all six foot six of him, had asked her why she was crying.

Eck ready to give somebody a *fucking good smack*. His usual term for what he would do if he caught some wee junkie climbing over the window sill. And that was just if he was coming into the house. If said junkie actually managed to make it into the living room and had the audacity to put his grubby fingers on Eck's TV, he'd *rip his fucking nuts off and shove them up his arse*.

What's wrong? he had asked. *Has that wee bastard touched you?*

Ruby hadn't known if Eck meant sexually touched her, or skelped her one, but she'd quickly defused the situation by turning it around on him and making him feel guilty.

No, he dumped me. That part was true. She'd edited out the part that she'd called him a wanker and thrown a drink at him, before she and Mo had left the pub and gone night-clubbing, leaving Ritchie behind to shout *We're finished! Crazy cow!*

I knew he was a piece of shite. I'll break his fucking legs, Eck had said.

Just leave it, dad.

That had been a couple of months ago, and then Ritchie had come to see her, sporting a bunch of roses in one hand, and a black eye. It seemed that Ritchie had had an epiphany and *did* want to marry her after all. Maybe he'd thought that this was the less painful of two options, the other one being having a pickaxe handle surgically removed.

Things weren't the same after that. She'd felt that Ritchie was forcing himself on her, not in a physical way, but forcing himself to tell her he loved her. Then he'd suggested she move in with him before the wedding. So she did and things seemed to get better, until they'd had an argument earlier that evening.

So this time, she dumped *him*. She knew her father would kill him when he found out.

'It wasn't working anymore, Mo. I thought by moving in with him that things would be great. Like we were married.'

'Better finding out now rather than find out when you have a ring on your finger.'

'That's true.' She walked through to the kitchen without putting a light on and she saw a shadow moving about at the window. She screamed.

'What's wrong, Ruby?' Mo shouted down the phone.

'I thought I saw some bastard at the back window.' She rushed over and looked out, but the back of the tenement looked out onto the shared drying green, and across the back fence, sat St. Mark's park with the water of Leith flowing through it. Lights from the apartments on the other side of the river were on but between them was an expanse of darkness, the park and the Water of Leith being no man's land.

She couldn't see anybody.

'Probably just my imagination,' she said, pulling the curtains shut.

'It was in the papers that the police are looking for a peeping Tom,' Mo said.

'Wasn't that over in Redbraes?'

'He might travel. He might have a bus pass.'

They both laughed as Ruby took a bottle of wine out of the fridge, the light from inside illuminating the small room until she shut the door with her backside. 'I think I'm going to get pished tonight.'

'What if he comes back?'

'Who? The perv or Ritchie?'

'Is there a difference?'

They laughed again as Ruby went through to the living room.

Then Ruby heard a noise at the front door. 'Mo, I think he's coming in. Maybe I should just get him to sit down and we can talk.'

Mo laughed again. 'What are you two like? Oh, honey, I'll be here if he tells you where to go.'

'You're a pal.' Ruby hung up and put the phone back on the

receiver. Went to the front door and waited. And waited. Then she wondered why Ritchie was taking so long to come in. Maybe he'd blootered back a few beers with some chasers. He'd been gone for a few hours, so it wasn't impossible.

She opened the front door. The communal stair was empty but a wind was blowing in. She looked at the front communal door that led into the street. Somebody had jammed it open.

Christ, it was meant to be a secure place. There was no point in having an intercom system if some twat was going to leave the front door open for all to walk in.

She walked along the corridor and kicked the sliver of wood out and let the front door close. Then she went back to the flat, closing her front door behind her.

She felt disappointed that it wasn't Ritchie. Usually, she got angry with him, but then she calmed down and then they had make-up sex. She would talk to him when he came in.

She went into the living room, then remembered she'd taken out the bottle of wine and left it in the kitchen. She went back through.

He was standing waiting for her in the dark.

'Ritchie? Christ, you scared me,' she said, reaching for the light switch. But the bulb was gone.

And it wasn't Ritchie.

THIRTEEN

'How are you enjoying yourself?' Jimmy said, sitting back down and getting wired into his lager.

'Never had a better night in my life,' he replied, sarcasm in his voice. The women were at the bathroom again.

'Come on, mate, it's just a laugh.' Jimmy was sweating and wiped his brow with a hanky. He'd been dancing with Candy to almost every tune that had been played.

'I'm having a good time. I've been listening to Flo tell me in great detail how they make the biscuits in the factory in Sighthill. Which is handy for you, if you're ever off work and want to pop over for a Jammy Dodger in her lunch break.'

'Is that a euphemism for...?'

'It most certainly fucking is. And *you'll* be fine, because she gets half an hour, so that leaves you twenty minutes to talk about the finer points of Custard Creams.'

'She's not that bad.'

'How would you know? You've got your tongue down her daughter's throat every five minutes.'

'You're in a hoor of a mood tonight. This is supposed to be fun, you and me out on the lash, giving it laldy.'

'My mother's been getting on my wick again. She brought up Dawn tonight.'

'Ah. Dawn.' He drank some more of his pint. 'She was a doll, let me tell you.'

'I'm sick of living with the old cow. And now Beckett's back.'

'Your brother? I thought he was in the army?'

'He was. He's been discharged. Then he fell and did something to his knee in London, so now he's poncing about in a wheelchair. Getting mummy's sympathy at every turn.'

'Don't be too hard on him. He's a good guy. Look on the bright side, he's going to get your mother's attention now too, so if she's bugging him, then she's not bugging you.'

'Fuck me, Jimmy, that was very philosophical. True though. I never thought of that.'

'Plus, you told me you're going to see that bloke tomorrow, what's his name again? Len Shitter.'

'Chatter. Len fucking Chatter. He writes the *Ben Goode* thrillers.'

'*Ben Doon?*' Jimmy said over the noise of the music starting up again.

'*Ben Goode!*'

'I can't quite hear you – *Ben Dover?*'

'I'll fucking bend you over in a minute,' Vince said, just as Flo and Candy came back.

'Not interrupting anything, are we?' Candy said with a raised eyebrow.

'No, we're just talking about a TV show.'

'Oh, okay. You boys want a drink? My friend's paying.' She looked at Flo, obviously calling her *friend* when they were out, which sounded a hell of a lot better than *Mother*.

'No, we'll–' Jimmy started to say, until Vince kicked him under the table.

'I mean, that would be great, thanks.'

The women walked away.

'Magic,' Jimmy said. 'Not only will they think I'm a tight bastard, they think you want to bend me over a fucking table. There goes my chance tonight.'

'Pish. Candy's hot for you. At least she's a looker. Or she will be after another six pints.'

Jimmy laughed and drank more lager.

'So, as we were saying, I'm going to meet this author tomorrow at the book festival. He's famous, and I was lucky to get a ticket.'

'What's his name again?'

'Oh, fuck off, Jimmy.'

'I'm serious, I forgot.' He was looking around, seat dancing to the music again.

'Candy obviously thinks you've got a big tadger or you're loaded. She's going to get a shock on both counts when I tell her.' Vince drank some of his own lager. 'Anyway, his name's Len Chatter.'

'Len Chopper?' Jimmy said, a sceptical look on his face.

'If I have to say his name one more fucking time, I swear to God–'

'I'm kidding. But if he's that famous, how come I haven't heard of him?'

'Because you only read magazines with fannies in them.'

'I've read books.'

'Name one title.'

'Fucked if I know.'

'Never heard of it.'

'When are you seeing him?'

'Tomorrow. He'll be at the book festival, and I've been invited along to a dinner afterwards. Just a select group of fans. He does that sometimes. Do you want to come along? I'm sure he won't mind.'

'A free scran? Count me in!'

'But no lewd jokes or getting your willy out in public.'

Jimmy shrugged, making no promises on either front.

'But get this, he's going to write a few new series of books, but he obviously doesn't have the time to write them himself, so he needs other writers. He's having a competition, and those who are selected will get to write with him. I got through to the next round, where he reads the whole manuscript. And since I'm going along to the dinner, I can personally hand him the finished manuscript.'

'Sounds good, mate.'

'It's life-changing, Jimmy. There's going to be a lot of entries, but this is me getting in the back door.'

'It would be better than working for the DVLA, that's for sure.'

'That's why I wanted today off, so I could polish my chapters. Christ, I'm excited, mate, I don't mind admitting.'

'Good. Now get into the spirit for tonight, and we can take Candy and her Ma back to my place.'

'Well, it sounds inviting when you put it like that. Can't you just say, her fucking sister?'

'Language,' Candy said, coming up behind Vince.

'Sorry, love. I forgot I was in the company of a beautiful woman.'

Candy blushed and smiled. Flo was standing behind him and cleared her throat.

'Sorry, I meant two beautiful women.'

'That's better,' Flo said. They put the drinks on the table and turned to look at the dance floor. Vince stuck two fingers up to his mouth, making vomiting gestures.

'Cheers,' Jimmy said, when they turned back.

It was getting to the time of night when the music slowed and the arse-grabbing started.

'Are you going to take me on the floor?' Candy said to Jimmy with a grin.

'I'd take you anywhere, darlin',' he said, taking his jacket off and hanging it on the back of a chair.

'We'll watch the handbags,' Flo said, sitting down. 'There's a lot of thieving bastards in here.'

Christ, imagine taking this thing back to meet my mother. She'd pop her clogs on the spot.

Vince turned to look at the dancefloor for a second.

'You taking us home then?' Flo said.

Vince made a noise that was almost a laugh. 'Oh, I don't think so. *Ma*.'

Flo suddenly stood up from the table as Jimmy and Candy came back.

'What's wrong?' Candy asked.

'That twat is about as much fun as a jellyfish.' She turned to Vince. 'Go fuck yourself.'

Then they stormed out.

'What happened?' Jimmy said.

'I got snippy with Flo and she took the huff.'

'What? Aw, away man, play the fucking game.'

'They were minging anyway.'

'Now you're just being a you-know-what.'

'A what?'

'Starts with C and ends in *T*.'

'Count?'

'Close.' Jimmy stood shaking his head. Five minutes later, he was dancing with somebody else, Candy all but forgotten. But Vince hadn't forgotten about Dawn.

FOURTEEN

Frank Miller wasn't sure where he was when he was woken up by his mobile phone ringing. In a strange room, like a hotel room, but this wasn't a hotel, this was–

'Are you going to answer that?' Carol said. She was wide awake and sitting up.

He reached over to the nightstand and answered it. 'Miller.'

'Wakey wakey, sleeping beauty. We got a shout.' The dulcet Irish tones of Paddy Gibb cackled in his ear.

'Serious Crimes as well?'

'We did indeed. All hands on deck. Bring Carol with you, orders of your old man.'

'Will do. What's the details?'

'I'll text them to you. Be there in ten.'

They were up, dressed and in Carol's Beetle in five minutes, heading along to Warriston Road. *The Powderhall end*, Gibb's message said. The barrage of emergency vehicles lit up the street like a Christmas tree by the time Carol pulled in behind a patrol car.

The text had simply said *SD*. Sudden Death.

'You're a jinx, Miller,' Paddy Gibb said, coming across to meet them as they ducked under the police tape. 'We haven't had an on-call shout for the longest time, and now you've joined the boots and suits, we get called out. And on a Friday night, no less.'

Miller looked at his watch. 'Saturday morning, sir.'

'Splitting hairs, Miller. Your old man's inside with a young fella who's crying like a gi...' looking at Carol, '...goldfish. It's the boyfriend.'

'What do we have?' Carol asked.

'Our peeping Tom just promoted himself to murdering Tom.'

'You say that like it's a real thing,' Miller said.

'Listen, son, when you've been in the job as long as I have, anything can be made real.'

Inside the flat, he was led past the living room where the boyfriend was. Forensics were busy getting ready to go to work, but Miller was shown into the bedroom where a young woman was lying at the side of the double bed. Jack Miller was looking at the woman and waved his son over.

'The boyfriend came home and found her like this.' He nodded down at the corpse. The young woman was naked and had multiple stab wounds, but there was a gash at her neck that looked far bigger than the other ones.

'He look good for it?' Miller asked.

'He's our number one just now, but it's fifty-fifty. I've had the team look through the house for bloody clothes, but we can't find any.'

'Doesn't mean to say he didn't dump them already.'

'We'll get a search done round the back in the morning when it's light, which is only a couple of hours.'

'Does he have an alibi for last night?'

'He does, which we will check out.'

'What's his version of the story?' Carol said.

'They had a fight. He was up front about that. Her name is Ruby Maxwell and he's Ritchie Sanderson. They have a love-hate relationship he says, but deep down, he loved her. They were going to get married but he asked her to move in before the wedding. Her family hates him, apparently.'

'So where was he tonight?'

'Out drinking with his friends. He only got back about half an hour ago. Said he went to a mate's flat where half a dozen of them were drinking. He's still a bit drunk, but he mostly sobered up when he came home and found her like this. He wouldn't have found her in the dark, but this is his side of the bed.'

'How do we know it's the peeper?' Miller asked.

'We checked her mobile phone which is on the coffee table in the living room. The last number was to a friend of hers called Maureen. We called her, and she said that Ruby told her that she thought she saw somebody peeping in her kitchen window yesterday evening.'

'It might have been Sanderson trying to put the wind up her. Pretending he was the Tom, so she would rush into his arms.'

'Unlikely, given the time of the call. if his story adds up.' Jack Miller looked up as one of the city pathologists came in. Jake Dagger. 'Hi, Jake. How's things?'

'It's the early hours of Saturday morning and I'm still sober. That should answer your question.' He looked over at Miller. 'Hi, Frank. How are you doing?'

'Sober,' said Miller.

'It's an exclusive club, this Friday night sobriety. I feel we're letting the Scottish *Over 21 Imbibing squad* down.'

'Saturday night's got my name written all over it,' Miller said. 'So, in 24 hours' time, I'll be a fully paid-up member.'

'I used to like you, Frank,' Dagger said, putting his bag down 'I'll still be on-call.' He looked at Carol.

'This is my girlfriend, PC Carol Davidson.'

'I know your father well. Keeping it in the family, eh? Soon, all of CID–'

'–will be made up of family members,' Miller said. 'It's what everybody says, despite the fact there are dozens of detectives.'

'So, let's see what we have here,' Dagger said. The overhead light was on, as well as a bedside lamp. He had his coveralls on and knelt beside the victim as the detectives moved out of the way.

After his initial examination, he stood back up. 'I haven't seen this frenzied an attack in a long time. It looks to me like the cut at the neck might be the fatal one, as there are no stab wounds near her heart, but obviously I will be able to tell better when I have her on the table.'

'Time, doc?' Jack said. His six-foot-five frame looked huge in the small bedroom.

'I would say five or six hours, give or take.'

'That would fit in with the time of the call to her friend,' Jack said. 'It could have been shortly after that. She saw the peeping Tom and he came in and killed her.'

'Maybe she recognised him,' Carol said.

'Or maybe it's just the fact she could identify him,' Miller said.

'Either way, maybe he was just practising with the pervy stuff, intending to escalate to murder all along,' Jack said. Then he looked at Miller. 'Get all of the boyfriend's alibis checked out. Then we'll have a debriefing in the morning.'

'Yes, sir.'

'Not only has your Friday night been screwed, but your Saturday too. Welcome to CID.'

FIFTEEN

'You're not going to get fed up with me, are you?' Marcie said, pouting.

'What?' Calvin said, pouring another couple of glasses of champagne. He was standing in front of the dresser, his back to her. 'Of course not.' He didn't normally drink in the morning, but the sun was up, it was a beautiful day, it was Saturday, and there was a blonde in his bed who wasn't going to say she was too tired.

'I love being with you, Calvin.'

He turned to her and smiled, holding the glasses. 'I love being with you too; we have the perfect love life; we satisfy each other without having to worry about what the other one is doing. I was just busy, that's all.'

'That's true. You do know how to satisfy me in a way that my husband never could. His idea of risky sex is doing it with the light on.'

Calvin sat on the bed and handed her the glass. This was their intermission, time to get their breath back. Light was starting to show through the curtains. Calvin loved the summer, with the late sunsets and early sunrises.

After she sipped at the bubbly, she giggled and pulled him on top of her. His love-making was frenzied, and Marcie was making her usual loud noises and if Calvin hadn't finished, he might not have heard the phone ringing.

'What do you mean, she's not there?' he said as he answered. He started to shake a little bit as the voice on the other end spoke to him. He knew he'd never be able to walk into a bank with a sawn-off shotgun and keep his voice calm.

'*She didn't turn up for her flight to Sydney. We had a stand-by crew member take her place. We were expecting a phone call, saying she was sick or something, but none came.*'

Calvin wondered what the *or something* would be if somebody was calling to say they wouldn't be in. *Sorry, I won't be in because I can't be arsed.*

'I'll call her mobile and then call you right back.'

He hung up and looked at Marcie. 'That was somebody from the British Airways office saying they can't locate Bree. I'd better call her mobile.

Calvin called the number and it went to voicemail. He left his wife a message telling her to call him and to call her work as they were all worried.

He called the BA office. 'I've just called my wife and there's no answer on her mobile. Now I'm worried. We don't always call each other before her flight, but now that you've alerted me that she's not turned up for work, I'm worried. Can somebody go round to our flat down there? I can give you the address.' He rattled it off to the woman. 'And please let me know if she's alright. She might have fallen asleep or something. Please call me. I'll try her phone again but please let me know.'

'I will. I'll send one of the manager's round there.'

'Thank you.' He hung up and looked worried. 'You don't suppose she knows about us and is creeping about outside, watching us?

Knowing we're in here. Maybe she's trying to catch me out. I'd be screwed if she caught me.'

'You worry too much. She's maybe away to Ibiza with her boyfriend.'

'I should be so lucky. I wonder what the bloody hell she's up to?'

'It could be anything. They'll locate her I'm sure, then they'll call you back.'

'What will we do meantime?'

'I can think of a few things,' she said smiling at him.

SIXTEEN

'Well, if this is how well you're going to treat me, I think I'll keep you, Miller,' Carol said, coming into the kitchen as he rustled up a cooked breakfast.

'Good to know.'

'What is it?'

'The Scottish heart attack special; eggs, bacon, black pudding, potato scones, and beans. Washed down by lashings of coffee.'

She smiled and kissed him. She was wearing an old shirt of his. 'Lashings, huh? I'll have to make it just the one, my dear. Otherwise... well, you fill in the blanks.'

'Say no more.' He smiled at her. 'I remember what it was like to be out on patrol and drinking too much coffee.'

'My last week. I can't believe it. There were times when I never thought I'd get through probation, never mind make it to CID. And here's you finished your first month. You're an old pro at this game now.'

'Ha-ha. I've been called worse.' He looked at her and felt something that he'd never felt for any woman he'd ever gone out with before; a desire to spend the rest of his life with her. Even with her hair still damp from the shower, and without any make-up, she was gorgeous. And it wasn't even six am yet. An image of the razor surfaced in his mind, but he forced it away.

'I don't know about you, but I feel like I haven't even been to bed yet,' Carol said, pouring the coffee.

'I have to admit, I'm feeling a bit knackered, but I'm going in after you, so I can sit with my feet up for a little while after you've gone.'

'I'm finished at three so maybe I'll have a nap this afternoon so I can be refreshed for my dinner date tonight.'

Miller switched the gas rings off and started to dish up the breakfast. 'Dinner date, eh? Anybody I know?'

'My boyfriend.'

'Lucky guy. You'll need to introduce me to him sometime.'

'Unlikely. He thinks you're my staff. You only come in to cook my breakfast.' She laughed. 'God, I love you, Frank Miller.'

'I love you too. Now sit yourself down and your manservant will dish up the food.'

The sun was coming up and the forecast was for a warm day.

He put both plates on the table.

'I've never had any man cook for me before,' Carol said.

'You've never had a man move in with you.' He didn't want to mention the razor. Not yet.

'Don't worry, I didn't have the Royal Scots stay over,' she said, smiling, as if she'd read his mind.

'I wasn't thinking that,' he said, feeling his face go red.

'Liar.'

'The defence rests its case, m'lud.'

'I obviously had boyfriends before you, sweetheart, but none of them ever came up to your level.' She forked up some food. 'Besides, don't you think my dad would have been all over them if he thought they were trying to take advantage of me?'

'I don't think anybody would take advantage of you.' *Least of all me* he wanted to say, but he felt she already knew that.

Suddenly, her expression changed.

'What's wrong?' Miller said.

'I'm just thinking about Sherri.'

'I'll make some phone calls today. I'll talk to my dad, see if he has any ideas.'

She nodded. 'I would talk to mine, but my mum insists he takes some time away from work when they're on holiday. He'll be champing at the bit and I'm sure he calls your dad every day.'

'Some guys just can't get away from work. It's in their blood, your dad's and mine.'

'Every time we say that our fathers are in CID together and now we're working together, they think it's a family business.'

Miller laughed. 'If it wasn't for our dads working together, we might not have gone out with each other.'

'I know. It doesn't help that my brother is already in CID, but thank God he works in Corstorphine.'

'Let's not forget your sister Julie. I'm sure people don't believe that she's a pathologist.'

'If you listen to some people, the whole of Lothian and Borders is made up of our two families like we're one big clan.'

'When people ask if Jack's my dad, I'm going to tell them we're not related.'

She put her knife and fork down when she was finished. Looked across the table at him. He was almost finished but stopped eating when he saw her looking at him.

'Have I got egg on my chin? Literally?'

She laughed. 'No. I just can't believe that you're here with me now. I've had some lonely nights in here. Don't get me wrong, there have been times when I've had peace being on my own, but this is so much better.'

'I understand we both need our own space, and that's fine.'

'I know. But this makes me feel good. Life's lonely as it is. And I want to spend the rest of mine with you.'

'You will.' He looked at her with her hair still slightly damp and couldn't imagine spending his life with anybody else. He considered himself lucky to have her. Other guys he knew would brag about their conquests when they were out, especially at the treble-nine balls they held in the Police Club, where members of all emergency services would get together. Miller had been to a few but then Carol had come into his life and he felt happy.

Carol stood up and looked at the clock on the kitchen wall. 'Come on tough guy, I still have plenty of time to get to work if you drive me and bring the car back.'

'Okay. What do you have in mind?'

'A girl has to work off a big breakfast.'

'I think I may be able to help with that.'

Less than an hour later, Carol yawned as she walked into the canteen of the police station on the High Street.

'Oh man, I should start using Red Bull,' she said to her patrol partner, Jeff Knight as they stood in line in the canteen before their shift started.

'Coffee will have to do. Although now Frank has moved in, I'm guessing that maybe Red Bull should be on your shopping list.'

'Cheeky.'

'Hey, I'm just being honest. When I moved in with my girlfriend, it was like–'

Carol held up a hand. 'Jeff. I haven't had my coffee yet.'

They got their coffee and sat at a table, Knight snagging a bacon roll as well.

'How did Frank's mother take it?' Knight asked.

'Why do you ask that?' She smiled at him.

'I just wondered if all mothers were like my mother. Mine cried, and then made me promise to take my dirty laundry round any time I wanted. But I thanked her and said I could manage. Well, my girlfriend manages.'

Carol's eyebrows rose. 'You don't wash your own clothes?'

'Technically a machine does that, but she knows what goes where.'

'You are going to learn though, right? You won't be expecting her to wash and iron your clothes.'

'Of course not. My mother will still do that.'

'Indeed she will not, Jeff Knight. You'll learn like every other man has to.'

'My dad doesn't.'

'He would if he lived with me.'

'I think Genghis Khan would, if he lived with you.'

'Your girlfriend needs to come out on one of our ladies' nights out. We'll soon put her straight.'

'I'm sure she wouldn't like that.'

'What are you like? Don't wash your own clothes. This is the twenty-first century, isn't it?'

'Carol, we delegate jobs around the house. You're looking at the chief shelf-erector, a skill honed only by many years of practise.'

'It's not hard. I did my own in my flat.'

'I was a joiner before I joined the force. It's a skill that can't be mastered by many.'

'Hold up a piece of wood, bang in a nail. That's how it's done.'

'You've just broken it down to its most basic level.'

'Sure, sure. You'll say anything to get out of household chores. If you lived with me, I'd whip you into shape within a week.'

Knight shook his head and wiped the tomato ketchup off his lip with a napkin. 'God help poor Frank. *He's* the one who needs to come out for a drink so the boys can put him straight.'

She reached over and slapped his arm. 'Don't you dare.' She drank her coffee. 'But we were up late last night. We got called out to a murder scene.'

'The lassie down at Warriston?'

'Yeah. Poor thing. Lying battered by the side of her bed. Young, too. Her boyfriend was a wreck.'

'The boyfriend did it.'

'What?'

'I don't want to go into CID, but I've watched a ton of shows where the boyfriend did it. Most people are killed by people they know.'

'They think it was the peeping Tom who did it.'

'That was my second choice.'

'No it wasn't.'

'You're right. Tell me more.'

'Now, now. I can't talk about it.'

'Mum's the word, eh? I understand. This is my last week with you and I know you don't want to tell me anything and risk your move to CID.' Knight drank more coffee. 'Tell me.'

'Sod off, Jeff.'

'Is that code for *I'll tell you later?*'

'No, it just means sod off.'

'Message received and understood.'

Just then, a young man in uniform walked over to their table. 'PC Davidson? I have a message; the duty sergeant wants you both upstairs right away.'

'Thanks.' Carol watched the young man walk away.

'Saturday morning and they want us to work. It should be against the law.'

'Come on, let's go and see what old grumpy wants.'

SEVENTEEN

'I should be able to walk without my brace in the next couple of weeks,' Beckett said, rolling his wheelchair into the kitchen. 'Then I can scoot around more on crutches instead of being stuck in this damn thing.'

Vince was sitting eating a fry-up, a large cup of coffee in front of him. 'I thought you said last night you used crutches now?' He crunched on a bit bacon.

'I do, but it's awkward. I don't walk around on them if I don't have to. I go to physiotherapy and the girl is helping me strengthen my leg. Any more of that bacon?'

'Yeah. In Tesco.' He saw Beckett make a sad face. 'Here, for fuck's sake.' Vince lifted a few slices off his plate and put them on a side plate.

'I hope you washed your hands.'

'Do you want the fucking bacon or not, Ironside?'

'Of course I do. And it's bad form to slag off somebody in a wheelchair.'

'You're not disabled. You might be a fanny, but–'

'Oh, Vincent, what kind of talk is that?' Mother said from the kitchen doorway.

Beckett grinned as he tucked into his bacon.

'He started it,' Vince said, pointing to Beckett with his fork.

'I did not.'

'Listen to the pair of you. Arguing like a couple of spoiled brats. Enough of that language. Mummy's tired. She hasn't had enough sleep.' She walked over to the kettle.

Vince stuck two fingers up behind his mother's back.

'I saw that,' she said, without turning round. Like she had eyes in the back of her head.

Vince ducked his head down and ate more breakfast.

'It's a bit late for breakfast, isn't it?' Mother said.

'It's called *brunch*.'

'It's called ten thirty.'

'It's ten thirty-five.'

'Don't be pedantic,' Mother said. 'Your father would have had his breakfast finished long before now, and been away doing something for the day. Something useful. Like Beckett. He's got plans for today, haven't you my darling?'

'I'm going with Vince later on.'

'Where to?'

'To see the author.'

'Oh my goodness, don't tell me he's roped you into this nonsense as well,' she said, standing next to the table. She was wearing a green twinset this time, and the fake pearls were round her neck, her fingers going to them like they were rosary beads.

'It's not nonsense. It's very interesting.'

Vince jammed a piece of bread into his mouth and chewed for a moment before washing it down with his coffee. 'If you weren't such a philistine, then you would be able to appreciate our way of thinking.'

'I do read, and I'll kindly thank you not to talk to me like that, young man.'

'You do colouring books. It's hardly the same thing.'

'I get *Reader's Digest* every month.'

'You look at the pictures. That's not reading.'

'That's beside the point. I don't want you filling Beckett's head with all this nonsense. Books. Writers. What a way to make a living. *If* you can make a living, that is.'

'I think Len might have something to say about that. Besides, if I don't get chosen, then there's self-publishing.'

'It's called *vanity publishing*.' Mother gave him a smug look.

'I won't need that after Len reads my stuff.'

'Your father would be so disappointed.'

This was part two of the nagging that she'd started when he came home in the wee hours. He'd tried to be as quiet as he could, but she was wide awake when he got up the stairs.

'What time do you call this?' she had said from her bedroom.

'Greenwich Mean Time,' he had answered. Her door was wide open and her face was staring back at him from the darkened room.

'You've been up to no good, m'lad. Out carousing with your friend, drinking alcohol, and no doubt talking to young women of the night.'

'What? Have a word with yourself. I'm *thirty*-five, not five.'

'Nice boys are home, tucked up in bed by now. Nice boys don't stay out late.'

'Nice boys? What the fuck are you talking about?'

'Don't you talk to me like that! Get to your bed and we'll talk about this in the morning.'

And so here she was, her face looking like an old washcloth.

'So, you excited to see Len later, cock?' Vince said, looking sideways at his mother as she poured herself a cup of tea.

She sucked in air at the sound of *cock* and Vince, not for the first time, wondered how he and his brother had ever been conceived.

'I am actually. These four walls are boring the hell out of me.'

'Beckett!' Mother said. 'I expect that kind of talk from cesspit mouth there, but not from you.'

'It's only *hell*.'

'And so you repeat it as if saying it the first time didn't shock me enough. I swear you two boys will put me in an early grave.'

'No pun intended,' Vince said to her. 'He's a great guy. He's lived in London for a while and now he's making our fair city his home.'

'I don't know why,' Beckett said. Mother took her tea out of the kitchen and floated upstairs like the resident ghost.

'He comes from here originally. It's a beautiful place to live. And it's an advantage for me, living here.'

'How do you mean?'

'Well, if he chooses some other writers who live elsewhere in the world, they will communicate with him by email or Skype, but I can have lunch with him, or go for a pint and we can chat about my work face-to-face.'

'I'm sure being on Skype will almost be like face-to-face for the other writers.'

'Live the dream with me, Beckett. Sometimes it's nice to ride on a carpet of dreams.'

'Sure. Sorry, pal. You're right of course; if you're chosen, then that will be great for you.'

'Have you read my first three chapters?'

'Not the polished ones.'

'I'd appreciate it if you could do that before we go. And the synopsis.'

'You had to write the whole thing, didn't you?'

'Yes, the novel is finished but I've been polishing the first three chapters again and again.'

'You have to let them go sooner or later.'

'I'm letting them go this afternoon, Becksy. Then Len won't be anything but impressed, I'm sure.'

'You've got just as much chance as the next man.'

'The next man is a useless twat. He's whittled it down to the final ten and he's going to pick three. I'm going to be his top co-author.'

'You will be. If you don't think negative, then nothing will happen. It's mind over matter.'

'For a daft squaddie, you've got something between your ears.'

'Thank you. I think.'

'Right, I'll get those chapters and synopsis printed off and you can have a squint at them before we go. Oh, and wee Jimmy's coming tonight. You remember him, don't you?'

'I do. He's sound as a pound.'

'Great. I'll get going as soon as I've finished this lot.'

EIGHTEEN

'Have you ever fancied living down here in Barnton?' Carol Davidson asked pulling into the parking spot in front of the new townhouse. It was a modern design, the facia a pink colour.

'This is the first place I'd think of if the lottery came up,' Jeff Knight said.

'Really?'

'Yeah, but maybe further down towards Cramond.'

'In the flight path for Edinburgh Airport, you mean?' She smiled at him. It was true; nice, expensive houses with airliners flying low on final approach.

'Maybe here instead then.'

He rang the doorbell and a woman answered. Late-thirties, blonde hair, obviously looked after herself.

'Yes? Can I help you?' she said with a worried look on her face. It was the mostly standard look they got when they turned up unannounced on somebody's doorstep.

'We're looking for Mrs Marcie Lincoln.'

'That's me.'

'Can we come in and talk to you?' Carol said.

'Yes, of course.' She stood back and Knight and Carol stepped over the threshold. Marcie closed the door behind them and led them through to the back of the house into a small living room. French doors led out into a small back garden.

'What's wrong?' she asked as they all stood in the middle of the room.

'Please sit down,' Carol said, and Marcie did. She and Knight sat on a couch opposite her.

'You're scaring me,' Marcie said.

'Is your husband Norman Lincoln?'

'Yes. Why?'

'I'm afraid we have some bad news,' Carol said. 'Your husband was involved in an accident last night in London, and he was pronounced dead in the hospital.'

'Oh my God!' Marcie jumped up out of the chair. 'Norman? Dead? No!' Carol stood up and put her arms around the woman. Knight stood up and was silent until the sobbing subsided.

'Mrs Lincoln, is there somebody we can call?'

'Maybe my friend next door, but tell me, what kind of accident? What happened to my Norm?'

'He was hit by a car, and unfortunately, the driver didn't stop.'

Marcie put a hand to her mouth. 'Somebody killed my Norm? Oh my God. Did you get him?'

'No. It was in a quiet side street near his hotel. The Metropolitan Police took a few hours to trace where he was staying.'

'Oh, no, I don't know what to do.'

'We have an officer who is a family liaison officer who will come round and help you make contact with the Met.'

'I'll go and see about your neighbour. Is she on the left or the right as I go out?'

'Left.'

When Knight came back with the woman a few minutes later, Carol had made tea.

Marcie was held by her neighbour as Knight and Carol left.

'It never gets easy, does it? Telling a loved one about a dead spouse.'

'It only gets harder,' Carol said. 'Even having money doesn't mean you get to skip out on the realities of life.'

They got back into the car and drove back to the station.

NINETEEN

'You look like a half-shut knife,' Paddy Gibb said as Miller walked into the enquiry room. Carol was with him at the request of DCI Jack Miller.

Miller could never fathom out what Gibb's expression meant; tired? Hungover? It was another of his colloquialisms. *You look like Paddy's Market* he would say, when somebody was dressed a bit scruffily.

'Good morning to you too, boss.' He sipped his coffee. Looked at the clock: 9.57 am. Jack had told him the meeting would start at ten, to give the search teams a chance to look around Ruby Maxwell's property, and so they could check up on Ritchie Sanderson's alibis.

The other detectives were starting to fill the room and there was a hum of conversation in the air.

'A half-shut knife,' Carol said, her voice low, talking into her coffee cup. 'I told you we should have gone straight to sleep when we got back.'

Miller grinned and turned away from the other detectives. 'Get used to it, lady. I'm a well-oiled machine.' Carol had been in the mood when they got back, and since he had knocked her back earlier that night, he didn't want her to think he had gone off her.

She shook her head and laughed. 'You've been watching too many movies. You're a snoring machine.'

'The good outweighs the bad, I'm sure.'

'I'll give you marks out of ten at the end of the month. See if you can live up to your reputation.'

'So, I have a reputation? Tell me more.'

'Wrong choice of word, big head. But you know what I mean.'

'You'll need a calculator to count the notches on your bed post.'

'Are you saying I had a lot of lovers?'

'From me! Just from me!'

She laughed.

'How's your morning been so far?' he asked her.

'We had to do a death message. A woman in Barnton lost her husband.'

'It never gets easy, delivering a DM.'

'The thing is, her husband was working in London when he was killed in a hit-and-run.'

'Did they get the driver?'

Carol shook her head. 'Plenty of witnesses but nobody saw anything. A dark car. It was raining, the roads were slick. You know the story.'

'Poor sod.'

'It's bad enough losing your spouse, but knowing they were hundreds of miles away and you didn't get to say goodbye? It would break my heart.'

DCI Jack Miller appeared at the front of the room like the compère in a club, about to introduce the first act.

'Ladies and gentlemen, I know a lot of you have other things you'd rather be doing,' DCI Jack Miller said from the front of the room, 'but unfortunately, murderers don't have a timetable to work with. Some selfish sod went and killed a young woman in her flat last night, and now we have to track him down and throw away the key.'

He pointed to the whiteboard on the back wall. 'Ruby Maxwell. Twenty-seven. Lived in Warriston Road. At the Powderhall end. As some of you may know, Warriston Road itself carries on up to the crematorium and beyond, to connect with Ferry Road. There have been reports of a peeping Tom in Redbraes, so now it would appear he moved. Underwear has been taken from some washing lines over the last couple of weeks.'

'Has anybody else apart from Miss Maxwell seen him?' Miller asked.

'The answer is yes and no; he's been spotted by women looking through their windows, but nobody has been able to identify him. He's white and has dark hair as far as anybody can tell, but it was hard since they had put a light on and the light's reflection was on the glass when his face appeared. We got nothing of any significance.'

'What about forensics?' DS Andy Watt said.

'They took fingerprints away but there hasn't been a match. And there's no sign of forced entry.'

'So, she may know him?' Miller said.

'We're not ruling that out.'

'How did the search go in the back gardens this morning?' Carol asked.

'Nothing was found. It's been dry so there were no footprints in mud. Nobody else has reported seeing anything. Nobody saw him creeping about last night, except Ruby Maxwell.'

'What about the friend who she spoke to on the phone?'

'You're going round to talk to her after this.'

'Could the friend have been involved? Made up the story about Ruby calling her?'

'We want an alibi from her,' Jack answered. 'Ruby did call her. It was on her phone with the time she called. But if this Maureen was the killer and was very clever, she could have spoken to Ruby and been outside her front door. We'll find that out. You'll be accompanying DS Watt and DI Gibb to speak with Ruby's family.'

'Will do.'

'We're pulling Ruby's life apart. See if there's anybody that would do her harm. Now, DI Gibb will give you your detail. Carol, can I have a word, please?'

'Of course.'

All the suits moved and Jack took Carol into his office.

'You were to start CID orientation on Friday, correct?'

'Yes, sir.'

'That's been brought forward to Monday. We have one of the team off sick, and your dad is away on holiday. I'm authorising your orientation to be brought forward. You've already completed your two years' probation. When was that again?'

'Back in June, sir.'

'Right, so we're covered. I'm assuming that this is okay with you, coming here a few days early?'

'It's fine by me, sir, but I'm not sure how the duty sergeant will take it.'

'Your father gave it the green light. Besides, you've been seconded to us before, so you know when we need extra bodies, uniforms are brought in. This is just like this. Plus, I already checked and there's two uniforms who are moving from orientation into regular duties from tomorrow, so they won't be short. I have a feeling we're going to need extra bodies this time round as well.'

'Then I'd be glad to come to CID early, sir.' She smiled at the man who would one day become her father-in-law.

'Off the record, I'm glad you and Frank are living together. It will be good for him. His mother's treated him like a kid long enough. And make sure he knows how to switch your iron on.'

'Way ahead of you there, Jack. I'm glad you're not one of those men who think their wives should run after them.'

'Steady. I'm talking about Frank, not me. My wife would kill me if I burned something with an iron. I used to iron my uniform shirts then I made the mistake of destroying one of her work blouses.'

Carol laughed. 'I'll be sure to keep your son away from my blouses.'

'Right, you can get back to duty now. I just wanted you sitting in on this briefing because as of Monday morning, you'll be in civvies.'

'Very good, sir.'

Carol left the office and went over to where Miller was standing with Watt and Gibb.

'Give you your jotters, then?' Watt asked.

'As much as some of you wish he would have, my orientation has been brought forward to Monday.'

'Behave yourself,' Watt said. 'We're glad to have you on board. This is not the eighteenth century. You don't see any females in here because one transferred and one retired, and now we are looking for more women to join.'

'I know, Andy.'

'Don't apologise, love, go and get us a cup of tea.'

Carol's eyes went wide.

'Carol, he's joking,' Gibb said.

Watt nudged her with his elbow. 'You'll get used to me.'

'I'm sure I will.'

'Then you'll wonder what you ever saw in *him*.' He winked at Miller.

'You've got the good looks, wit, *and* a way with the women, Andy,' Miller said. 'I think Carol will think she hit the jackpot.'

'Hey, don't knock it, son. It takes years of practise to be this perfect. You'll learn though.'

'You going back on patrol?' Gibb said to Carol.

'Yes. My partner's waiting for me downstairs.'

'Good. I'll see you in here with Frank on Monday.'

'Okay. I can't wait.' She left the incident room.

'Right you two, with me,' Gibb said, grabbing his suit jacket from the back of a chair where he'd left it. 'And then you can explain to me why you weren't at the crime scene in Warriston in the wee hours of this morning,' he said to Watt.

'I already told you, my car wouldn't start. Then my phone died. The cat had unplugged it. It wasn't my fault.'

'Bloody car wouldn't start,' Gibb said as they made their way downstairs. 'And I thought your wife took the cat?'

'I get him at the weekend.'

'Christ, listen to me; as if the bloody cat *could* unplug the phone.'

'It was the charging cable. He must have unplugged it when he was taking a benny round the living room. They do that you know. One minute they're sitting there all quiet, the next minute, they're tanking about like they're on crack–'

Gibb held up a hand as they left the station through the back door. 'Enough, Andy. I might look daft, but...' Gibb left the sentence unfinished.

'I'm saying nothing,' Watt said under his breath. He tossed the car keys to Miller. 'Here, you can chauffeur us around. I feel hungov... I mean, I have a headache.'

'Don't be teaching Carol any of your bloody bad habits,' Gibb said as Miller opened the doors.

'As if...' He nudged Miller. 'That's what she's got you for.'

TWENTY

'Up there on the left,' Watt said as Miller drove the car up Easter Drylaw Avenue.

He pulled the car into the side of the road.

'This place is certainly changing,' he said.

'A lot of people are buying their houses,' Gibb said. 'They take pride in it that way.'

Miller thought he had a point. The people in this street were certainly taking pride in their properties.

It would seem like an up-and-coming neighbourhood, except for the uniformed officer standing outside the front door of the house. The family liaison officer took them inside.

They were greeted by the sound of people crying. The death message had been delivered shortly after Ruby's death, but now it was time to look into her background.

'It's not fair!' Ruby's mother screamed when Paddy Gibb walked in. He made the introductions. The room was in semi-darkness, the curtains having been drawn, keeping out the morning sunlight, and no doubt some snoop with a long lens.

'I'm sorry for your loss, Mrs Maxwell,' Gibb said, hoping the woman wasn't in the mood for taking her frustration out on the first person she saw.

'Are you sure it wasn't that wee bastard Ritchie?' Mr Maxwell said. 'If I think he did this...'

'He has an alibi,' Watt said. 'It's been checked out. He was with six other people at the time.'

'He's cut up about it,' Miller said, and didn't flinch when the father rounded on him.

'Just as fucking well. I'd rip his nuts off if I thought he'd hurt my Ruby.' Then he looked towards the door of the living room. 'Mandy! Get the kettle on. Your mother needs another cup of tea.'

He eased his wife down onto the settee and the detectives sat down.

'We need to talk about Ruby, Mr Maxwell,' Gibb said.

The man looked at them with tears in his eyes. A hard man, not quite so hard in front of his family. 'Fire away.'

'Where were you last night? Evening time, between seven and ten?'

His eyes narrowed for a moment and Miller tensed, getting ready to step in between the two men. Then Maxwell relaxed. 'I was in the pub. Down in the Ferry Boat.'

Miller knew the pub, down on Ferry Road, not far from Drylaw Police station. 'We're going to need some names.'

The man nodded, resigned to the fact, as if this wasn't his first rodeo.

'I know this is painful, but we need to talk about Ruby.'

'Ask away.'

Miller looked up as a young woman came into the room.

'Mandy, you shouldn't be here,' Maxwell said.

'She was my sister.' Tears were streaming down her face. 'I want to know who hurt her.'

Miller wondered if the young woman couldn't bring herself to use the word *murdered*. The liaison officer came in, herself looking to be not much older than Mandy. She was dressed casually, making her job look less officious.

'Do you know anybody who would want to harm Ruby?' Gibb said. He had his notebook out.

'No. Everybody loved Ruby. She was best friends with Mo. They were like sisters.' He looked across at Mandy. 'Like another sister. They would all go out drinking together. Tell them Mandy.'

Mandy sat on a high-back chair near the window, like it was kept there for when the number of visitors outnumbered the comfy chairs. 'I didn't go out with her all the time, but we went out frequently. To the Docker's Club in Leith. Up town when we wanted to go on a pub crawl.' She looked over at her father as if expecting an admonishing for her drinking habits, but none came.

'Did she ever get into any trouble when you were at any of these places?' Watt asked.

'Trouble?'

'I mean, did she get into an argument with anybody, or were there any men there who she knocked back and who didn't take kindly to being rejected?'

'No, not that I knew of.'

'Where did she work?' Miller asked.

'She was a physiotherapist at the Western.'

'Could she have had any enemies there?'

Mandy tucked her head down and started sobbing harder.

'I'm sorry, I know these questions are tough, but we need every bit of information so we can build up a picture.'

She sniffed and lifted her head up. 'She always spoke about her work when she got home, but there was never any mention of a problem at work. But then she moved in with Ritchie, and we didn't see her as often. When I spoke to her on the phone, she seemed happy enough.'

'And she would tell you if there was anybody giving her hassle?' said Gibb.

'Oh, yes. The only one who she argued with was Ritchie, but she always said they loved each other.'

'We're not concentrating our efforts on him just now, although we're keeping an open mind.' Gibb looked across to Maxwell to see if he was going to butt in. 'No patients that were giving Ruby a problem?'

Mandy shook her head. 'Not that I know of.'

Miller could see that there weren't any pointers and as such, the case would be classed as a random act of violence. Until they knew whether or not Ruby was targeted.

Outside, reporters were gathering and there was a news crew further along from the pathway. The detectives brushed off questions as they got in the car, Miller behind the wheel again.

'Do you think Iris Napier's killer murdered Ruby Maxwell?' Miller said.

'Not a chance,' Watt said. 'I think we've got two nutters on our hands now.'

TWENTY-ONE

If anybody saw Calvin pull up to Marcie's house, so what? He was just a colleague and friend from work who was calling round to offer his condolences. If they had a problem, what were they going to do? Tell her husband? He smiled at the thought but then immediately changed his expression.

He didn't want some nosey parker to see him smiling away to himself in the car when this was a sombre occasion.

He parked next to Marcie's car. She opened her front door, tears streaming down her face, a hanky in one hand. He stepped over the threshold and she shut the door quietly behind her.

'God, Marcie, I'm so sorry,' Calvin said.

Then she smiled. 'What for? Our marriage was dead in the water. I fell out of love with him years ago. I couldn't wait until he had left for London every Monday. Weekends were a nightmare. I was so glad he wasn't coming home this weekend.'

'Aren't you going to miss him?'

'Of course not. He was loaded, Calvin. We have large insurance policies. The house will be paid off. We can be together.'

'What about Bree?'

'When she does decide to show her face, maybe you should just divorce her. That way we can do whatever we want.'

'Jesus, you're so clever.'

He kissed her passionately on the lips.

'And don't you forget it, mister. I'm the brains behind this operation.'

She took him by the hand and led him to the living room upstairs. They sat on the settee and Calvin was all over her, pushing a hand up her jumper.

'Easy. I'm the grieving widow, remember?'

'Plenty of time for grieving later.'

She moved away from him. 'We have lots to think about.'

'Like what?'

'Like keeping things cool like we've been doing. A transition period. I don't want to arouse any suspicions.'

'What suspicions? Your husband was killed in London. It's not as if the police were called after you found him in the bath with a radio plugged in.'

'I know that. But in a case like this, it takes a bit of time. Plus, you haven't had the police knocking on your door asking where Bree is. You need to be on the ball when that happens. The police are already going to get Norman's dental records to compare them down there. I don't want them to think we were involved.'

'We *weren't* involved.'

It was the subtle change in Marcie's eyes that chilled him. 'I know, but they're trained to think suspiciously.'

'I'll have to get in touch with the funeral directors. I'll tell them I don't know what I'm doing and they can deal with it all.'

'Did they get somebody for knocking him down?'

'No. It was raining. All witnesses saw was a dark car. But let's talk about Bree.'

'What about her?'

'Like, is she going to give you any hassle over the divorce?'

'What divorce?'

Marcie laughed. 'What divorce, he says. You're so funny.' Marcie poured herself a whisky, for *medicinal purposes*. 'Did she call you when she was away?'

'At first, but not in the latter years. We weren't teenagers in love anymore.'

'Tell me about it. I'm sure Norman had a slapper in his room every night. I can't tell you the last time I made love to him and felt something.'

Calvin felt a pang of jealousy inside at the very thought of somebody else touching Marcie. Even though this man had been her husband, he hadn't deserved her. Marriage wasn't a game, but a commitment you made to another person. Then he thought how ironic that was. If that was the case, then why wasn't he treating his wife like a princess instead of shagging around behind her back?

Then another thought struck him; *this isn't going to be fun anymore. The sneaking around, the screwing around behind his wife's back.* He stood up suddenly.

'You okay, honey?' Marcie asked.

He nodded and rushed through to the bathroom where he threw up. He hadn't seen it going like this; him on his knees in one of Marcie's bathrooms, puking his load. He felt his whole body starting to shake.

Christ, what have I done? He whispered to the inside of the bowl. The shiny white porcelain didn't have the answer.

He couldn't control the shakes. It felt like the morning after a good drinking session, where he felt cold and empty. And sick. *What was happening to him?* Regret? Shock? Fear? Probably a lethal mix of all three. It was the *regret* that was frightening him. He couldn't change what had happened. He felt like he was in a movie and was waiting for the director to shout *cut!*

This was real life. No second take, no stunt double taking the bullet and falling to the floor dead. Only to get up for the next scene.

This had really happened. People said they just got swept up in it all, and now Calvin was feeling this for the first time.

He lifted his head and flushed then puked again. And more, until he was dry heaving. His stomach was empty and there was nothing more inside to come up.

Flush again. He spat into the running water as the tank filled. *What have I done?* he asked himself again. Has living with Bree been so bad?

Of course not. She was his wife. He loved her. Not this whore he was having it away with. Realty hit him in the face like a freight train. She was so casual about the way her husband was now dead.

He took a few deep breaths, flushed again, and got up. Splashed water on his face at the sink then rubbed it dry with one of the guest towels. Bree would have killed him if she caught him using the downstairs lav and drying his hands on the guest towel. He smiled at the thought.

Marcie had made tea.

'It'll calm you down,' she said. Like she understood.

This relationship was a big ship at sea and Marcie had just climbed into the captain's chair.

TWENTY-TWO

Vince Rutherford threw his head back, chugging on his pint of Stella. Then he looked at his brother, who was taking his time with his bottle.

'I'm telling you something, Becksy, I'm shiting myself. I've had a whole fucking packet of Imodium and still I feel my sphincter giving it laldy.'

'Try and relax, bro.'

The Spiegeltent was getting busy with patrons having a swift beer before going to see whatever author they'd come to see giving a talk.

'My whole future is riding on this, Becks.' He nodded to his feet where his manuscript sat, taped up in a cardboard box. 'This is my masterpiece. You did read it, didn't you?'

'I've already told you ten times I did. And it's bloody brilliant mate.' He was balancing on one of his crutches, the other one leaning against the high table they were standing at.

'You're a good brother, I'll give you that.'

'Listen, I have something to tell you. I was waiting for the right time, but now seems as good as any.'

'Look, it's accepted nowadays. It's not like in Mother's time when they used to lock you away for being a pansy.'

'I wasn't sure you'd come tonight if you knew beforehand... wait, what? No, not a fucking pansy. And I know it's normal in society today, that's not the issue. Why would you think I'm gay, anyway?'

'I never thought you were gay.'

'Anyway, I was giving it some thought–'

'Becksy, spit it out for fuck's sake.'

'Dawn's coming tonight.'

Vince drank some of his pint, feeling the interior of the tent go round in circles for a moment. 'For a minute there, I thought you meant *my* Dawn was coming here.'

'I did mean her. *Your* Dawn.'

Vince put his pint glass down a bit faster than he wanted to and several guests looked at him. Beckett put a hand on his arm. 'Before you tell them to fuck off, remember they could be your fans one day.'

Vince smiled and apologised. 'I'd better see those twats sitting in the front row when I'm on the stage giving a talk,' he said.

'You might never be invited.'

'Have you seen some of those weasels who come here?'

'Again with the loudness. Calm down, Vince.'

'Calm down? You've just told me that the one and only woman that I ever loved is coming here toni... wait a minute; how the fuck do you know this?'

'She emailed me.'

Vince grabbed the pint glass and squeezed it. Then released the pressure before the liquid exploded out in a wave of flying glass. 'She emailed you? How the fuck did she have your email?'

'I've had the same email for years. I never changed it or got a new one.'

'So get to the good bit before I set fire to this fucking place.'

'She emailed me to let me know she's coming up with Len Chatter.'

'What?' His words were accompanied by beer spittle. 'How in God's name is she coming with Len? Christ, don't tell me he's fu–'

'She works for him.'

Vince drank some more. This was a dream he was having. He'd had a leftover Scotch pie for his dinner, and it had been a toss-up whether it was off or not, but he had cooked it thinking, *how bad can it be?* Now he was finding out that he had dozed off for a minute, the pie was rank and he was having a bad nightmare because of it.

'Punch me in the balls, see if I'm awake.'

Beckett started positioning himself.

'Figure of speech, Christ,' he said and Beckett relaxed. No, he was awake after all.

'How in the name of fuck did all this come about, her emailing you? Start at the beginning and don't leave anything out.'

'She was doing acting, but that didn't pan out. She met Chatter through a friend of a friend, and he was needing an assistant, so he offered her the job. She's been working for him for about a year now, and she's the one who's been overseeing the writer's competition. She saw your name, and saw you had been invited along to have dinner with this group of fans from Edinburgh, so she wanted me to tell you that she'd be here, in case you were uncomfortable.'

'Uncomfortable? Hell, the chance to see her again? Mother was just talking about her last night.' He drank some of the lager and looked at his brother. 'She doesn't know about Dawn, does she?'

'No, of course not. I wouldn't tell her anything. She gets wired into me when you're out, you know. Nagging all the time. When are we both going to settle down, find a couple of nice girls? Get married and have kids. I hear it all the time. You know what she said to me one night? She said–'

'Tell me later. Tell me more about Dawn.'

'Well, I wrote and told her I didn't think you'd be uncomfortable. She said that was good as she'd love to see you again.'

'She did? You wouldn't make that up, would you? 'Cause if you would–'

'What do you take me for, Vince? I swear to God that she asked me how you were and she looks forward to seeing you tonight.'

'Jesus. I can't believe it. It's been five years since I saw her. Dad dying buggered my relationship with her.'

'Well, I'm sure he didn't mean to have a stroke.'

'I know. I'm not meaning it that way. I meant that the timing was unfortunate.'

'Now you can sit and have dinner with her. She's obviously coming along to the meal.'

Vince banged the glass down again. 'Wait; is her husband coming along?'

'I didn't know she was married.'

'She was living with a sound engineer guy. I just assumed that she might have married him.'

'Fifty percent chance she did. Fifty she didn't.'

'She could have married somebody else. Fuck me. I don't know if I can see her, Becks. I mean, what would I talk about?'

'How about your book for a start?'

'Brilliant! At least I can talk about that and ease the conversation round.'

'If she is married, her husband might be with her, just be prepared.'

'Fucking give it with one hand, take it away with the other.' He took a deep breath and tilted his head back. Then looked at his brother. 'You should have fucking asked her.'

'How would I have brought that up?'

'Oh, I don't know. How about *Are you fucking married?* Something along those lines.'

'Well, too late now. I didn't. So if she tells you she is, don't go throwing a benny in the hotel.'

'When I got the invite to go along, I didn't know it was Dawn who had sent it to me. It was just initials *DT*. Dawn Tait, who would have thought?'

Vince felt his stomach turn inside out. He knew he had to play it cool. Dawn wouldn't be impressed by him going into a mood. Besides, what if she *did* have a husband? Vince going into a strop would just enforce the idea that she had made the right decision. No, he'd play it cool, tell her he had a girlfriend now. No, a *fiancée*. That sounded so much better. He would pick out the name of a woman at work and describe her physically, that way he wouldn't feel like an arse if she asked him later and he'd made something up and couldn't remember what he said.

Just then, Jimmy came in, wiping his brow with a hanky.

'Jimmy, you remember Beckett, my brother?'

'Of course I do. Good to see you again, mate.'

'Likewise,' Beckett said and they shook hands. 'Call me Becks. Everybody does. What you having? Vince's round.'

'Lager, thanks.'

'Why are you sweating?' Vince asked. 'The thought of opening that moth farm you call a wallet?'

'Who paid for the chippie on the way home last night?'

'Touché.'

Vince got some drinks in and Jimmy went to help him. 'Guess what?'

'You decided you're going to be a woman.'

'If I did, you wouldn't get a look in. No. Take another guess.'

'Does it involve a measuring tape like last time?'

'No, smartarse. Dawn's coming tonight.'

'Dawn Tait? The woman you dumped?'

'First of all, I did not dump her. We decided to go our own way.'

'Oh, I forgot; she dumped *you*.'

'Never mind who dumped who, fuckwit. The point is, guess who she works for?'

'Len Chatter.'

'Did Becksy tell you?'

'No. It was easy to figure out, considering we're going to see him tonight. It wouldn't have had the same impact if you said she works for Marks and Spencer.'

'You're right. Len Chatter. She works for him as some kind of assistant.'

'How are you with that?' Jimmy asked as they made their way back to Beckett.

'I'm nervous as all hell, to be honest. First of all, I'm going to give Chatter the book, and now knowing that Dawn is going to be there, I should have worn my brown trousers tonight.'

'It'll be fine. Play it cool though,' Jimmy said.

'That's what I was telling him,' Beckett said. 'Be all nonchalant.'

'You have to let her know you have a girlfriend,' Jimmy said. 'Let her think dumping you didn't have much effect on you.'

'I know.' He could hardly tell Dawn he had cried when he heard the sound engineer's voice on the phone.

'I'm going to play it cool. And if she's married, well, fuck her. I'm over her.'

'Sure you are, pal,' Jimmy said, clapping his friend on the shoulder.

'Besides, what's-her-face in the office is always asking me if I want to go for a drink. Zoob. The new girl.'

'What kind of a fucking name is *Zoob*?'

'She said it's ancient Greek or something.'

'Ancient horseshit, if you ask me,' Beckett said. '*Zoob*.'

'Oh, fuck off, you two.'

'There you are,' a female voice said from behind them.

Vince froze for a second before turning round. Dawn was standing looking at him, smiling.

'Hi.'

'It's good to see you again, Vince. You too, Becks. And who's your friend?'

'This is Jimmy. My work mate and best pal. You remember him, don't you?'

'Oh yes! Hi Jimmy.' She smiled wider and shook his hand.

'You're looking good,' Vince said, and she was. Hair cut shorter, she still had a good figure and she looked like she hadn't aged a second since he'd last seen her.

'Thank you.'

'Becks tells me you're here with Len Chatter.'

'I work for him.'

'Oh, excuse my manners; would you like a drink?'

'No, thank you. I just wanted to make sure you were here before I go and do my assistant thing. Basically, it's making sure he's remembered to have a pee before he goes on stage and tell him how good he looks and to make sure he's flossed. That kind of stuff.'

'Sounds really interesting,' Vince said, not meaning it.

'You don't mean that.'

'It doesn't sound interesting to me,' Jimmy said, grinning.

'That's because you're a moron,' Vince said.

'Is that your book?' Dawn said, pointing to his feet.

'It is indeed. Although I feel foolish bringing it along now. Nobody else has done that, I bet.'

'No, they haven't but it shows initiative. And if he has it right now, he'll probably read through it while he's in bed.'

Vince looked at Jimmy before he could come out with any quips about Chatter chugging over his manuscript.

'Thanks for putting my mind at ease.'

'I'll take it now if you like. He has other people with him as well, and one of them can lug it around.'

'That would be great.' He picked it up. The box itself was in a carrier bag. He handed it to her, knowing this was it.

'I'll personally see to it that he knows you brought it with you.'

'Will I see you later?' he blurted out before she left. 'I mean, at the dinner?'

'Of course. We'll have a drink. Catch up with old times.'

'Great. I look forward to it.' He couldn't help but notice the gold band on her left finger as she took the bag from him.

'You see that?' he said when she was gone.

'What?' Beckett said.

'You make it sound like she just nicked your book,' Jimmy said.

'No, not that; she has a fucking wedding ring on.'

'There was that possibility my friend,' he said, putting on a look that people used when flushing their child's dead goldfish down the toilet.

'I don't care, as long as he's not up here with her. If he is, I'm going to make a quick exit. I don't think I could take watching somebody put his arm around her, or kiss her.'

'Me and Becks could give him a kicking if we get him on his own.'

'That would look good, especially since she's seen you and would be able to pick you out of a line-up. I just don't want to see him, not make Dawn have to decide if she wants to switch off his life support or live with a vegetable.'

'Well, the offer's there, mate.'

'You know Beckett was in the army catering corps, don't you? He wasn't one of those ninja blokes who jump out of helicopters on ropes.'

'Well, he knows his way round a set of kitchen knives.'

'Jimmy, get a grip of yourself. We'll play it casual, then fuck off early if Mr Dawn is there.'

'Roger that.'

'Right, time for a wee chaser before we go to see Len. And remember, no heckling. This isn't a Jimmy Carr concert.'

TWENTY-THREE

Miller was tired, but having a can of Red Bull would see him through to tonight. He had told Carol that it was a surprise where they were eating, but the truth of the matter was, he had thought he would take her to the Ping On Chinese restaurant in Stockbridge, round the corner from the *Savoy*. Carol had taken him there the first time she'd brought him back to her place. It had good memories for him.

Unlike finding another man's razor in her bathroom cabinet.

It was almost like he'd found a bloodied knife under the mattress.

Just the thought of it being there made his stomach do flips.

'I was thinking we could choose some colours for the living room together,' Carol said, plonking herself down on the couch with a cup of tea. 'I think it needs a bit of new life in it. What do you think?'

He had been staring out of the window at the summer sky. The window was open and he could hear people down on the bowling green below.

'I'm sorry, what?'

'New paint for the living room.'

Do what you want. It's your place. 'Fine.'

'Well, don't get too excited, Miller. I know it's only paint, but we can make this place ours.'

He stood up. 'It's yours, Carol, not mine. Do what you like. I'm going to shower before we go out. Assuming you still want to go out with me, that is.'

'What...?' she started to say, but Miller had already left the room.

He undressed in the bedroom, wrapping his towel round his waist. How long would he be able to keep up this pretence? Not long. Maybe after tonight, he'd tell her to go fuck herself. *Christ, listen to yourself. What's wrong? Missing mummy? The first bump in the road and you want to go running home? It's not even a fucking bump! It's something that's in your own head. So you found a razor in her bathroom cabinet. Did you think she was a virgin before she met you? She had boyfriends just like you had girlfriends, but do you see her getting all antsy?*

He sat on the bed, trying to boot himself up the backside, but the feeling was deep inside. He remembered a friend of his from another station saying he had met a nurse and was dating her. Things were going fine but he started to notice that she seemed to know everybody. They got in a taxi one night and the driver knew her. She bumped into a guy in a pub who she knew. Even walking down the street, she bumped into somebody she knew. When they were out in a foursome one night having a meal, she knew the waiter and her friend made a comment about her knowing everybody.

Miller's pal had jacked her in after that. He fancied her, the sex was fantastic, she was good fun, but deep down, he knew there had been many boyfriends in her past. Like, battalions of them. And Miller's friend was worried that his girlfriend would still want boyfriends if she became his wife. Pre-emptive strike, he'd called it. She had been furious, but he had braved the storm. Now he was married to a boring but dependable woman who loved nothing more than to be at home with her two little boys.

Miller didn't think for one minute that Carol was like that, but the little voice in his head that kept him up at night spoke out... *what if?* He thought he would just call it a day if he thought she'd been like his pal's nurse. Maybe some guys could deal with it, but Miller knew he couldn't. He would be faithful to Carol, of that he was confident, but he wanted somebody who would feel the same way about him.

Maybe he should just go out and get pished with Andy Watt. The older sergeant would keep him on the straight and narrow.

He walked through to the bathroom to have his shower, and when he closed the door, he saw it, sitting there on the sink.

The razor. *What the hell?*

There was a knock at the door. 'Can I come in?' Carol asked.

He opened the door, the towel still wrapped round his waist.

She stepped in. 'I found it when I was looking for some ibuprofen. I'd forgotten it was still there but I noticed it had moved and figured you'd found it.'

'That?' he said, looking at the razor. 'I didn't give it another thought.'

'Liar. You thought it was my old boyfriend's, that I'd forgotten to throw it out.' She smiled at him. 'I thought there was something wrong with you and then I connected the dots earlier. I want to tell you something; both of us have a past. We don't have to tell each other all the little details about past relationships, and so what if I have a razor in there? But it doesn't belong to who you think it does. It's my dad's.'

'What?'

'Last year, before I started dating you, I went on holiday with a friend of mine – female – and Harry said he would retile my bathroom over a couple of days one weekend. He stayed here and did it all for me. Although he didn't shower, he still shaved. You know what he's like; he's old-fashioned. He said he felt cleaner if he had a shave. He left it in the cabinet and I found it not so long ago. I meant to clean the whole cabinet out, but as you can see, I haven't gotten around to it yet.'

'I wasn't thinking–' he started to say but could feel his face go red.

'Yes you were. And that's fine. We'll always be finding out things about each other. But let me tell you something, I had boyfriends, not a ton of them but a few, but not one of them stayed over. Not one of them. I didn't feel right letting them stay. I think I'm old-fashioned that way myself, and of course one or two wanted to, but I said no. You were the first one who stayed over, because I was falling in love with you. Nobody has ever come close to you. I love you and I trust you. I want you to feel the same way about me.'

'I know you trust me. Even if I came home in the wee hours, blootered, you wouldn't question me.'

'No, I'd just show you some 5 am love, dear.'

He raised his eyebrows but she didn't elaborate.

He looked down at the floor for a moment, before looking in her eyes. 'I'm sorry. I shouldn't have thought badly of it.'

'Don't do it again. I don't have any secrets. I have a past, but no secrets.'

'I won't think that way again. I promise. Now I feel like a twat.'

'So you should. But I won't hold it against you.'

'Jesus, Carol, I'm sorry. I love you more than I've ever loved any woman. Sometimes I feel so possessive.'

'Well, don't. Sometimes you just have to take a step back. And we have to build our relationship on trust. Okay?'

'Yes, ma'am.'

'Now get that towel off and get into the shower,' she said, unbuttoning her shirt.

'Dad, I want to run something past you,' Miller said, holding the phone with one hand, a drink with the other. Freshly showered and dried and feeling better about his relationship than he ever had.

'Go ahead, son, but make it quick. I don't want my beer to go flat.'

'We were talking with a woman last night.' He went into detail about meeting Sherri and her mentioning Perry MacKinnon. 'My thing is, now I want to look into him. I wanted some advice on how to do that.'

'First of all, you have to take a step back and see it from an outsider's point of view. Did this woman give you any proof that she wired money to the doctor? Any proof that she's been writing to him, or that he was writing to her? You saw a man arguing with her in the street; do you know for a fact that it was him?'

'No, I don't.'

'I've heard of Perry MacKinnon. He has ties to Holyrood. I wouldn't go poking your nose in just yet. This Sherri woman might be a crank and you don't want to be on anybody's radar at HQ for the wrong reasons. Just tread lightly, that's what I'm saying.'

'Thanks, dad. I will.'

He hung up and gave Carol the gist of what his father had said.

'I don't know about you, but I believe her. I'm going to ask her if she has copies of money orders she sent to him. There has to be a paper trail.'

'The thing that gets me, if he's loaded, why would he go to such lengths to take money from a woman he doesn't even know, risking his reputation?'

'We'll have to find a way to ask him.'

'What do you mean she's disappeared?' Calvin Baxter said into his phone. He was standing in the lobby of the *Savoy* hotel in Stockbridge.

'She didn't turn up to check in for her flight. We had to get a stand-

by to take her place and when we sent somebody round to her flat, there was no answer.'

'There was no answer? That doesn't make sense. There's no reason why Bree would miss work. Are you sure you went to the right place?'

'Yes, Mr Baxter. It was the correct address. If you don't mind, I'm going to call the police and get them to force their way in.'

'Of course. Go ahead. Do whatever it takes. I tried calling her like you suggested earlier, but there was no answer. Please call me and let me know what they find.'

'I will. I'm sure there's nothing to worry about.'

'Famous last words,' Calvin said, after he hung up. He went back into the packed bar and over to the window where Marcie was sitting.

'Still no joy?' she asked.

He shook his head. 'Keep it to yourself. I don't want Perry to know just now. It might be nothing. Dozy cow went out for a swift one and got laid by a brickie or something. Lost all track of time.'

Marcie giggled. 'Don't be like that. She's not like you, after all.'

'How do you know?'

'Just from what you've told me.'

'She might have taken a flight back up here to catch us out. Maybe she'll be waiting back at the house, hiding in a closet, waiting to jump out with a kitchen knife to do us both in.'

'Now you're just being *Creepy Calvin* again. Like when you put your underpants on your head and pretend to be a burglar. I prefer *Civilised Calvin*. Bring him back.'

'Sorry. I'm just worried that she's going to catch us.'

She reached over and squeezed his leg. 'That's the fun part, don't you think? Snogging in the back of a car, wondering if you're going to get caught.'

'Not really. I'm more a *My wife's going to cut my dick off* sort of man. One who worries about sharp implements coming into close contact with his pride and joy.'

'What about the buzz you got when you thought my husband had come home early? Now we'll never have to worry about him again.'

'Jesus, Marcie.' This wasn't the first time he'd thought she was a callous cow. But that wasn't the only thing nibbling away at his guts right now; *her husband's dead, Calvin old boy. You know what that means, don't you? No more sneaking around to her house. You can come and go as you please, no Norman to come home and find you keeping his wife warm. But she hated him anyway, and guess what? She wants her hooks into you now. And isn't it just a good old co-winky dink that your wife is missing? Who would have thought? Both of them gone just like that! Poof! Puff of smoke and abracadabra, now you see them, now you don't. And that's what's eating your guts inside out, isn't it? The fact that she's free to do what she likes. And you're not, not yet. But Marcie is hoping so, because that way she'll have you all to herself. The new Mr Marcie. You won't be creepy Calvin then, oh no boy, you'll be castrated Calvin. You won't be able to blow your nose without asking her first.*

'Oh, fuck off,' he said.

'What?'

Calvin looked at her. 'I mean, trust us to bump into MacKinnon. I want you all to myself.' He smiled at her like a letch.

'You'll get enough of me later. Steady, he's coming.'

'Dear, oh dear, this place is getting busier by the day,' Perry MacKinnon said, putting the drinks on the table and sitting down. 'Sure you don't mind if I join you?'

'Not at all,' Calvin said, raising his glass in salute.

'Cheers, dear,' Marcie said, smiling at him. 'So what brings you in here on a Saturday?'

'Oh, I have somebody I want to see.'

Calvin raised his eyebrows. 'A woman?'

'Yes, as a matter of fact,' he replied, looking around. 'But it's not what you think.'

'You old dog.'

'Less of the *old*, Calvin. I'm only a couple of years older than you.'

'So, what's she like, this new one?' Marcie said.

'This is purely business. But she's not here at the moment so I'll have to come back some other time. Anyway, what are you two doing in here?'

'We're just having a quiet drink. This used to be our old haunt, remember?' Calvin said.

'How could I forget? We had some fun nights, right enough.'

'It's a pity about you breaking up with Amelia. She was very nice. What is she going to do now?'

'God knows. She's not talking to me at the moment. But she's moving back to her own place, so says she. I couldn't care less, to be honest. She was becoming a whiney bitch.'

'Aren't they all?' He winced as Marcie nudged him in the ribs. 'Present company excepted, of course.'

'That's better,' Marcie said.

'What about Bree?' MacKinnon asked.

'Bree does her own thing, you know that, Perry.'

'I do. But she was much happier when you were working with me. Part of the team. Living on the edge.'

'It was hardly Formula 1 racing.'

'Having somebody's life in your hands, that's a far bigger rush than racing round a track in a tin box.'

'And now you reshape people's faces.'

MacKinnon laughed. 'You make it sound like I'm a hired thug.'

'I never thought of it like that, but that's a pretty good description; Perry MacKinnon, thug for hire. *If your name is on his list, your time is up.* Sounds like a badly written novel.'

'You should have jumped on board with me, Calvin. You could have been making a lot more money.'

'But then I wouldn't have met my delectable co-worker, Marcie.' He smiled at her and winked.

She beamed back at him.

'Why aren't you working in one of your bigger places?' Calvin asked.

MacKinnon drank some of his whisky. 'They might be modern and efficient, but they don't have the same character as the Dean Terrace clinic. I just love the atmosphere of the place. In fact, my wife expressed an interest in buying a house in Ann Street, just further up the hill. There's one for sale, and she wants to put an offer on it.'

'Isn't that too close to Amelia?' Calvin said with a smile. 'Or do you like the idea of sewing your own dangly bits back on?'

'Amelia's history. Attractive, yes, but too fond of Walter Scott, if you know what I mean.'

'I do,' Calvin said, knowing that MacKinnon was referring to the great Scottish writer's face on a one-hundred-pound note.

'Sometimes diamonds are not a girl's best friend,' Marcie said. 'Diamonds don't pay the rent.'

'And you can't blow up your nose with a diamond.'

'I never touch the stuff, dearest,' Marcie said.

Just then, MacKinnon was nudged forward on his stool. He turned around to see a man with a walking stick looking at him.

'Oh, I'm sorry, guv'nor,' he said, his London accent thick. 'Let me buy you another one.'

'No, it's okay,' MacKinnon said, looking at the stick. 'No harm.'

'Very good of you, guv'nor.' The man walked away, leaning heavily on his stick, his half-empty pint glass sloshing.

The TV was in the corner and the man had been looking at the football results. Now he finished his pint and left the bar, waving over to the barman. 'Catch you later.'

MacKinnon expected to see the man leave the hotel, but didn't catch sight of him. 'What a life, working in your old man's bar. Miles is such a sad loser.'

Calvin sniggered. 'Who would ever have thought that he would end up working in a bar, considering.'

Marcie nudged him. 'Stop. That's being cruel.'

'It's true though. An alkie, who turned himself round to work in a bar.'

'His father owns this place apparently,' MacKinnon said. 'Can you imagine him selling this place to me? I could knock through and double the size of the clinic.'

'It would cost a pretty penny,' Calvin said.

'And I would charge a pretty penny for glamour work. I could even make an ugly sod like you pretty again.' He laughed.

'I'm fine with what I have, thank you very much.'

'Yes, leave him alone, Perry.'

'Seriously though, I want this place. I'm going to make him an offer.'

Calvin saw her smile at him, and it was a smile he knew from a long time ago; the one he called her *hunger* smile.

'Right, lady, let's go and get us something to eat. This was just a pit stop.'

'Off so soon?' Stay for another.'

'Yes, let's stay, Calvin. We can eat later.' Marcie smiled again, but it wasn't directed at Calvin.

'I need to go for a pee first,' he said. He got up and fought his way through the crowd. He knew there was a toilet in the hotel reception that would be quieter, so he went out of the bar, and back into reception. As he was walking over to the men's, he saw Miles through the back, talking to the clumsy clot with the walking stick who had bumped into him.

The man was laughing and joking now. He was very familiar with Miles. It seemed that Miles knew him.

'I won't be serving dinner tonight, but if you're in your room, I'll get somebody to give you a shout.'

'Thanks my friend. You're a good guy.'

'No problem. You helped me in the past and I'll never forget it.'

Perry MacKinnon walked into the toilet, a feeling of utter disbelief washing over him. It couldn't be him, could it? He pictured the scruffy man with the walking stick, the unkempt hair, the scruffy beard.

Yet, MacKinnon knew it *was* him.

A face from the past.

TWENTY-FOUR

'There he is,' Vince said, nudging Jimmy. 'Over there.'

'Which one? I see a lot of old geezers.'

'Didn't you look at his website? I told you to have a butchers so you would know what he looked like.'

'I was too busy.'

'Too busy doing what?'

'I have things that need to be done. I don't have the luxury of having my old dear wash my skids.'

'Hey, we do that ourselves, eh, Becks?'

Beckett was standing in front of the other two in the line, waiting to get into the marquee theatre. The sun had dipped below the Georgian townhouses in Charlotte Square and a light wind had sprung up.

'Speak for yourself. Mother does mine.'

'Since when?'

'Since I came home.'

'Fuck me, she makes me put all my dirty laundry into the machine.'

'I do my own,' Jimmy said.

'Anyway, that's him over there.'

'Where?'

'The one with the straw hat and cravat on. He's hovering around near the writer's tent.'

'I see Dawn near an old bloke. That him?'

'Considering there's only one with a straw hat on, that narrows it down a bit.'

'God, I hope this is fun.'

'Just focus on the steak you can have at the dinner afterwards.'

'I hope he knows you invited us along,' Beckett said, turning to face them again.

'He'll be fine. He's minted. He'll whip out his piece of plastic and think nothing of it.'

The doors opened and they shuffled forward. Vince felt the excitement grab hold of him. One day, he'd be the one walking onto the stage, and people would be excited to see him. They would actually pay money to come and see him.

He had been so focused on the crowd moving that he didn't notice Dawn standing next to him at first. He did a double take. 'Oh, hi. Everything okay?' he asked.

'I was wondering if I could sit with you?' she said. 'I have to sit in the audience anyway.'

'Of course.'

She slipped an arm through his. 'It really is good to see you again, Vince,' she whispered to him.

'You too. You wouldn't believe how good I feel inside right now.' He winked at Jimmy. He could ask Dawn about the wedding ring on her finger later. Right now, he was going to see the man who he would be co-authoring with and the woman that he'd never stopped loving was on his arm.

Life was good.

'This is such a nice place,' Sherri said, sipping at her orange juice. A live band was playing on the small stage.

'Have you ever been to the Spiegeltent before?' Carol asked Miles.

'I have. I'm a big book reader and I've been here many times.'

'You only read big books?' Miller said.

'No, I meant–'

Miller laughed. 'I'm kidding, buddy. Just pulling your leg.' He drank some of his lager.

'Good one.'

'I'm a big book reader as well.'

'Now I don't know if you're still taking the you-know-what.'

'I meant I read a lot of books.'

'I bet you're good in the interrogation room. Both of you.'

'I'm not there yet,' Carol said.

'So who's your favourite author?' Miller asked Sherri.

'Len is. I met him in New York one time. In a little crime bookstore in Chelsea. He's very down to earth. What about you?'

'I like Grisham, but Chatter's a close second.'

They listened to the music for a few minutes.

'So where did you have dinner?' Sherri asked.

'TGI Fridays.' He'd skipped the idea about going to the Chinese place.

'Nice. One of my favourite's back in the States.'

'Nobody can say my boyfriend doesn't know how to treat a lady,' Carol said, laughing.

'I wanted a posh place on George Street, but what the lady wants, the lady gets.'

It was true; after making a fool of himself earlier, he'd wanted to make it up to her and treat her to a special place, but Fridays was one of her favourite restaurants. He felt so much better now, but still felt a twinge of embarrassment at his behaviour.

Miller turned at the sound of a man banging his glass down on a standing table. The man looked at him then apologised.

'Did you hear from Doctor MacKinnon again?' Carol asked.

Sherri shook her head. 'No, and I don't expect to. But my knight in shining armour here has told me to give him a shout if anything happens. Since he lives in the apartment down in the basement, he isn't far away.'

'She makes it sound like I should be locked away in the attic,' Miles said, smiling. 'It's an apartment down there. And civilised; we even have a TV.'

Sherri laughed and nudged him. 'Thank you all for taking me under your wing. I don't know what I would have done without you. However, I know this is just a hiatus. I still need to find direction in my life. I'm only in the hotel for two weeks, so I need to decide whether I want to go back to North Carolina, or stay on here for a while.'

'What's back there for you?' Carol asked.

'Nothing. I don't have anything left there at all. Not even my job. I could try and get it back of course, but by the time I went back, they would have filled the position.'

'What's your line of work?' Miller asked.

'I worked as a duty manager in a store. There are four of us and the general manager. They were planning on promoting one of the other members of staff, who I helped train before I left.' She looked down at her shoes for a moment before looking at Carol. 'Before I made a fool of myself.'

'Not made a fool of yourself, but were made a fool of. There's a big difference.'

'Let's enjoy tonight, then we can put our heads together,' Miles said. 'We don't want you to meet Len Chatter with your mascara running.'

She smiled. 'You're such a sweet man.'

'I've been called worse.' He smiled back. 'What about you, Frank?'

'Much worse.'

'You two are ganging up on me now,' she said, laughing.

'Well, us girls are going to make sure they pay for the rest of the evening,' Carol said.

'Uh oh, now see what you've done,' Miller said.

'Guilty as charged. Talking of which, we've got time for another before we have to go in. What's everybody up for?' Miles said.

Miller went to the bar with him. 'How has she really been today?' he asked Miles.

'Surprisingly upbeat, but I have the feeling she's just masking it. I can't believe some old catfish would take her to the cleaners. I feel sorry for her.'

'We can put our heads together and see what we can do for her after she leaves the hotel in a couple of weeks.'

'Don't worry, I won't see her in the street.'

'What will your father say about that?'

'He won't say anything. I run the hotel for him. He's away in Tenerife with my mum just now. I'll talk to him, but he's the most laid back man I know. We're best buddies to be honest. He's kind hearted, so he wouldn't want Sherri sleeping rough.'

'That's good of you, Miles.'

'It's what we humans do for each other. Or what we *should* be doing for each other. I'm not a tree hugger or anything, but I wish to Christ we could all live in peace instead of bombing the shit out of each other.'

'I hear you, pal.'

They got the drinks and went back to the women.

'I have to say, you do look better without the running mascara,' Miles said, handing Sherri another orange.

'I think I've just been complimented.'

'Knight in shining armour, remember?'

'You're not going to let me forget that, are you?'

'Maybe tomorrow.'

They chatted about books and authors before Miller looked at his watch. 'Time we were joining the queue to get in.'

They moved out of the bar and walked round to the theatre.

The show was on for an hour and Miller thought Len Chatter was a smooth operator. He sat on the stage with authority. Had a good sense of humour and was very entertaining.

After the talk, he sat at a table off to one side, where he signed copies of his latest novel, *Spearhead*.

'Who do you want this made out to?' he asked when it was Miller's turn.

'My friend, Sherri.'

For Sherri – hope you enjoy this! Len. 'Thank you.'

Miller had another copy. 'Could you sign this for me? Detective Frank Miller.'

Chatter raised his eyebrows. 'Detective? Not here to arrest me, are you?' he smiled.

'Not unless you've broken the law, Mr Chatter.'

Chatter laughed. 'Only my wrist.' He lifted the brace on his left wrist, then signed the book and handed it back to Miller. 'Thanks for coming along tonight, Frank.'

'The pleasure was all mine. But I hear you're coming to live here? I read it in the *Edinburgh Evening Post*.'

'I just moved into my new place this week. I had somebody look for a house for me and I got a nice one down at Trinity. I love the sea and I have a perfect sea view.'

'Fabulous. And welcome back to our fair city.'

'It's nice to be here. To smell fresh air again.' He laughed and took the book from Miles, signing it.

'He's such a nice man,' Carol said.

'He is.' He turned to Sherri. 'I got him to sign it for you.'

'What? No. I wasn't going to get his new one. Watching the pennies and all that.'

'It's a gift from us. Here. Enjoy it.'

'Oh, thank you, Frank.' She reached up and kissed him on the cheek.

'He beat me to it,' Miles said.

'Sorry, mate.'

'Don't worry. But I was going to buy you a copy.'

'I'm in the company of two gentlemen. I'm being spoiled tonight.'

'Anybody fancy coming back to the hotel for a nightcap?' Miles said.

'Sounds good to me,' said Carol.

Outside, it was cooler. The two women were walking arm-in-arm as they made their way downhill, so they could connect with Moray Place and Doune Terrace.

'I feel my life revolves around this hotel now,' Miles said.

'There are worse things in life,' Miller said.

'Like finding the body of a dead woman at St. Bernard's Well. Which doesn't make people want to come into Stockbridge. It could affect business.'

'We're trying our best to get him but it's not easy.' Miller didn't mind talking shop as long as it was within the parameters of what Miles could have read in the papers or saw on TV.

'And that other poor woman in Warriston. What the hell is this place coming to, Frank?'

'I hope we don't see any more murders,' he said. But in his heart he knew this was wishful thinking. It was only a matter of time.

Little did he know the clock was ticking for a woman he didn't know existed. Not yet anyway. But in the next few days, he would get to know her very well.

TWENTY-FIVE

The Malmaison hotel was down on The Shore in Leith. Len Chatter was in a taxi with some of his associates, including Dawn. Vince, Jimmy and Beckett were in the one behind. Chatter himself had asked Vince if he could stay behind and make sure everybody knew where they were going.

'Like fuck I will,' he had told Jimmy when Chatter's fast black departed Charlotte Square for Leith. 'If those ponces don't know where they're going, that's tough. Come on, I don't want to be far behind them.'

The cab was right behind Chatter's. Vince could see Dawn sitting with some of the others. She was facing the front and didn't turn around.

'Remember, wee man, try to be on your best behaviour.'

'I'm always on my best behaviour. What makes you think I'm going to make an arse of myself?'

'Your reputation precedes you.'

'Just relax,' Beckett said. 'You were fine when she spoke to you. We'll have a nice dinner and if it's not obvious she's married, I'll give her a bit of chat and find out.'

'I would have given her one if Vince wasn't going out with her,' Jimmy said to Beckett.

'She was something special. Real woman.'

'I'm right fucking here,' Vince said. 'Don't you pair of bastards go asking her if she wants a ride back to wherever she's staying.'

'Chatter's house,' Beckett said.

'What?'

Vince's brother looked at him. 'She's staying with Chatter. She told me in her email.'

'Christ, is there anything else you haven't told me?'

'No, that's it.'

'Well, if she's staying with him, then it's likely she hasn't got somebody with her.'

'It's a five-bedroom house. Plenty of room for her and her husband to stay. If she has one.'

'Where is this place?'

'Along the road in Trinity, not far from Ocean Terminal shopping centre.'

'You seem to know a lot about Chatter. Does he have a wife?'

'No, he isn't married.'

'Maybe he isn't attracted to women,' Jimmy said.

'No, he is. He just never got married. Why have some woman spend all your hard earned when you can have any woman you want?'

'Oh, magic,' Vince said. 'What if he has his eyes on Dawn?'

'She's worked for him for a year. She told me it's strictly business even though she'll be staying at his place.'

'She might just be staying at his gaff until she finds her own flat,' Jimmy said.

'She lives in London,' Vince said.

'Didn't you tell me that he's moving up here? If she works for him, then maybe she's moving back here too. Fifty-fifty chance.'

'Jesus, Jimmy, I hadn't thought of that. You're right. If she isn't married, and moving back here, I wonder if she would be interested in going out with me again.' The cab trundled along the setts of The Shore and the driver went straight through on the green light, until they reached the end of the street and the Malmaison Hotel. They'd lost the other cab and now there was no sign of Chatter and Dawn.

'I'm sure she would,' Beckett said.

'Nah, who am I kidding? I screwed it up five years ago. Let's face it lads, she's got somebody keeping her bed warm down in London, waiting to go back down to him to play the nice wife.'

'I'm going to ask her when we get in,' Jimmy said, reaching for the door handle. Vince put a hand on his arm. 'No, Jimmy. Thanks pal, but it's okay. I'll just have a pleasant evening with her and then we'll go our separate ways.'

'You're forgetting one thing,' Beckett said.

'What's that?'

'What if you win his competition? What if you're one of the lucky ones he chooses to be a co-writer? You'll see her all the time.'

'I never thought of that. Jesus, that would be a real bastard if she was married and I had to see her and her twat of a husband. Aw, man, what the fuck am I going to do now?'

He paid for the taxi and they stood at the water's edge, the Water of Leith gently flowing into the harbour up ahead. It was dark now, time for the adults to come out and play. Several large boats were moored opposite the bars and tenements. One was a floating restaurant, the *Blue Martini,* rumoured to belong to Robert Molloy, an Edinburgh businessman with a penchant for having blokes set about anybody who stood in his way. If they didn't just make you disappear.

'You need to have a plan,' Jimmy said. 'Let's say you win, and you get regular contact with her, and she has a husband – then you have to win her back.'

'Yeah, I'm a high-flying office clerk in the DVLA, just what she's looking for.'

'Not after you win and show them what you're made of,' Beckett said. He was balancing nicely on his crutches.

Jimmy turned and saw the small convoy of black cabs caught at the lights further back. 'Come on, let's get inside before those mutants get here.'

'Or as Vince likes to call them, *fellow scribes*,' Beckett said.

'I'm not a hundred per cent sure, but I think I'm having the pish ripped out of me here.'

Beckett laughed. 'Not at all, chum.'

Inside the hotel, there was no sign of Dawn or Chatter. 'Now what?' Vince said.

'Leave it with me,' Beckett said. He caught the eye of the concierge. 'We're with the Chatter party,' he said.

'Really?' he said, raising an eyebrow. 'Your name?'

'Captain Beckett Rutherford, British Army. I'm here with my brother Vincent and his other guest, James.'

The concierge looked at a list he was holding. 'Oh, very well, sir. They're through in the bar if you'd like to join them.'

'Thank you.'

They walked towards the bar, where Chatter was standing with Dawn and two of his assistants.

'Captain?' Vince whispered. 'That was a good one.'

'You liked that?'

'Very impressive,' Jimmy said. 'Maybe you could use that to snag us a bit of fan–'

'Christ, you've started already,' Vince said. 'Try and get through the meal without thinking about your dinky.'

Vince looked at Dawn's back as they went into the bar, Beckett hobbling on his crutches but getting into a rhythm. Even from behind, she looked spectacular. Her black trousers fitted perfectly, and she still had curves in all the right places. Beauty *and* brains. The whole package.

She was standing next to a tall man, skinny, with gelled hair. The sort of guy who could pull off that look and use it to attract a woman.

She turned as Vince got closer. 'Oh there you are!' She smiled at him and he could see the warmth in her eyes.

Christ, if she introduces stick man as her husband, I'm going to take Jimmy up on his offer of giving him a kicking he thought, but smiled. *Be the better man,* but it was hard.

'Here we are,' he said. 'Would you like a drink? Jimmy's getting them in.'

'No, no, Len's got a tab running.'

'Dawn!' Stick Man said and she whirled round. 'Len's needing another whisky.'

'Be right back,' she said, red touching her cheeks. She went to the bar and ordered more drinks. Turned to Vince and held up a bottle of Stella Artois. He gave her the thumbs up.

'Never mind those pricks,' he heard Stick say. 'See to Len first.'

Beckett looked at Vince with his eyebrows raised in a *did you fucking hear that?* kind of way.

'I did indeed,' Vince said. Now he was definitely going to slip Jimmy off the leash.

Dawn was busy dishing out the drinks when Vince moved forward to grab the three bottles. Stick Man didn't move so Vince bumped him, spilling his drink.

'Sorry, mate,' he said.

'Careless fucker,' Stick hissed.

'What did you call me?' Vince said. He was over six foot but Stick was way taller, but what Vince didn't have in height, he had in stature.

'You heard. Wanker.' His East London accent made it sound like *Wankah.*

Vince tensed, forgetting where he was for a moment, and he felt somebody grab his arm. Beckett. 'Got that beer yet, bro? What's a man got to do for a bottle round here?' He laughed and gripped

Vince's arm tighter, which wasn't easy seeing he was balanced on his crutches.

Vince turned with the bottles in one hand, gritting his teeth. He moved away from Stick. Len Chatter was surrounded by more of his assistants.

Dawn came over to them. They'd moved away from the group. 'Sorry about that. I'll introduce you to Len before we go through to the meal.'

'I hope you don't mind, me inviting Jimmy along. He's a good friend.'

'Not at all.'

They all had a drink. 'So, you going to formally introduce me to your husband?' Vince said. He wasn't in the mood for pussy footing about now.

'My husband?'

'The big guy there.'

Dawn turned around to look at Stick then back at the three men and she laughed. 'He's not my husband. He's one of Len's,' finger quotes *'inner circle.'* She leaned in a bit closer. 'One of his *yes* men.'

'Is your husband with you tonight?' Jimmy said.

Dawn gave him a wry smile. 'I'm not married.'

'What about the ring?' he said.

'I only wear that to stop men hitting on me every five minutes when I'm in a bar.'

Vince hoped his face wasn't going beetroot.

'Let's have a drink after the meal, Vince, just you and I. Catch up with old times. Sound like a plan?' Dawn said.

'Sounds good to me.'

'Dawn!' Stick Man hissed.

'I'll see you shortly.' She turned and walked over to Stick.

'Never mind those cretins, darlin', you're here to serve Len. Don't forget your place here.'

'Sorry.'

Vince turned away. 'I'm going to break a fucking bottle over his face in a minute.'

'Take it easy, brother,' Beckett said.

'Hear the way he fucking talks to her? Maybe I'll just go over and nut the bastard now.'

'Leave it just now,' Jimmy said. 'Right now, he's the prick. You're the good guy. She's going to have a drink with you after the meal. You don't want to ruin it.'

'You're right, Jimmy.'

'Besides, if anybody's going to smack the shit out of him, me and Becks will do it. That way, it'll keep you in the clear.'

More of Chatter's guests arrived.

'Now I'm starting to feel out of place,' Vince said. 'Bunch of snobs. I wonder how many of them are the potential co-writers?'

'All of them,' Beckett said.

'What? How do you know? Oh, don't fucking tell me my competition is here?'

'I didn't want to say. Dawn told me.'

'Is there anything else you haven't told me? I mean, I don't want to be walking into the fucking lion's den.'

'That's it, I swear. I thought you would go off on one if you found out those other twats were going to be here.'

'How many?'

'He whittled it down from ten. There are six of you altogether. He's going to choose three. But don't worry if you don't get through this time. Chatter's going to be writing a series of quick read books next year, and he'll be needing more co-authors then too. Dawn told me.'

'I'd be playing second fiddle to those jumped up narcissists? I don't think so. If I don't get through now, he can shove it up his juke.'

'That would be spiting yourself,' Jimmy said.

'You don't think they would give me a second look for a new series, do you? Coming in second is just being the first loser. They're not going to use the losers. They'll have another competition. It's all about marketing.'

'At least you'll get to see Dawn,' Beckett said. 'She's not married, so maybe she might be interested.'

'Why would she be interested in me when she's got big poncy boy over there to serve her every needs?'

'You've a lot to learn about women if you think Dawn would be interested in that stick insect. Besides, there's a chance she's coming to live here.'

'Jesus, if I thought she was interested in seeing me again, I'd do anything.'

'Start off by being nice to Chatter's assistant, no matter how shitey he is. Be the better man.'

That phrase again: *be the better man.* He didn't think he could.

'Are we all ready to go through to the private room?' Dawn announced.

There was the general murmur that they were indeed ready.

'Well, here goes nothing,' Vince said. He saw Chatter walk ahead with Stick.

'Skinny malinky,' Jimmy said. 'I swear to fuck if he gets in my face, I won't hold back.'

'Go for it,' Vince said, getting a bad feeling about the whole show. This was supposed to be a great night out, but it was rapidly turning into a circus.

Vince saw Stick walk away from the carrier bag with his book in it. 'What the fuck?' he said to Beckett. 'Somebody might nick that. What the hell's he playing at?'

'Look after it yourself,' Jimmy said. 'Give it to Dawn.'

'Again? I thought somebody was going to take care of it.'

'I reckon that lanky sod knows it's yours and was trying to lose it.'

They were at the end of the line. 'Everything okay?' Dawn asked, smiling.

'No, it's not, Dawn, hen,' Jimmy said. 'That big skinny sod left

Vince's manuscript lying at the bar. Anybody could have taken it. If he doesn't want to give it to your boss, there's no need to make an arse of Vince.'

'Oh, God, Vince, I am so sorry. I'll have a word with him.' She looked flustered and her cheeks were turning red.

'It's not your fault,' Vince said. 'I couldn't feel more of a prick if I tried. Sorry guys, I'm not going in there. They're obviously all hoity-toity. I can't compete with them.'

Dawn turned on him so fast that he flinched. 'That's not the Vince that I knew and loved. That Vince would have said, *fuck 'em*, and he would have marched in there and had dinner and held his head up. Are you still that Vince, or are you going to let them walk all over you?'

'I don't belong here.'

'Of course you do. I am not going to let you walk away. We're having a drink after that poxy dinner whether you like it or not, Vince Rutherford.'

'That does it for me,' Jimmy said, and started walking along the corridor.

'Me too, mate. If you leave, you're on your own. Show us where the steak is, Dawn, love.'

'Show me up why don't you?' Vince said. 'You're right, Dawn.'

She smiled. 'I'm sorry about your manuscript, but I'll hand it to Len personally.'

'Don't worry about it.'

They were the last two walking along. After everybody was in the room, they were the only two in the corridor and it felt like they were the only two in the world.

'God, I've missed you so much, Vince. You won't believe how much.'

'Christ, Dawn, I hate to admit this, but I've never had a steady girlfriend since you left. Yes, there have been other women, but none of them even came close. I'm ashamed to say, I've never had a long-term relationship.'

'Nothing to be ashamed off. Tell me all about it after the dinner.'

'Lead the way.'

She slipped her arm through his.

TWENTY-SIX

'I'd like to start off by saying how much I appreciate you all coming along to the big dinner tonight,' Len Chatter said. 'This is a first for me, having a competition to find some co-authors. As you all know, ten of you are on the shortlist, and I am going to choose three to work with. But if you don't make it through this round, please don't be disheartened. Nobody's a loser.'

'Except that Neanderthal you know,' Stick whispered to Dawn. Beckett was on the other side of her and couldn't help hearing. 'I mean, imagine bringing a fucking manuscript along to the dinner. I'll damn well make sure he's not in the running.'

'Why are you being such a pig?' Dawn said.

Stick laughed. 'I just took an instant dislike to him. I can't stand the fucker. There's no way he's going to be working with Len.'

Chatter was still standing, smiling at his guests. Dawn looked at Beckett, tears in her eyes. Beckett took her hand for a moment and squeezed.

'So I'll ask each of you, one by one, to introduce yourself and give us all a description of your work. Your *elevator pitch*.'

'I doubt that arsehole even knows what an *elevator pitch* is,' Stick said.

'Shut up, you cretin.'

'That's it, honey, talk to me like that when we're here. You damn well won't be talking like that to me back at Len's place.'

Dawn shook her head and a tear rolled down her cheek.

'Well?' he said to her.

'Well what?'

'Where's my apology?'

She shook her head at him. 'Don't hold your breath.'

The writers were starting to get up one by one to give their pitch to Len, who was seated again, King of the Hill.

When Vince stood up, Dawn beamed a smile at him.

'I'm going for a slash. That fucker's voice is grating on me,' Stick said. He got up and left the room. Beckett got up a minute later.

'I need to go as well. Vince won't mind. I've heard this many times.'

The toilet was down the hall.

Beckett hobbled in, the metal foot of his brace clanking on the tile floor. Stick was washing his hands and preening himself in the mirror.

'Ah, here he is, peg leg. You're that twat's brother aren't you? You need to get him to back off Dawn.'

'Oh, really, mate? Why's that?'

'I don't want her getting distracted. She belongs to Len and he always wants a hundred per cent from his staff.'

'You want her for yourself, is what you're really saying?'

'I've been around Len for a long time, long before that whore turned up. I wouldn't fuck her with a barge pole. Fucking slut.'

'You're a nasty piece of work.'

'Yeah? And what are you going to do about it, little man?' Stick poked Beckett in the chest.

Beckett let go of his crutches and grabbed Stick's finger, bending it back. He then thrust the tall man into a cubicle, bending him over, shoving his head down the toilet and flushed.

'That was very anti-social,' he said as the man screamed. 'I was in the army. Captain Beckett Rutherford. My brother thinks I was in the catering corps, because I wasn't allowed to tell him what regiment I was really in. Now, I could cause you a lot of damage, and as I'm temporarily disabled, that wouldn't look good for you; having your arse kicked by a smaller man on crutches. Do you get my drift?'

Stick screamed some more. 'Yes, yes. Let my fucking finger go.'

'If you get up and lay so much as the tip of your finger on me, I will break you in two. Do I make myself clear?'

'Yes.'

'And you're going to go back in there and apologise to Dawn. Tell her you've had too much to drink, or tell her you're a complete ignorant fucker, I don't care, but you're going to apologise to her. And if it gets back to me that you've upset her when you all go back to Chatter's place, you and I will talk where there's no witnesses and no cameras.'

'Okay, okay.'

Beckett let his finger go. 'And tidy yourself up before you go in there. And pick my fucking crutches up.'

Stick, still on his knees, reached for the crutches and handed them to Beckett.

'Remember, one fingertip on me and you'll learn to wipe your arse with your foot from now on. And if you think I'm kidding, go right ahead and try it.'

'I won't touch you.'

Beckett hobbled out and saw Jimmy coming along the corridor.

'He was fucking brilliant. Our Vince is going to blow them all away,' Jimmy said, beaming.

'Great. Where are you off to?'

'I'm going for a pish.'

'Use the one in the bar. Somebody fell into a toilet in there and he's drying himself off. It's a real mess.'

Jimmy nodded and smiled. 'This is a great night. One of Len's other assistants is giving me the eye. She wants some of Jimmy, I can tell.'

'Good for you, buddy. I'll see you back in there.'

Inside, Vince was sitting back down again. He had been the last to go and it was all over now.

'Thank you all for coming. We will of course let you know the outcome. Best of luck to you all.'

They all shook hands with Chatter and filed out.

'Sorry, Dawn,' Stick said, then moved away.

'We can find a little pub if you like?' Dawn said to Vince. 'Your brother and Jimmy won't mind if we skip out on them?'

'Not at all. Let me just tell them where we're going.'

They left into the warm night air and once again Dawn slipped her arm through his as they walked away from the hotel. Vince turned and saw Stick standing watching them. Crowds were milling about, enjoying the opportunity to have a drink outside.

'How about the *Blue Martini?*' Vince asked.

'Sounds good to me.'

They went onto the floating restaurant and headed into the bar. After getting them both a drink, they sat down at a table.

'I bet there's no trouble on here, considering who owns it,' Vince said.

She sat and smiled at him. 'I meant it when I said it was good to see you again, Vince.'

'Me too. I've never stopped missing you.' He took a sip of his beer.

'I knew you wouldn't be able to leave your mother, that's why I made the decision to end it. I knew you couldn't.'

'You were being kind?' He let a little bitterness creep into his voice. He was shaking inside, a mixture of elation and anger. Like somebody gets angry with a loved one who's died.

'I knew you were hesitating. Understandably after your dad passed on. I thought it was the best thing to do.'

'Best for who, Dawn?'

'For both of us.'

'What about the sound engineer? It didn't take him long to move in.'

She sighed and looked at the glass in front of her. 'I'm sorry I did that now.'

'I couldn't blame you. You were lonely, you needed a man-'

She put a hand on his. 'It's not what you think.'

'I think it's exactly what I think.'

'It wasn't. I knew you would be sitting on the fence about leaving your mum, so I had to make you believe I had another man in my life. That way, you'd stay with your mum.'

Vince drank some more, unsure of what to say next. He had to take a minute to collect his thoughts. 'He wasn't your boyfriend?'

'No. He was just somebody I worked with. He was my flatmate, that's all. He had a girlfriend.'

'What about after him? Is there nobody special in your life?'

She smiled a sad smile, her mind filling with memories of the last five years. 'Yes, there is somebody special in my life.'

He looked at her. 'I knew there would be. You're gorgeous, and always have been. You're intelligent and smart, so it stands to reason there'd be a man in your life. What's his name?'

'Vincent.'

He raised his eyebrows, feeling like he'd just stepped into an elevator shaft. 'Who would have thought? Somebody with the same name as me. Is he younger? Better looking?'

'He's younger, yes. Better looking? Definitely.'

'Dawn, it was nice catching up with you, but I don't think I can do this.'

She was raking about in her bag and came out with a photo.

'For God's sake, Dawn, I never stopped loving you, and now you're torturing me like this.'

'Just have a look.'

He took the photo and looked. It was a little boy.

'He's four and a half now. Vincent junior.' She looked at him. 'He's your little boy, Vince.'

'What? You're kidding. Mine?' Something caught in his throat and he couldn't speak for a moment.

'I was three months pregnant when I went to London. I was going to tell you when you came down.'

'You should have told me anyway.'

'You had your mum to look after.'

'I would have left her in a heartbeat.'

'I know you would. And that would have been wrong.'

'Where is he now?'

'He's with my nanny at Len's house. I'm looking to get my own place. I want you to meet him, Vince. Are you up for that?'

'What? God, of course I am.'

'I don't want you to hate me for not telling you.'

Vince looked at her and leaned over to kiss her. 'I've never felt anything but love for you.'

'I've never had another boyfriend. I mean, I went on a few dates, but nothing serious, and as soon as they found out I had a little boy and wouldn't sleep with them, that was it, over. I just stopped going out and centred my life around our little man.'

'I have to be honest, I did go with other women. I didn't fall in love with them. I just, well, you know—'

Dawn put a finger on his lips. 'You were living the life I'd forced you into. That was then, this is now.'

He looked at her and smiled after she took her finger away. 'My God, a son. Who would have thought?'

'Can we have lunch tomorrow? I'd like you back in my life, Vince. If you want me.'

'I am dreaming, right? My Dawn wants me back? Christ, I've dreamed of this day, knowing it was never going to happen. Of course I want you.'

'Let's have lunch. Then we can talk things through.'

'Good idea. Give me your phone number.'

She did, and told him where Chatter's house was.

TWENTY-SEVEN

'Well, that was quite a success, wouldn't you say?' Len Chatter said to Stick Man.

'On the whole, it went very well. Apart from one thing.'

'Oh? What was that?'

'One of those writers. I don't think he'll be suitable for you to work with.'

Chatter was in the living room of his house in Trinity. It was built in the 1800's, for a fishing Captain. It overlooked the Forth from the back, yet it was secluded from the great unwashed.

'Do tell.'

Stick was pacing about the large room, holding a glass of whisky. 'That woman you chose to hire, she's-'

'Not this again. Is it because she won't be your girlfriend? I already told you, I don't encourage relationships between my staff.'

'No, no, I get that. But she's having a relationship with one of your prospective new co-authors. The one called Vince.'

'Really? The man who gave me his manuscript?'

'The very same.' He drank more of the whisky, which he had been drinking since they came in.

'I think if he proves to be a valuable member of my team, then we might be able to overlook it.'

'The thing is, sir, he has a mental brother who attacked me in the toilets tonight.'

'What do you mean, *attacked you?*'

'He followed me into the toilet, and said in no uncertain terms what he would do to you if his brother wasn't chosen. Then he attacked me to prove his point. He stuck my head down the toilet and flushed it.'

'What? Good God. That is nothing short of outrageous.'

'It was scary. He's seriously off his head. I'd hate to think what he would do if he was to carry out his threat.'

'I can't have that. Tell him he wasn't chosen. Make up some excuse about how good it was but how we won't be using him to co-author.'

'I'll wait an appropriate amount of time then email him.'

'I still want to read his stuff. You never know, it might be quite good. How many ideas did we garnish?'

Stick laughed. 'Believe it or not, we got over 350. Not including the ideas from the last ten.'

'Right, I'm sure we can find a decent three from those writers we had at the meal. We can bring them on board and then start pumping those books out. By Christ, I can feel the excitement now. The money will be pouring in and then in six months' time, we can do it all over again. More stories, more saps to write my stuff. All I'll have to do is write the synopsis and they can do the donkey work.'

'Sounds good to me.'

'Where is Dawn just now?'

'Upstairs.'

Chatter looked thoughtful. 'Do you think that she was having a relationship with him before tonight? I mean, I think she might have said something.'

'I don't know who he is or how she met him, but they left together.'

'And this was after his brother threw you about?'

'Yes.'

'Was he a big bloke, this brother?'

'Size doesn't matter. He knew what he was doing.'

Chatter laughed. 'So a little man slapped you about and flushed your head down the toilet? I wouldn't go saying that out loud too often.'

'Doesn't change what he did.'

Chatter sighed after he had stopped laughing. 'You're right. Maybe we should tell Dawn to stop seeing him as it's a conflict of interest.'

'I'll gladly tell her in person.' Stick made to leave the room then Chatter put a hand up.

'Wait. Let's do it after we announce the winner, which is going to be in the next few days. It's been a long day and I'm tired.'

'As you wish.'

'And see that I'm not disturbed for the rest of the night. I have a lot of thinking to do.'

Chatter sat and smiled to himself. He'd just mined so many ideas that would keep him in books for the next few years to come.

Little Vincent ran into the room, shouting and laughing. Dawn came in behind him. 'I'm so sorry.'

'Keep the little bleeder under control,' Stick Man said.

'What did you say?'

'You heard.' He turned to look at Chatter. 'I told you it wasn't a good idea having her live here with her ankle biter.'

'Ankle biter? Don't talk about him like that.' Dawn leaned down to her son. 'Go and find nanny.' The little boy ran out into the hall.

'Let's not get upset here,' Chatter said. 'If you two want to argue, go into the kitchen or something, but keep it down. I have a lot of thinking to do.'

Dawn left the room and Stick followed. He grabbed her by the arm.

'Let me go, you fucking twat.'

'You watch your mouth, bitch. I've worked for Len for a long time. You're just some slapper who blew her way into his life.'

'What did you say?'

'You heard. Fucking tart. I'll see to it that your arse is out of his life soon enough. He doesn't need you now. I've already interviewed people to replace you. You're finished here.'

'Oh really? And when were you going to tell me this?'

'After we chose the new co-author's. Of which your boyfriend isn't one.'

She sneered at him. 'Is that right? Well, give me his book back.'

Stick laughed. 'You obviously didn't read the small print; any entry become the property of Len Chatter, to do with whatever he fancies.'

'You're going to stick Vince, then keep his book?'

'That's the way it works. The other authors need to have a lot of ideas to work with. Be sure and thank him next time you're giving him a blow.'

Dawn lifted her hand to slap him but he caught her arm. 'You know what, darlin'? Just fuck off now. Get out tonight. You and that little bastard. If you're not gone in the next half hour, I'll personally boot you both out.'

'Are you kidding me? Where the hell am I going to go at this time on a Saturday night?'

'I don't care. Get your stuff and get the hell out.'

'I'm going to talk to Len about this.'

'Who the fuck do you think told me to tell you to get out? He can't even look at you now you've betrayed him.'

Dawn looked puzzled. Then the penny dropped; Stick had been after her for a long time and when he saw her with Vince, his jealousy overtook him. 'So that's it then? Fired and out on the streets?'

'You got it.'

'I sold my place in London. I don't have anywhere up here yet.'

'Too bad.'

He left her standing in the hall, dumbfounded.

She went upstairs to collect her son and her things.

'What are you going to do now?' Beckett said.

'We're going to have lunch and she's going to bring my little boy. Jesus, I don't think I've ever felt more nervous in my life.'

'You'll be fine,' Beckett said as he got another beer from the fridge.

'I have to say, I keep thinking I'm dreaming. Cheers.'

'You're not. This is what you wanted.'

Vince took the photo out of his jacket pocket again. Looked at the little boy smiling into the camera. It was only taken a few weeks back.

'I always wanted to be a dad, but I thought my life's purpose was to be going out with Jimmy at the weekend, getting pished and picking up slappers.'

'I'm so glad for you, mate. And now I have a nephew.' He was smiling when he stiffened slightly.

'What's wrong?' Vince asked.

'There's somebody outside.'

'What? I don't hear anything.'

'Listen.' Although they lived in Craigcrook, a decent neighbourhood of Edinburgh, they were perfectly aware that housebreakers preferred to travel from their own hovels to the rich pickings of upmarket areas.

Beckett took his brace off.

'What are you going to do? Hit them with it?' Vince said.

'I can fight better with it off. My knee's healing but if I have to fight a housebreaker, I want to be more mobile.'

'I hear you,' Vince said, opening the kitchen pantry door and bringing out a baseball bat. He kept them all over the house. *No point in keeping one in the living room if they come through the kitchen and vice versa* he had told his brother. Becket picked up a kitchen knife and Vince looked at him. Maybe Jimmy had been right about Beckett knowing his way around a set of kitchen knives.

Then he also heard the noise just outside the front door. Then they both saw the security light come on, through the glass panel at the top of the door.

'Let me open it,' Vince said. 'Keep the knife handy just in case. If it's some of those tossers from the schemes, we'll let them know they picked the wrong fucking house to break into.'

Vince grabbed the door lock, keeping the lights off, and with one hand, opened it quickly, letting it swing open while he grabbed the bat, preparing to strike.

'Hello, Vince,' Dawn said.

Beckett put the lights on behind him.

'Dawn. What are you doing here?' Vince said.

'The bat, Vince,' Beckett said when he saw the little boy standing behind his mother.

'Oh, you know, I was just in the area and since I was passing, I thought I'd pop in and see you.'

Vince was silent as he stood looking at little Vincent.

'Come in, Dawn,' Beckett said, nudging his brother out of the way. He saw she was carrying a small suitcase and he stepped forward to take it from her, keeping the knife hidden behind his back.

'Oh, Vince I don't know what to do,' she said, almost in tears.

'Come away in. Go through to the kitchen.' The little boy looked up at him as they came into the house.

'Couldn't wait for lunch?' he said, smiling. Then he saw the tears. 'What's happened?'

'Len's assistant got me fired. He kicked me out. Me and Vincent.'

She looked down at her son. 'This is Vince. He has the same name as you.'

Vince knelt down and smiled. Held out his hand. 'Good to meet you, Vincent. Would you like a lollipop?'

The little boy shook his hand and nodded.

'No lollipops, I'm afraid,' Beckett said. 'How about a biscuit?'

'Yes, please,' Vincent said, and Vince hurriedly put the bat back in the cupboard and Beckett slid the knife back unnoticed.

'Sit down and I'll put the kettle on.' He looked at the clock; 11.37 pm.

'Decaf, if you have it,' Dawn said. Her little case was sitting beside her.

Beckett took care of it, pouring a glass of milk for the little boy and took him through to the living room to find some cartoons on Netflix.

'Why would he do that?' Vince said as he poured three coffees.

'He's jealous of you. He's been trying to go out with me for months, but I kept it strictly professional.'

'I'm afraid it's all my fault,' Beckett said from the doorway. He was standing where he could keep an eye on the boy. 'I had words with him in the toilets. He tried to have a go, but I got the better of him and flushed his head down the toilet. He wasn't happy but he knew where he stood with me.'

'Can I have another biscuit please, Uncle Becks?' little Vincent said from the living room.

'Sure you can, buddy.' Beckett fetched him one.

'Uncle Becks?'

Beckett came back and stood at the doorway. 'You'd better tell him, Dawn.'

'Tell me what? What's going on?'

'Vince, please don't get mad, and I was going to tell you at lunch tomorrow. But I met Becks in London. I knew I was coming home to live and work, and I just couldn't throw this all at you, so I asked your brother's advice. He said he was coming home to live here, and he said he would break it to you gently. If you had said you didn't want to meet me, I wouldn't have turned up at the festival gig.'

'You know I would never refuse to meet you.'

'I know that now, but I don't know what I would have done without your brother to lean on. He's been such a fantastic help to me.'

Vince looked at his brother with pride. 'You really are a Captain, aren't you?'

'Was. I resigned my commission after I buggered my knee.'

'What? You can't stand at a cooker anymore?' he grinned at him.

'I can't jump out of helicopters on a rope anymore.' He walked away to be with his nephew.

'Was he…?'

Dawn nodded. 'Yes. He really was. I saw him in uniform.'

'And he only flushed Stick insect's head down the toilet? I reckon that bloke got off lightly.'

'Anyway, I wanted to come around to tonight to say that I don't know if I will make it to lunch tomorrow. I don't know where me and the little man will end up. I've been trying hotels but a lot of them are booked.'

Just then, they saw a figure appear in the kitchen doorway.

'I thought I heard your voice,' Mother said.

'Hello, Mrs Rutherford.'

'What are you doing here?'

'She brought somebody to meet you,' Beckett said from behind her. She turned round and saw little Vincent. Looked at her younger son.

'Mum, this is your grandson, Vincent.'

Mother turned to Vince and her mouth opened but no words came out at first. 'Is this true?' she finally said.

'Yes,' Dawn said, 'but don't worry, Mrs Rutherford, we won't be staying long. In fact, we were just leaving.' She stood up from the table.

'Why are you coming round so late?'

'She was asked to leave her temporary home tonight. She's house hunting up here. She's going to be living in Edinburgh again.'

'I'm trying to find a hotel for me and Vincent.'

'You're going to be staying in Edinburgh again? With my grandson?'

'Yes.'

'And now you have nowhere to stay?'

'I will have soon, I just need to find a hotel just now.'

'Oh, here we go,' Vince said, but Mother held up a hand.

'We have a perfectly good room upstairs. You won't have to search for a hotel at this time of night. And you can stay as long as you want. You and my grandson.' She turned and smiled at the little boy, a tear running down her face.

'That's very good of you, but I couldn't impose. I don't need money, I just didn't feel safe traipsing around Edinburgh late at night on my own.'

'Nonsense. These boys tell me nothing. Get the little boy to bed and we can sit down and have a nice chat over lunch tomorrow.'

'Thank you, Mrs Rutherford.'

'Call me mum, if you like.' She smiled at Dawn. 'The boys will put clean sheets on the bed.' She smiled again. 'A little grandson. I can't believe it. Dawn, go and put your things away and get a good night's sleep. We can catch up tomorrow.' Mother left the kitchen.

Vince smiled at his brother and held onto Dawn. 'We're going to work it out this time.'

'I know, honey. I've been out of your life for too long. Thanks to your brother for giving me the confidence to approach you again.'

'What about the rest of your things?' Beckett asked.

'He said they would dump them. Oh, and by the way, you didn't get picked as a co-author. Sorry, Vince.'

Vince shrugged. 'It doesn't matter. I'll just send my book to an agent.'

Dawn shook her head. 'Sorry, but when you signed the application form, you agreed to let him keep the book to do with what he wants. I had nothing to do with the contracts, that was the guy who kicked me out. I just communicated with the writers. They're stitching a lot of writers and keeping their ideas.'

'Bas...' he started to say and then saw his son.

'So, he's going to throw out everything I have, and keep your book. Sorry, sweetheart.'

'Like hell he is,' Beckett said. 'You forget what Regiment I was in. I know more ways to get into a house than you would ever dream about. Not only are we going to get your stuff back, Dawn, but we're going to get your book back, Vince. He's not keeping it.'

Vince knew his brother was right. But first of all, he wanted to go to bed. Time to sort out Stick Man later.

TWENTY-EIGHT

The physiotherapy department in the Western General was bustling. Patients sat in chairs, waiting to be seen, wishing they were anywhere else but here. Some had casts on legs, arms, wrists. Others, braces.

The woman at reception was smiling, but it was forced. News of Ruby Maxwell's murder had filtered through. There was an air of sadness, tinged by fear. *If it could happen to her, it could happen to anybody*, seemed to be the thought of the day. It wasn't the best way to start Monday morning.

'I'm DS Watt, this is DC Miller. We'd like to speak with whoever's in charge.'

'Is this about Ruby?'

'Can you get us a manager, please?' Watt said, ignoring her.

'I'll call somebody.'

The two detectives turned away as she got on the phone. 'I hate hospitals. It reminds me of when my old man died. The smell gets to me every time.'

'I don't think anybody likes hospitals.' Miller remembered when his mother had taken him in to see his gran when she was up in the Royal Infirmary. The old building was like a museum. It was almost like ghosts still walked the corridors. Footsteps echoing along the ancient hallways. The smell of death lingering in the air, not far away. He remembered his gran's face, wrinkled and creased, her mouth tired, her eyes watery.

The old woman had been dying, but his mum had only told him that she was sick. That she was getting better. The lie of the protective parent. But Miller had known the old woman wasn't going home. Wasn't going to leave the bed. The beds had been in a long row, on either side of the ward. A big room, like the size of an aircraft hangar, to the eyes of a small boy. The overhead lights were harsh. A clock was on the wall, above the double doors that they had come through after waiting outside, like they were waiting to go into a concert or something. Then the nurse would come along and open them. Letting the flood of fans inside, where they peeled off for each bed.

He had sat and read a comic, played with a toy car he had brought along, and he was sure the clock hands were only going at half speed. Until finally – after what felt like ten hours – the bell would ring, indicating that it was game over. Time to put the coat back on, kiss a cheek and promise to be in the next day, taking a note of the requested items to be brought in – Lucozade, a magazine, grapes (green not purple, and no seeds!), maybe a bag of boiled sweets, and a cardigan because it gets cold at night and the nurses are all bitches who moan if you ask for another blanket.

'...manager here.'

Miller felt an elbow in his ribs. Looked at the woman standing in front of them. 'I'm sorry. I was thinking about the case.' He looked at Watt, thinking for a moment that the woman might have elbowed him.

'I'm the case manager for the department,' the woman said, as if Miller was special. She didn't offer a hand to shake. 'You can come along to my office.'

It was barely larger than a broom closet with a window. But they all squeezed in, the detectives sitting down opposite the woman.

'This is simply awful,' she said. Miller didn't know if she'd said her name or not, but Watt came to his rescue.

'Mrs Willow, we'd like to know more about Miss Maxwell.'

'Anything I can do to help you.'

'What was she like to work with?' Watt had his notebook out and looked at the woman expectantly.

'She was very nice. Such a pleasant girl. We were lucky to get her.'

'What do you mean?'

'After the other hospital closed down. St. David's in Dunfermline. Ruby used to work there. When it closed, she came over here.'

'How long has she worked here?'

'A few years. She was a nurse over there but retrained and got in here.'

'Any problems with anybody here at work? Patients or colleagues?'

'Not that I know of.'

'Would you be able to get us a list of names of her patients?'

'Yes, I can do that.' She messed with the mouse and keyboard on her desk and a printer spat out a sheet from the printer on a table behind her. She grabbed it and gave it to Watt.

They thanked her and left the office. 'Well, well, what do you know?'

'What is it?' Miller said.

'Guess whose name is on the list?'

'I don't know.'

'I said guess.'

'Oh, I don't know – Lord Lucan?' He tried to grab the sheet and Watt whipped it out of reach.

'*Lord Lucan*. You would be detective of the year if you did find him. No, it's that writer geezer you went to see on Saturday.'

'Len Chatter?'

'The one and only.'

'He was wearing a brace on his left wrist.'

'We should go and have a word with him.'

'He might not take too kindly to being questioned as a suspect.'

'Who says he's a suspect? I just want to see what kind of gaff he lives in. *And* I'll bet he drinks tea out of a china cup.'

'Yes?' the tall man asked as he opened the door.

Miller and Watt were holding out their warrant cards. 'We'd like to speak to Len Chatter,' Watt said.

'About what?'

'Is he in?'

'Yes.'

'Well, either let us in or go and get him.'

The tall man stepped to one side and let them in. 'Wait here. I'll go and tell him you're here.'

'Lurch,' Watt said under his breath, and kept staring at the man as he turned briefly, unsure if he'd heard Watt's comment or not.

He came back a few minutes later. 'Mr Chatter will see you in the drawing room.'

'Are you his butler?' Watt asked.

'I'm one of his assistants,' he said, his rough East London accent more pronounced as he glared at Watt. He showed them into the room and announced them, closing the door behind them as he left.

'Gentlemen, what can I do for you?' Chatter said, smiling. 'Don't I know you?' he said, pointing to Miller.

'We met on Saturday night after your talk at the book festival.'

'Yes, yes, I remember now. Sorry, I didn't recognise you.'

'Don't worry.'

'Have you brought your friend along to have another book signed?'

'Er, no, we're here on business.'

'I'm kidding of course. Would you like a cup of tea? I've just brewed.'

'Thank you.'

Chatter turned round to the tray that was sitting on a side table next to his desk. Watt nudged Miller and nodded to the china cups.

An iMac was sitting on the desk with a document open.

'I do enjoy being mother. It's not often I get guests dropping in unannounced. Milk and sugar?' he said, turning round to face them for a second.

'Just milk for me, thanks,' Miller said.

'Same for me,' Watt said, looking at the paintings on the walls as if he were memorising where they were hung, for when he came back after dark with a flashlight and a canvas sack.

They sat down, and Miller was trying his best to not let his pinkie stick out as he drank his tea.

'Right, so what is this about?'

'Ruby Maxwell,' Watt said, drinking the tea and letting his pinkie stick out and be damned.

'Awful news. They called me this morning to cancel my appointment. They're scurrying about trying to get a replacement, but you know how these things are.'

'How well did you know her?' Miller asked.

Chatter looked thoughtful before answering. 'In what way?'

Watt put his cup down, looked around for a tray of biscuits, and seeing none, settled back in the chair. 'How did she seem when she was working with your wrist? Was she a bubbly person, or reserved?'

'Very bubbly. What a great sense of humour.'

'It must have been fun, seeing her again. Hurting your wrist and then getting paired up with Ruby. Especially when there were other clinics you could have gone to.'

'I don't know what you mean.'

'You were a surgeon, weren't you, Mr Chatter? At St. David's hospital in Dunfermline. Where Ruby was a nurse.'

'Yes, I was. Before they closed the place down.'

Miller had clued Watt up on the story of Len Chatter as they drove to his house. He'd known about Chatter from his website, knew he was a surgeon before becoming a writer.

'Where did you go to work after that?'

'St. John's, in London.'

'That must have been a culture shock after working in Scotland.'

'It was a bit.'

'Can I ask you how long it was after leaving Scotland that you got published?'

'I got a contract after six months. My novel was already written and I got an agent. Then I got a three-book contract.' Chatter drank more tea. 'Can I ask you what this has to do with Ruby?'

'We're just trying to build up a picture,' Watt said with practised ease.

'It must have been nice seeing her again, as I said.'

'It was. She was a nice girl.'

'It seems strange that a nurse would retrain to become a physiotherapist,' Watt said.

'Physios are in demand. When the hospital closed, there were a lot of nurses looking to transfer. Ruby didn't say why she did what she did.'

'Was there any connection between you two?' Miller put his cup down. He was a coffee man and had only taken the tea to be polite.

'In a sexual way?'

'Yes, in a sexual way.'

'No, there was nothing like that. Ruby and I talked about all sorts. She asked about my books and told me she was engaged to be married. She was enjoying her job at the Western.'

'She didn't confide anything to you? Like, if her fiancé was throwing her about or anything?'

Chatter smiled. 'Ruby? No, she was tough. Her and her boyfriend were at it all the time, she said. Arguing, that is. I have a feeling he would come off worst if he lifted his hands to her. But she loved him and she was still getting married to him.'

'Can you tell us where you were between 7pm on Friday night and 4am Saturday morning?' Watt said, sure he could taste a rogue tea leaf in his mouth but not wanting to pull at his tongue in front of the writer.

'Here. Working. Until late, then I went to bed.'

'Can anybody confirm that?'

'Yes, my assistant, who showed you in here. He made me a hot chocolate before I retired. You can ask him before you go.'

'We will.'

The detectives got up to leave and Stick Man appeared as if my magic. Or he had been listening at the door.

Watt asked him about Chatter's whereabouts the previous Friday and was told the same story as Chatter had said.

'I wouldn't have minded getting him to sign a copy of *The Goode Times* before we left,' Miller said.

'Did you bring it with you?'

'No, I didn't know we were coming here, did I?'

'There you go then. You worry about the smallest stuff.'

They got in the car and Miller started it up. 'There was something that bothered me. Something that Chatter never mentioned.'

'What was that?'

'That he worked with Perry MacKinnon in Dunfermline.'

'Who?'

'A man whose name came up in conversation, that's all.'

He drove away.

Monday night and still the bar in the *Savoy* hotel was busy. Maybe the owner wouldn't want to sell, or he'd want an over-inflated price. He could see Miles was behind the bar.

'Perry. What can I do for you?'

'Hey, Miles. Is Sherri in?'

Miles looked at him for a moment. 'I don't think she'd want to see you after the other night.'

'I think she would. Especially when I tell her I got her money back.'

Miles lifted his eyebrows. 'Really? I won't ask.'

'Please don't, seeing as how it's none of your business.'

'I'll call down to her room.'

While he was on the phone, MacKinnon looked around the bar. There he was again. The scruffy sod who had bumped into him the other night. *Him.* Christ, he was sure it was the old face, but he couldn't be a hundred per cent.

'Perry. She says you can go downstairs. Second landing, go through to the back. Second on the left.'

'Thanks, Miles. Still keeping off the sauce?'

'As always.'

'Good man.' MacKinnon left the bar and went through to the hotel reception and took the stairs to the second landing as instructed. It was darker down here, a place where normal guests didn't go.

He approached Sherri's room door and knocked.

It was opened a few moments later and Sherri stepped to one side. 'Are you going to tell me it was all a mistake, that you really did take money from me?' she said.

He smiled as he came into the small room. It was one of two rooms that had once been staff rooms when the hotel was just a home. 'No, Sherri, it wasn't a mistake. Not on my part, anyway. You see, I have a son who is lazy and thinks he's entitled to get everything without working for it. After university, he came home and didn't get a job. His mother spoils him. Apparently, his new scheme was to be a *catfish.* Taking women's money from them.' He looked at her. 'He's quite good at it. Good at moving money around undetected into offshore bank accounts. If only he'd use his talent for better things.'

'You have my money?'

'Yes. Not on me, of course, but it will be deposited into your bank account soon. I need the details. However, I need you to agree to something first.'

Sherri's eyes went wide for a moment but MacKinnon held up a hand. 'Nothing like that. I'd like you to forget this happened. To get your money back and not report my son to the police.'

'He hurt me. Badly.'

'And I have chastised him, trust me, but reporting him would just make him dig his heels in. I would rather him learn a lesson from this.'

'I'll get all my money back?'

'Every penny. Right back into your bank account.'

'I'd like to be there when you wire the money.'

'Fine. How about tomorrow morning at 11? I'll take you to my bank and we can transfer it then.'

'Okay. Where will I meet you?'

'I have a private bank. There are no signs outside. Here, let me write the address down.' He took out a piece of paper and pen and scribbled down the address. 'It's next to a lawyer's office.'

'Thank you.'

'Eleven o'clock sharp.'

'I'll be there.'

Perry MacKinnon let himself out of the room. He saw the scruffy man coming up the stairs.

'Evening, guv'nor.'

'Good evening.' MacKinnon stood to one side and let the man pass. He'd been completely wrong about this man. He had been so sure… but no, it wasn't him. Just some old duffer down on his luck. Kudos to Miles for helping him then.

TWENTY-NINE

Detective Chief Inspector Jack Miller pulled his sunglasses on as he got out of the car. 'Second day back after his holiday and the boss is thrown this.'

'It's only Tuesday. I woke up thinking it was Wednesday,' DS Andy Watt said, hauling himself out of the passenger side.

'It could have been worse; you might have thought it was Friday.'

The ambulance sat at the front of the line of cars in Portgower Place, a narrow, dead-end street at the side of Edinburgh Academicals Sports ground. At the far end was one of the entrances to Inverleith Park, at the Stockbridge side.

They walked down to the police tape where Frank Miller was standing.

'Have you seen her?' Jack asked his son.

'Yes, sir. It's gruesome.'

'Do you think it's one of his?'

'The *Surgeon?*' Miller nodded. 'She's just like the last one.' He held up the tape for the two detectives to walk under.

'This place brings back memories,' he said. 'Beth and I used to bring Frank here when he was a little boy. We used to feed the ducks in the pond,' he said to Watt. Then to Miller: 'Is Carol here, too?'

'She is.'

'Christ, her orientation started yesterday, and now she's been thrown in at the deep end.'

A large, black barrier was open. It usually sat across the wide pathway, used by the council gardeners. A smaller, yellow barrier was across the footpath to deter anybody who thought of using it as a shortcut in their car. Two suited forensic officers were going through two bins, one of them a small green bin for litter, and a battered black council bin on wheels.

Another uniform was standing at the yellow barrier. 'Morning, officer,' Jack said.

'Good morning, sir,' PC Hazel Carter said. She was another uniform who was a friend of Frank Miller's and said she wanted into CID one day, but she hadn't long started her career in uniform.

Over on their left was the large pond. Big enough for people to use radio controlled boats on. Benches lined the perimeter, perfect to bring the kids down to feed the ducks in summer, while the grass area could be used for kicking a ball around.

'Fuck me, I can't wait to get my hands on this sick bastard,' Detective Superintendent Harry Davidson said, shaking his head as he came over to them.

'Frank says it's our boy again,' Jack said.

'Fucking right it is.' He was in his fifties, his hair going thin on top, which made him look even harder than he was. He was a big man, a rugby player at one time. Some of his muscle had gone to fat, but that just added to his stature. He was two inches shorter than Jack's 6' 5" frame. They looked a formidable force, standing side by side.

'Do we have an ID for her?'

'Nothing. She was found naked this time.'

'He's getting more confident,' Watt said.

Jack nodded, looking around him.

'Come on, she's up here.' He started walking away, Jack at his side, Watt and Miller behind. 'The fucker cut the padlock on that barrier. Drove up here. The driveway turns to the right, tucked away behind some bushes.'

They turned right onto a pathway that went up an incline. A black coloured plate attached to the railings announced they were in the Sundial Garden.

The sundial itself was situated in the middle of the pathway, flanked by two benches. A pathway ran around the perimeter of the garden, bordered by high bushes. It would be perfect for dumping a body, which the *Surgeon* had obviously figured out.

Where visitors would normally see the stone sundial surrounded by more green fencing, they would have been greeted by a large forensic tent erected over the scene, had they been allowed in here. As it was, the only visitors on that warm, August morning, were police officers, forensic officers, and Professor Leo Chester, head pathologist.

'It looks like his work,' Chester said, coming out of the tent. 'I won't know for sure until we open her up again in the mortuary, but I'd put money on it.'

'Morning, doc,' Jack said.

'I wish it was a good morning, Jack. It never is though, when a young woman is found like this.'

'Who found her?' Jack asked, going inside the tent.

'A jogger,' Davidson said. 'He came in from the Arboretum Road entrance and was making his way down through here after doing a circuit of the park. We're running him through the system just now and he's up at the station giving a statement.'

'Morning, Carol,' he said.

'Morning, sir.' She had been crouching looking at the body. Somebody with an acetylene torch had cut the railings to let them get access to the location.

Watt knelt and looked at the naked woman's body. She had been opened up, one incision down the length of her belly, then stitched back up again. Almost like the incision a pathologist would make, minus the top part of the Y. The same cut as Iris Napier had been given.

'Looks like she's been cleaned, obviously,' Jack said. 'I don't think we're going to get any fibres or DNA off her.'

'Just like the last one. The clothes Iris had on had been freshly laundered and they weren't hers. Now this woman doesn't have any clothes on at all,' Davidson said.

Watt straightened up. 'So he knows the park. He knows he can drive up past the entrance to this garden, and take the woman from out of whatever vehicle he's driving and have enough cover so he's not seen.'

'How long do you think she's been dead?' Jack asked.

'I'd say between twenty-four and forty-eight hours,' Chester said. 'He took his time cleaning her after he killed her.'

Davidson left the tent, followed by Jack and Watt.

'The council grass-cutting crew are based in a yard on the other side of that wall,' Jack said. They could just make out the wall behind the trees.

'Get somebody onto it, Jack. I want the names of everybody who works there and I want to know where they were the last two nights. Watt? Co-ordinate the uniforms and have them talk to people in the park. See if they come here at night, 'though I doubt many people do. Unless they're up to no good or shagging in the bushes.'

'Bit nippy for shagging outdoors, even in August, but I'll get onto it, sir.'

'We're ready to transport her down to the mortuary,' Leo Chester said. They stood by as two technicians entered the forensic tent with a body bag. Jack leaned on the gurney to stop it from running away downhill. Uniforms helped lift the body onto the gurney and Jack watched as it was wheeled down the pathway.

'If he's getting more confident, we know he's only just starting,' Jack said. Davidson just nodded. He had two daughters of his own, Carol being one of them. He couldn't even imagine outliving them.

'Good morning, sir,' Julie Davidson said to her father, preferring to keep an air of professionalism between them at work. She was one of the three pathologists who worked in the Edinburgh city mortuary.

'Morning, Julie.'

Davidson and Jack were wearing coveralls as they stood round one of the stainless-steel tables on the first floor of the grey building down in the Cowgate.

The woman lay on the steel table. Her skull cap had been taken off by Gus Weaver, one of the older assistants.

'As you all know, this is where we usually take out the organs to weigh them,' Chester said, 'but we all know what to expect if this is indeed our man.'

Chester inserted the slim, steel scalpel into the flesh, cutting from the right clavicle to the sternum, repeating the move from the left clavicle. As he joined the two cuts, he carried on down, cutting through the skin alongside the crude stitching that had been used by the killer to stitch the woman back up.

'She's been photographed, top to bottom by Gus, and we'll let the lab have the stitches,' Chester said, not taking his eyes off the woman. Davidson ignored him, transfixed on the killer's cut.

Jack Miller was holding his breath, as if watching a magician, and the corpse was going to disappear any second.

As Chester opened the woman up, they all saw that this was indeed the work of their killer, the man Edinburgh residents knew and feared as the *Surgeon*.

Her main organs had been removed, and like the first woman, a plastic driving license had been left inside. Chester didn't want to wash it but he could clearly make out her name.

'Amelia Arnold,' Julie said, peering closely at the credit-card sized license. 'Age 26, from Wester Drylaw.'

'Fuck,' Davidson said. 'That isn't far from Hillpark, the address of the first one.'

'There seems to be bruising on her arms,' Jack said. 'Possibly taken by force.'

Chester looked at him. 'Possibly. But they don't look like they're from somebody grabbing her wrists. Maybe she just bumped herself.'

'We'll locate next of kin,' Jack said.

Davidson nodded. 'See if there's any connection to the first one.'

The Sundial Garden wasn't that far from St. Bernard's Well. Nobody had come forward with any useful information, but there were hundreds of calls from people who *thought* they had seen something. Nothing useful had come of it.

'If he's getting more confident, then hopefully he'll make a mistake,' Jack said.

'Meantime, we have to pull out all the stops to get him before he strikes again.'

'St. Bernard's Well is accessed by walking along the Water of Leith footpath, so he would have had to carry her there somehow. You can't get a vehicle along there. Now, we're assuming he drove onto the driveway at Inverleith Park, because of the cut padlock. It was easier to leave his victim naked.'

'How long between them going missing to them turning up dead?' Chester asked.

'They weren't reported missing. I'll have to run this woman's name through the system, see if we get a hit. Meantime, pick up Watt and go to her address and see if we can find a relative.'

After another ten minutes, Jack and Davidson were changed out of their scrubs and heading to Amelia Arnold's address.

THIRTY

Wester Drylaw Park was on the north side of the city, spitting distance from the waters of the Forth lapping at the shore of Silverknowes.

'Ever played golf down at Silverknowes?' Jack asked Watt.

'What makes you think I like sports, boss?'

'Doesn't everybody play golf at one time in their life?'

'Nobody I know. However, in the interests of full disclosure, I did try it one time. My mate harped on until I caved. He'd sponsor me for his club, says he, so like a twat, I go out and buy a second-hand set of clubs.'

'Did you have a handicap?'

'My only handicap was, I couldn't hit the ball in a straight line. And I didn't have the patience either, as it turned out. I played two rounds and jacked it in. Grown men hitting a wee ball about a park. I ask you.'

Jack was driving, and they skirted the centre of town, going past the Western General Hospital and he took a left at Crewe Toll, past the fire station and was in the street they wanted five minutes later.

It was a little dead-end street, in the Wester Drylaw estate.

Smart, four-in-a-block flats. The one they wanted was on the ground floor in the second block in. A hedge was round the front garden but it wasn't this that caught Jack's attention. It was the *For Sale* sign in the front garden, on the right-hand side of the building. And a similar sign in the living room window.

He and Watt walked up to the window but curtains were drawn across it.

'There's curtains there, but I think the sign is a dead giveaway for burglars,' a woman said as the glass-fronted stair door opened.

'Housebreakers,' Jack said.

'I'm sorry?'

'They're known as housebreakers in Scotland, not burglars,' Watt said, explaining for Jack. 'We're police officers.'

They left the garden and stood on the pathway in front of the woman. Showed her their warrant cards.

'Come in, I've got the kettle on.'

They followed her into the stair hallway and into her flat. She lived on the opposite side to Amelia Arnold.

The doorway led into the living room. A TV sat in one corner of the room. A talk show was on before the woman muted it. A small couch, armchair, and coffee table made up the rest of the furnishings.

'I'm Karen, by the way. Have you come about Dick?'

Jack looked at Watt before answering. 'Dick?'

'Him next door. Dick. The one who died.'

'No, we were looking for Amelia Arnold's flat.'

She indicated for them to follow her. The back wall was made up of a door and a wall with frosted glass. They went through a door to the back where the kitchen was. The kettle was indeed on.

Karen opened her back door and lit up a cigarette. The warm air crept in. 'My husband hates it when I smoke in the house. He says it makes the paintwork yellow.'

'Not to mention your lungs,' Watt said, pointing to the kettle. 'You want me to be mother?'

'Sure. If my husband was here, you could train him to do it. Lazy sod doesn't even know how to switch it on.'

The coffee jar and all the other beverage-making paraphernalia was sitting next to the kettle. He spooned coffee into two mugs and held up a third.

'Tea for me, love,' Karen said, blowing smoke out of the door and then decided it was too warm and nipped the cigarette like a boss and shoved it back into the packet.

She looked to be in her early to late forties, with hair that badly needed a bottle of colour through it. Maybe done by the hairdresser she needed to go to.

Watt made her a tea with the instructions to add a coo and two. Milk and two sugars.

'So, did you know Mrs Arnold from next door?' Jack asked, sipping at his coffee. Watt, if nothing else, was a good coffee maker.

'Of course I did. We sometimes went to the bingo together down on Granton Road. What a laugh she was. She's alright, isn't she?' She looked at the two policemen and sipped her tea.

'We're just looking into some background, that's all,' Jack said, lying. A formal identification would have to be made first, before her name was given out, and sometimes they had to outright lie to people. 'Who was Dick?'

'He was Amelia's boyfriend. A real clown. She was too good for him, so I'm glad she left him. They lived here for a long time. She's brilliant. We became good friends, but my husband never associated with him. Don't get me wrong, we were civil to each other, but he hung out with the wrong people.'

'What happened to him?' Jack asked.

'He died of an overdose. Heroin. He always looked high when I saw him. He never used to be like that, and he was always happy. One of those people who smiled all the time and laughed at his own jokes. I suppose that's why Amelia was attracted to him. He knew how to have a good time. But then he started snorting coke.'

'How do you know that?'

She laughed. 'He told me. He worked on the rigs, see? A month away at a time. Made plenty of cash, and when he was home, he would get blootered all the time, go out with his mates, show Amelia a good time. To be honest, she told me she was knackered when he was home. Plenty of the old *how's your father*. She was glad when he was away again.'

'How was their relationship?'

'Rocky. I mean, they got on really well, but he was a party animal. Made a ton of money. She wanted him to settle down. Take it easy with the drinking and the coke.' Karen sipped more tea and looked between the two detectives. 'What woman doesn't want a man to settle down? She wanted to start a family, but Dick wasn't ready. Then he died. And she felt she couldn't live here anymore.'

'I can understand,' Jack said. He sipped more coffee. 'Do you know where she moved to?'

'A flat in Stockbridge. Dick left her a lot of money, and there was the insurance. Plus, the money from the sale of this place. She lived above a pub, she told me when I bumped into her a couple of months ago. She looked really good. Said she had a new fella in her life. They were going to be moving in together.'

'Did she give you his name?' Watt asked.

'No, but she said he was a doctor. Which suited her down to the ground, considering she was a nurse. That's something you don't often see, doctor's going out with nurses, but Amelia is so good looking, a doctor would be lucky to have her.'

'Where does she work?' Jack asked, remembering to keep the questions about Amelia in the present tense, to make it look like she was still alive.

'The Western General, but she was also a bank nurse.'

'What's a bank nurse?' Watt asked, looking around the counter top for a biscuit tin but seeing none. If he had been in here on his own, he would have raked about in the cupboards but the woman gave no indication that they should transfer back to the living room.

'They register with an agency and then they work their day off at whatever hospital they get sent to.'

'Did she get sent to any hospital in particular?'

'I don't know. She'll be able to tell you though.'

'Do you know if she had any problems with anybody?' Watt said.

'No. Everybody loves her. She's a good-looking woman with a great spirit. Great outlook on life.' She looked at Jack. 'She's not in trouble, is she?'

'No, nothing like that.' He drank more coffee. 'Did she get on with Dick's family?'

'As far as I know. They live up in Dundee where he came from, but I don't remember her saying anything about them not liking her.'

Jack made a mental note to run Dick's name through the system too, and see if any of his family had a grudge against Amelia.

They chatted some more and then Jack handed her a business card. 'If there's anything else you can think of, please give us a call.'

Back in the car, Jack cranked up the fan as Watt started the engine. 'I want uniforms to start spreading out door-to-door. I want to find out where she lived. Karen said Amelia lived above a pub, and there's a few in Stockbridge, so let's get them onto it.'

'Some of them won't have to be asked twice to go on a pub crawl,' he replied, pulling away.

THIRTY-ONE

The Command Centre trailer was parked in Comely Bank Road, on the double yellows next to the bus stop, opposite the entrance to Portgower Place, where Amelia Arnold had been found. It was used as a mobile base and somewhere people could come to if they wanted to report something. Somebody seen, or something unusual. If they'd been the last one to see Amelia alive, apart from her killer.

There were a dozen uniformed officers cramped into the small trailer, with Andy Watt standing at the end, beside Carol and Miller.

'Spread out. The basic information we have is that Amelia lived above a pub, but that might not be the case. There are a dozen bars within spitting distance of each other. Unless you hear a radio call telling you to call it off, carry on up into Howe Street, which I know is stretching it a bit, but you never know. We need to find out where she lived so we can get a next of kin. Any questions?'

'Is somebody checking where she worked?' one of the uniforms asked. 'See if they have an update on her address?'

'Already been done,' Miller said. 'They have the Wester Drylaw address as well. It seems she didn't want to update that information for reasons known only to her.'

He looked at the sea of faces. 'If there's nothing else, let's move out. Stick to your given area and check in with the operator here. Move out.'

The uniforms moved out and Miller and Carol were left.

'Miller,' Watt said, 'a word before you go.'

'I'll see you outside,' Carol said.

Miller nodded and turned to Watt. 'Yes, Sarge?'

Watt took him aside. 'Everybody knows you and Carol both have senior officers as parents, and they'd love nothing better than to see you fall flat on your face. Just watch your back.'

'Thanks for the heads up.'

'No problem, son. Go to it.'

Miller stepped out into the warm air, but a breeze was shooting along Comely Bank.

'What's that all about?' Carol asked as they started walking along towards Raeburn Place.

'He said I was to keep an eye on you, as they think you need your hand held,' he said.

'What? Bugger off. That's what he told me about you earlier.'

Miller laughed. 'He said to watch our backs because of who our fathers are.'

'Really? That's magic. What if we catch the bastard though? That would certainly make them sit up and take notice.'

'Easy, Tiger. Don't let anybody get to you.'

'I know, this is only my second day with CID and most of the grunt work is done by us while Serious Crimes will step in and take the credit.'

'Let's just see if we can find where Amelia Arnold lived.'

Stockbridge was like a small village in the heart of the city. Raeburn Place was lined with shops on both sides, and there was an abundance of charity shops, one of them even dedicated to selling just books.

They came to the first pub, right next door to another one. It was

St. Bernard's Bar. The communal door to the shared stairway painted battleship grey. It was next to a small jewellery store which was neighbours with the pub, but there were windows above the pub, which meant people lived above it. A set of buzzer buttons with an intercom was set into the wall next to the door.

Miller looked at the names. None of them were Amelia Arnold.

'Let's try the next one,' Carol said, and they walked to the next stair door. It was slap bang in the middle of the two pubs, the other one being *The Stockbridge Tap*. Right on the corner of Raeburn Place and St. Bernard's Row. The pub wrapped right round the corner of the building.

This door was jet black, and it also had a set of names on an intercom system. None of them indicated Amelia lived there.

'There's a little wine bar across the road in Dean Street,' Carol said. 'We should try there.'

'You seem to know all about the pubs round here. Is this where you bring all your boyfriends?'

'I do actually. I hope you don't bump into any of them. They might get jealous.'

'I've got my truncheon with me. I can take them.'

They crossed the road at the traffic lights. Dean Street was a narrow, one-way street that connected Raeburn Place with St. Bernard's Crescent. *Good Brothers Wine Bar* was the first establishment they came to on the left. There was a communal door to the right of the bar and that's where they found Amelia's name on a buzzer.

Miller pressed some of the buzzers and took a step back. There were two windows on the ground floor, and two levels above that, so it wasn't a large tenement building.

'*Hello?*' a tinny voice said through the little speaker on the intercom system.

'Lothian and Borders Police. Can you let us in, please?'

The buzzer sounded and the door unlocked. They went into a

nicely kept stair and went to the top flat. Miller bent and opened the letterbox, peering through while Carol called it in to the Command Centre.

The door behind them opened and a young woman appeared, dressed in pyjamas, pulling a robe around her.

'Is everything okay?' she asked.

'We're just looking for Amelia Arnold's flat.'

'Well, you've come to the right place.'

'Does she live here alone?'

'Did. She moved out a while back.'

'Do you know where to?'

'Is something wrong?'

Miller looked at her for a moment. 'We need to gain entry into her flat.'

'Some of her stuff is there but she moved out. She still owns the place though.'

'Can we come in and talk to you?' Carol said, and the young woman stepped aside.

'Are you friends with her... Miss...?' Miller asked when they were seated in the living room.

'Faith Hope. Yes, I am. We work together at the Western General. I'm a nurse.'

'When's the last time you saw her?' Carol asked.

'Friday night.'

'What time were you with her?' Miller was taking notes in his electronic notebook.

'She came here, then we went round the corner to the bar in the *Savoy* Hotel, that little place with the big name. That was around seven. We were at the singles club along the road in the *Dean* Hotel. Got there about eight thirty. Any earlier and it smacks of desperation.'

'She doesn't have a boyfriend?' Carol said.

'Oh she did, but before she started going out with him, her and I used to go every Friday night if we weren't working, mainly for a laugh, but I'm single and well, you never know. She was my wingman, as it were. She just liked dancing and we'd have a laugh.'

'Do you know her boyfriend's name?'

'No, sorry. She wants to keep it a secret as he's still married.' She looked worried. 'Is something wrong with her?'

'We're not at liberty to say. Do you know if she has any family?'

'She has a sister in England. Do you need to contact her? Oh my God, has she been arrested?'

'Again, we're not at liberty at this time.'

The woman nodded. 'I understand. I have her sister's number. She wanted me to keep a hold of it in case of emergency.' She left the room and came back with a little address book and read out the name and number of Amelia's sister.

'At this singles club, did Amelia leave with anybody?'

'No, we never did. We would sometimes take a guy's phone number, but we made it a rule never to leave with anybody. There's some genuine guys there, but some weirdos as well. You can never tell.'

'Do you happen to know where she lives now?' Carol asked.

'Her boyfriend moved her into a little mews house.'

'Can you give us the address?'

'Dean Park Mews, just up at the top of this street and round the corner a bit.'

'What number?'

'Seventy-six.'

'So, at the end of the night last Friday, what did you both do?' Carol said.

'We went to her place. Had a few drinks and a laugh then I left and came home.'

'No men?' Miller asked.

'No. There were one or two nice ones, but we left before the end.'

'What time would that have been?'

The woman shook her head side to side, trying to think of the time. 'Around one-ish. I think it stays open until around four.'

'Did you walk home?' Carol said.

'Yes. It's a ten-minute walk in heels, from her place to here. I went back round at nine o'clock on Saturday morning. I didn't drink as much as her and I felt fine, but I knew she was rougher than a badger's armpit. I bought two coffees from a place round the corner but she didn't answer. I knocked, called her and sent her a text, but nothing. I sent her another text saying I'd been round and hoped she hadn't slept in for work.'

'I thought you said you didn't have work the next day?' Carol said.

'Oh, I meant we didn't have work together at the Western. Amelia snagged a shift at the little clinic she sometimes worked at as a bank nurse, but I thought she wasn't working until noon. I thought she'd maybe been called in early and couldn't use her phone at work, so I left.'

'Do you know which clinic?'

'The *Stockbridge Wellness Centre.* A fancy name for a women's and men's clinic. They give men the snip there, I know that, but other than that, I think it's mostly private work. Plastic surgery and the like. Amelia gets paid well for working there.'

'Thanks for your help,' Miller said, leaving a business card with her.

'She's dead, isn't she?'

'What makes you say that?'

'You didn't say, *give us a call when you hear from her.* You know she's not going to call.' Her lips started to tremble a bit.

Miller looked grim as they left the flat.

'Christ, I hate doing that,' Carol said when they were outside in the street.

'What?'

'That. Lying to them.' She put up a hand before he could answer.

'I know we have to, until we get a next of kin, but that woman is going to be devastated when she finds out.'

Miller contacted the Command Centre and let them know what they had found.

'This Dean Park Mews is near you, isn't it?' Miller asked.

'Just round the corner. And it's *us* now, remember?'

'She meets this married man, and he moves her into there, while he's still at his house with the wife. And he's told her he's going to leave his wife for her. Just as well she kept her other flat on.'

'You're so cynical, Frank.'

'More of a realist. They never leave their wives. However, if he can afford to put her into a place like that, he must have money.'

'We'll have to try and locate him.'

'We? Serious Crimes will be all over this. We won't get a sniff at it.'

'Don't be so sure, Miller. Those women were at the singles night, which is every Friday. If nothing comes up by next week, there's nothing stopping us going.'

'People will wonder why we're going to a singles club together.'

'Not together. As singles. I'll let you pick me up.'

'I'll be the envy of the place.'

They started walking up the road to the top of the hill. St. Bernard's Crescent was round to their left but they carried straight on into Dean Park Mews. Once old carriage houses for the big houses on the main road, they were now homes for people who wanted relative seclusion.

They turned right and walked down, looking for the number. They found it near the bottom. Miller had called Andy Watt and the detective pulled his car round just as Miller and Carol got to the front door of the house.

'Here's the cavalry,' Carol said.

'That'll be us, one day,' Miller said. He looked at the front of the old, stone property. It had recently been refurbished, that was obvious. The stone was clean, sand-coloured, and where a garage door had once been, there were thick, glass sliding doors. The main entrance door was next to it. One of the windows above the garage door had been extended height-wise and had been replaced by a door. It had a Juliette balcony now, enough to have the door open but not big enough to step out on.

'You sure this is her place?' Watt said as he got out of the car and locked it. The sky was overcast and the temperature had dropped.

'According to her friend. Amelia's boyfriend lets her live here.'

'Did you get a name for the boyfriend?'

'No, she didn't know it.'

'He's a man of mystery,' Carol said.

'Perry MacKinnon,' Watt said, trying the door handle and finding the door unlocked.

'What?' Miller said.

Watt turned to look at him. 'I'm not just a pretty face, son. I had the nerd in the Command Centre do a property check after you called me, and it was bought by Dr. Perry MacKinnon. The guy you mentioned yesterday after we spoke to Len Chatter. Get your gloves on.'

'That's the man who Sherri says screwed her out of a lot of money.'

'No wonder he can afford a gaff like this then.'

Miller and Carol pulled on their gloves and they stepped into the little hallway. There was another door that led into the living room, where once the garage was. Everything was new. Blinds had been drawn across the tall windows and the daylight struggled to get through, but there was enough to show them the place had been turned over.

'Get onto forensics,' Watt said to Miller, who then got onto the Command Centre, passing on Watt's request.

'Looks like we came to the right place,' Carol said.

'Her friend said she didn't know who Amelia's boyfriend was, but it's looking like this Perry guy is the one,' she said.

'You're right,' Watt said, making his way through to the open plan kitchen, which was a continuation of the living room. 'He must be minted, buying this place for his piece on the side.'

'Christ, Andy, that's a bit of a jaded outlook on life. Piece. Like she was cattle or something.'

'That's how these jokers see women. They woo them, give them the fancy car, the jewellery, the flat. Use them, abuse them, lose them. I've seen it a million times. The bigger the wallet, the more they can't keep it in their pants. You said she kept her own flat on?'

'That's what her friend said.'

'We'll get the fingerprint boys to go through that as well. See if moneybags was in there.'

Nothing was out of place in the kitchen. There was a bathroom off the kitchen area, with a toilet and a washbasin. Upstairs, the bed was a mess in the master bedroom, and the other two rooms were empty.

Miller walked up to the side where it was obvious that a struggle had taken place. There were little droplets of blood on the pillow. 'Looks like she could have been taken from here.' He looked at Watt. 'Her friend Faith, who we just spoke to, said she put Amelia to bed as they'd been drinking.' He saw the plastic bucket lying over by the window, which was the one that had been converted to a door.

'I'll have Maggie Parks and her crew go through this place. I'll get a list of all the contractors who had access,' Watt said.

'Amelia sometimes worked as a bank nurse on her days off. Especially at the *Dean Wellness Centre.*'

Watt looked at him, turning away from the window. 'The one in Dean Terrace?'

'Yeah, why?'

'That's where Perry Winkle works. He owns the place. The one who owns this house.'

They heard a noise from downstairs.

'We're up here!' Watt shouted, just as two of the Detective Constables entered. 'I've put in a request for forensics to come here. Don't touch that bed. We think the girl was taken from here.' He looked at Miller and Carol. 'Right you two, with me.'

They left the flat and another two uniforms were outside, with more arriving in a van.

'Get a door-to-door going. We know Amelia Arnold lived here,' Watt said. Then he indicated for Miller and Carol to get in his car.

'You did well, finding out about this place. I'll make sure I put that in my report. See those two DCs in there? They won't last six months. They need each other to tie their shoelaces. They couldn't find a cup of coffee in Starbucks. You two though, you've got what it takes; initiative. Let's go and talk to Dr. Death.'

He started the car up and moved up the lane, heading for St. Bernard's Crescent. The clinic was literally a two-minute drive, three if they got stopped at the end of the road.

'They do plastic surgery there,' Carol said.

Watt looked in the mirror then across to her. 'Maybe I could see if they'll give me a discount on a nose job.'

'Your nose is fine the way it is,' she said.

Watt looked in the mirror at Miller sitting in the back. 'What do you think, Frank?'

'I think you'd need to take out a mortgage, the amount of work they'd have to do on a conk like that.'

'Cheeky sod. Why can't you be more like her?'

'I'm just being honest.'

'So was she!' He pulled out into the crescent. 'You were, weren't you?'

'I was, Andy. Frank was just doing his pitch for *I don't really want to stay in CID*.'

'Well, it's bloody well working. That's the best one I've heard yet. It'll be traffic for you, laddie.'

'There's nothing wrong with traffic.'

'Just wait until you're on the M8 in the pissing rain, trying to flag down tax dodgers. Then you'll wish you had sucked up to me like young Carol here.'

'Sorry, Mr Andy, sir.'

'Piss off, Miller. Too late now.' He pulled up in front of the clinic and parked on double yellow lines on the corner. One of the officers from the Command Centre contacted Watt and told him that Amelia's sister in England had been traced by officers down there and been told the news.

There was no sign of the heat letting up and there wasn't a cloud in the sky as they got out of the car. 'Right, listen up; when you're out with me, there are a couple of rules I like underlings to adhere to. One, no drinking. That's a big no-no. Plenty of time after hours to buy me lager and whisky chasers. That will do your CID career no end of good. You listening, Miller?'

'Something about drinking.'

'And two, keep your eyes on me in case I give you the nod.'

'What kind of nod?'

'The kind that says, *get over by that door now, the fucker's trying to get away.*'

'Is that the only nod you have?' Carol said. 'Or do you have a few different ones?'

'Oh, you know what? You two are just taking the piss now. Let's get inside, and for God's sake, keep your eyes peeled.'

Carol laughed as they climbed the small staircase in front of the Georgian building.

'You might find this funny, lady, but it's by being alert all these years that I haven't had my face broken.'

'Why do you need a nose job then?' Miller said.

'It's a family thing, not because I didn't duck.'

The building was being refurbished, the outside clad in green netting with a sign outside saying *Business as usual!* and another one with the name of the clinic on it.

Inside, where once a coat rack might have stood for the master to hang his coat, was a small reception desk, manned by a young woman with immaculate hair and even more immaculate teeth.

'Good afternoon. Do you have an appointment?'

'I'd like to see Perry MacKinnon.'

'Do you have an appointment?' she asked again, as if he hadn't heard her the first time round.

'I have a warrant card and two other detectives with me. I don't need an appointment.'

'Can I ask what it's about?'

It's about MacKinnon shagging his girlfriend. 'You can ask, but I think MacKinnon might want to talk to me. Call him please.'

'*Doctor* MacKinnon's prepping for surgery just now. Do you want to call back?' Her smile didn't miss a beat.

Watt leaned in closer. 'Call him and say this one word to him: Amelia.'

She picked up a phone and dialled a number and said the code word. Hung up. 'He'll be with you in a minute. If you'd like to take a seat in the waiting room.' She nodded to a door on their left.

Miller looked at Watt, about to ask if the receptionist's nod was the same as his and should he stand guard at the door in case MacKinnon made a break for it.

'We'll stay here,' Watt said.

Two minutes later – a minute later than promised – Perry MacKinnon appeared in reception from the back of the building, looking like he had a ferret stuck down his trousers.

'Officers, if you would like to follow me through to the back. I'm busy prepping a patient, so this will have to be quick.' He turned and they followed him along a dimly-lit hallway, past a set of stairs that led to a basement, past other doors.

'I'm prepping a cell in Saughton prison right now, so we might be a little bit longer than you thought,' Watt said to the doctor's back. 'Get your jacket on and call your lawyer.'

THIRTY-TWO

Perry MacKinnon had composed himself and was looking more confident as he sat next to his lawyer.

Jack Miller was sitting beside Paddy Gibb. The interview was being filmed, and behind the scenes, watched by Harry Davidson and other detectives.

'You're not being charged with anything, Doctor MacKinnon and we appreciate your help with our enquiries,' Jack said.

'Unfortunately, the public will think I'm guilty, and that by *helping with enquiries,* I'm one step away from being charged.'

'Nobody knows you're here.'

'So what is it you want to know about Amelia?'

'Can you account for your whereabouts over the last few days?'

'When specifically?'

'From Friday night until this morning,' Gibb said, glad that he'd had a smoke before he came in here.

MacKinnon sat back in his chair and looked up at the ceiling for a moment before looking back at the two detectives. 'Let me see; Friday night I was at the Rotary Club. My wife and I. We attended a dinner for somebody who's been elected to the board of some company.

Saturday morning, I was lying in bed with a hangover and in the afternoon when I'd sobered up sufficiently to drive, I played a few holes of golf. I went home, had dinner then Saturday night, I went back to the golf club. Had a few drinks with some of my golf buddies.'

'Which one is that?' Jack asked.

'Ravelston.'

'And you have the names of people who can confirm that?'

'I do. I can write them down.'

'Don't you go out with your wife on a Saturday night?'

'No, do you?'

'No, I don't go out with your wife, I go out with my own.'

'I meant your own wife.'

'I know what you meant. Do you go to the club every Saturday on your own?'

He stared into Jack's eyes for a moment. 'I think you know the answer to that.'

'Tell me anyway.'

'I usually spend Saturday night with Amelia.' His eyes dropped to the table for a moment, and Jack thought he was going to start crying, but he kept himself composed.

'Sunday, Monday?'

'Sunday I spent with my wife. We had lunch at *The Bistro* in George Street, followed by a leisurely couple of drinks before heading home. I wasn't out of the house again until Monday morning.'

'Why didn't you spend last Saturday night with Amelia?' Gibb said.

'I couldn't get hold of her. I thought she'd maybe got a shift somewhere. She was a very popular nurse, liked by everybody.'

'Clearly not everybody,' Jack said.

'Most people. Certainly everybody at my clinic.'

'Where does Sherri Judd fit into all this?'

'Who?'

'Oh, you know, the woman you were fighting with in the street.'

'Oh, her. I don't know who she is. Some kind of nutter trying to fleece me out of money.'

'How did she get your address?'

'I'm in the papers. It doesn't take a law degree to find out somebody's home address nowadays.'

'She seems to know a lot about you. Are you saying she picked your name out of the phone book and decided to scam money out of you?'

'Exactly.'

'And then she spent thousands of dollars on a plane ticket, and booked a hotel, just so she could come over here to try and scam you out of money, face-to-face?'

'That's what it looks like to me. Why are you talking about this woman anyway? Do you think she murdered Amelia?'

'No, we don't think she murdered Amelia. She has an alibi.'

'Still doesn't make her sound sane though, does it?'

'I took the liberty of making a call to North Carolina, where she comes from. Somebody did some research and found out that she did indeed send money over here. In your name. She sold her car, gave up her apartment and sent you money to get your clinic off the ground. That's what she claims and it seems to me her claim is backed up by evidence.'

'This is preposterous. I don't need money from some American woman. I have a bank for that. I bought the house that Amelia lived in for God's sake. Why would I con some woman? It doesn't make sense.'

Jack thought that it didn't make sense but for some killers, things like this were a deflection.

'You like sleeping around with other women, Doctor MacKinnon.' It wasn't a question.

'I believe we all have the right to lead our lives as we see fit. My wife has known about my indiscretions for a long time now.'

JOHN CARSON

'Were you also seeing somebody else apart from Amelia? Somebody who might have gotten jealous over your relationship?'

'Like this American woman, for instance?'

'Yes, like her. Maybe somebody else who sent you money.'

'I told you, I didn't take any money from a woman. And no, there wasn't anybody else. Just Amelia.'

'We have the bank records of money being paid to a Perry MacKinnon. Sherri Judd hasn't been lying to us. I think you are though.'

MacKinnon's lawyer looked at Jack. 'My client is here helping you. Please remember that, detective.'

'How about Iris? How did she fit into all of this? Wasn't she worthy of a bought flat?'

'Iris who?'

'Napier.'

'Iris worked for me a long time ago.'

'In what capacity?'

'She was one of my surgical team at the hospital where I worked.'

'Which was where?'

'St. David's Hospital in Dunfermline.'

'And when was the last time you worked with her?'

'The hospital closed five years ago. I started up my own clinic after that.'

'How long have you been in your clinic in Stockbridge?'

'Well, let me see; I knew St. David's was closing, so instead of moving to another hospital, I decided to branch out on my own. I looked for premises, found the Dean Terrace townhouse, got all the necessary funding, had it refurbished and moved in, all within six months. And I haven't looked back since.'

'And the other members of your team?'

'Some of them located to other hospitals. Others went to do other things. Iris went to work in the Western, I believe, because that was closer to where she lived.'

Gibb looked at him. 'Her husband said Iris had affairs. Would you know anything about that?'

MacKinnon turned his lip up. 'Not with me she didn't. We were work colleagues, that was all.'

'You said you had an open marriage,' Jack said.

'No I didn't. I said my wife turned a blind eye to my indiscretions. She couldn't care less if we ever had sex again.'

'What was Amelia getting out of this? Apart from a fancy place to live. A promise of marriage after you left your wife for her?'

MacKinnon smiled as if Jack had just told a dirty joke. 'Nothing like that. She was with me and no promises were given or expected. I own the mews property and I suggested that Amelia move in there so we could have privacy.'

'It was a control thing. You didn't want to go back to her flat, even though she lived on her own and you wouldn't be disturbed. You moved her into the mews property, so you could call the shots.'

'Why would I want to do that?'

'Insecurity. You wouldn't expect her to be seeing somebody else behind your back if she was living in a place owned by you, and not just some manky little flat somewhere but a mews in Comely Bank that's just had a fortune spent on it doing it up. If she was in her own little flat just along the road, well, she could have every Tom, Harry and no doubt Dick in there whenever she wanted. Isn't that correct?'

'Nonsense. I just felt–'

'What? More at home? Surely she could have had other men in her life if she wanted, since you have another woman in your life; your wife.'

'It wasn't like that. It was just a bit of fun.'

'Then it was reasonable to think she could have been having fun with other men. She didn't need an old man like you when she was living in a nice place. She could entertain any man she wanted to.'

'She wouldn't do that to me.' MacKinnon's face was starting to turn a shade of red.

'Of course she would. We've spoken to her friends, and that's exactly what she would have done. In fact, she was at a singles club on Friday night. Is that what pissed you off enough to kill her?'

'No, of course not!'

'It didn't get you riled enough to teach her a lesson? How fucking dare she go to a singles club! How dare she even go out without you! She should be in the house, the house that you bought and paid for, waiting for you to call, or to come round. She had no right going out without your say-so. Isn't that right Perry!'

'Fuck you!' MacKinnon screamed. 'She was fucking history anyway. Fucking slag, just like the other one. I bought her nice things, lavished gifts on her, took her on holiday and how did she repay me? By sneaking off to a singles club with her fucking friend! We argued and I told her we were done! Finished!'

MacKinnon's lawyer put a hand on his arm. 'You don't have to say anything. You aren't here under caution.'

MacKinnon shrugged the hand off. 'No, I'll tell them. Let's get this out in the open. Amelia was a slag, just like her friend, Iris. I fancied her from the get-go, ever since I worked with her. She was a flirtatious cow, always winking and smirking, a real fucking cock-teaser. I knew one day I would have her, but she was married to that knuckle-dragging arsehole. When he was away on the rigs, she went out partying like it was going out of fashion. I even made it back to her house one night, and we were about to go at it, when we heard the sound of a taxi pulling up. It was her husband. She'd lied and told me he was away, when he clearly wasn't. She later told me it was a thrill to almost get caught. When he came in, we had to pretend that I was talking about her work. Her husband believed me.'

'Was she a tease with other men?'

'Probably. But when I had her, I didn't want her going out with other men.'

'You were buying her affection?'

MacKinnon laughed. 'Do you think I need to buy sex from

women? I'm hardly a God, but I get by. When they've had a few, I tell them I'm a surgeon, they can see the kind of watch I wear and the car I drive, and they fall at my feet.'

'How long were you seeing Amelia?' Gibb asked.

'Just over a year. Then things started to get a bit more serious.'

'You mean if you were going to spend money on her, you wanted exclusive membership to the *Amelia club*,' Jack said.

'Wouldn't you? Spend all that damned money, you don't want anybody else eating at the kitchen table.'

'She was just a commodity, then? Did she want more from you?'

'Like what?'

'Marriage. For you to leave your wife for her. That's what mistresses want sometimes.'

'She had talked about it.'

'And this wasn't something you were going to do. Did it lead to a fight? Maybe you smacked her out of anger, accidentally killed her.'

'I didn't touch her! I just told you that! I have an alibi. Check it out.'

'You just said she was a slag a moment ago.'

'She was. I found out the hard way. I told her that maybe we should call it a day. She still had her own flat, that she should move out. And yes, I know you might think that's a reason for me to kill her, but I didn't touch her.'

'You didn't see her at all over the weekend?'

'I just told you I didn't.'

'We'd like you to give us a DNA sample and your fingerprints.'

'Fine. But obviously they're going to be all over the bloody place. And in her little flat.'

Jack terminated the interview and MacKinnon was asked to wait until an officer came in with a DNA kit.

In Harry Davidson's office, Jack stood looking at the boss.

'What's your impression, Jack?'

'I'd like it to be him, sir, but my gut tells me it isn't. God knows, he has means and motive, but he's giving us DNA and has supplied an alibi, which has yet to be checked out, but he's got to know it holds water or else he wouldn't have given it to us.'

'I agree, but check it out anyway. It's his wife, isn't it?'

'Yes.'

'Get onto it. The sooner we eliminate him, the sooner we can move on.'

'Will do. But I was thinking about MacKinnon's mews place; if we find that the blood spatter is Amelia's then we have to think she opened the door to somebody she knew. There were no reports of her leaving the club with a man, and she and her friend left early and went to the mews house.'

'Unless somebody followed them and waited.'

'That's a possibility. If it was just somebody he wanted to attack, and he was waiting, why did he wait so long? For all he knew, the two women were in for the night. Or if he was content to just stand around and wait, then he would have seen Faith, her friend, leave the house to walk home to her own flat along the road.'

'You think somebody like Perry turned up when she was on her own and she let him in and he killed her there before dumping her.'

'He didn't kill her there or else there would have been a hell of a lot more blood. I think she was at least incapacitated there and taken somewhere else to be opened up.'

Jack left, feeling that Perry MacKinnon was lying through his teeth but not being able to do a damned thing about it.

THIRTY-THREE

Calvin Baxter was in his office, staring out of the window onto Lothian Road. What a complete fuck up this was. Things were going along fine until that fucking phone call. Calvin was having trouble eating and sleeping, never mind doing the business with Marcie. Where the hell had Bree gone? Why was she doing this to him? Had she found out and this was her way of pissing him off?

Well, it was working!

Christ, he hadn't realised just how much of a bitch Marcie could be. Her husband wasn't even in his box, yet here she was, laughing and joking like it was nothing. It was spoiling his performance, that was for sure. It had been fun shagging her behind her husband's back, but now the poor sod was dead, the risk wasn't there. Or at least, fifty per cent of the risk wasn't there. Getting caught by Bree wasn't off the table yet, so when she decided to stop playing silly buggers and come back home, the risk would be there again. Or would it?

He had been having second thoughts about seeing Marcie now. Maybe he should think about cooling his jets with her. Tell her that seeing as how her husband wasn't even pushing up the daisies yet, maybe they should postpone their behind-the-scenes activities for the foreseeable future. Yet, he didn't see her taking it lying down. He smiled at his own pun. He'd thought about breaking up with her before, and had actually gone to her house with that very intent, but he had told himself, *One more shag, then that's it.* He wasn't proud of himself for thinking that way, but it was there, in his mind, more and more these days.

Norman getting mown down in London was a selfish thing to do. Why couldn't the clumsy bastard be more careful? Christ, all he'd had to do was go to London, do whatever it was he did, then come back to Marcie. Then he, Calvin, could slip in when he was gone and keep his side of the bed warm.

What the hell was he going to do now? He didn't want to be stuck with Marcie the rest of his life. It was like buying a pie from your favourite bakery then buying the shop. Suddenly, there was nothing to look forward to anymore. It was all there, and it would be good for a while, but then he would eat the pies every day, and he'd get sick of them, and then he wouldn't be able to eat another pie. That would be life with Marcie. The hunt would be gone. He wouldn't get that feeling like he'd just jumped out of an airplane and wondered if he'd strapped on his parachute or his backpack. No more driving on the autobahn in a car with no brakes. *Please come home, Bree.*

There was a knock at his door. The walls and the door were glass, and although there were blinds, they were up just now. Marcie stood there, smiling at him. He waved her in.

'How's my sexy boyfriend?' she said, smiling.

'I don't feel too good, but thanks for asking.'

'Oh, you need a little bit of *TLM: Tender Loving Marcie.*'

'Marcie, not for nothing, but people might start talking unless you start acting like a grieving widow.'

'Oh, what do they know? I'm sure they know about us.'

Calvin's eyes went wide. 'How would they know that? Have you heard anybody talking about it? What are they saying?'

Marcie laughed. 'Nobody's saying anything. Relax. I'm just assuming that they might start talking when they see us together, that's all.'

Then Calvin sat back in his chair as he saw the police officers coming along the corridor, following a young female assistant.

'Oh Christ, this is it,' he said.

Marcie looked but kept smiling as the officers stopped at his door and one of them knocked.

'Stay cool,' Marcie said through clenched teeth. She got up, opened the door and left the room.

'Mr Baxter?' a young woman said.

'Yes?'

'I'm Detective Constable Carol Davidson. May I talk with you for a moment?'

'Please, come in.'

She was followed into the room by a uniformed officer. 'This is my colleague, PC Jeff Knight.'

'Is this about Bree? Have you found her?' Calvin didn't have to fake a concerned face.

'It is about your wife, but no, we haven't any information regarding her whereabouts. Do you mind if we have a seat?'

Calvin indicated for them to sit.

'An officer from the Met called us and asked us to come and talk to you regarding your wife, Mr Baxter. They wanted some more information.'

'Anything I can do to help.'

'Has she done anything like this before?'

'No, never.'

'Did she often stay in London on her own?'

'All the time. When she was on long haul. Sometimes she would do short haul and she would come home after them. But when she was on long haul, like, say, going to Australia or something, she would stay down in the little flat we bought years ago for her to use.'

'Did she seem upset or anything when she was down there?' Knight asked. 'Did she indicate to you that anything was wrong?'

'No, nothing like that. She would call me to say she was settled in and we would talk after she got back from her flight. We didn't constantly chat when she was away, because of the time differences, and she was busy working, of course. She would call me when she was coming back up from London.'

Carol looked at him. 'None of her things were there when officers checked your flat; her purse, her phone. All her belongings. It's like she disappeared into thin air. Any idea why she would do that?'

'None at all. I'm worried sick about her.'

'Was she having any problems with anybody that you know of?'

Calvin looked at the young, blonde detective, at her face, her eyes, trying to see if she was leading up to something. 'If she was, she didn't tell me. Have they asked her colleagues if she had any trouble at work? With staff or a passenger?'

'Her colleagues didn't report any problems. It seems that she didn't go out partying with some of the other young women.'

'Well that's good to know.'

'What's her personality like?'

'She's a happy person. Always full of life.'

Carol looked at Jeff before staring at Calvin. 'Mr Baxter, we have reason to believe that your wife never left Edinburgh.'

'What?' Calvin shot forward in his chair. 'What are you talking about? She got a domestic down to Heathrow last Tuesday morning.'

Carol shook her head. 'There's no record of her being on the plane. She was due at a meeting on Tuesday afternoon, which she missed. There were other work commitments, which she missed. Then she missed her flight.'

'There has to be a mistake.'

'There's no mistake. After we received this information, we

checked your wife's mobile phone records. They show her phone never left the Edinburgh area.'

Calvin looked like a fish out of water for a moment. He sat back and ran a hand through his hair. 'Let me get this straight; you're telling me my wife is still up here?'

'We're not sure. Her phone was turned off Tuesday afternoon.' Carol looked at him. 'Did you actually see your wife leave the house on Tuesday?'

'No. I was at work. She sent me a text to say she was leaving. Here, let me show you.' He took his iPhone out of his pocket and opened it up to the messages. Showed Carol the screen. 'See? There it is.'

'We have the records as I said. We already checked. There were no text messages sent from her phone after last Tuesday. One week ago, your wife dropped off the planet, Mr Baxter.'

Calvin closed his eyes for a moment. Leaned his hands on his desk. 'I'm not getting any of this at all. Why would she do this?'

'We were hoping you could tell us.'

'How would I know?'

'You see, I spoke to an officer from the Met, who had spoken to some of your wife's colleagues down in London, and they seem to think that she wasn't happy in her marriage.'

'What? That's fucking ridiculous! We're as happy as anybody else. Sure, we had our fights, but nothing that would make me...'

'What? Make you what?'

'Make me want to leave her for another woman,' he said softly.

'Somebody like Marcie Lincoln?'

'What? No, that's absurd.' But there was no conviction in his voice.

'I was the one who delivered the news about her husband dying in London.'

'She told me. We were at my promotion do. Who knew her

husband would be dying the very evening we were celebrating? It sort of took the shine off things.'

'What night was that?'

'Last Friday.'

'Mr Lincoln was killed last Tuesday, not Friday. It took the police a few days to identify him. Somebody at our end got their wires crossed.'

Calvin looked blank. 'Tuesday?'

Carol nodded. 'Tuesday. What made you think it was Friday?'

'I... I just assumed, I think.'

'Do you know a woman named Iris Napier?'

Calvin shook his head. 'Doesn't ring a bell.'

Carol took a photo out of her pocket and pushed it across Calvin's desk. 'She might have been using another name when you took her home from the singles club in Stockbridge.'

'She was the one who was murdered, wasn't she?'

'Yes.'

'Christ, I didn't recognise the name when I heard it on the news.'

'Did you take her home to your place?'

'What? God, no. She was living in a rented mews place, not far from the hotel. She said she knew the owner, and he was going to have it refurbished. I took her home, we did, you know, and then I left.'

'Did you ever see her again?'

'I saw her at the singles night, but we didn't hook up again. We said hi to each other, but that's the beauty of that place, you can meet somebody and know it's a bit of fun.'

'It's amazing how a bit of fun can get out of control. Mr Lincoln suspected his wife was having an affair. We talked to his colleagues, and they said he wasn't happy in his marriage and he was planning to divorce his wife.'

'Jesus. I don't know if Marcie knew.'

'Maybe not. But you must admit it's more than a co-incidence that your wife went missing on the same day that Norman Lincoln was killed in a hit-and-run.'

'I... I don't know what to say.'

'Start by telling us where you were, Tuesday of last week.'

'I was here. I wasn't in London. Why would you even ask that?' He looked at his computer screen and moved his mouse around before swivelling the screen so the two police officers could see. 'I was in a meeting Tuesday morning. I had lunch and then I was back in here working. They'll be able to confirm I was in here,' he said, pointing in the general direction of his colleagues.

'We're still looking into this, Mr Baxter. We'll be in touch,' Carol said, standing up. She and Jeff Knight left the office.

'What did they want?' Marcie said, when they were gone.

'Nothing. Just to talk about Bree being missing. They don't have a clue where she is.'

She smiled at him. 'Dinner tonight?'

'No. I'm going to have an early night. My stomach's churning now.'

Marcie looked unsure of herself as she left.

Calvin thought that he had got himself in deeper than he had ever been.

'Did Norman Lincoln's co-workers really say he knew about his wife fooling around on him?'

'I thought one of them did,' Carol said, getting into the passenger seat of the patrol car. 'But I might be wrong. What I'm not wrong about is, Baxter is having it away with Marcie Lincoln. Call it woman's intuition. She and Baxter are behind this. And I'm going to prove it.'

THIRTY-FOUR

'Won't your boss be annoyed that you took a week off at the last minute?' Dawn said as she and Vince walked hand-in-hand through the Ocean Terminal shopping centre, down in Leith.

'Wood's a donkey. I've never liked the man. He was always sweating, as if he was up to no good. You remember him from the nights out we used to go to, don't you?'

'I do. Him with his crummy little moustache. Thought he was God's gift.'

'He hasn't changed.'

The centre was busy with locals and tourists alike. They sat upstairs with a soft drink, looking out at the Royal Yacht Britannia, now moored as a tourist attraction.

'Your mum is taking things very well. She didn't even ask me for little Vincent's DNA.' She laughed when she said it.

'Becks and I are both surprised by that. I don't think you need to prove it; the wee guy looks like his dad.'

'He does that.'

'What did you say to him? About me, I mean. Like, where was I and why wasn't I around?'

'I just said that you lived far away in Edinburgh and that he would meet you one day.'

'I feel like I'm having a dream. That I'm going to wake up any moment now.'

Dawn leaned over and kissed him. 'I can assure you that this is real. And I want you to come with me to find a flat. I've been in touch with the estate agents and they're going to find some places for us to look at. I'd like you there to help me choose. And I know this is all moving fast, but you can move in with me, Vince. We have a lot of time to catch up on. No pressure though; I'm not forcing you into a corner. If you want me to move in on my own with Vincent, then that's fine too. The door will always be open.'

'I'd like to move in. If Mother's not happy, then too bad.'

'Don't be mean. She's being very understanding. And Beckett is such a treasure.'

'I have a question for you.'

'Shoot.'

'If Chatter hadn't been moving back to Edinburgh, would you have stayed down there with him?'

'No. Without question. I wanted Vincent to go to school in Edinburgh. London is fine, mind, but I wanted him to be up here.'

'Where was he born?'

'Up here. In Edinburgh. I wanted him to be Scottish.' She looked away for a moment. 'I'm sorry. It was a hard time. You know why I didn't tell you.'

'I understand. He speaks with a London accent.'

'I know. It's what he's used to being around.'

'I'm not complaining. It was me who messed up.'

She squeezed his hand. 'We're only looking forward now. Sure, I'll tell you anything you want to know, but I'm not rehashing the past to lay blame. It is what it is, so let's just move forward.'

He smiled. 'Okay. I can live with that.'

'There she is now.' Dawn stood up from the table and waved at a young woman walking towards them.

They hugged when the girl got close.

'I am so sorry things didn't work out, Michelle,' Dawn said. She turned to Vince. 'I'd like you to meet my nanny, Michelle. This is Vince.'

'Ooh, handsome,' Michelle said, shaking Vince's hand. 'Good to meet you at long last. This one hasn't stopped talking about you for the longest time. Vince this, Vince that.'

'Do tell me more. Would you like a Coke or anything?'

'No, thank you. I'm catching a train this afternoon and I don't want to be needing the lav while I'm standing on the platform.' She giggled as they sat down.

'This is not how I saw things going down,' Dawn said. 'I was going to take you with me when I found my new place. You can still come with me.'

'You're a love, you really are, but I don't want to stay in a place that's home to that old tosser. And his bloody sidekick, Lurch.'

'What will you do now?' Vince asked.

'I don't know. I'll find another nanny job eventually.'

'Look, why don't you stay on as my nanny? I have enough money to pay you.'

'I couldn't do that. Len was paying me. Besides, you'll have enough on your hands, starting a new life with Vince and little Vincent.'

'I could still do with a hand.' Dawn turned to Vince. 'What do you think?'

'Sure. But I must admit, I still work for the DVLA. I don't earn a fortune.'

'I have savings. Even though I don't work for Chatter anymore, I get money in from some scripts I wrote for the show I was working on. You're not the only writer in the family, Vince Rutherford. I have plenty more ideas, and I'm going to use my contacts in London to see they land on the right desk.'

'I'd be a third wheel. You and Vince are starting a new life together.'

'I still need somebody to look after our little boy. And the others when they come along.'

Vince raised his eyebrows and smiled.

Dawn laughed. 'I intend for us to be a proper family, Vince. In fact, I think I should tell the estate agent to look for a house, not a flat. May as well start off properly. We'll get a place that has room for a nanny.'

'I don't know what to say.' Michelle was smiling but a tear ran down her face.

'Just say yes.'

'Okay, yes!'

Dawn looked at Vince. 'Thank you. Don't worry about the money; the price I got for my house in London will more than cover the price of a house up here. We won't even have a mortgage.'

'I want to be able to provide for you and my family,' Vince said.

'And you will. I read the parts of the book you sent in to Chatter before you brought the whole book along. It was superb. I even had lunch with an agent friend of mine, who said she thought it was fantastic. You were wasting your time sending it in to that old vulture.'

'And now he owns the rights to it. Jesus. Just my luck.'

They both heard Michelle clear her throat and turned round to look at her. She was holding up a key.

'Chatter said that I'm responsible for getting rid of your stuff, since I don't have anything better to do with my time. Cheeky old sod. I said I would arrange for a pick-up, but I haven't called yet. I wanted to speak to you first. Like I'm going to just get rid of your stuff.'

'He won't like it if you give me the key,' Dawn said.

'Don't worry, I'll be there. The old tosspot is out this afternoon with Skinny. He's doing some talk for students up at the university.' She looked at her watch. 'He should be gone by now. But if not, you can be sitting round the corner. He's not expecting you back in the house, but he's expecting me.'

'We came down on the bus.'

'I have my car. Let's go.'

They walked to the car park and Dawn felt excited as she got in the back of the Volkswagen. This was the start of her new life.

THIRTY-FIVE

Miller, Carol, and Watt were sitting in the canteen. The lunchtime rush was on, but they sat at a far corner. They could see the TV from there.

'Cheer up,' Watt said to Carol. 'Or have his personal hygiene habits shocked you already?'

'Nothing that I wasn't expecting.'

'Just wait until he farts in bed for the first time. Then you know it's true love.'

'Jesus, Andy,' Miller said.

'It's the sign of true love. Me, I used to blame it on the dog. We had a German Shepherd. It was cute when he was wee and wanted up on the bed, but when he turned into a hundred-pound farting machine that left me six inches of bed space, it wasn't fun anymore. That was the only good thing about him though; I could blame the farts on him.'

'Christ, I'm trying to eat my fruit and custard here.'

'I'm only talking about farting, not puking.'

'Oh, for fu...' Miller pushed his plate away, leaving half of his dessert.

'Do you mind if I have that, since your appetite has gone?' Watt said.

'You may as well.'

Watt took the spoon out and produced one from the side of his plate. 'I always pick one up in case one of my colleagues has a change of heart. But I don't go round all the tables, you understand.'

'Fat sod.'

'That's it, work your anger out. When you're done sulking like a wee laddie who wants his ball back, I'll be here to listen.' Watt got tucked into the fruit and custard.

'Never mind the big, nasty man; Carol will fix you something nice for afters,' Carol said, reaching across and patting his hand.

'You two are in bloody cahoots, I swear to God.' Miller shook his head and washed down his lunch with a bottle of water.

'We're just toughening you up, Miller,' Watt said, pushing the empty plate away and sitting back, rubbing his belly.

'Let's just hope we don't get a call to chase somebody this afternoon,' Miller said to Carol. 'Billy Bunter here will be well stuffed.'

'That's why I have you. Me, master; you, prodigy.'

'The only thing I'm learning from you is how to snag a free lunch.'

'No, you had your first lesson in using psychology; I put you off your food so I could have it for free. You'll learn how to use that to your advantage when you're interviewing somebody.'

'So, if they're not spilling the beans, I can talk about my dog farting.'

Watt laughed. 'Now you've got it.'

'I was at an office today, talking to a man whose wife is missing in London,' Carol said.

'Sounds interesting,' Watt said, feigning interest.

'Hear me out; I just thought it was a co-incidence that I was at a woman's house a few days ago, delivering a death message. Her husband was killed in a hit-and-run. Also in London.'

'I know I don't believe in coincidences,' Watt said, 'but that sounds a bit thin to me.'

'You might think so, but the woman who I gave the death message to, was in the guy's office when I went there with Jeff Knight. She left his office just as we got there.'

Miller and Watt both sat up. 'Now, that *is* a coincidence,' Miller said.

'It is indeed. And she wasn't looking like the troubled widow, missing her husband.'

'She should be thinking about her husband's funeral by now, don't you think?'

'I do think. I mean, it might be nothing. Maybe she's just putting a brave face on it, but something about the way she was smiling when she came out of that guy's office got to me. And now his wife is missing. She didn't even make it down to London to the BA base. A mobile phone tower pinged her phone in Edinburgh. Then it went dead.'

'Maybe she switched it off for the plane ride.'

'She didn't get on the plane. And she was supposed to be going to London a week ago. Her phone pinged in Edinburgh last Friday.'

'Maybe we should go and have a talk with the husband at home,' Watt said. 'We can go tonight, if you like. Sort of surprise him. We can give him some bullshit about the Met wanting us to ask some more questions. The two of us can go and put the wind up him.'

'I can get on board with that,' Carol said.

'Good. We can meet up after dinner.'

'Maybe it would be best not to let your father know about this,' Watt said. 'He'll give you a skelped arse, but me and the boy here will get our jotters.'

Carol laughed. 'He's just a big teddy bear.'

'A teddy bear with teeth.'

'Why does this feel like we're breaking in?' Dawn said.

They were parked outside the big house in Trinity. A large wall ran around the perimeter of the property. It was one of the things that Chatter had been attracted to.

'It's not breaking in, silly,' Michelle said. 'I have the key. I'm getting help from you to get rid of your stuff. You worry too much. Am I right, Vince?'

'She has a point, love. It's your stuff.'

'And yours. We're getting your book back.'

'You already told me that by sending it to him, I was agreeing that he could keep it. I have no right to it now.'

'Listen, all the submissions were sent to me, at an email address that I made up. When you sent your first chapters, they were stored on the hard drive and on an external hard drive. I already have the external hard drive. I just need to get my laptop. It belongs to me. I bought it. I asked the tight old sod for a new one, but he knows how to save a few quid, and by me using my own laptop, he saved himself over a thousand. So I want it back, and that way, he won't have any of your chapters any more. Like they won't even have existed. He'll have copies of the others but he can keep them, they're not our property. He only reads printed stuff, so he has all those entries on paper. We need to get the version you printed off for him then he won't have any of your stuff.'

'Sounds good to me, if you can pull it off.'

'We can.'

'If we can just run through the plan one more time–' he started to say, but Michelle already had the car door open. Followed by Dawn. 'Oh, shit,' he said, getting out of the back. They all walked up to the front door as if they belonged there.

'Here goes nothing,' Michelle said, putting the key in and opening the front door.

The large house smelled of furniture polish. There was a large stairway in front of the door to the left with a hallway leading through to the back. There were several doors off the main entrance hall.

'Where's your laptop?' Vince said.

'It was upstairs in the room I was staying in.'

Michelle handed him a pair of latex gloves. 'We keep them for doing dirty jobs around the house. Maybe best if you wore a pair. So no fingerprints are left behind.'

Fuck, I knew it, Vince thought but just put the gloves on in silence.

'It's optional of course. Otherwise, we can just look for your stuff.'

They nodded and started. The house had three levels, and on the ground floor was a huge drawing room. A working area was set out in one corner with an iMac sitting on it.

'Len doesn't like to sit in a cramped office. He likes to work in a big room. There's another living room where he has a TV so he mostly has this place to himself,' Dawn explained.

'Nice. I hope I can get an office like this one day,' Vince said. 'I'll have to settle on my living room for the time being.'

'Don't worry, when we buy a house, I'll make sure it has a big office for you.'

'I just can't wait until I can pack that job in. I know I can make money at my books, despite what Mother says.'

'I have every confidence in you, honey,' Dawn said, smiling. 'Now, let's see where your manuscript is.'

They were all wearing gloves now, and Dawn started looking through filing cabinets and on the bookshelves, that lined the back wall. They couldn't find it.

'Where the hell is it?' Dawn said.

'Didn't you say he might take it to bed with him, last Saturday night?' Vince said.

'Yes, I did! Let's go and have a look in his bedroom.'

There were two bedrooms on the first floor with another four upstairs. Chatter's bedroom was on this floor. The biggest one with the en suite. Dawn opened the door and they went in. The bed was a super king and had a nightstand on each side. On the left-hand side, Dawn saw a pile of papers. She picked them up and flipped through them.

'No, sorry, this is one of his own stories.'

'It has to be somewhere,' Vince said, beginning to feel that Len Chatter would indeed be the new owner of his book.

'Here!' Michelle shouted from the office. Vince and Dawn went back through.

The nanny was holding up a brown parcel, the size and shape of a ream of paper. On the front was taped *Death Heights by Vincent Rutherford.*

'That's it! I made sure the book didn't run past 500 pages so it wouldn't use more than a ream of paper. Look, the old twat hasn't even opened it!'

Michelle was holding it in her hands but she had a worried look on her face. 'I know you said you wanted this back, but in the eyes of the law, you gave it and all the rights to it to Len Chatter.'

'So what?' Dawn said. 'He's an old cheat.'

'Hear me out; what if Vince took the book and had it published? Chatter might sue him for all the money it makes.'

Vince looked at Dawn. 'She's right. I'm stuffed.'

Dawn looked angry. 'No you're not. He hasn't opened it, so he doesn't know what's in it. Here, watch this.' She walked over to the back wall where there was a load of boxes with reams of copier paper in them.

'He was going to print all the entries off so I had to make sure that he had a load of paper.' She took the lid off a box and took out a ream of paper and opened it. Laid it down on the desk and carefully opened the wrapper that Vince's book was in, carefully peeling the Sellotape back. Then parted the paper enough to get her hand in and take Vince's manuscript out. Then she put the ream of blank paper in and carefully pressed the Sellotape down to shut the wrapping up again and then she put it back. 'Even if it springs open, he'll think it was because it's been manhandled.'

She put the manuscript in the copy paper packet. 'One book back. And if he did have the gall to question you, all you say is, you wanted to get his attention. To get your name noticed and by putting in a ream of blank paper, he would remember your name when you finally got round to sending in your book. Unfortunately for you, you missed the deadline and didn't get your book sent in. The deadline was last Saturday, by the way.'

'I also sent it in by email.'

'And I'm going to take care of that. As I said, it's on my laptop. He doesn't know his way around his email. I had to answer everything for him. I'm sure he'll have somebody else answer his emails, but I had a special one just for the competition. He doesn't have access to it.'

'Brilliant. Let's go and get it.'

They went up to the next level where the other bedrooms were, including Stick Man's. There were four and a bathroom. Michelle went into hers and started packing her things.

Dawn stood in her bedroom and looked around.

'Does it make you feel sad?' Vince asked from behind her.

'It does in a way. You were meant to win that competition and make a name for yourself.' She turned to face him. 'You know what? You'll still make a name for yourself. I'll see to it. Come on, let's get my stuff. You start throwing my stuff in my suitcases and then we'll work on Vincent's, although he doesn't have a lot. I'll look for my laptop.'

Vince started taking Dawn's clothes out of the wardrobe and drawers and roughly folded the items before putting them into her suitcase. Skirts, sweaters, trousers, shirts. He didn't feel comfortable touching her underwear, so he left the drawer open so she could deal with that herself.

He checked on top of the old wardrobe and pulled off a shoebox. CD's. He put it on the bed. Then he got down on his hands and knees and looked under the bed. There was a black bag under there, tied with the plastic drawstrings. He pulled it out and took a few minutes to fiddle with the handles to untie them. It felt like a bag of clothing.

He opened it up and saw it was an article of clothing. He pulled it out. It was a long, black coat, but it wasn't this that caught his eye; it was the knife that came out with it. Vince didn't touch it but merely stared at it.

The weapon was covered in blood. Then he saw the dried-on blood on the coat. Christ, had Dawn killed somebody?

Then he remembered the peeping Tom murder. And the murders of the two other women. How was Dawn involved in that?

'What's that?' he heard her say from the open doorway.

He twisted his head round. He hadn't touched the knife so it wouldn't have his prints on it. 'A knife with blood on it. I found it under your bed. Along with this coat.' He stood up. 'Listen, it's okay, we can work things out. Get you help–'

'Okay, honey, before you go any further, they're not mine. You're letting your crime-writer imagination run away with you.' She stepped into the room and he involuntarily took a step back. 'For God's sake, Vince, I wouldn't have left them under the bed for you to find if they belonged to me. I would have had you go to Vincent's room and get his stuff while I made sure I got the bag and nobody opened it.'

'I know. I'm sorry. It's just a shock.'

'What's that?' Michelle asked, coming into the room.

'Vince found that stuff in a bag under my bed.'

'Jesus, what is it?'

Dawn looked at her. 'I'm not sure, but I think it's what we would call a *murder weapon*.'

THIRTY-SIX

The *Savoy* hotel wasn't too busy when Miller walked in. Carol was away with Andy Watt. Miles was behind the bar with Sherri, who was helping out.

Miller raised his eyebrows. 'This is a surprise.'

Sherri smiled back at him. 'Miles and I have come to an arrangement.'

'Don't say it like that,' Miles said. 'He'll think I'm some kind of weirdo.'

'I already think you're some kind of weirdo,' Miller said.

'Cheers, Frank.'

Sherri indicated for him to go to the end of the bar. 'Miles spoke to his dad. They have a couple of rooms in the basement level that aren't rented out except to long-term guests. There's one resident there and the other room is empty, so I'm getting to stay in there if I help around the hotel. Cleaning, helping in the bar, that sort of thing.'

'That's very good of you, Miles,' Miller said.

'Technically, she's not working as no money is changing hands, so she's here on a six-month visitor's visa. But I'll see she wants for nothing.'

Sherri turned to look at him. 'My knight in shining armour.'

'Och, away woman, I'll be getting all embarrassed now.'

'Nobody else would have done this for me.'

Miller looked serious for a moment. 'We had Perry MacKinnon in for questioning on another, unrelated matter, and we've been doing some background checks on him. Money was indeed sent to him, but the thing is, and this is where it gets very strange, none of the bank accounts belong to him. It seems that somebody created bank accounts online and had the money deposited, and then transferred the money and closed the accounts down.'

'Thank you, Frank, but I got it sorted.'

'What do you mean?'

'Perry MacKinnon came to see me here last night. He gave me my money back, as long as I don't press charges against the man who took it in the first place.'

'Did he tell you who conned you?'

Sherri looked unsure for a moment. 'His son. He left university but he's lazy. Then he decided to take money from me. I suspect it was to get back at his father, and I just got caught up in it all.'

'When did he give you the money?'

'This morning. I met him at his private bank up in Moray Place.'

'His son should be taught a lesson instead of just getting a slap on the wrist from daddy.'

'I know, but I really needed my money back.'

'And he's probably covered his own tracks very well,' Miles said.

'You can still press charges.'

'It's fine, Frank. Where's Carol tonight?'

'She has to go and interview somebody on an unrelated case.'

'And here's me thinking all you coppers had nice, easy, nine-to-five jobs.'

'One day when I make Chief Super maybe. Until then, we're just foot soldiers in suits.'

'How's the search going for the *Surgeon*?'

'We're making headway. I can't go into details, but we all know he's a coward. Attacking women like that and hiding them.'

'We have them like that in America, Frank. They're just a bunch of little boys who can't deal with real women. Scum, the lot of them. I hope you catch the bastard soon. Before he chooses his next victim.'

'You and me both.'

A man walked up to Miller's side and put his glass on the bar. He was leaning heavily on a walking stick. 'Anything else, Robert?' Sherri asked.

He smiled at her. 'No. I'm going down to my room. Watch some TV.'

'Cheers,' Miles said and watched as the man left the bar, leaning heavily on his walking stick.

'So how did Carol's dad enjoy Spain?'

'Harry finds it hard to relax. So he hit the ground running by the time he stepped off the plane.'

'It's awful though, not only a man killing in that way, but a peeping Tom murdering a woman too,' Sherri said. 'Nobody's safe nowadays.'

'At least you're in a hotel surrounded by people,' Miller said. 'Safer than most, I reckon.'

'Baberton was as far out of town that I liked,' Andy Watt said, as Carol drove past the road that would lead into Balerno village. 'This is way out in the sticks. Next stop down the road is the psychiatric hospital.' She slowed down, looking for Calvin Baxter's house. 'Until they close it and build flats on the grounds, that is.'

'It seems that everywhere is closing now. The population is getting bigger every day, yet, we still have only one Accident and Emergency.'

'Try telling that to the politicians, Carol. Unless their pockets are bulging with handouts, they couldn't give a monkey's.'

They saw the number on the right-hand side and Carol pulled into the driveway. A little red Corsa was sitting next to an Audi TT. 'I wonder what size his manhood is to want to drive one of those penis envy cars.'

'What do you drive, Andy?' Carol said as they got out.

'I don't have a car. You can raise your eyebrows all you like. And now your boyfriend drives this girly Beetle, well, that just says it all really.'

Dusk was settling over the west side of the city and the automatic light came on above the door, although it wasn't full dark. Watt leaned on the bell for a good few seconds.

Calvin Baxter answered the door, looking flustered.

'Whatever it is you're selling, I have one,' he said, but then looked at the two people in front of him, holding up warrant cards.

'DS Watt. I believe you've met DC Davidson. We'd like to come in and speak to you for a moment, if you don't mind.'

Baxter looked back into the house before opening the door.

'This won't take long, will it?'

'I don't know. Will it? I know it won't take half as long if you let us in.'

Calvin stood back and let the detectives inside. There was the smell of Chinese food hanging around in the air.

'Through this way,' he said, staggering slightly. Watt quickly followed, Carol right behind him.

Calvin went into the living room where he slumped down onto the settee. 'What can I do for you fine officers?' He reached over to a side table and drank from the glass of wine that was there. 'Have a seat.'

They both sat in chairs.

'We want to run through some things again, regarding your wife,' Watt said.

'Have you found her?'

Carol looked at him. 'No, sir, but we just wanted to ask you a few questions, if that's all right?'

They could see just how much Calvin had been drinking. He was swaying slightly as he sat, his words slightly slurred. 'Go right ahead, honey.' He drank some of the red and stared into the glass.

'Usually when somebody goes missing, they are walking away from an old life to start a new one. Or there's foul play,' Carol said. 'You told us that Bree had nothing to worry about, so we have to err on the side of caution and think now that there was foul play. Unless you know otherwise.'

He looked at her, his eyes getting bloodshot. 'Foul play? You mean something happened to her before she left for London?'

'It's looking more like that.'

He drank some more. 'I don't know. She was an enigma.'

'What do you mean?' Watt asked.

'Bree was Bree. What Bree wanted, Bree got. What Bree wanted to do, she did. My opinion counted for sweet fuck all. I love her but when she sets her sights on something, nothing I say will stop her. She's very strong-willed.'

'You were having marital problems then?' Carol said.

Calvin laughed. 'No. We were just like any other, boring married couple. We would argue, she would sulk for a few days, then we'd have at it like we were on honeymoon again, and then she'd fuck off to New York for a week. She's very tough, my wife.'

'How did she get on with her colleagues?'

He drank more wine and looked down into the glass again, as if the answer lay at the bottom. Then he looked at her. 'She always had to be the big cheese. *Oh, look at me! My name's Bree and I want to be the centre of attention. Laugh at my jokes. Look at my cleavage. Do you think I have nice legs? I spent a fortune on my teeth, do you like them?*' He looked over at Watt. 'You married?'

'Yes.'

'How would you feel if your wife was a stunner and men looked at her and you knew that every one of those men in the room wanted to fuck her?'

'How do you know my wife isn't a stunner?' Watt said, his eyes boring into Calvin's.

'No offence, mate. But you're a copper. Men like me, good-looking, worth a few bob, we're the ones who marry stunners. But answer my question.'

'I think I'd be quite happy if other men looked but knew they couldn't touch.'

Carol looked at Watt, thinking that Calvin was getting the upper hand, making the sergeant answer his question.

'It starts off that way; you're proud that you have a beauty on your arm, sort of, *Look at my missus! Isn't she gorgeous? But you can't have her, because she's mine!* Then it turns into the cow putting some extra weight on, wearing cheap red lipstick so men will look at her lips in case there's the vaguest chance they'll be interested in what she's saying instead of them looking down her tits. But she also wants them to check those out too, because although they're fighting gravity, she's popped them into a push-up and they stick out just like they used to, albeit with a little help nowadays. But it's in her head that she's still 21, not 41. Oh yes, that was a bastard, turning the *Big four-oh!* God forbid we should say *forty*.'

Both detectives let him ramble on. Sometimes people would let something slip.

'But it's her party and she's had more champagne than she normally has. Oh yes, she's taken to drinking champagne now, not the white wine spritzers that she used to drink. She thinks it's what the young girls drink, but she's so out of touch. It's what girls drink who are being bought by some wanker with loads of dosh. Like me!' He laughed at himself for a minute. 'But Bree is going around the hall like she's the Queen bee. *Queen Bree* they were calling her. She was telling everybody to drink as much as they could as the bar was free and hubby was picking up the tab. And all her friends are there, but they're work friends now, as she's driven all the other ones away with her *I'm better than you and I earn more* attitude. And you know what I caught her doing?'

Both detectives shook their heads, affirming that they were in the dark as to what Bree had been doing.

'Fucking snogging that tosser, what's his name? You know, the one everybody thought was gay but he was faking it. The ladies thought he was Mr Fun, and he went along to the women's night out. *Guess what thingummy did tonight? He danced on a table top. What a laugh. He had us in stitches. I've never had such a laugh.* Well, thingummy wanted to sleep with my wife. I caught them snogging near the toilets. She said it was just a bit of fun, but if I hadn't gone for a pee, God knows what would have happened. I got all stroppy of course, and I didn't get my way with her that night, but neither did thingummy. But I was the one who deserved it!' He poked himself in the chest. 'I'm her fucking husband! I should be the one who sleeps with her, not some jumped up, wannabe pilot who couldn't guide a fucking drinks trolley down the aisle if it were on rails. She was mine.'

Calvin finished his wine and got up to get another and almost fell over onto the couch. Watt stood up but Calvin waved him away. He walked over to the drinks cabinet where the opened bottle sat and he poured himself another healthy measure. Then sat back down.

'Bree was the funny one. Bree was the smart one, the one who everybody talked about at parties. In our younger days, she could party all night, but as age got its grip on her, she still wanted to party all night but her body creaked and groaned just a little bit more than it used to. She used to sit in front of the mirror crying sometimes. Another crows foot had appeared round her eyes, or maybe the elasticity was leaving her skin on the back of her hand faster than she approved off. There was nothing wrong with her! It's called aging gracefully!'

'What do you think's happened to her?'

Calvin started crying the cry of the drunk. 'I love her. I really do. I overlooked all the faults, all the little idiosyncrasies, the mood swings, the tantrums. *Queen Bree* they called her, did I tell you that? Everybody wanted her but nobody could have her. Not truly have her.' He drank and sniffled, wiping the tears with the back of his hand.

'Do you think she wanted to just up and leave?'

Calvin shook his head. 'No. I'm the only one who came close to taming her, although I accepted long ago that I could never own her. Nobody can own another person of course, but own her in a way that a man should feel about his wife. He should be able to encapsulate her, make her the centre of his universe. And I did all that. But Bree wanted to be free. One of those women who want it all. The security of being married, not wanting to be stuck on the shelf, getting into her thirties without a ring on her finger. I put a ring on her finger and we exchanged vows and I promised to love her and I was so proud.'

He drank some more wine and looked at them. 'How could she do this to me?'

'Do what?' Watt asked.

'This.' He swept an arm around the room. 'Leave me alone like this. How could she do this?' His head flopped down on his chest and Watt thought for a moment that the man had passed out but then his head shot up as if he had been jolted by electricity. 'Was she looking for eternal youth?'

His eyes started drooping and he was about to let the glass fall when Carol jumped up and grabbed it. He sat up, startled. Looked at the glass in Carol's hand.

'I'm going to bed. I'm off work tomorrow. Who are you two again?'

'We're police officers,' Watt said. 'I'll leave a business card and if you think of anything that might be of interest to us, you can call us anytime. Okay?'

'Yeah, sure.'

'Will you be okay?' Carol said.

'I've had a lot more to drink than this before,' he said and left the living room. They heard a door shutting further down the hall.

'We can always come back,' Watt said. 'Maybe when he's a wee bit more sober.'

'I don't think he'll remember much about this conversation. Just as well I was recording it.'

They left the house and Carol took her phone out and snapped a photo of the number plates on the cars.

'And remember, not a word to your dad. I wouldn't want him to think we were trying it on with the overtime.'

'I know,' she said, getting into the driver's seat of her Beetle. 'This is on our own time.' She backed out and drove away.

Calvin sat on the edge of his bed, crying again. Marcie came out of the en-suite toilet and sat down beside him, putting an arm around him.

'It's going to be alright, Calvin, just leave it up to me.'

'What are you doing here?' He sniffed again, his eyes now red and puffy.

'Don't worry, we're both off for the rest of the week. I have a funeral to arrange, and you're distraught about your wife going missing. Nobody at work will question it. But I have a few things to do.'

Calvin was looking at her but he was beyond listening. Marcie got him to stand up for a moment, pulled back the covers, and then helped him get into bed. He could get changed in the morning, after he had sobered up. She was glad she'd only had one glass of wine as she had to get up early. Way earlier than Calvin.

'Just drop me off at Tanner's bar if you don't mind,' Watt said as Carol was driving along Lanark Road. She pulled in opposite the pub. It was well lit and she could see a few patrons inside, mostly locals she assumed.

They had been dissecting Calvin's rant. A drunken ramble after he realised that his wife wasn't coming home? Something else?

'Did you see the second wine glass on the drinks cabinet?' Carol said.

'I did. There was nothing in it though. Maybe it was the wine glass that his wife used.'

'There was the tiniest spot of wine in the bottom of it. And a smear round the edge as if somebody had finished the glass but hadn't got round to pouring another before we got there.'

'Very observant. I just noticed it, that's all, because it was on the drinks cabinet.'

'I could see you were starting to foam at the mouth just looking at it.'

'I swear we were married in another life.'

'It might be nothing,' she said, looking at Watt. 'Why don't I come into the pub with you, and you can pretend to all your mates that you've picked up a young chick?'

'No thanks.'

'Why?'

'Because none of them are zipped up the back. Young chick indeed. I'm not ready for a mid-life crisis.'

Carol laughed. 'We'll know soon enough about Calvin Baxter when you run those plates tomorrow.'

Watt opened the car door. 'Me? Oh I see how it goes. You're a bad lassie, Carol Davidson.' He got out and leaned back in. 'But with that attitude, you can be on my team any day.'

Carol drove the car away, thinking not only of the empty wine glass but the smell of the expensive perfume that had still been lingering in the living room. That and the feeling she'd seen the black Audi TT somewhere else recently.

And it wasn't Calvin Baxter's.

THIRTY-SEVEN

'I've been looking online at houses, and there are a few that I've liked so far. I've made an appointment to start viewing them,' Dawn said to Mother.

They were sitting at the kitchen table, having a cup of tea. Beckett was in his room, and little Vincent was having a nap.

'Listen, I know we got off on the wrong foot all those years ago, but I'm hoping we can make up for lost time. I know Vincent wants to make a life for you and his little boy, and I'm so glad that you don't hold a grudge against me.'

'Of course I don't!' Dawn said, reaching over to take her future mother-in-law's hand. 'I wasn't sure if you would even want me on your doorstep. But I can tell you with all my heart that I love Vince.'

'I know you do. And he told me over breakfast what you did for him five years ago. That was a very selfless thing to do, especially knowing you were pregnant with his child.'

'I know my own mum was lost when my dad died. I didn't want you to feel that way.'

'Bless you. But I was thinking; why don't you and little Vincent stay here for a while? You and Vince can even share a room. I might appear old fashioned to the boys, but I know what goes on in the world. That way, Vincent would have his own room. I should probably call my son Vince now, just to save confusion.' She smiled. 'What do you say? I promise you I won't bother anybody. There are five bedrooms in this old pile, and I would just rattle about in it. I mean, just until you find the right place. It would give you time to save up for a deposit.'

'Mum, that would be great. Have you spoken to Vince about it?'

'Not yet. I wanted to see what you thought first.'

Dawn didn't have the heart to tell the old woman that she didn't need to save for a deposit. Her London home had gone for a fantastic price, and it would allow her to buy a decent house in Edinburgh for cash, and still have a lot left over.

Her job with Chatter had been about getting her foot in the door. Not only had she been given a speaking part in the soap opera, but she had been invited to be on the writing team. It had been little Vincent's schedule that had made her think that a job working from home would be best, although she wanted Michelle to come along too, to give her time to write. And Len Chatter was quite willing to bring Dawn on board. He wanted to get into TV scripts as well as his books, and he saw Dawn as a wealth of experience, so he had hired her as his assistant. It was only Stick Man who treated her like crap.

In retrospect, she might have got an agent for her books if she'd pursued it, but one night she had met Len. They'd got talking. And after all, he had worked with her in the past when she was a nurse.

'I think it's a wonderful idea, but we'll contribute to the food bill, and I'll take care of the electricity bill. That's the least I can do. And we'll give you money for our room too–'

'Dawn, relax. I'm not thinking for one minute that you don't want to help out, and that's fine, but the idea is for you to save money.'

'Look, Mum, I got a good pay cheque from the BBC. I sold my house in London and made a fantastic profit. We'll stay here for as long as you can put up with us. But we'll pay our way, me and Vince.' She smiled at the old woman. 'I'm sure he'll agree with me.'

'Beckett is doing his best to look for a job, and he'll contribute when he can.'

'He doesn't have to worry. We'll make sure we have everything we need. I appreciate you putting a roof over our heads in our time of need.'

'You're family. It's what we do.'

'Would you mind if Michelle came here? She's Vincent's nanny. I'll make sure that the bills are paid and that we have plenty of food delivered.'

Mother smiled. 'Why not? This house has seen too much misery over the past few years. Vince deserves some happiness.'

'Thanks, Mum. And we'll do lunch. I have a surprise for Vince, but don't tell him; I'm just on the verge of publishing my own thriller. I've always done some writing on the side, and I thought it was about time I made money from it. That, along with my acting money and money from my house, we'll not have to worry about the bills. And listen, Vince's book is good. I read his submission to Len Chatter's competition, and he's got talent. He's going to make a fortune.'

'I know he is. I read the stuff he printed out, and I told him it was rubbish, but it was the exact opposite. I'm a bad mother; very selfish. I thought if I encouraged him, he would make a lot of money and move out. I'm a very selfish old woman. I hope he forgives me.'

'There's nothing to forgive. You were just being a mother. And now I know what that feels like.'

'I do have one question; do you think that you and Vince will get married?'

'I'm 29, Mum. I want to be Mrs Rutherford by the time I'm 30!'

Mother smiled.

'Mum, I have to call Michelle, my nanny, and tell her the news.'

'That's fine. I'm meeting a friend of mine in town for a tea. I'll see you later.'

Dawn went upstairs to her room and took out her mobile phone. Called Michelle's number and listened as it went to voicemail. 'Michelle, I was hoping we could meet up. I want you to come here and live with us. I've cleared it with Vince's mother. She's happy to let you. You won't have to live there anymore.' She hung up. Then headed out to the rented car she'd hired.

And headed down to Trinity.

She parked outside Chatter's house, feeling a buzz in her stomach. *What's wrong with you? You're not afraid are you? No, not of Len. I've known him for a long time, but it's that other skinny freak who bothers me.*

She couldn't put it off any longer. She went in through the wooden gate that was set in the high, stone wall and went up to the front door.

It was ajar.

Going against every instinct, every warning that was shooting through her mind, she nudged the door open. The hinges creaked. She had overheard Len asking Stick Man to oil them, but the skinny man had said it was a good early warning sound. Nobody could gently open the door without it being heard, so he hadn't oiled them.

Now they squeaked and the noise sounded like it was being played through an amplifier.

'Hello? Len? Michelle? It's Dawn.' No answer. Maybe Chatter was typing away with his earphones in again. He did this sometimes, telling her that he wanted to feel detached from the world. She didn't want to tell him that when the house got burgled, they would be in and out with his TV and he wouldn't even know it had happened.

She walked through to the back of the house. The drawing room door was closed. She knocked on it. 'Len? You in there?'

Nothing. The house was deadly quiet.

She turned the handle and opened it, making it look like she wasn't creeping about.

The room was empty.

Christ, what if he was in his bed, sleeping?

With the front door open, Dawn, love?

And was his car there? She hadn't seen it. Maybe the man-of-the-moment had taken it. To get some more Brylcream. And a deodorant stick if he had any sense.

Through to the living room, the kitchen, the front room which had another TV in it. Some place he could escape to and binge watch shows on Netflix. Probably shove some porn on when everybody else was in bed.

The ground floor was dead.

Empty, Dawn, empty. Don't say dead.

She walked up the stairs, a fairly wide set of sturdy wooden steps, with dark wood panelling on the walls. There was a door straight in front of her, and the hallways led off to the left and right. Michelle's room was down on the left. It was a large room at the back of the house. Stick Man's was opposite, his bedroom looking out to the front, onto the lawn and the perimeter wall.

'Shell? You there?' She couldn't even hear a clock ticking in the house. Knocked on Michelle's door. No answer. She tried the handle. Pushed the door.

The room was empty.

She backed out and turned to Stick's room. She knocked on the door. 'Len? You in here? It's Dawn.'

'Come in,' she heard a faint voice. Was he sleeping? Had she disturbed him? So what if she had? She didn't work for him anymore.

'I'm coming in, Len. You decent?' She thought that if he wasn't, that if he was walking about in his underwear, she would act all indignant, and demand she get her stuff back. Even though they had already taken it.

She opened the door. Len Chatter sat in a chair. He was dressed as if he was going out for a drive. *Smart but casual.* Maybe he was going clubbing at the old folks' home, she thought.

'Len. You okay? I just came to go with Michelle. Your front door was open.'

He nodded and his mouth moved open and closed a few times.

'Is Michelle here?' she asked, taking a step closer into the room.

'Y-y-y-yes,' he whispered.

'Where is she? Is she okay?'

'She'll be... okay... if they don't make a fuss.'

'They?' What was he talking about?

'Her and him.'

He meant Michelle and Stick Man. 'Where are they, Len?'

'I... they'll be okay. He promised me.'

'Who did?' Dawn looked puzzled and took a step closer.

'He did.' He was looking past Dawn now, at the open bedroom door and she could feel somebody behind her, moving as silently as a ghost and she hesitated, like she was frozen with fear for a moment, and before she could turn round, she felt a hand roughly snake round and grab her face and the needle slide into her neck.

'I'm sorry, Dawn,' Len said. His voice was distant as if he was in a different room. And now he was sideways, like he had moved his chair and it was stuck on the wall. Then she realised that she had fallen over and was lying on the carpet, looking up at Chatter. His face was crumpled, like he was crying.

She was shouting in her head, screaming at him to help her but he didn't move.

Dawn saw the other figure moving about the room but her eyes were starting to go blurry. Suddenly she was rolled onto her face so that she smelled the dust in the carpet. Rough hands grabbed her arms and pinned them back. She was being tied up.

Dawn couldn't move.

But she could feel everything.

THIRTY-EIGHT

'She should have been back home by now, surely?' Vince said, putting his car keys down on the hall table.

'She went out hours ago,' Beckett said. 'I mean, you know what it's like when two women get together, but considering that she wanted Michelle to come here and live, why not go down there and then just bring her back here right away?'

'Maybe she has a lot of stuff?'

'Maybe. But I called her to see what we should make little Vincent for his dinner and she hasn't replied.'

'Now you really are scaring me, Becksy.'

'She wouldn't just go out with Michelle on the piss, would she?'

'No, mate. I don't believe she would do that.' Although for the first time since last Saturday night, he felt a nagging doubt creeping in. What if it had all been a lot of guff? Spinning him a line about how she loved him and how she wanted to get back together. How she had sold her house and had a ton of money in the bank. What if it was a load of shite? She was skint, knew she was going to get booted out of a job and needed somewhere for her and her boy to crash?

Jesus, what if Vincent wasn't really his? *Do you want to go down that road? If you do, then now's the time to bail.*

'I'm going down to that old wanker's house. If she's there, fine, no harm. If not, then we'll have to see what she's up to.'

'Christ, don't do anything hasty, Vince. Maybe her phone's dead.'

'As I said, if that's the case, then no harm. but we found some stuff at his house when we were there getting Dawn's belongings.'

'Like what?'

'Like a blood-stained overcoat and a knife.'

Beckett stood looking at him. 'Why the fuck didn't you tell me? I never would have let her go there alone! Christ almighty. She didn't say.'

'I think she's in trouble, Becks. You with me?'

'Too right I am, brother.'

Vince grabbed his car keys and after making sure Mother was alright looking after the little boy, they left the house.

'Well?' Carol said, walking up to Watt.

'Well, what?'

'The car from last night,' she said, pulling up a chair.

'I admire your audacity, but sometimes being a detective is a slow, deliberate process. A perfectionist can't be rushed.'

'Neither can a procrastinator.'

'That too. I knew they both started with a *P*.'

'Did you do it though?'

'I did, and to be honest, I passed the result to Jack. I told him you were suspicious and that we'd questioned him. The Audi TT in Calvin Baxter's drive last night belongs to Marcie Lincoln.'

He nudged her when Harry Davidson walked up to the front of the room. 'I just wanted a brain-storming session with you all. Give you an update and see where we're at.'

Miller was standing off to one side when Jack took centre stage.

The whiteboard had photos of the murdered women on it.

'We've been doing some background research and we thought our killer was targeting random women. One had been at a singles club in Stockbridge. Now we have Amelia Arnold found dead in Inverleith Park. A nurse. Just like Iris Napier. Ruby Maxwell wasn't a nurse but a physiotherapist. At least that was our line of thinking. Then we did some background checks.

'It turns out that Ruby *was* a nurse at one time. Not only that, she worked with Iris and Amelia. Coincidence? We don't think so. Carol had cause to give a death message to a woman whose husband was killed by a hit-and-run driver in London. Tuesday of last week. At the same time, a woman called Bree Baxter went missing. She's a flight attendant and was due to fly to London, but then her husband gets a call from her employer saying she never turned up for work. In fact, there was no record of her getting the BA shuttle down to London at all and her phone was pinging in Edinburgh, before it died.'

'Where does she fit in with the three murdered women?' Watt asked.

'Bree Baxter used to be a nurse. All of them worked at St. David's hospital in Dunfermline, before it closed down five years ago. Some of them carried on with their medical careers, while some of them went on to other things, including Ruby and Bree. Ruby was a theatre nurse like Bree, but she re-trained as a physiotherapist.'

'Isn't that a bit of a climb-down from being a nurse?' Miller asked.

'Don't be a snob, Frank. Some might look at it that way, but for whatever reason, she chose to do that. Maybe she couldn't find a nurse's position in Edinburgh, or just wanted a change. Whatever it was, that was her decision.'

'So now Bree's missing and she worked as a nurse. That could still be coincidence.'

'Tell him, Andy,' Jack said, looking at Watt.

'There's no such thing. I mean, very rarely, but in this job, you find out that somewhere there's a connection.'

'Good. And there is. Bree worked with Iris, Ruby, and Amelia in the same surgical team. Carol saw Bree's husband in his office with a woman called Marcie Lincoln. She's the one whose husband was just killed in London. Nothing wrong with that, and nothing wrong with her going to see a colleague after work. But here's where there's another connection;

'Baxter used to work in St. David's alongside the nurses. He was an anaesthesiologist, on the same surgical team. When the hospital closed, Baxter took up a position in a finance company, and we think he started having an affair with Marcie Lincoln.'

'Do you think Baxter's involved?' Carol asked.

'There's nothing to indicate that just now. He was at his own promotion party on the night of Amelia's abduction and murder. Marcie Lincoln was there too. We checked. They both have alibis.'

'So his only connection to the murdered nurses is that he worked with them?' Miller said.

'Right now. But one name keeps popping up; Perry MacKinnon. He was on the surgical team too. The head surgeon was none other than celebrated author, Len Chatter. He moved to London to take up a post as consultant after St. David's closed, then he got a publishing deal and hasn't looked back. However, he did something to the tendon in his left wrist, and he's been getting physiotherapy for it. His physiotherapist was Ruby. Who he already knew.'

'Who else worked as part of Chatter's team?' Miller asked.

'Another surgeon, Miles Laing. He doesn't work in the medical field that we know of, but he's dropped off the radar for the moment. We'll find him though. Another surgeon, Hugo Flynn. He's dropped off the radar too. Not working in the medical field, or else he would be registered somewhere. We'd like to find him. Also Dawn Tait. Went to work at the BBC after the hospital closed, and lastly, a nurse called Faith Hope. She was a next door neighbour to Amelia Arnold.

She's a nurse at the Western. So that's six women who worked with Perry MacKinnon, who as it turns out, was accused of swindling money out of a woman. Now, two of those women we need to speak to. One of them, Faith, has already been spoken to by DC Miller, but we need to bring her in and see if she can help us further. Dawn Tait we're still trying to track.'

'We know a Miles Laing,' Miller said. 'It's an unusual name, so it's probably the same man.'

'You know where he is?'

'His father owns a little hotel in Stockbridge, called the *Savoy*.'

'Good. DS Watt will take you and DC Davidson. Go and speak to him. Get some background on MacKinnon and Chatter and all the rest of them. The surgical team consisted of six women and five men, four of them surgeons and the anaesthesiologist.'

'I notice that the women are all nurses,' Watt said. 'Why didn't they have a female surgeon?'

'I have no idea, Andy. That was just Chatter's team. There are some very fine female surgeon's but there just happened not to be one on that team.'

'The Old Boy's network, no doubt.'

'No doubt. But that's all changing. DCS Davidson's daughter is a pathologist in the city, as you know. It's not like in Florence Nightingale's time.'

'Not far off it. I would rather trust a woman poking about inside me,' Watt said.

'And that's just a Friday night in the pub,' Jack said.

Laughter exploded around the room.

'It's true though,' Jack said, when the laughter died down. 'Andy does have a point. Those teams aren't just thrown together last minute; they're hand-picked. Maybe Chatter and MacKinnon are misogynists. MacKinnon had bought a mews flat and had Amelia Arnold move into it. She was his girlfriend, before they split up.'

'Which would give him even more of a reason to kill Amelia,' Watt said.

'He has an alibi. But I want somebody to go and talk to his wife again. I'll go with DI Gibb. Meantime, try and see where Hugo Flynn is. Maybe he can shed some light on MacKinnon. Andy? You talk to Chatter. Go and see him again. I want more info on what MacKinnon was like outside the hospital, what he was like in a social situation.'

Jack looked around the room. 'Any more questions?'

There were none and they were dismissed.

THIRTY-NINE

'Plan of action,' Watt said when they were in the car. 'We go and speak to your pal in the hotel, and then we'll see if we can track down Faith Hope, either at home or at work. I don't suppose you got her number?'

Miller nodded. 'I did actually.' He reached into his wallet and pulled out a business card with Faith Hope's number on the back.

'See that, Carol? Got another woman's number and keeps it in his wallet.'

Miller felt his cheeks going red. 'I just got her to write it down instead of me putting it into my notebook.'

'That alright, son, you don't have to explain it in front of the future missus. Next it'll be, *Oh, it was a wrong number.*' Watt laughed. 'You should see your face. I could make toast on it.'

Watt drove down the Mound and along and up over Frederic Street, heading down to the *Savoy* hotel. They were there in five minutes.

'Don't you think it's a bit funny, a man goes from being a surgeon to a bartender?' Watt said, locking the car.

'Not really. It's a family business. He probably enjoys it and I don't think he chose it. The hospital closed down so he opted to help his father run the place.'

'This whole place must have cost a fortune,' Watt said, nodding to the empty townhouse between the hotel and MacKinnon's clinic.

'That's what working in private medicine gets you,' Carol said.

In the hotel, Miles was behind the bar. 'Hi folks! How's business?'

The place was busy but not packed. A few tourists and a scruffy man with a scruffy beard, sitting in a corner.

'We need to talk, Miles,' Carol said.

'Uh oh, that sounds ominous, Carol.' Miles' smiled slipped a bit.

'Somewhere a bit more private.'

'Sure. I was just about to knock off anyway.' He looked at the young barmaid and told her he was finishing and would be back on for the evening rush. Then he led them through to the back, where Miller and Carol had sat with Sherri in the dining room. He didn't offer them a drink this time.

'What's this about?' he said as they stood beside one of the tables.

'Perry MacKinnon,' Watt said.

'What about him?'

'We know it was him who took Sherri's money, but that's not what we want to know,' Miller said. 'We wanted to know what he was like in a social situation.'

'How would I know?'

'We know you were a surgeon, Miles,' Carol said. 'On Perry MacKinnon's surgical team. We just want to know how he behaved when he was outside. If he ever socialised with you. We know he socialised with the nurses.'

He indicated the seats round the table. 'Please, sit down.' They sat.

'Perry was very outgoing. Loved going out with women, and God knows how he didn't get caught, but it was like a drug to him.'

'Did he ever get angry with people when he was out?' Watt said.

'I didn't see him like that. I mean, we didn't go bar-hopping, but sometimes we would get invited to his golf club.'

'How did you all get on as a team?'

'We were fine. Everybody knew what to do. Some of us were trainees but Perry and Len were excellent teachers.'

'Do you know why Calvin Baxter didn't want to work in another hospital? I mean, he must have been making a lot of money.'

'I'm sure he's making a ton now. Without the stress. I would have made that decision if I was in that position.'

'You were though, weren't you?' Watt said. 'That's why you run this hotel.'

'Well, yes, but I mean… you know… if I was like him. The chance to make a lot of money.'

'How long has MacKinnon had the clinic?' Miller asked.

'He bought that place maybe a year ago. Then the place next to it. He wants to expand.'

'Do you know Bree Baxter?' Watt said.

'Bree? Yes, of course. She was part of our team.'

'Do you know she's missing?'

'What? Missing? No, I didn't know that. How did she… like, when did she go missing?'

'A week ago.'

'What? A week? Why haven't I seen this on the news? Why didn't Calvin tell me?'

'You've spoken to him recently?'

'Yes, he was in the bar with…' His voice trailed off.

'Marcie Lincoln?' Carol said. Looked him in the eye. 'We know all about them.' It was a lie but she made it sound convincing.

'I told him it wasn't a good idea, an office romance. I didn't see him for the longest time. Then they came in here one night, the two of them.' He looked at Carol. 'He's a fool. Bree is a wonderful woman. She'll be gutted to find out he was playing around behind her back.'

'Did Len Chatter have a roving eye?'

'Len? Not really.'

'You don't sound too convinced.'

Miles looked down at his feet for a moment. Then back at Carol. 'He tried it on with Bree once. When he was drunk. It was nothing. He got angry, because he was drunk. This was at a party at Perry's golf club. He stormed out. I remember thinking how lucky he was that Calvin wasn't there, and to be honest, I expected Calvin to have it out with Len, but there was nothing afterwards. I think she kept it to herself, put it down to a clumsy, drunken pass. I'm not sure Len thought it was that though, but he didn't pursue it. There was a cool air between them after that. Then the hospital shut down not long after.'

Carol looked up and saw the scruffy man who'd been in the bar, standing looking at them before he moved away and walked out the door at reception.

'Can I ask you why you decided to quit being a surgeon?' Watt asked.

'It was my father who put the idea into my head. He told me I could buy him out, have this place to myself. I'd make a lot more money than a surgeon and although it's hard work, you have a lot of people helping you. I sort of liked the idea, rather than applying for a surgeon's job all around the UK. And the rest is history.'

Watt nodded and stood up. Miller and Carol followed suit. 'Thanks for your time, Miles,' Carol said.

Outside, they left the car where it was, rather than driving for thirty seconds and spending twenty minutes trying to find another space.

'Her flat is up here,' Miller said, stopping at the door next to the pub.

Carol stepped forward and pressed the buzzer. No answer. Then again, and this time somebody spoke to them and buzzed them in when she explained who they were.

Up on the top floor, there was no answer.

'Maybe she's in trouble. Or maybe he's done something to her,' Miller said.

Watt looked at him. 'Well, you're a lot younger and uglier than I am – get the door in.' He turned to Carol. 'Get on the radio and tell them to send a patrol round here. We'll be needing this scene secured after we're done, so get them to send–'

'A joiner. It hasn't been that long since I was sitting in a patrol car, Sarge.' She turned and got on the radio while Miller shouldered the door and it sprang open.

Inside, the flat was empty. Some mail was behind the door, pushed to the wall by the door being forced open. There was a stale smell in the air, like something had been cooked days ago and a window hadn't been opened. They split up and had a look around.

'In here,' Miller said from the bathroom.

Watt came through and saw what Miller was looking at; the glass in the medicine cabinet door was cracked into a spider's web pattern. And there was blood in the sink. And on the tile floor.

'Looks like he smashed her face into the cabinet,' Miller said, turning to look at Watt.

'Jesus Christ. I'll get onto forensics and get them down here. I hope it's not too late.'

'Faith Hope said she went to the singles club with Amelia Arnold. What if he watched them both?'

'This is not random, Frank. This bastard is targeting them, for whatever reason.'

FORTY

'My father was shaken up by it all,' the young woman said, sitting down opposite Jack Miller and Paddy Gibb.

'We were gathering some names, people who worked at St. David's before it closed. We were looking at people associated with Perry MacKinnon. One name that came up was your father's, Hugo Flynn.'

'He doesn't use the name Hugo anymore; he uses his middle name, Robert.'

The house was a detached bungalow in Craigcrook Avenue. It was very well kept but Jack could see dust floaters in a ray of sunshine coming in through the living room window. No doubt the woman would be out with a duster after they were gone.

She hung her head and wrung her hands together. Then looked Jack in the eyes. 'Is this about the murders of those nurses?'

'It is, yes.'

'Oh, God, do you think my father's responsible?' Her lip quivered as she spoke.

'We just want to talk to him about Perry MacKinnon.'

'God, MacKinnon. I can't believe any of them would do this. They were all so tight, you know what I mean? Until the incident.'

'What incident?'

More wringing of the hands. 'Until my father killed a woman.'

Jack looked at Gibb before carrying on. 'What woman was this?'

'A patient. In for surgery. It was something he couldn't talk about for the longest time.'

'Tell us what happened,' Gibb said.

'It was a routine surgery. You have to understand, I don't know the whole story. He wouldn't talk to me. Wouldn't open up and talk about it. All he said was, a woman died because of him. That's why he called it a day when the hospital closed. He retrained in computers, something he was actually quite good at. But he couldn't live here anymore.'

'Where is he now?'

'He was living with a friend, just renting a room. Then he found a small hotel where he was renting a room on a long-term basis.'

'Do you know the name of it?'

'The *Savoy*, in Stockbridge.'

'How did he get on with his colleagues when he was a surgeon?'

'He didn't talk about his work much. He was pretty devastated when the hospital closed. He seemed a different man. He got angry a lot. Started drinking more. But it was the anger I remember most.'

'Was there anybody else who lived here with you at the time?'

'No. My mother died a long time ago and I spilt with my fiancé, so I moved back in here with dad. He sold the house to me when he moved out. I told him he could have stayed here with me, but he didn't want that.'

'Did he ever socialise with people he used to work with?'

'No, not after he left. He became like a recluse.'

'Did he ever talk about having a grudge against those he worked with?'

'No. Never. He never had a bad word to say about anybody.'

'You said he retrained,' Gibb said. 'Where does he work now?'

'Freelance. He's a contractor. Or was, the last time I spoke to him. He worked from wherever he was living.'

'Do you know if he ever had any contact with his former colleagues?'

'If he did, he didn't say. He wouldn't talk to me much, especially after the incident.'

'Was he investigated after the woman died?' Jack said. 'Maybe that's what caused his depression?'

'Oh no, nothing like that. It wasn't like that at all. You don't understand.'

'Help us to understand,' Jack said.

And the woman started telling them what had happened.

FORTY-ONE

'Well, you're not very chatty. Not feeling up to it?' the surgeon said as he stepped into the room. 'Not surprising really; your tongue will be a bit woolly for a while. Oh, and if you feel your leg getting a bit itchy, I can get you a knitting needle to get right under there for a scratch.'

Dawn couldn't speak but he could see her eyes wondering, looking into his eyes. He was wearing his full scrubs, including the face mask. She couldn't see who he was, but even if she could, it didn't matter. She wouldn't be going home again.

'I just popped in to see how you were before your surgery tomorrow. And guess what? Len will be watching. I'm making him watch this afternoon too. He won't be invited to participate of course, he'll be here just as an observer. I might let him in on your surgery. Would you like that, Dawn?'

Dawn tried to talk but nothing was coming out.

'The gang's all here. I thought it would be very fitting for the finale. I wanted to string things out a bit but the ending was always open to interpretation.'

Dawn looked at him with fuzzy eyes. He smiled at her but she couldn't see him smile behind the mask. He was dressed head to toe in his scrubs.

'Well, Dawn, my sweet, as much as I would love to stay and chat, I have a lot of things to do. I fear the police are snooping too closely, and things must be wrapped up sooner than I anticipated. You just relax though. It'll be your turn tomorrow. Aren't you excited? I wish you could stay and see what I have in store for Len, but I have a tight schedule. By this time tomorrow, this place will be a funeral pyre.'

He walked out of the room and down the corridor. The hospital was warm from the day's heat but he didn't feel it. All he felt was an electric buzz as he walked, his shoes squeaking on the floor.

He turned down another hallway, this one a little bit darker than the other ones. The surgical suite was always kept a little bit more muted. He hit the button on the wall and the doors into the first suite opened. He walked in and sucked in the antiseptic smell. It was like an expensive perfume, or a fine wine. Intoxicating. He'd missed this smell for the longest time. He washed his hands in the scrubbing area. Not that he needed to of course, but it was just part of being a surgeon. He opened one of the other doors that led into the operating room itself.

The room was in semi-darkness, just a few select lights on, but it was the main one above the operating table that shone the most light.

Highlighting the woman lying on it.

The surgeon stood on one side of her, a man on the other.

'Why are you doing this?' Len Chatter asked him.

'Simple; I'm going to show you that I'm a better surgeon than you ever were. *Old man.*' He wiped his hands with a towel.

'I always knew you were a good surgeon. You were better than me.'

'I know I was! I was better then than you ever were. And now I'm going to show you.'

Chatter staggered back from the table, his head swimming.

'Whoa there, Lenny. Anybody would think that you've been drinking.' He laughed at his own joke.

'You don't have to do this.'

'Oh, but I do. My hand was forced years ago. I didn't choose to go down this road. I was pushed onto it and told to get on with it.'

'It was a mistake.'

'Yes it was. And now you're all paying for that mistake. Sucks for you, doesn't it?'

Chatter closed his eyes and swayed for a moment.

'Len, if you don't look at what I'm doing, I'll cut your eyes out.'

Chatter opened his eyes and looked at the surgeon.

'That's better. But then, you never did have any manners, did you?' He looked at the older man but Chatter said nothing. 'Answer me!'

'No, I didn't have any manners.'

'Better. Just remember who's in charge here now.'

The patient on the table looked back at him. Her eyes weren't moving, which was a good sign. He knew her muscles couldn't move, so there was no chance of her body moving.

'Watch and learn, Lenny. Watch and learn.'

The woman had been prepped for surgery. She was covered in a green surgical sheet and a rectangle revealed her front. The surgeon took a scalpel and held it up for Lenny to see. 'Where would you start the cut?'

'What?'

'It's not a hard question. Where would you start the cut?'

Chatter sneered at him. 'Forgotten, have you?'

Laughter behind the face mask. 'That's funny. You should have written comedy novels. But just for that...'

He moved towards the woman's face and ran the scalpel down her cheek. Blood ran from the wound, coursing down her cheek to her neck.

'Now, you do know that she can still feel but not move, don't you?' he said to Chatter. 'She's probably screaming in her head now. And that's all on you, Lenny. Do you want me to take her eyeball out next?'

'No, please don't. I'm sorry. Please leave her alone. You don't have to do this. You've made a point with the others. It can stop here.'

The surgeon looked at the author. 'Can it? What do you think they would do to me if they caught me? They can't do any more than they already will. One, five, ten, it's all the same. I'll get the same punishment. So why should I stop now? Every one of you had the chance to stop five years ago. None of you did though. All of Lenny's little group decided to close ranks. That's how it worked, didn't it?'

'You know it wasn't like that.'

'I beg to differ.'

'It was a mistake. She's got nothing to do with it.' He nodded to the prone woman on the table.

'She had everything to do with it! Her and the rest of them.' He looked away from Chatter and down at the woman. A single tear had escaped her eye and was running down her cheek to mix with the blood.

'Right, Lenny, time to get this show on the road. I've got a full roster.' He looked at the old man. 'The top, just below the ribcage. Right?'

Chatter just stared at him.

'I said right?!' The surgeon's scream was loud in the room.

'Right.' The answer was spoken softly and was barely out of his mouth when the surgeon made the first cut.

'Christ, where is she?' Vince said, knocking on the door again. Dawn's car was outside, so he knew she had at least been here. He looked around for his brother but he was nowhere to be seen. He'd slipped round the side of Len Chatters house a few minutes ago.

'Vince, quick.'

Vince turned round at the sound of his brother. 'Jesus. Fucking creeping about like that.'

'Come on. The back door's open.' He had taken his brace off, feeling like his leg was eighty per cent better.

Vince followed him. The back door was indeed open but whether it had been that way when Beckett got there, was debatable. The small broken pane of glass suggested that it might not have been.

'We'll sweep each room, and if that big twat comes at us, I'll let him have it good and proper this time,' Beckett said.

'Hey, it's my turn. You already flushed his head down the lavvy. I want to boot him in the nuts now.'

'He's all yours.'

'Dawn!' Vince shouted. 'Chatter! We're here for Dawn, then we'll leave.' Nothing.

They made their way through the rooms downstairs, but saw nothing. No sign of Dawn.

'Let's get upstairs,' Vince said, eager to get on.

They walked up to the next level. 'Dawn!' Vince shouted again. Then they heard the thump.

'It's coming from there,' Becket said, stopping outside a door. They heard it again. The door was locked. Vince stood back and kicked the door. It flew open and he reached in and turned on a light. The curtains had been drawn.

He and Vince stood still for a moment. There were two figures in the room. Only one of them was alive.

'You know, people with money always land on their feet,' Watt said, parking the car outside Len Chatter's house. 'It's up to us to trip them up.'

He got out with Miller and Carol close behind. They walked

through the wooden gate and up to the front door but there was no answer.

'If in doubt, check round the back,' Miller said.

'Looks like somebody already has,' Carol said when she saw the door open and the broken glass.

They took out their extendable batons and went inside. They began searching the ground floor. Miller went into the drawing room. Chatter's Mac was on but there was no sign of him. 'Looks like he might have been disturbed,' he said, seeing the type on the screen where it had been left open at a page in a book.

'Let's get upstairs,' Watt said.

Along the landing, a man stepped out and Miller raised his truncheon. 'Police, stay where you are.'

'Christ, that was quick.'

'What do you mean?'

'Vince, is that them now?'

'Yes. I think.'

'Who are you?' Watt said, stepping forward.

'Vince Rutherford. I'm the one who called you.'

They heard the sirens outside as a patrol car pulled in.

'What's going on?'

Vince showed them inside. Michelle had been untied from the chair she'd been bound to. Stick Man was still in the other chair. It was clear he was dead by the pallor of his skin. There were no obvious wounds.

'Somebody tell me what's going on here. And keep your hands where I can see them.'

'We came here looking for my girlfriend, Dawn Tait,' Vince said, as Beckett sat with Michelle on the bed. Two chairs were sitting back-to-back. 'We didn't find Dawn, but we found Michelle tied and gagged.'

Watt looked at the woman. 'Did Chatter do this?'

She shook her head. 'No. Another man. He was dressed like a

surgeon. He injected me with something. He came into the house and he and Len were arguing. I saw Dawn, but my head was starting to swim by then.'

'And he tied you up in here,' Watt said, wondering why he hadn't just killed her.

'Yes. I woke up and felt myself tied to him. I banged the chair on the floor when I heard Vince and Beckett shouting. They came in and untied me. I think he's dead. He has asthma. Maybe he had an asthma attack.'

'That's why we called the police and an ambulance,' Beckett said. 'Dawn's car is outside but there's no sign of her. This surgeon guy must have taken her and Chatter.'

'Any idea where?'

Michelle looked at them. 'I don't know, but I do remember him saying one thing before I passed out. He said, *We're going home, Len.*'

FORTY-TWO

Carol stayed behind at Chatter's house in Trinity, to supervise the incoming patrols until a uniformed inspector could get there.

'Jack, slow down,' Miller said, pressing his mobile phone harder to his ear. He was trying to hear his father above the noise of paramedics working on Stick Man. Even if he was dead, they had to show they tried to revive him.

'We spoke to Hugo Flynn's daughter. Get to the *Savoy* as quickly as you can.

'He's a what?' he asked again, letting go of the seat and putting a finger in his ear.

'A surgeon. He was a surgeon. He fucked up an operation, a woman died and they all covered for him. It was swept under the carpet, but he was a broken man after that. He didn't go back into medicine after the hospital shut down.'

'Then where is he?'

'At the hotel. He's been staying there.'

'We'll be there in five.'

Watt floored the car, while Miller held onto the side of his seat, holding his phone with the other hand. The lights and sirens cut through the traffic as they rounded the corner at Goldenacre, heading down Inverleith Row.

Dean Terrace was blocked with police cars so Watt pulled behind a patrol car parked on Deanhaugh Street. He and Miller ran along to the hotel.

Jack was there with Gibb. 'There's no fucking sign of him. He's gone.'

'What does he look like?'

'Scruffy bastard. Walks with a stick.'

Miller was silent for a moment. 'Dishevelled hair, beard, talks with a cockney accent?'

'The description's right, but he's not cockney. Far from it. Upper class Edinburgh. Snooty as they come.'

'Unless he was faking it.'

'Could be. We're waiting for the warrants now. I want that fucking hotel ripped apart.'

'What makes you think he's the *Surgeon*?'

'I don't. Not a hundred per cent, but we're going to damn well make sure.'

'Tell me why you're thinking he fits the frame,' Miller said.

'He worked with those nurses. Worked with Perry MacKinnon. Maybe he was pissed off that they had careers and he was washed up. So he took his revenge on them.'

'Christ, sir, he walks with a stick. How could he have climbed over the railings to dump Iris Napier at St. Bernard's Well?'

'He doesn't need a stick.'

'What?'

Jack turned round as one of the other DCs came up with the warrants. 'His daughter says he uses the walking stick as a mental as well as a physical crutch. He hides behind it.'

'It still doesn't make sense.'

'Neither does killing three women.'

'Why wait all this time?'

'God, Frank, who knows why those bastards do what they do. But Hugo Flynn has the motive.'

'Where did he kill Iris and Amelia? Then wash them?'

'In his fucking room, Frank. He has his own bathroom. And see that down there?' He pointed over the railings into the basement of the hotel. 'That's the draymen's entrance. The barrels of beer are dropped off here and then they slide down there, and get taken into the cellar. He can come out there with a body at 3 am and up those stairs.' He pointed to a little gate that led down to the basement. 'There's very little foot traffic and no cars coming past since they closed the end of the road off to through traffic. This bastard picked this hotel. He had it all planned. He was getting back at the people he worked with because he was jealous.'

'Christ, he's taken Len Chatter and Dawn, his assistant.'

'When was this?'

'I tried to tell you; a couple of hours ago. He left behind Dawn's nanny and one of Len Chatter's other assistants. A man. He died when he was tied to a chair. He had asthma and the nanny reckons he died from a severe asthma attack.'

'That just goes to prove my point; he isn't killing people who aren't involved. He's just taking revenge on those he worked with. They covered for him at the time, but he knew life for him was over. It was enough to put him over the edge.'

Carol pulled up in the patrol car that she'd driven from the Western. She ran over to Miller.

'Did you find Faith?' he asked.

'No. She's taken some time off. They don't know where she is.'

'God Almighty, where the hell did she go?'

Miller watched as more uniforms piled out of two vans.

'Guests can leave if they want, but I want every room searched. Nobody gets in the way. If they do, restrain them.'

They piled into the hotel, starting with the bar, and patrons were told to leave. The barmaid ushered them out, telling them their drinks would be okay and they could wait outside while the police did what they had to do. Miller looked at her, thinking she was familiar, but he couldn't place her.

'Gibb, get upstairs with Watt and supervise emptying the rooms. Frank, with me.'

He went through to reception where a young woman was sitting behind the desk. 'Where's Miles Laing?'

'He's out at a meeting with the brewery, I think. Or maybe he's at the cash and carry.' She shrugged. 'He's somewhere.'

'Okay, you're it. I need to know how many guests are in their rooms. And here's the copy of the search warrants.'

She took the warrants and checked the keys. 'All the keys are here. Nobody's in their room.'

'What about Hugo Flynn?'

'Who?'

'He goes by the name *Robert*.'

'Oh, Bob. He's out. At least his key's here.'

'Where's his room?'

'Downstairs. There are a few rooms there but only two of them are used at the moment; Bob and the American women are in them. Sherri Judd.'

'Where are the rooms?'

She pointed behind her. 'The stairs are there. You go down, turn right, along the hallway and round the corner.'

'Christ, rooms down in the dungeons. I hope they get a discount.'

'They're not the honeymoon suite, if that's what you mean.'

'Keys. Or we can take the doors off their hinges. Your call.'

She handed over the keys.

'Now you can go upstairs with the keys and unlock all the doors.'

Jack turned to one of the uniforms. 'Stay here.' Then back to the receptionist. 'No phone calls to anybody in here warning them we're here. That's accessory to murder.'

'No photos for Facebook either?'

Jack ignored her and led the way to the stairs. 'I don't care how old she is, if she was my daughter, she'd be going across my fucking knee. People nowadays have no respect for the law.'

Miller let his father ramble on, thinking he had a point.

Uniforms were leading the charge downstairs. The light was definitely more low-key down here. They followed the instructions they were given; turn right, along the hallway and round the corner.

Two doors faced them. Jack looked at the uniform who was in the lead. 'The door facing you. Get it open.' He handed him the key. The door was opened.

It was Sherri's room. The window looked out onto the shared back gardens with the other townhouses. There were bars on the windows. It looked more like a prison cell. They searched everything but nothing stuck out.

Next was Hugo Flynn's room. The ex-surgeon's room was unremarkable. Nothing of interest was in his drawers or his wardrobe. It wasn't until they opened up his laptop that things got interesting.

I'm not sorry for what I've done. The pain they endured was nothing to what I've had to endure. I couldn't stand to see them getting away with it anymore. It's done now. By the time anybody reads this, it will all be over. We all went home. Back to where it started. Hugo.

Jack turned to Miller. 'Does that answer your question?'

Miller read the words again. 'What did his daughter say again?'

'That his scalpel slipped and he nicked an artery in the woman's chest. She bled out. But Miles Laing took the fall. They blamed him. He was ruined after that.'

'Why did they choose Miles as the fall guy?'

'He was an alcoholic. He was the easy mark. However, a nurse saw what happened and spoke up. She was railroaded as well.'

'Bree Baxter?'

'No. Faith Hope. She works here part-time.'

'Christ, I saw the barmaid a few minutes ago, and I thought she looked familiar. I think it was her.'

'Christ, Frank. She doesn't have a clue what danger she's in.'

'She's outside with the guests.'

'I'll go and get her.' Carol took off running. Miller went upstairs, following her.

Outside, some of the customers from the bar were milling about. Others had decided they would sacrifice their drink and go find a new watering hole.

Carol was standing looking around at the small crowd, trying to see the barmaid. She couldn't find her. She went down the steps and got hold of one of the customers.

'Have you seen the barmaid who came out with you?'

'No, I don't know where she went.'

Miller came down the steps. 'Do you see her?'

'No. She's disappeared.'

'Oh, Christ. Something feels off about this.'

'What do you mean?'

'I'm not sure. Just something buzzing about on the edge of my brain.' He looked at her. 'You read the message in there. Do you think Hugo Flynn's gone somewhere to kill himself? Or was he waiting for an opportunity to take Faith?'

'God knows. Maybe both, Frank.'

'Let's go along to the clinic.' He started walking further along, Carol beside him. Inside, the reception area was cool. 'I'd like to speak with Doctor MacKinnon,' Miller said, holding out his warrant card.

'He's not here.'

'Where is he?' Carol asked.

'He got a phone call a little while ago. He said it was urgent and that he had to go out.'

'Did he say where he was going?'

The receptionist looked at them. 'He said he was going home.'

FORTY-THREE

'By Christ, that was fun!' the surgeon said. The face mask was blowing rapidly, in and out, in and out, like he had just run a marathon.

He looked over at Calvin Baxter, still sitting bound to the wheelchair. 'I know you couldn't see the whole show sitting there, but Len is going to tell you how well I did.' He looked over at Chatter, who looked like he was about to fall over.

'Tell him how good I was, Len. You don't mind if I call you *Len*, do you, Len?'

Chatter shook his head.

'That's good. I feel we're all pals here now. Like the good old days. Now we're all back home. Just like we used to be. So, give me marks out of ten.' He looked across the table, across the bloodied corpse. Then quickly at Calvin again, just to make sure he was still awake.

'Ten,' Chatter said. 'It was a good, solid ten.'

'Well, did you hear that, Cal? A good, solid ten. What about you? How many marks? Pretend we're on TV. Give it a few seconds to build up the tension. How many marks for killing your wife?'

'Fuck you. That was the worst piece of surgery I've ever seen.'

'Aw, listen to him, Lenny; he isn't having a good day. You are though, aren't you?'

No answer.

'Len!' the surgeon screamed. 'Are you paying attention?'

'Yes, yes, I just feel a little tired, that's all.'

'That'll be all those trips you have to make to the bank. It must be a pain making all that money. I'll bet you could use a wheelbarrow, taking all the money to the bank.'

'Not quite.'

The surgeon laughed and looked at Calvin. And the other two men who were also sitting in wheelchairs, restrained. 'Listen to that, boys! *Not quite!* Can you believe that? This man has money dripping out of more places than I have places. And let me tell you, Perry, you thought you were going to buy the *Savoy*.' He looked at Chatter. 'Tell him who just signed on the dotted line, Len. Tell him who pulled the rug from right underneath him. Go ahead, we're all listening.'

'Me. It was me. I bought it.'

'It's amazing what you can do when you have amazing computer skills. You can look into places that normally you wouldn't get past the gate. And that's when I found out that Mr Nasty there bought the hotel. Not you, Mr MacKinnon, but the world famous author. So you see, your plan to extend your clinic into three townhouses, just came crashing down.'

'Is this true, Len?' MacKinnon said, ever the businessman.

'Yes.'

'Straight from the horse's mouth, eh? Don't take my word for it. And why don't you tell Perry why Len was able to do this, Cal?'

Calvin sat stock still in the wheelchair. 'I don't know.'

The surgeon laughed. 'Calvin doesn't know. Did you hear that Lenny? Calvin's memory is slipping gears now.' He looked at the other man in another wheelchair, but his head was still slumped over. 'He doesn't have an opinion yet, as he's still asleep. But let me tell you why Lenny boy here was able to buy the hotel; because Perry couldn't. Calvin didn't want to lend him the money. That's right, ladies and gentlemen, Calvin, the man who works for a finance company, wouldn't do his job and lend his old pal the money.'

'He's a big risk, and you know it.'

'No I'm fucking not!' MacKinnon screamed at the top of his voice.

The surgeon laughed again. 'Yes you are. I looked at your financial records. You took on too much by buying the townhouse between your clinic and the hotel. You were getting too greedy, Perry. You were starting to become a risk and Cal there knew it.'

Len Chatter winced. He knew this wasn't going too well. And decided to make a move.

'I'll give *you* the hotel,' he said.

The surgeon turned to look at him. 'I beg your pardon?'

'I said, I'll give you the hotel. For free. You can keep it and you don't owe me a penny. Just let me go.'

The surgeon laughed. 'Oh I see. Just like that? I kill some of you, and then you come up with the idea to give me the hotel. Wouldn't it have been better to give me it before I started murdering women? Oh, wait, that wouldn't work, would it? Something drastic must happen for you to give me the hotel. And when it's too late, you notice. And in order for me to get away without any witnesses, you're all going to die.'

'For God's sake, you don't have to do this. You've hurt us all enough now.'

'That'll be for me to decide. Now, if I did let you go, you'd be able to play around with your girlfriend, now that I've just killed your wife, wouldn't you?'

Nothing.

'Answer me, Calvin!'

'Yes, yes.'

'Then, that would mean you could go on with your life and you would be able to get the insurance money I'm sure you have on her. She was murdered by a raving psychopath. So why won't you do me a favour and finance me?'

'I will, I will, I promise! Now, just tell me where Marcie is.'

'Okay, I will. She's right here.' He whipped the green sheet from her face. Marcie's glassy eyes stared back at him. Calvin forced himself into a half-standing position and he let out a scream when he saw her.

'What have you done, you bastard!'

'You didn't think I'd let you off so lightly, did you? Kill your wife, indeed. You and I both know you wouldn't finance me, and you would be running about with Marcie, free as a bird. You see, I thought she would be upset when her husband died, but that's what you both wanted. No, Bree is alive and well. For now.'

'Where is she?'

'Not your concern now, Calvin. Just rest assured that you'll all be getting it.'

'Listen, we all have money. We can make sure you're okay. Calvin will damn well make sure you get a loan,' MacKinnon said, but when he looked over at Calvin, the financier's head was bowed and he was sobbing.

'Don't cry, Calvin, it will soon be over. We have another show starting in five minutes. However, you lot won't be around to see it. Sorry, folks, but for you, the war is over.'

He turned and picked up something from behind him. It was a roll of packing cling film, on a roller. Perry MacKinnon and Calvin Baxter began pulling against their restraints.

'What the fuck are you doing?' Calvin screamed. But the surgeon started wrapping his face. Round and round, laughing all the time he was doing it.

Dawn had pulled the needle out of her arm a while back, but kept the needle in place, against her skin, not under it. The tape held it in place so a quick glance would let somebody think that it was still in situ. The meds had worn off and now she was waiting her time.

Which was now.

After the last scream.

Whatever was going on, it wasn't good. A man dressed as a surgeon had come for Len a while back, and now the empty bed across from her was a constant reminder that she was next. Was the man torturing Len? She hoped not, but she knew she wouldn't be able to go and help him.

Not with the plaster cast on her leg.

Len had one on too. It was genius really; who could run away with a plaster cast on their leg, keeping it straight?

She was going to try it anyway. She might not get far, but maybe far enough to hide, until she could go and get help. She didn't know where she was, but she would figure it out. All she had to do was find her way out of this building first.

Her head swam for a moment when she got out of the bed. *Fuck me, I'll never get out of here. Just grin and bear it, Dawn. You've been through worse. Really? When? What's worse than getting taken by a fucking serial killer. Stop! Concentrate.*

She took some deep breaths. Steadied herself against the wall and pulled the door open. The corridor was empty. The place was quiet, apart from the screaming coming from further along the corridor.

Where the hell was everybody?

This is not a normal hospital, Dawn. You know that don't you? You realised that as soon as you woke up. Oh yes, it looks like a hospital, but this isn't a hospital that's used every day.

The smell hit her as she stepped out into the corridor. This place looked normal at first glance, but as she leaned against the wall, she could see the crude brushstrokes of paint slapped on in a hurry.

She could see the stairs at the end of the corridor. She got her legs to move, lifting the one with the cast on it and putting it forward, leaning on the wall for support. Sliding along the wall. Pushing away from it to get past a fire alarm box that had broken glass in it. Had somebody used it to summon the fire brigade a long time ago, or was it not part of the refurbishment program?

Her question was answered when she got to the stairs.

They were clean, but the debris from the ceiling above them had been roughly swept down to the bottom. She grabbed the handrail, hoping, praying that she wouldn't feel her bodyweight pulling her forward.

The stairs were made of stone. The handrail, polished wood, supported by iron railings. They probably looked good when the hospital was first built many moons ago. She hopped down one step, grabbing the handrail with her right leg sticking straight out. Her head swam again, and she was sweating. She realised she was wearing her clothes. Her jeans leg had been cut off for the crudely applied plaster to be applied.

She sat on the top step and began to bump her way down, her right leg straight, but using her hands and left foot to make her way down. Then she was at the landing where the stairs turned left at ninety degrees. She could feel the sweat lashing off her. Light was coming in from downstairs. Then a flash of memory shot into her head. As she scooted herself forward and got round to the big set of stairs, she looked down. The stairs were open to the corridor below. And to one of the doors that led outside. The memory was of Vince.

"Dawn!" he said, coming towards her, holding a small bunch of flowers.

"This is a nice surprise!"

'This is our six-month anniversary. I wanted to surprise you and take you to dinner.'

"That's so nice. But I didn't get you anything," she said, taking the flowers and smelling them.

"You're here with me, that's enough. Come on, I have a reservation."

He had been standing down at the bottom of these very stairs! How long ago had that been? Almost seven years. She could feel the tears coursing down her cheeks now. She was never going to see her little boy again. Or Vince. She had left it too late to get back together with him. The only little ray of sunshine in her heart was the fact that Vince would look after their son. Now she knew where they were; the old hospital where she used to work.

Then an explosion of anger shot through her. *No! I will not give up without a fight! You want to take me back upstairs, then fight me face to face instead of creeping about with your syringe!*

She knew she would quite happily take it off him and ram it into his eyeball. Faster down to the bottom of these stairs. She needed to get outside. Scooting round the corner now, the last flight, down to the bottom. Christ, she had made it. She pulled herself up into a standing position.

Had she just imagined this was the place Vince had come to her all those years ago? Her mind filling in the gaps in her terror with perfect memories to spare her from the horror of her situation?

No, this was real. This place was real.

The floor was littered with debris. Graffiti adorned the walls. She hobbled over to the double doors that led into a large vestibule. Cringed as one of them squeaked. The glass in the panes was cracked but had held up. Across more debris, then to the main doors. One was ajar. It opened easily. Then she grabbed a hold of the pitted hand railing. She held on and hopped down the steps, out into the open. She knew this place like the back of her hand. All she had to do was turn left and make her way down the hill. That would mean she was out in the open, but if her escape hadn't been noticed, then she might have plenty of time.

The sun was hot, making her sweat more. She could feel it running down her back like a river. Then she saw the temporary security fence running round the property. There had to have been a way in though. Maybe he had brought them in round the back.

She changed direction, turning right. Hobbling as fast as she could. This entrance was round the side of the building, and then she saw it; the fence had been moved. One of the fence posts had been pulled out of the concrete fastening and then put back, left to sit on the ground.

Her escape route.

Then she heard it. A car coming. Driving over the gravel, the tyres crunching. Christ, now what?

She saw an old communal bin. That wasn't where it lived when she worked here, but somebody had obviously moved it here for whatever reason. She hobbled over to it and ducked behind it.

The car drove past and stopped outside an old garage block. She kept down, heard the driver's door open then the sliding garage door open and then the car drove in. The engine was turned off and then the sliding door sounded again. She made herself look as small as somebody who was wearing a leg cast possibly could. She was looking under the bin. The fence was moved then put back again as the person came inside the boundary. That's when she saw the shoes walk past. And then she knew.

She stayed where she was, listening to the sound of the receding footsteps.

Then she tried to move. And couldn't.

FORTY-FOUR

'Hear me out,' Miller said to Jack when they got back from the clinic.

'What is it?' Jack was standing on the steps, talking to a uniform.

'Let me run this past you; what if Hugo Flynn wasn't working alone?'

'What? You mean he had a partner? First of all, we don't know if he's guilty. He's just a person of interest.'

'What if he was though? It always bothered me that somebody would struggle with a body at St. Bernard's Well. If there were two of them, then maybe they could have done it together.'

'Listen, son, there's no evidence to suggest he is.'

'I know that, but that timeline doesn't make sense. Ruby Maxwell and Amelia Arnold killed round about the same time.'

'Not exactly at the same time, but round about. It's not an exact science, Frank. He might have done them both, one right after the other.'

'Hugo Flynn? Have you even see him? I have. He's not a body builder.'

'Okay then, just suppose for a minute that he was working with somebody. Who is it?'

'This is a shot in the dark, but... Faith Hope.'

'What? The nurse? The one who's on his hit list?'

'We were in her bathroom this morning. The cabinet door mirror was smashed with blood all over it, like somebody's face had been rammed into it. Possibly to make us think that maybe she's a victim. We know he was working his way through the list. If that was the case and he attacked her, she would have her face messed up.'

'Probably. We are trying to locate her now, Frank.'

'I know where she is.'

'You do? Where?'

'Here.'

'He's right' Carol said.

'We met her in her flat when she told us about Amelia having moved out into a place her boyfriend bought, remember?'

'Yes, I read your report.'

'A dark-haired young woman.'

'I remember her, Frank. I didn't see her here.'

'You did. You just didn't recognise her, just like I didn't at first. Her face was familiar but I couldn't place it.'

'Where was she?'

'The barmaid. She was behind the bar when we came in.'

'But that girl's face wasn't marked,' Jack said.

'Exactly! It wouldn't be if she was working with Flynn.'

'Let me go and ask that lassie in reception.' Jack went inside, followed by Miller and Carol. The girl was still at reception.

'The barmaid,' Jack said. 'The one who was behind the bar when we came in. What's her name?'

'Faith.'

'Last name.'

'Hope. She's a nurse, but she works here on her days off. She's good friends with Miles.'

'Where is she now?'

'Outside.'

'No, she's not.'

'She was. I saw her go out with the guests.'

Miller turned to one of the uniforms and issued some instructions. He and some of his colleagues set off to search the hotel. The man came back and reported that Faith was nowhere to be found.

They went back along the lobby to the front door. Carol went to see if she could see Faith milling about. 'She's gone, and now Perry MacKinnon is gone as well.'

'What do you mean?'

'He's not in the clinic. We checked. He's not at his house. He told his receptionist he was going home,' Miller said.

'So? Maybe he stopped off on the way.'

'You're not listening to me; when Flynn took Len Chatter, he said he was taking him home.'

'Get to the point.'

'I think they're at the old hospital. The one where they worked before it closed. That's what it felt like to them, the surgical team; home.'

'That's a shot in the dark.'

'Have it checked out.'

'Christ, talk about wasting time, but I'll get onto Fife, have somebody swing by there.'

'Thank you.' Miller walked over to Carol while Jack got on his phone. 'Any luck?'

'She's nowhere to be seen.'

'Jack's going to have a patrol car swing by the hospital.'

'Okay, and if they're not there, where will they be?'

'I don't know, but we won't stop looking for Flynn.'

'I saw him. When we were in the dining room, he was hovering around outside, listening.'

They chit-chatted outside. It took the patrol car 15 minutes to swing by through the hospital in Fife and report back that the place was closed and had a security fence round it. No vehicles were on the property.

'Frank. Carol,' Jack said, coming out of the hotel. 'There's nobody there. They swung by and it's clear.' He turned and went back in.

'Fuck. It's the only place that made sense.'

'Did they check right inside the hospital, sir?' Carol said. 'I mean, get out of the car and have a good look inside?'

Jack stopped. Turned around. 'No. They said they just drove up to the perimeter. Gave it a cursory glance. But they did say the fence was there.'

'A cursory glance? They might be inside, being held by a serial killer and the foot soldiers gave it a *cursory glance?*'

Jack looked thoughtful. 'Both of you, go with Andy Watt. If anybody from Fife gives you hassle, get them to call me. We'll be busy here for a while. It won't take you long with the blues on. Don't waste any time and then get back here.'

'Thank you, sir.'

Watt came out of the hotel a few minutes later. 'Whose idea was this?'

'It was mine,' Miller said. 'I just thought–'

'Hold that thought, Frank. I just wanted you to know that I'll buy you both a drink next time we're in the club. I was bored out of my tits in there.'

Miller smiled as they walked along to the car. 'I won't argue with that.'

They got in the car and Watt sat in the back seat, after tossing the keys to Miller. 'Boot it. Let's see your driving skills in action.'

Carol sat in the front.

'You don't usually get bored raking through a woman's knicker drawer, Sarge,' Miller said as he pulled away.

'Just for that, the first round's on you.'

'Shit. I should learn to keep my mouth shut.'

'Don't,' Watt said. 'If it wasn't for you speaking up, we wouldn't be going on a hooly to Fife.'

'Should we alert them we're on our way?'

'And have them tell us to take a back seat? Fuck 'em.'

'You think Faith Hope could be capable of this?' Carol said.

'Nurses are strong, physically. So yes, I think she would be more than capable of helping Hugo Flynn.'

Miller headed for Queensferry Road, the siren blaring. It was two lanes on both sides, so he made good time out to South Queensferry and the Forth Road Bridge, expertly weaving the car through the traffic. Another few minutes and they were taking the slip road for Dunfermline.

'It's not far from here,' Miller said. 'It's in a country setting, in its own land. I read a while back that they're going to convert the main hospital into flats and build houses on the land.'

Left at the roundabout, then Miller cut the siren. Up ahead was the entrance to the old St. David's Hospital, the sign now faded and vandalised. There were stone pillars at the end of the driveway.

Miller took the car in, driving steadily, not roaring the engine. Some outbuildings were on their left as the road cut through the trees, which would have been kept trimmed, back in the day. Then they rounded a corner and saw the imposing main building in the distance. Smaller buildings – no less imposing – surrounded the main building like they were giant Lego buildings dropped into place. Wire fencing was indeed round the building, steel panels sitting in concrete feet.

'Maybe we got it wrong,' Miller said.

'This is what the patrol saw. Nothing seems disturbed or out of place. They didn't go in. But, we are going in.'

The main door at the front was boarded up, but Miller saw a side entrance that looked like it didn't have boards on it. 'Over there, Andy.'

Miller pulled up opposite the door, stopping outside the fence. They got out.

FORTY-FIVE

Dawn stayed where she was, unable to move at first, but she knew she had to. They would discover she was gone, and then they'd come looking for her, knowing she couldn't have gotten far. Then they'd find her and kill her.

Then she thought about her boys; her baby and the man who was going to be her husband. The two Vince's. That was what spurred her on. She got to her feet, her right leg sticking out at an awkward angle. She leant on the communal bin for a moment, the big, steel container on wheels supporting her. Its wheels were locked so it didn't move. She wondered why it was still here.

She moved round to the side of it and knew she would be visible from any of the windows above her. She tried to figure out where the ward was, in her head, running through it like a 3D model on a computer. The side door, back in, turn left, upstairs, turn right, right again and then onto the landing. The front. The room she had been in faced the front. She was on the side. Of course there were other windows they could look out of but they wouldn't know where she was or what direction she'd gone in.

She lifted the fence panel, and it wouldn't move at first. She looked down and saw it was clamped at the bottom. Stuck into its concrete boot. How the hell did that other person move it?

Then she noticed she was at the wrong bit. The panel she needed to move was already out of its boot, but further along.

Closer to the door.

There was nothing else for it. She was going to have to move it or else she was going to die. And this way, if she got caught, then she was going down fighting.

She looked at the door. Anybody else coming here and looking would think it was locked. The boards covering the windows in the doors would give her some cover but if somebody looked out, they could see her. Just like how she'd seen out. But she couldn't see in for the daylight reflecting on what little glass was visible.

She grabbed hold of the panel and pulled it open, careful not to let it scrape the ground. It was surprisingly light, but trying to move with the cast on her leg was awkward. She grunted as she lifted and turned. Then she was out, and picking it up again, doing it all in reverse. Then she hobbled over to the garage block.

The door was on rusted rails and no matter how quietly she tried to push it, it squealed. She pushed it far enough just to squeeze through. Then she was in.

A car and a white van sat parked next to each other. The car was a Vauxhall. Black, and the badging on the back said it was a diesel. Funny, she hadn't even noticed the diesel noise as it had gone past. Maybe because of the sound of rushing blood in her ears. Facing death was funny that way.

Then Dawn froze on the spot. She could hear another car coming in the distance.

Then she heard a shoe scrape on the dirty concrete floor behind her. She turned round.

'Hello, Dawn.'

FORTY-SIX

The door was open. The top halves were boarded up but somebody had opened it.

'They obviously didn't come round here to check,' Watt said.

'It might not have been open,' Miller said.

'Or it might have been. We'll never know.' He walked forward and gently pushed the door. It swung open easily but the hinges creaked alarmingly. 'Remember, this fucker has a knife and he's not averse to using it. If he comes at us, we take him down hard and ask questions later. We can always fudge the report about how we tried to persuade him to come quietly,' he said, without turning to look at them. Taking your eyes off the ball and being attacked was just for the movies.

A shaft of light speared into the vestibule and on into the hallway of the hospital. It was mostly in darkness as the windows on the ground floor were boarded up. Debris littered the floor. Miller saw an old doll lying in a corner, covered in dust.

They saw him when they walked into the hall. The man hanging by his neck from the railings on the next floor, away from the steps.

'Hugo Flynn,' Watt said, looking around him, in case it was a trap. Divert the attention then when you weren't paying attention, you were eviscerated. Something inside him wished that Flynn had just come at him with the knife. Andy Watt had been brought up in Niddrie and had been in many a fight when he was a boy. Still had the scars to show for it. Four years in the army had honed his fighting skills, but he didn't get to use them much nowadays.

Miller started running up the stairs. 'Christ, he might still be alive,' he said, but Carol gave Watt a look that said this was wishful thinking. She ran up after Miller anyway. Watt stayed and grabbed hold of Flynn's legs, taking the strain. Miller and Carol reached through the railings and grabbed the rope, but it was difficult to start pulling him up, but with Watt pushing, they managed to haul him up and over the balustrade.

Watt came up the stairs as Miller fought with the rope around Flynn's neck.

Then they heard a scream coming from outside.

'What the fuck was that?' Watt said.

'I'll go and find out,' Carol said, running for the stairs.

'Carol, no!' Miller said, jumping up.

'I'll be fine. You see to that bastard.'

'He might be out there!'

Carol stopped. 'He's right there, Frank, and by the look of him, he's not going anywhere. Somebody needs our help.' She ran down the stairs.

Christ, where did that scream come from? Somebody was obviously trapped. Or being attacked. Jesus. The only person she knew had been taken was Dawn Tait.

The hallway was dank and smelled. Carol was aware of her surroundings, her senses on high alert. Paint peeled off the walls, dripping like dead skin. Graffiti covered the walls in parts. Drawings, initials, warnings of death. An old wheelchair sat in the middle of the hallway, not looking as dusty as its surroundings. Maybe it had been a plaything for vandals. Joyriding around the inside of an abandoned hospital. No wonder they grew up to be guests of Her Majesty.

The floor was littered with rubbish as well as debris from broken walls. Old office equipment was strewn around the corridor. Papers littered the floor like giant confetti. She looked in the rooms as she went further along. Examination rooms with tables in them. Dusty chairs, some of them rusty. Still the smell of dampness. The hallway was in shadow, only slivers of light falling between the boards that were on the windows. The debris crunched under her feet, her boots scraping along the vinyl floor.

She'd reached the halfway point, where the big doors were when she heard the scream again.

It was faint, not as loud as it had been when they had first heard it.

It was coming from outside, where they had just come in.

She ran back along the way she had come. At the landing, she turned and looked up. Watt and Miller were gone.

She heard the scream again, this time louder.

She ran outside.

FORTY-SEVEN

Dawn didn't know who the woman was but she was focused on the knife she was holding.

'Let's go back inside, Dawn. We can talk there.' This woman knew her name, but Dawn didn't know *her*. The knife was still uppermost in her mind though. The woman walked towards her.

She was wearing scrubs, but this wasn't a nurse; this woman was wearing heels. Not stilettos but not the flats that nurses normally wore. She walked slowly towards Dawn who was standing by the driver's door of the car. Dawn knew if she backed away, this woman would think she had the upper hand. That she, Dawn, was running away, and this would give her the psychological advantage. She wasn't going to relinquish anything.

'Give me the knife and I'll let you walk away,' Dawn said.

The woman smiled. Big, bright teeth and red lipstick. Not what a nurse would wear.

'You're very funny. But I'm not going to stand here and negotiate with you. I am going to give the orders and you're going to do as I say.'

'Why? So you can kill me like the others.' Dawn felt herself shaking, but she forced the image of her little boy into her mind. *How much do you want to live?! How much do you want to go home and see your baby again?! Do you want him to be brought up by another mummy? Have Vince find somebody else and have that woman tuck your little boy into bed every night? Well, do you? Or are you going to fight? Stand there and let her gut you like the others, or fight the bitch.*

The woman was still smiling, the hunting knife unwavering in her hand. She started walking slowly towards Dawn. 'Come on now. We can talk about this inside. We can even have a nice cup of tea. You like tea, don't you, Dawn?'

'I'm not going anywhere with you. Just put the knife down and I won't hurt you.'

The laugh was almost comical had it not been for the situation. 'I have to admire you, I really do. You're the only one who has any guts. Well, I shouldn't say that; Ruby Maxwell was a fighter. If she hadn't fought so hard, she would have had the pleasure of seeing the surgeon.'

'You killed her and put the bloody clothes and knife in Len's house.'

'I did. Just to throw the police off the scent. Play with their minds.' She smiled and moved closer. 'She was fighter, as I said. Are you going to be a fighter, Dawn?'

'Why don't you come closer and find out?' She took a step back, leaning against a work table against the back wall. It was full of rusty tools. She leaned her arms on it, making it look like she was just balancing, but her right hand wrapped round an old, rusty spanner. It looked like it could have taken the lug nuts off a truck.

'I was quite prepared to give you a second chance, Dawn. I mean, it's not everybody who can manage to escape the hospital, and while wearing a leg cast. So, kudos for that. And for your reward, I'll tell the surgeon to give you a little something to numb the pain. Not too much. After all, we don't want to spoil the fun. But enough to take the edge off, just before he slices into you. What do you say?'

Dawn was at a disadvantage; the light streaming in from the open door into the darkened garage made her pupils contract to compensate. This woman's pupils were doing the opposite.

'Go fuck yourself, bitch. And you'd better know how to fight, because I do.'

The woman's laugh was harsh as she tilted her head back. It was a move that was meant to throw Dawn off. But it didn't.

The look on the woman's face was pure hatred when she looked at Dawn again. At the same time, she pushed off on her back foot, raising the knife so by the time she got to Dawn, her arm would be on the downward arc, momentum driving it.

A lot of women panic when they are attacked. Fear grips them, and then it is all over. Their attacker is on them, and all they can do is try and curl up into a ball to protect themselves. As a nurse, Dawn had seen the victims of such crime, and vowed that she would never be caught out like this. Sometimes, all it took was a moment to focus, to let the fear dissipate, and to channel the fear and turn it into anger. Most men who attack women are cowards and the last thing they want is a victim to fight back.

Dawn saw the stance more than the knife but as the vicious blade came arcing through the air, she put up an arm to block it, leaning into it while bringing her right hand up. The big, rusty spanner was heavy but not so heavy that she couldn't swing it. The adrenaline helped her. As the woman's knife-hand connected with her arm, Dawn brought the spanner down full force onto the side of the woman's skull.

Her attacker let out an almighty scream as she fell over, blood exploding from the gash on her head. The knife fell out of her hand and Dawn kicked it under the car. The woman recovered quickly and rolled away from Dawn, then she reached under the car, her hand scrabbling. Dawn balanced on the leg with the cast and then kicked her. The woman grunted and realising that she was in a vulnerable position, got up on all fours and then stood up.

Dawn grabbed her after throwing the spanner aside. This fight was going to be hand-to-hand. She was more worried about losing control than using a weapon. The woman grabbed her and tried to head butt her but Dawn turned her face down and the butt connected with the top of her skull. The woman grabbed her clothing and brought her in close.

Dawn made a fist and extended the knuckle of her middle finger so it was pointy and sticking out further than the other fingers, then she punched the woman as hard as she could. She was aiming for the solar plexus to wind her, but her attacker moved sideways at the last minute and Dawn's fist connected with the ribcage. She pushed away from Dawn and then let out an almighty yell. One of hatred and frustration.

Dawn grabbed the woman as she got in close. Used her hand to pat her down as they were struggling but she couldn't feel the car keys. Then the woman twisted Dawn around and pressed her face against the window of the driver's door. It was almost as if she was showing her where the keys were.

Still in the ignition.

And why not? Who was going to take it from here?

Dawn rammed her elbow into the woman, and was free again. She pushed her and as she fell, Dawn turned and started hobbling towards the door. Maybe she could get out and lock this woman in.

As she got to the large garage door, she turned, expecting to see the woman right behind her but the nurse had got in behind the wheel of the car. Started up and put her foot on the gas pedal, the engine roaring.

Dawn squeezed out of the gap and into the sunlight.

The engine screamed in protest and then the gearbox crunched as it was put into reverse.

Dawn looked away from the door for a second, just in time to see somebody running right at her.

FORTY-EIGHT

Hugo Flynn's face had cuts on it, like something had smashed into it. Or it had been smashed into something. He was long dead, so they left him where he was and made their way across the landing.

'Christ, it looks like this place was given a coat of paint,' Watt said as they went through the doors into the hallway.

'I wonder why?' Miller said.

'Maybe he wanted it to look like a real hospital for his patients.'

'Patients?'

Watt nodded to the room on Miller's right. It was just like a regular hospital room, with a bed and monitors. The sheets were thrown back as if somebody had recently been in it and had been taken from it.

'You were right about this place, Frank. Sometimes it's hard to see the woods for the trees.'

'It was a lucky guess.'

'Nothing lucky about it, son. It was bloody good detective work.'

'You're embarrassing me now.'

'Pish. I told you, some day, sooner rather than later, you'll be my boss.'

They both heard a metallic clatter from further along the hallway and they took off running. It got darker along at the far end and the sound of a commotion came from the right. A sign hung from the ceiling: *Operating Theatres.*

Miller battered the swing doors first, Watt following closely behind him. They could see into the operating theatre itself. A man dressed in a suit was in a hospital wheelchair, struggling as another man tried to wrap cling film round his head.

Miller burst through the door and the surgeon turned to face him. Dressed in green scrubs with his head and face covered. He let Perry MacKinnon go and moved away towards the tray of surgical tools that MacKinnon had manged to kick off a side table.

'Go near a fucking knife and I'll break your face,' Watt said, standing with his extendable baton out. 'And if you're thinking this old bastard can't move as fast as you, go ahead and try it.'

The knives and scalpels were scattered on the floor, the closest one being halfway between them.

The surgeon backed away from MacKinnon as Miller moved forward, taking in the scene before him; a woman, by the looks of her anatomy, lying dead on the table, having been opened up. His last victim. Another man tied to another hospital wheelchair, cling film round his head. From the colour of the man's face, Miller guessed he was already dead.

An older man lay on the floor, not moving, his skin the pallor of the dead. Len Chatter. Miller got to MacKinnon and unwrapped the cling film. 'Help me! he's a fucking lunatic!' He took in deep gasps of breath.

The surgeon was backed into a corner. He looked at his watch.

'You expecting somebody?'

'Nobody you'd be interested in.'

'Keep your hands where we can see them,' Watt said.

'Or else?'

'Or else you'll find out what we're capable of, Miles,' Miller said.

The surgeon laughed. Pulled down his face mask. 'I'm still going to get away with it, you do know that, don't you?' Miles said, his smile not slipping. Watt stepped forward and twisted him round, putting the speed cuffs on him. Miller undid the leather shackles that had held MacKinnon to the chair.

'No, you're not. You're not getting past us.'

'Oh, I wouldn't count on it.'

'Shut your fucking mouth,' Watt said. 'Frank, get on the phone for an ambulance and back-up. I'll even take the Fifers at this stage of the game.'

Miller was about to make the call when his phone rang. He answered it.

'Frank, we have Faith Hope,' Jack said.

'What? That's good. We have her boyfriend, here. The surgeon. We got him, sir. It's Miles Laing, the owner of the *Savoy* hotel.'

'No, son, listen; you don't understand. Faith Hope isn't working with him. I didn't arrest her. She was round at her flat, shocked that somebody had smashed her mirror. She doesn't know who would have gotten in there, but she's scared shitless. She thinks that the killer is coming for her now. And she's horrified that Hugo Flynn was here.'

'She could be a good actress.'

'She could be and I might have gone with that line of thinking if I hadn't just confirmed her alibi for the night Iris Napier was murdered.'

'But I already said she could have been the one who murdered Amelia Arnold, just telling us she left her alone after they'd been to the singles club together.'

'You're forgetting one thing son.'

'What's that?'

'I've been able to read people's body language for a long time now. You should see the lassie; she's a wreck. If she's acting, then she's the best fucking actress I've ever seen. I'll get Fife to get help to you there. Don't let the bastard go, for fuck's sake.'

'Christ,' he said when he hung up.

'What's up?' Watt said.

Miller looked at Miles. 'We have Faith Hope in custody. Now you're both caught.'

The irritating smile was still there. 'Oh, well, you've got both of us now.'

'What are you talking about?' Watt asked.

'Hugo Flynn was a competent surgeon, not a brilliant one,' Miller said. 'He made a mistake one day. His scalpel slipped and a woman died on the table.' He looked at Watt. 'Flynn's daughter told Jack all about it. Flynn knew what he had done, but Perry MacKinnon and Len Chatter there covered for him. Blamed our friend Miles here, because Miles had a drink problem. It would seem plausible that an alcoholic could make a slip. He was railroaded. Miles even doubted himself for the longest time. Isn't that right, Miles?'

'I was the best surgeon on his team.' He nodded to MacKinnon, who was still strapped to the chair, but his breathing was coming back to normal. 'Faith saw what really happened, but they didn't believe her, especially since the whole surgical team backed up MacKinnon and Chatter. Lying bastards every one of them.'

'Why now?' Miller asked.

'I was working in my father's lousy hotel. Then one day, he said he would sell it to me, as there was a mortgage on it. He couldn't just give it to me, but you saw how busy it gets; it makes a fair bit of money. So I go to the finance company after the bank knocked me back, and who should be the loan officer? Calvin Baxter. I could see he was embarrassed about me being there, but we went through the motions and I applied, thinking that maybe he would swing it in my favour. How wrong was I? I got knocked back. Life just sailed along. Then earlier this year, who came into the hotel, looking for a long-term room? Hugo Flynn. Somebody he knows had been staying at the hotel. It's a crappy little room but if it can make some money rather than be turned into a closet, then why not? I gave him a break. I mean, you saw him. He was a broken man.'

'What made you target the nurses?'

'They would come into my bar before going along the road to the singles club in the hotel. It was almost like they were rubbing my face in it. I don't think they knew who I was. I lied and gave them a false name when they asked. But if they did know who I was, they didn't say anything. Then MacKinnon came in one day. I knew the clinic had opened just a couple of doors along, but it was his. And when I Googled him, it turns out that isn't his first. Then he bought the place next door.

'Next on his list was the hotel. He wanted to add them altogether. But Chatter there stepped in and bought it from my father. He was a spiteful old bastard. He just didn't want MacKinnon to have it.'

MacKinnon looked at him with contempt.

'It just made me mad. Then my girlfriend said I should get back at them all. She has a mean streak. I wasn't convinced at first, but when I found out that Chatter had bought the hotel and I would be homeless anyway, it was enough to tip the scales.'

'Except it wasn't Faith Hope.' He looked at Watt.' She's in custody but she's a wreck, Jack says.'

'If it wasn't Faith Hope, then who is it?' Watt said, looking at Miles.

'I'm not going to do your job for you, detective.'

Miller looked at him for a moment, thinking. 'If it isn't her, that just leaves one unaccounted for; Bree Baxter.'

Watt turned round and whipped the cover off the dead patient's face.

'Marcie Lincoln,' Miller said. 'She was Calvin Baxter's girlfriend.'

'She wasn't part of the team, but I wanted Baxter to feel pain,' Miles said.

'So where's Bree?' Miller said, taking a step forward.

'Dawn Tait's a nurse too, and you haven't found her,' Miles said.

'No, she was taken with Chatter. We have witnesses. We need to find her, but I don't think she was working with you.' He looked at MacKinnon. 'You've been drinking in that hotel recently; have you seen Bree Baxter in the bar in the past few weeks?'

'No, I haven't seen her for years.'

'Call Jack, let him know,' Watt said.

Miller took his phone out when a thought struck him. 'The scream. Carol went looking.'

'Go look for her, Frank. I've got things under control here.' Watt nodded to MacKinnon. 'Check the old boy's pulse. Frank, get going. We'll be right down.'

Miller took off running. Past the lifeless body of Hugo Flynn. Then a thought struck him: Flynn had retrained in IT and was good at it. And Miles knew he had been putting on a fake accent. He wondered if Miles had planned to use him from the word go.

He ran down the stairs two at a time. 'Carol!' he shouted, knowing her life was in danger.

FORTY-NINE

Dawn saw the nurse get into the car and tried to get the garage door shut, but it was stuck. She heard the car's engine kick over and then being revved. She turned and started hobbling back the way she had come.

'Dawn!' Carol said, shouting her name when she saw her.

Dawn, in a panic, turned back and started hobbling towards the garage. Carol ran across the yard, towards the garage, just as the car had been put into reverse. It came smashing through the garage door at speed, just as Carol pushed Dawn.

The car hit Dawn's plaster-cast leg and spun her sideways. Carol wasn't so lucky. The back of the car clipped her, but she had no protection on her legs. It caught her upper thigh and she was thrown through the air to land on her back. Her right wrist smacked the ground hard, breaking. She lay winded, unable to get a breath and pain was shooting through her whole lower body and her arm.

She heard someone approach her. Her eyes were blurry with tears and she tried to scream in pain but couldn't. She didn't know if her leg was broken or not. It was a woman wearing nurses' scrubs. That's all she saw as she was roughly grabbed and dragged towards the car. Then she was manhandled into the passenger seat, unable to fight back, feeling she was going to pass out at any moment. The pain was unlike anything she'd experienced before.

She felt her head spinning, then she thought she was going to vomit. The nurse got into the driver's seat. The car rocked as she slammed the door. Then the car was put into gear and she drove away.

Carol couldn't move her leg and couldn't reach for the seatbelt. She was gripping the side of the seat. She wondered where Bree Baxter was taking her. But when she looked over and forced herself to focus on the nurse's face, she saw it wasn't Bree at all.

'I... I don't understand,' Carol said, her head still swimming.

'You don't have to.'

FIFTY

Miller skidded on a pile of debris and went crashing over onto his side, sliding a couple of feet. He was back up on his feet, trying to get his phone out as he ran through the doors to the outside where they'd parked.

Tyres screeching on the road caught his attention and a car came screaming towards him. He dived out of the way, but before he moved, he saw Carol in the passenger seat.

'Carol!' he shouted, feeling panic well up inside of him for a moment. She had been leaning against the window as if she wasn't fully conscious. He didn't see Dawn lying on her side near the garage.

He got up and sprinted towards the car they'd come in. Got the keys out and jumped into the driver's seat. By the time he turned round the other car was already out of sight. He floored it without bothering with his seat belt. The road was overgrown with weeds in places, but still relatively smooth. He picked up the mike and spoke to control, telling them to get a move on. His call had already gone through and sirens blared on the air close by.

He turned the corner in the driveway and raced towards the exit.

The other car was gone. *Silver Vauxhall Astra* he kept repeating to himself. He hadn't got the plate number. Couldn't remember if Miles drove an Astra or not. He looked right and left. Couldn't see which way it had gone until a car coming towards him swerved onto the wrong side of the road. He turned left, his blues flashing, his own siren splitting the air.

He floored it, trying to catch up before the Astra hit the roundabout ahead and split off without him seeing which way it had gone. He saw it had gone straight ahead. Heading through Rosyth. He relayed the details to control. Where were the patrols? The car reached sixty, Miller navigating past the other cars. He got stuck behind a bus for a second, before pulling round it. Then they were under the M90 motorway, heading towards Hillend, a sleepy little village with the main road cutting through it.

He was keeping up with the Astra. Then he saw it go straight over at the roundabout for Dalgety Bay.

Where are you going, Bree? he thought.

FIFTY-ONE

Except it wasn't Bree Baxter driving the car.

Carol sat up straighter in her seat, her right hand useless. It had felt like it was on fire at first, but now it was numb and the pain was radiating up her arm to her elbow and beyond. Her hip was painful but wasn't as bad as the agony in her arm.

The nurse was driving like she was on drugs. Her eyes were staring ahead and she was smiling. Carol's eyes cleared and she no longer felt dizzy.

'Sherri? What's going on?'

'Haven't you worked it out yet?' Gone was the American accent.

'You're Scottish. I don't understand.'

She laughed as she drove the car at high speed under the M90. 'It was Miles' idea.'

'Miles? You mean...?'

'He's the one the papers called the *surgeon*. Ironic since he really was a surgeon at one time.'

'But... you only just met him. Didn't you?'

'God, you're dumb. I've been his girlfriend for a long time now.

You just didn't meet me because I didn't drink with him in the hotel bar. We used to socialise somewhere else.'

'Why the accent?'

'When Miles first saw Hugo Flynn in the hotel with his stupid, fake London accent, it gave him an idea.' She looked across at Carol before looking in her mirror and seeing the blue lights following her. 'It was my idea to get back at them all. I didn't work with him, but they came into the hotel, practically mocking him. I told him he should make them pay. I even told him I'd help him.'

'Frank thought it was Faith Hope helping the killer.'

'No, Faith had nothing to do with it. She tried to help Miles, but they railroaded her as well. She was never in any danger. The rest of them, however, were going to pay.'

'What about all this story with Perry MacKinnon screwing you out of money?'

'That was a classic ruse. I got Hugo to help me with that one. He got a cut of course, but he set it up so we took money out of Perry MacKinnon's business account. Made up accounts in his son's name, and then we just pointed Perry in the right direction. Miles knew that Perry had a son who had just graduated university last year, but was too lazy to get a job. Miles told Perry a friend of his had tracked Sherri's money to an account that his son had opened. If I didn't get my money back, he'd let it be known to backers what a conman he really was. He'd do a number on him. So when Perry checked, he discovered the money. He was going to pay me back, he says. So I arranged to meet him, he paid me the money, had it wired into an account and then Miles took him. It was perfect. He was giving me his own money. And you and Frank certainly fell for it. The sob story, and how I got conned. I even got Hugo to make false accounts in the USA, where I supposedly came from. Jack Miller checked up and everything checked out. It was pure brilliance. So now we had the money and when we were done, we were going to disappear with our new identities.'

'But we caught onto you. Or more specifically, Hugo.'

'He had to die because he knew too much, but we also needed everybody to think he was the surgeon.' The car screamed through Hillend. 'Did you think the *surgeon* was working with a partner?'

'It was Frank who thought of that.'

'Why?'

'We suspected Hugo, but Frank didn't think Hugo could have lifted a body over the railings onto the base of the statue at St. Bernard's Well.'

Sherri's smile dropped. 'I told Miles not to leave her there. I said we should just leave her propped against the railings on the footpath, but oh, no, he wanted to be dramatic.'

Screaming straight over the first roundabout into Dalgety Bay.

'Sherri, you know you're not going to get away with this, don't you,' Carol said, being flung against the door and banging her head.

'Frank's behind us but I'll lose him. Then it's just me and you. Then I'll show you what happens to people who cross us.'

'Your name's not really Sherri, is it?'

'It doesn't matter.'

The car shot forward and she hung a right, the tyres screeching, and Carol felt the car sliding. She thought it was going to roll but it steadied, jerking them from side-to-side.

'Just stop, Sherri. We can talk about this.'

The laugh that came from her was more of a cackle. 'Thanks for the offer, Carol, but when we get out, I'm going to say a little prayer just before I kill you.'

Another roundabout. Straight over, heading more towards the coast. Sherri drove like there was nothing else on the road. Carol risked a look out the back. There was no sign of Frank. Christ, had she lost him? But then she saw the blue lights in the distance.

Another roundabout. Straight over this one again.

The car was roaring down the road. It turned round to the right.

She had slowed down a bit, then she put the brakes on and turned off the road onto a grass area, bumping up over the kerb.

Here it comes Carol thought, when she saw the copse of trees, right down by the water front. *This bitch knew where she was going all along.*

Carol had to dig deep. Go way past the pain barrier, to feel something that she had never felt before, a level of pain she didn't even know existed. She leaned down on her broken wrist, pushing herself up and forward and when Sherri looked at her, there was no smile, just surprise.

'Take this, bitch!' Carol screamed and head-butted Sherri in the face.

The woman screamed and Carol grabbed the steering wheel, expecting the car to stop.

It did the opposite. Sherri was in so much pain that she jammed her right foot down on the gas pedal. The car shot forward, jumping as it hammered over the uneven grass. Carol saw the sea looming towards them. She looked over at Sherri, a few little boats in a small harbour, bobbing up and down.

The car was going faster and Carol knew what she had to do and she couldn't think about it or else she was dead. Maybe ten seconds left to live if she didn't move.

She opened the car door with her left hand and threw herself out. Later on, she would be told that if she had done this on tarmac, she would have been more than likely killed.

But she rolled on the grass, her body going over and over. By the time she stopped rolling, she had been knocked unconscious. She didn't see the car accelerating towards the edge, where it shot over at high speed and dropped into the Firth of Forth with an almighty splash.

She didn't see it, but Frank Miller did. He had bumped his car onto the grass and stopped near Carol. He saw the tail end of the car disappear from view. The drop was maybe twenty feet into the sea.

He had been in touch with control and let them know where he was.

He jumped from the car and ran over to Carol and threw himself down by her still body. He felt for vital signs and found a pulse.

'Thank you,' he whispered. He didn't want to move her for fear of doing more damage.

Another patrol car came screaming round the corner and drove towards him. He identified himself before running over to the edge. It wasn't a cliff as such but a drop into the ocean none the less. There was no sign of the car. It had gone under the water like a stone. Still ignorant of who had really been driving, he was looking for Bree Baxter to surface, but there was nothing.

Little sailboats bobbed in the sea further out, and he saw some on land. A boat club.

The ambulance arrived and he ran back to Carol. Then more reinforcements. He wouldn't see Andy Watt or Carol's father, DCS Davidson, until they all met up at St. Margaret's Hospital in Dunfermline.

Miller sighed with relief as they lifted Carol into the ambulance.

Then she went into cardiac arrest.

And the ambulance doors closed.

FIFTY-TWO

TWO WEEKS LATER

'Are those for me?' Carol said as Miller came into her room with a bunch of flowers.

'Actually, they're for one of the nurses I just met.'

'You're a pig, Miller.' She was sitting up in bed. Miller thought that Carol had never looked more beautiful. 'How do I look today?'

'Beautiful as always.'

'Oh, I know that, but I meant the bruises.'

Miller took the old flowers out of the vase and took the new ones out of the wrapper. Put them into the water. It was dark outside now, but still warm.

'Your eyes are getting better. Just a hint of bruises now. How does your nose feel?'

'Like an elephant sat on it. It's healing nicely though.'

'It looks fine. It's your wrist I'm worried about.'

'The pins are holding it together nicely, and I'll get physiotherapy once the cast is off. The doctor said that I'll probably feel it in old age.'

Miller smiled and sat down on her left side so he could hold her left hand. The doctors had told her about the cardiac arrest and she had taken it well. No lasting damage. They had taken her to St. Margaret's in Dunfermline, but she had a concussion from hitting the ground at speed, so she had been brought over to the Western General in Edinburgh, where the head injury unit was. They had operated on her wrist, screwing it together.

'Your mum and dad's coming in tomorrow morning,' he said, gently squeezing her hand.

'He'll be clucking about like a headless chicken. Mum will have to reign him in. Still, so long as he brings grapes.'

The TV was on up on a shelf, but it had been muted. 'I've been watching the news, but there's nothing now. It's old news.' She looked at him. 'I know you're sick of me asking, but any news?'

He shook his head. 'Nothing. Your dad spoke to the Coastguard again, and they said that she most likely would have been dragged underneath by a current and drowned. She might have been hit by a ship's propeller or else she sank, to be eaten by fish.'

'And she wouldn't float?'

'Maybe in a river, with the body gases acting like a life vest, but not out there. She'll be at the bottom.'

'They recovered the car though and found nothing?'

She'd asked the same question, again and again, like she didn't want to believe the answer: they'd recovered the car out of the sea but there was nobody in it.

'I still can't believe we went out with them, Frank. Sherri and Miles. And I've known Miles for the longest time! I still find it hard to believe he did this.'

'Luckily the Procurator Fiscal does. However, we're still waiting for the results of the evaluation from the State Hospital. If they say he's unfit to stand trial, then he'll stay there until he is fit, but that might never be the case.'

'He was such a nice guy. We trusted him.'

He squeezed her hand. 'There's going to be a news conference tomorrow, but I didn't want you find this out from the news; we found Bree Baxter.'

'Jesus. Where?'

'In the basement of the townhouse that Perry MacKinnon had bought to add to his clinic in Dean Terrace. Some of the contractors found her. Your sister is doing the PM on her, but at a rough guess, she thinks Bree was dead a couple of days before we caught them. She hadn't been cut open like the others, but she had been murdered nonetheless.'

'Poor thing. I wonder what MacKinnon thinks about that?'

'Business as usual. It will be a seven-day wonder then people will get over it. We're getting desensitised to murder now.'

'I know.' She yawned. 'God, I am so tired. These painkillers are wiping me out.'

'I'll get going.'

'Can you call my mum and ask her to swing by the house and bring me my 3.5mm crochet hooks?'

'Where are they?'

'She'll know. She can grab them. She knows what they look like.' She smiled at him. 'I'm glad I learned how to do crochet years ago. It's perfect exercise for my wrist. I'm starting off slowly but I'm getting there.'

'Sure. I can call her tomorrow.'

'It's only gone ten. Can you call her now? She'll still be up.'

'Don't you want to call her?'

'Oh, God, she'll be asking me a thousand questions. I've already had her clacking at me today. Please. If you love me, you'll do this for me.' She smiled at him, the smile he couldn't resist.

'Fine. But you owe me.' He smiled, then went to make the call when a nurse came in to check on Carol and give her the meds.

There was a uniformed officer outside Carol's door. She'd had round-the-clock protection for two weeks now, but they were talking about reducing the hours. Harry Davidson was not happy, but with all the signs indicating that Sherri Judd was long dead, the threat level was reduced.

He made the call and spoke to Harry Davidson, Carol's father and his boss, and then he spoke to her mother, reassuring her that everything was alright, and that Carol only wanted crochet hooks. Then she told him she wouldn't be able to make it in the following morning.

'Your mum can't make it in until the afternoon,' he said as he went back into her room. 'A doctor's appointment and some running about to do. Sorry.'

'Aw, hell's teeth. I wanted to do some tomorrow.' She bit her lower lip and all but batted her eyelashes. 'I don't suppose you would run home and get them for me now, would you? It's not far. And I'll make it up to you when I get home.'

He smiled. 'Really? In what way?'

'I'll crochet you a pair of underpants.'

'Well, who could resist such an offer? I'll be right back.'

Miller left, and it took him almost 45 minutes to return because he couldn't find the crochet hooks at first. He didn't tell Carol he didn't know what they looked like. But he eventually found them and headed back up the road, which was literally a two-minute drive from the flat.

It was raining now. Miller parked inside the lower level of the car park and ran across the road. Up and round the corner to the entrance. He pressed the button for the lift. Upstairs, he stepped out and walked along to the ward, and then he saw the constable who had been guarding Carol, standing at the nurse's station, leaning on the counter, laughing.

'What are you doing here?' he said to the uniform.

'Oh, hello, sir. There was a telephone call for me, but when I came round, they had hung up. There was nobody on the other end.' His face was starting to go red.

'What? You stupid...!' Miller started running down the corridor, followed by the uniform, their footsteps sounding like thunderclaps in the quiet. He rounded the corner and saw a nurse going through the door to the stairwell, and he relaxed a bit. Nobody would have got past her.

He opened the door to Carol's room and slapped the light on.

'What's wrong?' Carol mumbled, drowsily, narrowing her eyes against the harsh light.

'Nothing. Sorry. I got your crochet hooks. I'll leave them right here,' he whispered He flicked off the light, managing to see by the shaft of light coming in from the corridor. He took the small hooks out of his pocket and laid them on the table. He kissed Carol on the forehead. She'd already drifted back to sleep, so he left.

He closed the door gently. The uniform was standing outside.

'You stay outside this door, or I'll damn well make sure you spend the rest of your career mopping out toilets. You got that?'

'Yes, sir.'

'That's a fellow officer in there, one who helped tackle a serial killer. Don't forget that.'

'I'm sorry, sir. It won't happen again.'

He walked over to the nurse. 'Sorry about the drama. I saw one of your colleagues go down that stair so at least Carol was safe. She's been through a lot, and I worry about her.'

'What other nurse? There's only two of us on through the night, and Karen's round at the station.'

'Would another nurse have reason to come on this level?'

'No. And if for some reason they did, they would let us know they're coming. And they would use the main stairs, not the ones along there.'

'Where do those stairs lead to?'

'They're fire exit stairs. They lead to a door at the bottom that opens out onto the car park.'

Miller went back to Carol's room. Opened the door quietly this time. He walked over to the window and looked out through the rain, over to the car park.

A nurse was walking over to a little dark car on the top level. She opened the door of her car then stood and looked up at Miller. They were looking right at each for a few moments.

She waved at him.

Then she got into the car and drove off.

FIFTY-THREE

EIGHT YEARS LATER

The day had started out a little cloudy, but the sun had come out in full force. Miller left his jacket in the car and walked across the grass, holding a bunch of flowers. He stopped in front of Carol's grave, now engraved with the name of their son who she had been carrying when she died. *Harry.*

He laid the flowers down in front of the black polished stone and stood up, reading her name over and over, as if he couldn't believe she was buried there. But she was.

'It was eight years ago today that we caught Miles Laing. I've thought about him often since then, mainly because he exercises his right to call me from the State Hospital. I remember how angry you were when the doctors said he wasn't fit to stand trial, that you thought he was faking it. Well, he must be good at faking it, because it's been eight years.

'I thought you were dead that day Sherri took you. But I'm glad we spent the next few years together after that, before you went away. You were destined for better things. You would have climbed the ladder so much faster than I would have. Until the day your life was cut short.' Miller's voice caught in his throat for a moment before he cleared it.

'You know, I often think back to the day I found that razor in your bathroom and how jealous I was. I didn't even want to make love to you that night, I was so out of whack. God, I wish I could turn the clock back. Hold you in my arms that night, hold you close and tell you how much I loved you. Oh, you don't know how many times a day I wish I could hold you again, to smell your hair, to look into your eyes, to see your smile. I wish I could go back and insist you didn't do the ransom drop that night. You would have been with me now, and I wouldn't be standing in a cemetery, talking to you and not being able to hear your words.'

He felt his eyes filling up with tears.

'You know, I'm shaking just now. I look at my little boy's name, and I feel guilt. It's been eating me up since the day I found out that Kim's pregnant. I'm sorry, I wanted a life with you, I really did. For the longest time, I wanted to take a bottle of pills and wash them down with a bottle of vodka. I couldn't see tomorrow. Now Kim and I are settling down and we're going to have a baby, and I should be over the moon about it, but I'm not. I feel a despair grab a hold of me. Like a dark veil. I miss you every day. The thing that gets me through is, I can say I was married to you. I was your husband.'

A light wind rippled the grass at his feet. 'People say that time is a healer, but it's been a few years since you left me, and I still feel the ache inside when I think of you. Think of the times we had together. I don't want to move on. I have to, I know that, but it's hard.'

He heard somebody behind him and he spun round. Dawn Rutherford was standing watching him.

'I'm sorry to disturb you, Frank. Your dad said you would be here. He said you come down to see Carol often.'

He nodded. 'I do.'

She was holding a bunch of flowers. 'I thought she might like these.'

He stood to one side to let her put the flowers down. She stood back. 'I heard that you're going to be a dad.'

I'm already a dad to little Harry, he wanted to say, but kept the thought to himself. 'Yes.'

'Congratulations.'

'Thank you. How're the boys doing?'

'Little Vince isn't so little anymore, and Frederic is going the same way.'

'How old are they now?'

'Twelve and seven.'

'When's Vince's new book out?'

'That's what I was wanting to talk to you about. It's being launched at the book festival. We'd like you to come along. It's been a while since we've seen you and Kim.'

'Thanks, I'll think about it.'

'No you won't, Frank Miller; you'll come along. I've already spoken to Kim and she wants to come. You've come along to every other one, so why should this be different?'

'Okay, I'll be there.'

'Thank you. For everything. If you hadn't figured out where Miles was keeping me, I wouldn't be here today.'

'Now, that's—'

'True. That's true. And Vince is eternally grateful too. In fact, he's got something for you.' She had a jacket draped over one arm, and from underneath it, she brought out a hardback book. *The Conflict by Vince Rutherford.*

'Open it.'

There was a paper bookmark inside. Miller opened it to the page. *For Carol.* 'Jesus, that's so nice.'

'She pushed me out of the way that day. The car clipped me but if it wasn't for her bravery, the car would have been right over the top of me. You both saved us.'

He had no words for a moment. 'Thanks for this.'

'I shredded every one of those story entries. With Len dead, we could have used them, but that wasn't fair on those other authors. I wrote to every one of them and told them to feel free to use their ideas if they wanted. They only belonged to Len while he was alive. If the ideas hadn't been used for a book by the time of his death, the idea would revert back to each author.'

'Vince didn't need anybody else's ideas. He had plenty of good ones himself.'

'That's what I told him.'

'Not only that, he's better than Len Chatter ever was.'

'I told him that too.'

'You're both better than Chatter. I read your stuff too, Dawn.'

He stood silent for a moment.

'I'll leave you alone.'

'I'll be there in a minute, Dawn.' He turned back to the headstone as Dawn walked away to her own car.

'I'll never forget the good times we had, Carol. And I will always love you.'

He turned and walked back to the track. Dawn's car was behind his. She was standing in front of it.

'Did you see the news this morning?' he said.

'Yes. Vince is worried that he'll come back and try again. What do you think, Frank?'

'I think that Miles Laing is a nutcase.'

'A nutcase who just escaped from a mental hospital. And he has a grudge. You said so yourself.'

'I'll come and talk to Vince.' He looked at her for a moment, thinking how she and Carol had become friends. 'Meantime, just be careful.'

'I will.' She stepped forward and kissed him on the cheek.

'Remember, the book festival. We'll go for a meal afterwards. Beckett proposed to Michelle and she said yes.'

'That's good. It's about time. But I was sorry to hear about Vince's mother.'

'Thank you. Lung cancer takes no prisoners. At least it was quick at the end.' She smiled at him before getting back into her car. 'Come and see Vince soon, Frank.'

Miller looked at the book again. He regarded Vince Rutherford as a friend now.

He got back into his car and glanced over at Carol's grave once more. He couldn't help but hear Miles Laing's words to him when they'd had their last conversation just a few days ago on the phone:

See you soon, Frank.